In the early 1800s, out of the  redcoats, gaolers, convicts and the fe none ventured much farther inland Sydney. Those who tried came back saying it could not be done, or did not come back at all.

Or so it was believed until the brazen escape of Desmond Kale after the final vengeance of his rival, the wildly eccentric 'flogging parson' magistrate Matthew Stanton: 'Kale marched a vicious mile, changed shape over a ridgeline and was gone. His face a shadow. His bootprints evaporations in the dirt.'

The Ballad of Desmond Kale is Roger McDonald's stirring novel of the first days of British settlement in Australia. At the centre is Stanton's pursuit of Kale – an Irish political prisoner and a rebelliously brilliant breeder of sheep in a place where 'even the land itself is a punishment'. When it is discovered that fine wool thrives in the country of pitiless desolation, the fledgling prison colony is galvanised by dreams and greed: 'Something was going on there you might say like new stars being born into the darkest corner of the sky.' Wool is 'a hoard of promise on yellow hooves'; currency in a colony 'where every hand is on the throat of another'.

From the back country comes rumour in the form of a ballad, disturbing proof that somewhere beyond the colony line, Desmond Kale is thriving – 'a boast to the downhearted, a bother to the secure' – and the finest wool in the colony along with him.

On both sides of the world, the alchemy of wool fascinates, threatens and transforms. This epic story of greed, conceit and redemption is also an exultant love story and a lively recreation of our past. Once the ballad is sung, the world can never be the same again.

'This is an historical novel in a grand, operatic style, an affectionate and bravura performance by a novelist at the height of his powers. Steeped in the lore of wool and bushcraft, it echoes a clutch of Great Australian and American Novels, from *Moby Dick* and *Tom Sawyer* to *His Natural Life* and *Such is Life*. It also recalls many of the best-loved works of English fiction, suggesting in its darker moments the mordant wit of Thackeray's *Vanity Fair* or, in its sunnier moments, the uplifting ethical vision of Fielding's *Tom Jones*. It shares something with those novels in its sweeping geographical scope, its rich cast of characters, and the rollicking pace of its events, which take us from the bush beyond Parramatta to the Houses of Parliament in London, from the sheepwalks of Yorkshire to shipwrecks and piracy in the South Pacific, from the chaotic settlement at Sydney Cove to the grim melodrama of the convict system at Macquarie Harbour.'

2006 Miles Franklin Literary Award judges' report

'. . . [an] exhilarating fable . . . a rollicking extravaganza that tells a ripping yarn . . . But it is the language – witty, colourful and evocative, extravagant at times, lyrical at others, a style that makes sentences rear up and gaze at themselves by means of cunning adverbs, adjectives and often unusual syntax – that sustains the novel and reminded me of the virtuosity those old authors sought to cultivate.'

Andrew Riemer, *The Sydney Morning Herald*

'Roger McDonald is a riot . . . He combines a love of intrigue and high adventure with a defiant, lyrical, vigorous way of telling. Here are art and excitement, mixed to magnificent strength . . . a full-blooded, pulsing tale . . . A *Sydney Morning Herald* critic wrote of

[McDonald] that he had a "subtle understanding of human motives and a clear eye on human savagery", and it's still going, this gripping insight, in this latest novel.'

Stella Clarke, *The Australian*

'. . . pitched to almost visionary intensity . . . written to be read at a breakneck pace, a looping, half-wild portrait of a world where wonder and squalor lie hard against each other . . . cascading energy and radical fervour . . . underpinned by a poet's understanding of the natural world. It is a world where meaning infers in every detail, and an intimate understanding of the land and its textures is revealed again and again, deepening the resonances of the novel's broader aspirations.'

James Bradley, *The Bulletin*

'What McDonald has created in *The Ballad of Desmond Kale* is a superbly paced book that absolutely steams along, leaving the reader scarcely a moment to draw breath . . . you soon find yourself completely seduced by the beauty and vigour of McDonald's writing. You'll read *The Ballad of Desmond Kale* for the magnificent story it tells. You'll read it again to savour its depths: the nuances of its language, and the abundance of the loves and landscapes McDonald brings so wonderfully to life.'

The Canberra Times

'McDonald is one of Australia's most accomplished novelists and this novel . . . eminently illustrates his gifts . . . McDonald writes in vivid, fast-paced prose that is witty, colourful and evocative.'

The Newcastle Herald

Also by Roger McDonald

Fiction:
1915
Slipstream
Rough Wallaby
Water Man
The Slap
Mr Darwin's Shooter

Non-fiction:
Shearers' Motel
The Tree in Changing Light

As editor:
Gone Bush

Roger McDonald is the author of seven novels and two works of non-fiction.

His first novel, 1915, won the *Age* Book of the Year and the South Australian Government Biennial Prize for Literature; his autobiographical *Shearer's Motel* won the 1993 National Book Council Banjo Award for Non-Fiction; *Mr Darwin's Shooter* won the 1999 NSW Premier's Award for Fiction, the 1999 Victorian Premier's Award for Fiction, the 2000 National Fiction Award and the 2000 SA Premier's Literary Award.

The Ballad of Desmond Kale won the Miles Franklin Literary Award 2006.

The Ballad
OF DESMOND KALE

ROGER MCDONALD

VINTAGE

A Vintage Book
Published by Random House Australia Pty Ltd
20 Alfred Street, Milsons Point, NSW 2061
http://www.randomhouse.com.au

Sydney New York Toronto
London Auckland Johannesburg

First published in Australia by Vintage in 2005

National Library of Australia
Cataloguing-in-Publication Entry

McDonald, Roger, 1941–.
The ballad of Desmond Kale.

ISBN 1 74166 114 5.
ISBN 978 1 74166 114 9.

1. Australia – History – 1788–1851 – Fiction. I. Title.

A823.3

Cover illustration by Lessing J. Rosenwald Collection, Library of Congress.
Copyright © the William Blake Archive. Used with permission.
Cover design by Christabella Designs
Internal design by Christabella Designs
Typeset by Midland Typesetters, Australia
Printed and bound by Griffin Press, South Australia

10 9 8 7 6 5 4 3

For Lorna McDonald
with love and thanks
for gifts of conversation, friendship, and example
over a lifetime

GLENDOWER:

I can call spirits from the vasty deep.

HOTSPUR:

Why, so can I, or so can any man:
But will they come when you do call for them?

— Henry IV, Pt I

Chorus of the First Part

WHERE KALE BEGINS IN THIS

AFTER DESMOND KALE WAS FLOGGED for stealing a ten-shilling metal rake he was cut down from the punishment tree and commanded to walk the ten miles back to the prison stockade of Toongabbie. So famous was Kale's conceit in Botany Bay, he was ordered to walk in ankle irons, holding his chains in his fists.

Eight flogged men were given a ride in the stone quarries' waggon. Kale was given an escort soldier, kept under view. It was said he might die — it was hoped by some that he would — just through the effort of lurching along in the bright morning, restrained by bolt, ring, rivet and rusty chain. The man who awarded his fifty strokes of the cat, Parson Magistrate Stanton (who was not present at the flogging, on a pretext of standing aloof), was quite as likely to agree in the denying fullness of his heart: that Kale could leak his gore into the earth, that the flies could swallow him.

'But fifty is nothing,' Kale was heard to say, spitting a tooth worked from the side of his jaw where it was cracked on a lump of tree during punishment. The back of his shirt flooded red while the next part of Kale's joy was to struggle forward of the bullock waggon and keep pace with his escort soldier, who said nothing from the time he flitted up from behind a log at the side of the track where he seemed to have been sleeping in sticks and grass and dirt.

That escort man, Moreno (answering to the name of Brown), kept his face turned to the road before him, the hard black visor of a regimental cap pulled over his eyes, the chinstrap tight and distorting his dark mouth and opossum cheeks. He was a stranger to the punishment detail but his written orders were exactly correct and his surly manner authentically iniquitous: more salt in the wound to Kale.

Redcoated Moreno stepped out feeling anxiety as much as Kale's in getting away — that man whose every shuffle made the sound of chains, whose back was striped like the marsupial wolf's from rib to shoulder, whose eyes were murk attracting too much interest beyond the forest walls. Fifty was nothing but tomorrow Parson Magistrate Stanton was quite as likely to come on with another fifty under more indictments against Kale, from a list as long as his malice, and the next day and the day after it, more.

It was a sandy track they walked, through tortuous white-trunked gum trees and bracken ferns. Every half mile they dipped, cut and crossed a shallow stream where the men in the waggon falling behind cried out for a drink. Kale grinned, satisfied as the distance led increased: 'Botany Bay aristocrats never cry out, but today they complain loud and long.'

There was no water in the stream six months of the year but this was mid-winter in New South Wales; it was June the ninth; the king's birthday: heat came in the middle of the day, the flogged men's thirst needed slaking, the purple blood they grew on their backs needed washing away. It was a tribute to royal clemency to offer prisoners a ride in a stone waggon at all, a drink when they thirsted hard.

Where fires had been, the winter grass was thinly greened up, the fringes of grasstree spears shone, their black trunks silvered in the noon light. Water in the stream ran shallow over rust-coloured sand. One great old tree still burned, it was over a low ridge before them, smouldering down into itself. Towards that pillar of smoke Moreno led Kale.

The quarry waggon came on through ferns, lurching up clay cuttings carved by wheel tracks, the flogged men rocking like so many sacks of corn and crying out, always making their noises, eight howling faces dripping as the guards relented and bucketed water over them. Far off through the open forest with its scattered grey sentinel trees and drifting smoke they saw Kale and his escort go, in glimpses less frequent until their crossings of the meandering stream were complete and the supposed redcoat and the suffering convict too far ahead to see.

When they reached the burning tree Moreno stopped where the smoke hung thickest. Grunting over the low ridge in a turn of clumsy speed Kale came hurling his lungs after him. Moreno raised his hand palm flat and Kale piled into it with his heavy gait's momentum.

Here was the place where they had some minutes to do what was wanted against the irons.

Smoke came from knot holes, tongues of flame burned high in forks of the tree. A hammer and tongs and chisel waited under a charred bush. A mound of white ash in heat waves lay at their feet.

Kale took another step — Moreno squealed warning up his sinuses. Kale believed the Spaniard courageous but a donkey's piece of work and told him stow his frenzy. Fire in this country of trees burned down roots, smouldered for weeks creating pits of glowing cinders into which a man might slide into hell very quick. It was awe piled on fear on danger that Moreno felt, of which they had both dared plenty. The moment of release was offered on wings of smoke, a few blows of steel on links already filed part through.

Kale crawled under the bush, fingering the tongs stowed according to the plot that was hatched with a third man waiting for them ahead. Kale took hold of the tongs' handles, raking them around in the ashes and grabbing the chisel. Moreno scrabbled for the hammer, raised it to his shoulder, ready to strike. All this metal filched and stashed was to save Kale condemned for stealing a metal rake: the weight of extra iron now plenty to hang them both, and that third man, too, if his aura of great advantage didn't save him.

Kale angled his shoulder, tongs upon the chisel:

'Strike!'

And the Spaniard brought the sledge hammer down, but missed, the head of the hammer thudding into the sand. The next stroke grazed Kale's forehead with moving air and Kale shrank his position into a beggar's cower, his elbows angled to maintain hold on the tongs and keep the chisel from slipping on the chain links where it wavered from the exertion of being held. If Moreno missed again, Kale's skull would splinter.

With better-aimed strokes Moreno shattered the chains.

In that forest the sounds rang sharp as musket shots, but the guards were distracted by the men in the waggon wailing Irish songs. Even a crooning lullaby in that treacherous tongue was foul noise enough. The guards broke out whips, unloaded the men from the waggon and sent them forward on foot, where it was a matter of importance between their convict souls to mess the track as much as they could in the clean winter light towards Parramatta.

Kale grinning across the broad strap of his jaw, throwing back his wild hair, drew Moreno after him, Kale wearing his ankle fetters split of their chains, until he came to a second known place and gave the signal to break off. They made their run over burnished kangaroo grass, one bent, the other bowed.

Across their tracks and around the ashy fire pit where the metal tools were dropped into the hell hole of the earth, the flogged men came drooling and messing the sand, for the sake of Desmond Kale and the life he wove into them.

After a half mile of bad going among rocks and confusing trees Kale stopped, lifted his head, stood still. Moreno whistled. A dog pricked its ears and came forward; a man appeared through the trees, a mob of sheep gathering at his back. It was Captain Tom Rankine of His Majesty's N.S. Wales rangers leading his horse coated in sheep dust and ash. There were always sheep criss-crossing the wastes of flatland forest. They would attract no suspicion driving a mob. This mob was Moreno's care, and the captain said:

'Here are your sheep for you, Kale. Here are three hundred of them, and five rams.'

Kale shook his head with haggard humour as if to say he would look at the sheep first and if they were any good get out of his ankle irons later. He lurched around feeling ribs, looking into mouths. Rankine and Moreno peered anxiously over their shoulders in the direction of the forest tracks.

'The rams are no good,' said Kale.

Moreno was astounded after the fandango of walking through the forest.

'He is my rams, I breed hims.'

'Very good, too,' said Rankine. '*Muy bien.*'

They called Rankine 'Ugly Tom' for his handsome poxy face in which there was now a strained affection as he stared down his shepherd, Moreno. With short-cropped prematurely grey hair and dusty pale eyes, Ugly Tom Rankine had an air of decisiveness and good humour that made him trusted by men, and liked in his adventures. That there were limits to his tolerance on many questions was never quite apparent, until he acted.

The three men cupped hands to their ears and listened for the sound of waggon wheels creaking, bullocks lowing and flogged men singing their national songs. Even the sheep stopped bleating and held the moment of quiet, into which flew, from branch to branch, and then onto a sheep's saddle back, a small black fantailed bird with a white vest and feet like starved black twigs.

'It is telling us we are safe,' said Rankine.

'That is the Mundowey bird,' said Kale, 'if you want to know what the first man that ever sighted it called it, and he said it was a forest friend.'

Moreno crossed himself for the shame of his dedication to Rankine and his needs. From a saddlebag Rankine took a bundle of clothes and threw them to the Spaniard. Moreno flicked off his cap, stripped himself free of his military jacket, shook himself out of the canvas trousers he wore. He clambered into his shepherd's rags, hopping around on one leg to get the other foot into the second leg. Last on was a grubby smock. Then he began his shepherding in a better mood of feeling.

Kale watched as the sheep broke from the trees in ones and twos and fours. The mob joined up and came funnelling down a length of track, throwing up sand and spreading it about. Kale counted the number by raking his eyes over them and moving his lips in rapid counts of ten. They were small ewes of Spanish blood, two hundred originally shipped to the colony without attracting the attention of stockmen better known than Tom Rankine. Arriving with the sheep eighteen months ago on the *Melanthus*, from Hull via Calcutta, Rankine had been deceptive in describing them as Bengali mutton breeders on a manifest of shipments — though few could have told any difference: that they were prizes from war in Spain; their wool smitten gold under pancaked pizzle-stain and wasted sores; that they were the king of Spain's own breeders — Rankine taking them first on a barge up the Parramatta river, then across mud flats through mangroves, and finally on a slow drive into rough bush where, for most of a year, they wandered with Moreno, growing out their coats. Their gaunt and unthrifty forms increased in that time from the appearance of starving rats to something better. Their two hundred became three hundred through every second ewe boasting a surviving lamb. At their first shearing they proved remarkable as promised. They were Rankine's hoard of promise on yellow hooves and were made to do better under the hand of Desmond Kale.

'The ewes are not half bad,' said Kale, 'six for each lash,' and he winked a droopy eye — the milling animals parting either side of the trio while Rankine, in a rush of feeling, looked at Kale's back, his lumpy darkening shirt crusted with busy flies. It brought him to quick tears that he brushed away with a shirtsleeve.

Kale turned, caught Rankine's glance, and the officer's mouth resumed its usual lopsided insouciant look. Tom Rankine was reliable mostly where there was provocation and dare, which was, here to say, a compound of love and mercy. Kale was Rankine's wish that what was done irreparably wrong in another part of life would be bettered by hopefulness in this one; that what was won in Spain by treachery would be improved in New South Wales. But no time for wishing — they'd better get on. It took another few minutes for the sheep to be bunched ready. Even then, Rankine was unfinished with feeling. For more than just sheep and repentance folded around Kale in the perilous matter they risked. No telling this to the convict — Rankine loved Kale's daughter, Meg Inchcape, whatever the threat to his skin and, what he cared for as much, his pride. But Rankine had only just begun a campaign of having her, of making his first moves upon the daughter in time with consorting with the father. He was further advanced with Kale than he was with her. With Meg Inchcape he was not even yet in danger. He was in love at first sight — and with Meg as a prophecy, you could almost say, to which he bent, idealising his life, though they had never spoken more than two brisk words to each other.

Kale did not know of any sort of connection. He'd fumed that Meg was ruined by an officer once, a matter he made difficulties about, without satisfaction. A regiment had no strategy on love, only its officers had tactics. Now by their look at each other you would think Kale and Rankine were merely stock dealing in this dangerous paradise past Toongabbie, where men worked in irons until they died foul deaths, or made escapes from the stone quarries of which this one was more finely calculated than most.

Kale got up on the horse behind Rankine and clasped him around the waist. Now he almost fainted. The dog working the sheep came into sight and brought the sheep around behind them, its tongue lolling conspicuously wet. Moreno tripped along on his small foreign feet. They moved off — the three men, the sheep and the dog through the white-trunked gum trees closing behind them.

A half hour later when the bullock waggon came through headed by the shuffling Irish, Desmond Kale was gone from the world of punishment, gone as if he had never suffered in it.

A WEEK AFTER KALE'S ESCAPE Parson Magistrate Stanton said to his wife, Dolly, of whom he pretended to be more afraid than he was of Irish convicts herding sheep in the bush and shaping daggers out of farming tools:

'Say, my precious darling, if you were in the way of spreading yourself as I am, with plenty of livestock and no sons, might it not benefit a boy, a prince of the breed, to be taken on and encouraged?'

In serving his own interests the parson magistrate was able to speak to a moral purpose — 'Whether it should benefit a boy' — and his wife had something the same way of thinking, but objected:

'You forget we already have Titus.'

'No, I am always thinking about Titus,' said Stanton, passing a hand across his face to brush away flies and express frustration, making a wish for new beginnings.

Titus was a boy they had rescued from a native camp when he was estimated eight years old, and sworn to raise in a civilised fashion as their own. The first of them to run sheep out their way, Aaron Tait, had worked Titus's parents as shepherds, and said they were king and queen of their tribe. Whether it was believably true,

Titus was allowed the distinction when spoken about. His parents were no longer living to testify what they were, except pitch black and scurrilous. Titus proved less a son, more a serving boy as he waited at table and otherwise amused guests, living in a hut at the back of the house while the rest of New South Wales looked on, Titus taming lizards, Titus spinning whistling tops, Titus making cat's cradles and throwing a native playstick that bounced on the ground and flew two hundred and fifty yards before it clunked to a stop. The Stantons made such great noisy show of being workers of Christian change that they took Titus with them wherever they went, usually to hold the horses, if he could be found.

Without Stanton being able to understand why, when Titus had all his advantages bestowed, the boy still went to his people who came up the creek begging sugar and flour; he remembered enough of their languages to keep their superstitions in his fickle heart; he lived in two worlds displeasingly to say, but each time deserting was welcomed back with a good scrubbing in the bathtub and a rule of Christian forbearance. Titus having recently turned an estimated fifteen it was doubtful if two women, mother and daughter, scrubbing him in a frothing tin tub was anything like a punishment but more a passionate delight to a wicked boy whose sense of shame never extended to wearing clothes, unless he decked himself out like a peacock.

Of course, there was a charitable motivation in the air all the time in the farmhouse parsonage and sheep yards. Travelling to Parramatta and Sydney, Dolly Stanton went around saving unwanted infants, those that weren't throttled and flung under the drain or in a sewer after unlawful birth to debauched convict women. She found wet nurses and planted babies in foundling care. They were given names to grow into, those of the Lord's disciples for boys, for girls the names of the foremothers of the house of Israel.

The boy Stanton now proposed to advance, Warren Inchcape, was the grandson of the flogged Irishman; a boy needing decent rescue, Dolly agreed, and how could she not, except she did not think of Kale continuously as her husband did.

There was always a whole nest of snakes under everything. Desmond Kale was Stanton's first shepherd when he came to the colony. Given his chances, Kale had squandered them. Bitterness, dispute, rivalry and scorn were the issue. No thanks, no reciprocal gratitude, no concessions, none to pride. More times in prison than out, more times flogged than healed. To lower one person and keep him down, to raise another and keep him up was Stanton's notion. In the circumstances, he could not skin a Kale without clothing a Warren.

But he decided to wait until his wife's temper on the question improved. Too fast a move on Warren would seem like blatant hostage-taking — though who should suspect it when the boy was so brilliant with sheep, superlatively suited without argument, and justified on sheep grounds absolutely? Anyone would want him on that strength, and this was proved when Stanton went to Aaron Tait's rough farm at Toongabbie, just for the pleasure of watching stout Warren at work. How splendid he was with livestock . . . Of course, no guessing, it all came down from Kale.

While wishing Kale blank, Stanton was frustrated not doubling the sentence from a bob to a canary — fifty to one hundred lashes — 'And flog him a tester each morning, until he confesses' — exactly to what, in the way of crime, it appeared only Stanton had the zeal, or the private information, to imagine. Something to do with sheep, you might guess, on every count. It was ten years since their sheepwork together ended and they had turned their backs on each other, master and convict. Kale spent those years mostly in confinement; both men brooded on wool. Tarry on the outside, yolky cream within, the wool sheep carried on their backs was worth a life and a reputation. It grew through the week and on the Lord's Day, when work ceased, kept growing. In Stanton's dry paddocks it grew dense and rich. He accumulated mountains of the beautiful stuff, sending it to England, but always remembered, with a stab of hurt, that the tar-tipped surface was a cover for insolence, secrecy, crime and disorder.

The governor ordered a police tracker's report and said Stanton would have a copy of the report soon enough. In that first week he rode ninety-six miles, two return gallops to Parramatta from his sheep station, Laban Vale, to be told the report was not ready. He was not the only person in this matter wearing out saddle leather and crossing tracts of countryside in a hurry day and night. Sometimes the two men, Matthew Stanton and Tom Rankine, came close enough to kick gravel into each other's teeth from the hooves of their horses, close enough to eat from the same dish, drink from the same cup, warm their two faces to the same minted breath of the same beautiful woman, but only one of them, Ugly Tom Rankine, was aware of the other's startling nearness.

Here was all Stanton knew so far. After years of disobedience, defamatory insolence, and hard service in chain gangs, Kale had won provisional freedom. On strict parole, he could not restrain himself from committing a fresh provocation upon his former master and chief punisher. That Laban Vale was off-limits only inflamed him. On the day Kale stole the rake it was proved he made his way from Stanton's ram shed where tools were kept to a pauper's graveyard. There he was found raking the rubble of a neglected grave and giving the impression of being a simple gravetender or humble mourner without guile. He was felled with a blow, dragged to the cells, and sent back to the stone quarries, from where he was in due course taken out and tied to a tree of gummy lumps and overgrown jagged limb-holes. Prisoners had their arms pulled around the trunk and their breasts squeezed against the trunk and so were denied the power to cringe. There Kale was flogged his due portion; from there made his escape according to exquisitely forged orders carried by a trooper answering to the name of Brown. Nothing else was known of him that day, except he marched a vicious mile, changed shape over a ridgeline and was gone. His face a shadow. His bootprints evaporations in the dirt.

Stanton was able to lay out the facts without putting himself too much at the centre of them as the one who went after Kale most ferociously: having him dragged before his bench; reclaiming his rake; having him sentenced before the taste of freedom ever swilled twice or thrice around his mouth. It was only when Stanton reached (in his thinking) those sheep, that a great cloud rose up impenetrable to investigation. Where had they gone?

One man was less helpful than Stanton wished while having the power to help absolutely: Sir Colin Wilkie.

It annoyed the governor to learn that Kale was flogged under a sentence that Stanton pronounced while quitting his court to get back to his sheep, throwing the number of lashes back over his shoulder as if half a hundred was the smallest of all numerals, a scratch.

'Has the man lost the compassion and manners of a Christian minister, through passing vindictive sentences on the triangle and putting the welfare of flocks over the needs of Christians? Suppose there's an extractive, not merely a punitive motive against Kale,' the governor said, 'putting the sentence into the category of flogging for admissions — what is that called now?'

'Judicial torture' it was called in the governor's camp — a libel of barely extreme malice from a man who called Stanton his 'quondam friend parson incendiary' in a treacle of amused dislike.

Stanton blurted he would see the governor in court, and empty that Scotchman's pockets in damages, if he kept talking loose.

But whether flogging for admissions was a libel in fact was an obstacle to Stanton's opening his mouth any wider — because, for more than a year past, rumours had reached him of a tightly run superlative flock, small, but better than his own, being led through the wastelands by an unknown shepherd in the manner of the trans-humants or migratory merinos of Spain. Here today, gone tomorrow, where they were grazed was the question. It was not on any good land. Their wool was said to thrive on hard ground like no other. They had now disappeared from reckoning. The only Botany Bay breeder with the gift of carrying great blood to rarer heights (if it was not Stanton himself) was the Irishman. But as if accursed Kale could have run sheep from a gaolyard or would cry into Stanton's ear the location of flocks and the progress of their breeding after a mere fifty stripes! — matters that Stanton would almost gladly flog any man to hear, bond or free, with no other crime involved needed as justification, there was wool on his mind so much.

Anyway, enough: couldn't it be seen that he didn't exactly ask questions of the flogged? For Stanton had a policy of never attend-ing a flogging in person. If confessions were blabbed they were blabbed to him unsolicited, not from intention. It was from the motive of keeping the vengeance of the law cold in his chest, the wrath of God in its proper place, beyond man's comprehension, that he only sometimes watched floggings from a distance as he rode past observing a proceeding — a cameo'd Lucifer in broad-arrow rags twisting before the arm of virtue, having evil strength mastered by greater clout.

What Stanton heard from that distance, more than the cries of the condemned, who appeared to have a sullen pact among themselves anyway never to bleat, if they could help it, were the sighs of the mob, their moans of sympathetic heart-wrenching so risen into a wave you would think they turned into fingers and plucked the cat from the flogger's hand.

Stanton hated the passionate stupidity of the mob but longed to forget himself and roar with them . . . Until one of them turned, seeing him sitting motionless on his white mare, under his round white hat, and threw out the curse of the Irish:

(It was a foul, purposeful, lewd piece of language made to scorch his ears.)

'Stanton, you horribilis —'

'What? Horribilis what?'

Better to spit bile between his horse's ears and ride on, leaving the curse unsplattered.

Kale was a stone, or a pebble, so called, an iron man in the parlance of convicts, with a back like terraced quartz. Rear view was the last angle seen of him, shambling through the forest flicking the tail of a government shirt. Although he bled copiously there was little slowing down of his escape. Blame was laid widely on convict plotters as yet unknown. Stanton knew better. It must have been an officer with sheep, he reasoned, who palmed Kale blacksmith's tools (those conjectured instruments remaining unfound); who organised an escort soldier, who slipped him the escort service roster; who forged signatures on orders; a double-crossing duplicitous blatant rogue in the king's uniform — officers being the ones most forward in sheep and established enough in their raving confidence to scorn the danger of being hung.

He suggested it was officers to the governor, who said, 'Which faction should I prefer, then?'

Stanton went through the roll of known breeders, trying to pin a name to the deed without success. His vainest rival was Major James Agnew, but neither guile nor cleverness marked Agnew whose boastful claim to genesis was in a few culled rams Stanton had leased him. From these he bred a perfect small animal whose wool became finer and finer until you would have to say, the view of the skin was preposterously good, but where was the fleece?

No. So many sheep used to cover a man's tracks and the whole lot swallowed into the wild was hardly an Agnew folly. It proved impossible to name names to the governor without stiffening Wilkie's regimental pride. 'If Stanton thought that N.S. Wales rangers were involved he had better prepare his ground ...' etc., etc.

That yellow-haired frowzy highlander, sensualist, whig, philosophical atheist insulting to Anglican forms by pretending Presbyterianism. What use was such a man in the maggoty dust baths and hot outer limits of the colony? General Sir Colin Wilkie went galloping home each afternoon to his rangers' dinners, no matter how far on kangaroo hunts he went towards the gates of the sandstone gorges where Kale was swallowed. At those dinners he ate, drank, recited verses in Gaelic with dubious Irish emancipists, put his hand up the skirts of maids, gossiped like a swamp frog, played cards till his eyes popped, and bloody-veined they were in the mornings.

Little help Stanton had from the law in conjuring up a gang. No help from the convict constabulary who were felons in uniform at best. When at last he received the government tracker's report, brought by express rider with the governor's dusty compliments, it contained little more than was already spoken about between himself and the governor.

Except Stanton saw that something was missing from the report. He read it through several times to be certain. Sure, before fully healing Kale had been tracked a good distance past Emu Plains — doubtless in a cloud of maggoty flies — setting off limping to some mythical China, heading into parts of New South Wales whence no white man had ever returned. Kale could not have been too badly striped to reach that far, Stanton reasoned, cutting his broad feet on razor-sharp rocks and curling his misshapen toes around boulders, scraping his broad forehead and shaggy wild hair on thorn bushes. It was said in the report that Kale took many sheep with him, but there was only a scatter of men's bones into the rampart of hills that stood to the west of occupied lands, where other like thinkers had perished. The sheep were gone up in smoke. Brought back was a shin bone, with a commotion over whether it was black, white or crossed, murdered or thankfully hacked or shot, eaten by cannibal Irish despots in a quarrelling band of escapees, and there was always the possibility of natural causes: heat stroke, lightning stroke, death by thirst.

Here was the puzzle, then. While sheep were mentioned, wool was not. Wool from travelling sheep was immemorially gathered on bushes, unpicked from grass, wherever flocks shifted along. Where were wool's traces here? All blown away?

Stanton, in his mind, went after the faceless cohorts of Kale in a storm of gathering wool. Men betrayed, wool rewarded.

Stanton had an eye for wool. 'Trust in God and breed like the Devil.' He estimated distances and places where to stick his nose, but only came up against cliffs and gorges in reports of where they had gone.

Rage and bafflement called for another head on this. And so Stanton cultivated a bush trader, a London Jew, whose crimes were forgery and the receipt of stolen goods in Whitechapel, who since transportation made himself known in the colony for selling merchandise up country from a lumbering waggon and rescuing his honesty from the dung heap.

ALTHOUGH DISCREET IN HIS TRADE Joe Josephs was a pliable source of information from many quarters gleaned. He was blessed with rampant curiosity, full of intense affections, ignorant in his wool buying when it came to the finer points — thus to be educated in wool by one who knew better. Joe was appreciative of Biblical arguments, which pleased Parson Stanton all right, the trader knowing his ancient texts better than any Christian teacher Stanton had learned from — his old Cambridge university professors spouting original Hebrew letters included. Old writings of *dalet* and *resh* were alphabets known to Joe, a Cockney criminal type as originally spawned. It was like he lived Biblical times as he made his observances on a Friday night and lay down in his camp of a Saturday morning smoking his clay pipe, doing little else to stir his skinny legs on his day of rest.

The minister had an intense motivation with the gingery-bearded Joe — an aim running through the veins of his worldliness back to the plug of his dark believing heart. It was to advance his wool, pursue Kale to the limit, and, in a smaller voice, ask Joe to drop his resistance to the Christian cross or throw him to the Devil.

There was a battle with Titus going on over the same subject. A good leather strapping was known in Yorkshire dialect as an anointing. Stanton brought anointings with him into his own house. After many anointings Titus went to Sunday school and learned his texts, but as to the sincerity of his catechism, Stanton had angry doubts. He felt he would never know the truth of that boy unless he split his ribcage open and held his heart to the light.

Stanton's branch of established religion, the evangelical, claimed that everything was possible to those who showed contrition and expressed a sense of mortal danger; though whether it would save them from the gallows tree or stay the flogger's hand was to bring the argument down from heaven a bit too far. When it came to Jews, they were stubborn as blacks resisting commands. It made Stanton justified in naming a hard God, 'wrath resisting mercy' when he struck refusals.

Finer points of theology escaping Stanton's capacity of brain, he argued by letter to his evangelical friends in Cambridge. It took almost two years to rotate the meditations over the seas and back. Some of those evangelical friends were become known names of English preaching while Matthew Stanton, their hoop-legged old amigo, after leaving Cambridge without taking his degree, stubbornly missionised among the bluebottle flies and johnny cakes of the thieving sheep camps of Botany Bay.

Gratifyingly to say, his advisors (all archdeacons now, and bishops' chaplains) endorsed his opinions back to him, agreeing on his need to flog sinners and buy land and make profits for the sake of independence from interfering governors. They were most soothing in their assurance that although the strait gate was narrow he was fitting through. The parable of the talents, where a man was justified increasing his wealth, aptly applied where he was. When he asked cunning Joe Josephs for a gloss on that, the fellow looked stoomped — and Stanton was pleased. For the parable was a story from the New Testament — a book that Joe would not accept even as a gift from a well-meaning friend to take with him on the waggon track, as a useful reminder of right from wrong if he ever felt the need to delve deeper into repentance after his life of crime.

It was two weeks after Kale's escape when Stanton rode into Joe Josephs's encampment near Parramatta, and after a sharp look around from under his floppy white hat, decided there were now a few more good reasons for seeking Joe's friendship than were already worked up between them.

It was late afternoon on a Friday, the sun about to set. Smoke from a cooking fire threaded into the trees and flattened among high spindly branches. Steam hissed from under the lid of an iron pot suspended by chains from a triangle of metal stakes. There was the smell of boiled fowl in the wintry air, spiced with green nettle.

As Stanton rode on into the compound a movement showed through the trees on the other side. It was a flush of rust-red greatcoat, a rider on a black horse, a man making off.

There was too much of that kind of flurry around Stanton since Kale was freed. Next time he roved, he would bring along an old black man, Mr Moon, who was able to lean down from the neck of a horse and waver his black nose along, reading bent grasses by the trackside and interpreting a wren's feather, knowing if it was disturbed by the passage of a rogue or not: to see better than Stanton ever could, anyway, in a gathering dusk.

The camp was a rough space of ground, grazed over by bullocks on a creekbank pugged by animal tracks. At the edge of paperbark trees, close hobbled, were five working bullocks. They doddered forward into better light. There was a brown and white with lopped horns wearing a large bell, two brindle and white, one with cocked horns, and a strawberry junior with snail horns sounding a bull-frog bell when lowering its glossy head. The brand was an indistinct MT.

'Those are Mick Tornley's bullocks,' thought Stanton, 'who Joe is in league with and plainly; he is clever as mustard to get on with that man. Everything Joe touches is blessed by a quantity of profit, with a contrived innocence when bartering, which I quite admire.'

The time of day had an air of contrivance in it of another sort. Nature was a subtle arguer against certainty when shadows fell. Behind an old tree Stanton found the bullocky sitting on a fallen log mending a whip. Mick Tornley greeted him with a brown, toothless smile. Stanton remained on his horse and lifted his hat.

'Good evening, there.'

'Mister Stanton, you ave come round to see us rather late.'

"Never too late for true friends, Mick, though aren't the days getting short as they can get, in this part of the world just now?'

'It is gettin too dark to see,' agreed Mick.

'Who was that horseman?'

'A redcoat.'

'So it was.'

There was no duplicity in the bullocky; more a sturdy feeling of limits. He made you doubt there was any wrongdoing within a fixed radius of himself — just regular business involved — which included this ground, those trees, and out as far as that departing rider lanky-legged in the saddle and making a clatter with something he carried. Mick was a man all at your service — or not, depending. You had to be one of the chosen with Mick, and Stanton believed he was.

Stanton strained his credulity to admit that a redcoat — any redcoat — had the right to do business with whomever he chose. It was quite possible to believe that whatever elaborate or nefarious business Joe Josephs was engaged in with officers, touched Mick Tornley only to the extent that it weighed on his waggon axles and decided on his bullocks' needs in fodder. He was square-necked, bushy black-bearded, with a thickly boned forehead as powerfully deep as a bull's brain plate. His cheeks were mahogany buffed from the winter sun. When he lifted his hat, his forehead, showing sweaty plastered hairs, was white as milk. Whatever went on in his head, he was quite devoid of curiosity about another person.

Mick stood with his legs planted wide coiling his whip. 'If you don't mind, reverend, with your horse, get away.' Tornley stepped out then, into the little light remaining, slithered the whip through his fingers, raised his whip arm and shook out the plaited leather like a dusty snake, first merely upon the ground and then lifting it clean into the air where it looped back and forth, and in a final moment, cracked.

'Good enough,' he assessed. 'Tis better.'

Another crack, and stars appeared in the pale evening sky. Tornley's five bullocks, ambling closer, reacted to the sound, their heads swayed, they stamped their stocky forefeet. Then it was like Tornley created flashing points in the air — star points — over the head, along the flanks, there at the tail and down to the feet of an imagined sixth bullock. Stanton's hands sweated to take hold of the whip handle and create from it himself! Then on the other side of the clearing there appeared that sixth bullock, real as could be, pale, enormous, that raised its head and bellowed with tormented strength.

'Ercules,' Tornley called it.

Stanton wanted to ask:

'When are you leaving for the outlands, Mick?' 'Who are Joe's trade goods for?' — but these were questions you did not ask a gentleman with bullocks.

A bullocky's wheels turned slow in a progress of lurching and leaning, straining and baulking, hardly to be described as progress at all. Yet the tracks of every bullock waggon ever hauling out from Parramatta remained deep cut in the ground years afterwards. It caused Stanton to consider coming on afterwards in the matter he was concerned with; not to rush but to follow and watch, as he was doing on the question of tempting the boy Warren Inchcape over to his service — to try not frightening up answers too much. It was how he worked his livestock — why not with men, for a change? Men left tracks of intention, they indicted themselves with their hearts.

Stanton dismounted and walked his mare around a stack, a hillock, of the most marvellous collection of valuable trade goods he had ever seen. His thoughts ran on:

'Here in our colony! — formerly starved — where a two-pound of iron, shaped to a rake, is taken from a shed in risk of a man's neck; yet here, here in the open air, under a bare sky, is metal worth a thousand guineas, guarded by a mongrel dog to be bought with a bone, a pat on the head, or a tickle. Get behind me, you yeller mutt!'

The trade goods were spread on the ground by category, size and weight, ready for loading onto Tornley's six-wheeled waggon. Stanton saw in a glance, from as close as he could step without being savaged, sufficient items for the setting up of a stock camp or the foundations of a veritable sheep station as big as his own or bigger. Quite possibly Tornley and Joe had better information than Stanton could have dreamed: that not just was somebody out there waiting for their supplies, but also their prime location was given. Allow Stanton a minute, and he would be able to calculate pretty exactly the number of head of sheep to be grazed by an ambitious settler from such a quantity of cast-iron pots, farming tools, boots, canvas buckets, sheep shears, tar tubs, tarpaulins, axes and big-toothed saws. It would be a fairly large clutch — around five thousand head! There was a quantity of corrosive sublimate, sulphur, bluestone, twine thread, gin, and also a trunk holding 'household linnen', securely padlocked. Of sugar and flour there were several one-hundred-pound sacks. There might not be five thousand sheep or anything like that number spreading through the landscape awaiting these stores as yet, but that was the number being perfected, he estimated. By the time the goods were run out, and further supplies were needed, it would be . . . say two or three years' time and a good few lusty matings and well-rated lambings and so forth bringing the numbers up . . . and by the thousands, yet . . . because whoever the goods were going out to would not be in a hurry getting themselves back.

O N THE FAR SIDE OF the waggon, under a canvas fly, Stanton found Joe Josephs sitting on a square of carpet, wearing a battered top hat and a weskit of gold threads and blue buttons, his legs crossed and reciting prayers with his eyes rolled back in his head. Stanton waited respectfully until he was noticed, while supposing he was noticed from the moment he rode into Joe's camp, and even now in all probability from behind those intelligently elevated eyeballs . . . 'It is Friday night,' he thought, 'their Sabbath begins, the shadows are chilly blue, the sun is gone, and over in their home tent (now Stanton could see it, from where he stood) all's as it should be. The women have lit their candles . . .'

'Amein,' said Joe, blinking up at his visitor.

'Here we are again, my very good friend.'

Joe Josephs was aged around forty, narrow-faced, straggly red-bearded, with deeply set tired eyes and a Londoner's sooty pallor enduringly staining his weathered skin. Joe had a bird's nest of wiry hair, touched with drab grey fringes, that dangled to the front of his ears in two jouncing ringlets. His chest was concave, his back slightly humped. A character of energetic contemplation burned in his eyes. When he unfolded himself from the ground, dusting his knees, doffed his top hat and stood fairly straight, he shone, you might say, shimmered, and you could see he was ready to get going, that he was a travelling man. He was forced by necessity to become a travelling man since being shipped to Botany Bay for the term of his natural life — and given few choices in working up a legitimate trade.

Joe walked ahead of Stanton taking long strides.

'You have a lot of chattels here,' said Stanton.

'Less than I did, since our governor took my best quart pots off of me. They all nested into each other, a proper bush man's kitchen.'

'Was that a governor's man come over to nab them, the rider who left?'

'And never paid me,' said Joe, 'except in promises.'

'Who was it?'

'Captain Tom Rankine.'

'Never heard of him. Rankine, you say?'

'Ugly Tom Rankine they calls him, he is our governor's boon companion. Rode off with them quart pots swinging from his elbows. They have a nitpick on the creek tomorrow, the swells, and must have the best ironmongery.'

'A picnic, you mean.'

'I stand corrected,' said Joe, putting his hand to his head, and leering intelligently at the minister.

Stanton mentally consulted his list of officers, over which he stood poised ready to strike off names, or else to double underline them. He considered the name Rankine, then struck it off after asking:

'Are any more of these items to be his — the camp ovens, the bluestone, the gin? Does Ugly Tom Rankine want them?'

'If he does, he's not asked me.'

'Who's are they to be, then, Joe?'

'All are mine, still, at present,' said Joe. 'They are my stock in trade, my inventory. They are not orders of anyone's in particular. They are available, my friend, first come first served to settlers in the bush. This here is a travelling store. When on the road, we make our house under one end of the waggon, Mick at the other. We shall get to your homestead by and by, but remember: the farrer out I travel, the greater the percentages I put on. One per cent each mile is a fairly good rule I am working up to my customers, a little less to my friends. So, before I gets too far out your way, cast your eyes over some pots and pans, gardening tools, dried peas by the loose weight, fish hooks, Batavian hatchets, flints, or if it's castor oil you wants . . . What is it you wants, now, less the twenty-four per cent I am entitled add for your twenty-four miles of road?'

'I think you know.'

'Not a new rake, is it?' said Joe.

'I have my good one. It is repaired since Kale broke it.'

'Mine are better made.'

'I have no doubt of it.'

'But as you mention that name, Kale,' said Joe.

'Yes?'

'Then I think — believe — it's a crystal ball you wants.'

'So,' said Stanton, lowering his voice disappointedly. 'You've heard nothing?'

'Nothing. Or nothing much. But I do have something for us to look at, after we've eaten our supper.'

'Must it wait?' said Stanton, taking Joe by the wrist and squeezing hard.

'Ouch! Where is that woman?' said Joe. 'Oi! Marfa! Give the man dinner!'

Inside the tent was a bench and a plain plank table. Stanton was told to put a hat on his head, and look foolish while Joe said a prayer over a cup of sweet wine. They munched on bread sprinkled with salt, to remind them of the bitterness of life.

At last their plates were wiped clean of chicken fat. The daughter, Leah, served them honeycakes, and the boy, Arthur, played the violin. A frenzied tune, then a sad one. The youngest boy, Solly, danced a sailor's dance on the dusty spot.

When all such rites were complete, Stanton took Joe by the elbow and steered him back outside. Joe threw sticks on the fire, making a blaze they could see by, brighter than a lamp, and keeping Stanton waiting no longer, withdrew from his pocket a staple of fleece.

'Wool,' breathed Stanton, his eyes following every movement of the mellow, waxy material.

He experienced a kick in the chest. An unappeasable appetite for possession. He watched Joe twirling the swatch of fibres, and thought, what a marvel Joe was with that element dangling from his fingers. To the inexpert eye the material was no more than a dusty rag, while Stanton saw otherwise. It was a magical worm, a necklace, a cloudy icicle, a misty knife. It was fine sheep's wool, the essence of distinction over the tawdriness of daily shapes. And surely it led back to Desmond Kale more certainly than search parties of mounted troopers and knavish blacktrackers.

'Aren't it pretty,' said Joe.

Stanton saw white sparks deflected down a tumble of greasy crimps as Joe layered it across his cupped hands, a gift.

'My deepest thanks.'

'You owe me nuffink, saving something I would like to ask of you, which is a few pointers, or lessons in wool, for me and my sons in telling good stuffs from bad. We have been badly misled in several consignments.'

'The first principle is the greatest.'

'Which is?'

'The hook.'

'I never heard of such a thing with sheep,' said Joe. 'Except at the butcher's.'

'THE HOOK — IT IS THE means of taking hold,' said Stanton, 'say between grasses, seeds, in the way they cling; among insects with their feelers, birds with their claws, fish with scales, man with his fingers, teeth, and his generative organs; God has decreed it among all with their scents and colours, down into in our cravings for attraction; and further in the affinity of thoughts as philosophies, in the mechanisms and mysteries of love, in the possibilities of accidents or otherwise deciding our fates. See this tiny filament or threadlet of wool?'

Stanton separated one out in the firelight.

'Stop there,' said Joe. 'It is more like a cobweb than an hook.'

'It is all in the catch and the tangle. A thread of wool is made up of scales, the scales hook threads together making wools and worsteds. The hook is the great binder of wool's existence; the catch is its means; the tangle is a natural state.'

'Tangles explains my life, at least,' said Joe. 'But I still don't understand wools.'

'It needs English mills to unravel it all. They are marvels at straightening threads to make them usable, and they need the best raw wools, and we can find them for them, Joe.'

'I'm not much helped.'

'You will be if you come to my place directly, but without your outrageous percentages stacked on. I will show you more what I mean. I shall unpick your tangle and make you rich.'

Stanton smoothed the sample along the length of his forearm. 'Where was it found?'

Joe could not say. His informants were out of their wits, he said, at the western limit of signs, at the tumbled sandstone ramparts on the far side of the biggest river. They found dead men's bones. They would have died themselves, except their tracker found a way. After a three-day return ride they came back where waggon tracks converged, and there they found Joe. A trooper, and his blacktracker, the two men bargained for gin and lapped it up like dogs did water. For which they paid in this handful of floss gathered from thorn bushes.

All they'd said was, that from where it was found, either all were perished — or they had maps to go on, to take them as far as China.

'Maps?' said Stanton.

'Except there ain't no maps, from what I have heard.'

'Correct. None that anyone has ever laid eyes on, Joe. Remember that. You are wise to say so. It is a vast impoverished *terra incognita* out there.'

Stanton rode off into the night, found a dry sandy spot, wrapped himself in his blanket and went to sleep in the bushes. Joe's staple of wool burned warm under his vest and tickled his armpit with its presence.

In the middle of the night he woke, the dome of the heavens sparkling overhead, his nose very cold. Every star cluster was a shred of shining fleece hanging in the sky.

Later he heard a horseman approaching, and raised himself on an elbow. Two horses went past, one a saddle horse and the other a packhorse outlined against the stars. The rider sat forward in the saddle, huddled in a greatcoat. It was the bearing of a military campaigner. Nobody came after.

Just before dawn Stanton woke with dried gum leaves in his hair, crusted sleep in his eyes. There was dirt on the palms of his hands, ants in the folds of his shirt, a scorpion in his boots. When he knelt to pray he kept his eyes open wishing for the rider, his night's passing companion, to step forward from between the trees. That would happen soon enough, he decided: he was armed for that rider now by a weapon of wool.

It was his very man, he was certain, and only lacked a name, that greatcoated apparition. For there was no reason for an officer to be riding south into unoccupied lands except the suspicion that Kale and his cohorts awaited him. They were not perished, Stanton reasoned, or walking to China — as the ignorant contended — but through feasible possession of maps had possibly doubled back this side of the biggest river, and found a way on, in the direction of wastelands, swamps, rocky ridges, and reedy coarse uplands known since the beginnings of settlement as a scramble of frigid dessications not worth the trouble of exploring.

'Not worth the trouble of exploring' — now there was a phrase that hooked in Stanton's brain.

These were, he remembered well, the words of a pestilential man who came to the colony some fourteen years ago, under letters of credence from Sir Joseph Banks. He was Stanton's fellow Yorkshireman George Marsh, a former blacksmith and weaver, who, by heeding herbal cures for sick horses, had come to studies of botany in a large way, in his home village by the moors, with a strong enough opinion of his self worth to gain a patron's appointment to Botany Bay.

George Marsh's influence had been strong in this particular: holding that while New South Wales rivalled North America in size, the only part worth cultivating was the circle of land out from Parramatta. The rest was only interesting to science, damnably rough and dry, realm of the hardscrabble black man and his bride. For many years until now it was truly sufficient land as it was, and Stanton himself had the pick of it (though he wanted more). Of the broken, tumbled sandstone country Marsh trekked, ringed to the north, ranged to the west, banked obscurely to the south, the best he claimed was that it was 'like walking on rooftops'. Botany Bay accordingly was a pastoral prison, where sheep might safely graze inside those wider crumbled prison walls of New South Wales.

George Marsh had held the government post of naturalist, bird fancier, and explorer manqué for around five years before decamping back to England after completing his botanical collections and vain explorations. He had irritated Stanton extremely with his manners.

One day Marsh's cockatoo attacked Stanton's whippet, when all lived in disharmony at Parramatta, and the fellow had the arrogance to curse Stanton for keeping such an imbecile pencil-thin-headed dog. 'If Marsh was a gentleman he would have been shot in a duel,' Stanton liked to say. Although married, Marsh had amours: it was said he left a child in the colony born to a convict Jezebel. Dolly was never able to find which one.

Then Kale, to crown Stanton's annoyance, finagled assignment as Marsh's servant for Marsh's great (but unsung) expedition to the south and south-west. They went with a native companion and guide, named Mun'mow. It was under a governor's mandate to allow Marsh to search for government cattle gone wild and bred up in the vicinity of Aleppo Mere, one of a bundle of names Marsh gave to untamed places that made them impossible for anyone to find later, and if they were found again, as these particular cattle swamps were (Stanton coveting them for his own grazing) the names were changed back to something more sensible.

But Marsh went far beyond those swamps, for certain knowledge — he was away two months. He came back fairly subdued, you might say, tired and starving. But smug. Vainglorious. His black-fellow, Mun'mow, he took along with him when he returned to England, with the hope of making a gentleman's valet of his attentiveness.

If Marsh had ever the decency to pass any discoveries around instead of holding them to his private self when he returned to England, he might have made profits. Stanton might have been his friend. If the heroics of settlement were ever to be written, Marsh's name might stand tall among them. Yet the most lasting consequence of Marsh's New South Wales life was the grinding suspicion that he'd gone many more hundreds of miles farther inland than claimed, and that Kale kept his secrets. So if there were maps, Kale knew about them, but of maps Kale had never spoken: a league of whips hadn't unscrolled maps out of him. Indeed about the one action Stanton liked of Marsh's was his declaration, over some matter of dispute, that Kale was an incalculable rogue, and had taken liberties disobeying decisions Marsh took on their meanderings, and had to be sent home.

When Stanton completed his ride to Laban Vale after his night in the bush, stumbling into his house stiff-jointed, dazed, but more than illuminated, it was still early frosty dawn. Dolly and their daughter, Ivy, and Titus their boy, and their convict servants, numbering five and twenty including bond stockmen and convict shepherds locked in the barrack rooms' sheds, were still asleep. Stanton bundled in beside Dolly, worked his arms around her, shivering from what he knew, from what the staple of wool would lead him to, if he trusted it, in its close readable wriggles. Let wool be his maps and damnation to maps on paper.

Dolly was aware he'd been gone all night, as he pressed closer for a warm touch of her. She trusted his absences, for when he slept in the bush, making his busy way through the wide country, it was to be getting on with his preaching and magistrating, his disputing over land and livestock. Bold enterprise made the two of them stronger.

There were plenty of reasons for being fearful, yet Stanton was never too afraid to lie down and nuzzle the stones. Let there be grunts, scratches, howls and shrieks alarming others. Night in this country was God's invitation to meet the Devil. Let escaped convict malcontents know that every shadowed log or lump of boulder might be their minister. Let their nights in the bush drive them mad with thinking of him. Likewise the native populations, till they found God.

U GLY TOM RANKINE WAS NO stranger to the game of riding out from Parramatta past the sleeping farms with their spike-collared guard dogs and man traps set for miscreants. But this was only Rankine's second time in full danger, counting the ride he made with Kale, Moreno, and the sheep, after the freeing of Kale.

There was a feeling of breaking free of oppression past Stanton's Laban Vale into the starry bigness of the south. There Rankine found he could breathe better, his heart calmer in his chest.

He rode with his packhorse on a short lead, setting a good pace. Saddlebags bulged with salt, sugar, tea, flour, small sacks of corrosive sublimate, sulphur, and bluestone — and strapped across that load were blankets, a precious axe, and a nest of metal canisters, each fitting one into another and promising a fine sort of camp kitchen to men owning nothing more to sup from than a tin beaker between them. That beaker they had fought over from the start: Kale said Moreno did spit in it; Moreno said Kale did piss in it, and down in his blanket roll, too, because he was a dirty drunk. To keep

Moreno happy there was a bag of confectionary ingredients, ground sugar, dried coconut, cochineal and concentrated flavours more treasured in a country of paltry gratifications than diamonds. With sugars and sheep's milk cheeses Moreno was the master of caramelos. He started out life as a starveling boy in a castle kitchen of Estremadura, where his mother was scullery maid, the pair of them scoffing fudges, toffees and jellies until his belly stuck out and she lost her teeth. There was also a canteen of rum Tom Rankine carried, and four bottles of French brandy. It was what Kale asked, at great expense, to be brought back for them, and whatever Kale wanted Rankine swore to provide — except, when Kale asked for a woman, Rankine was evasive.

'Any one mainly?' he'd said — as the colony was a market of tradeable females and whores.

Kale answered with a name: Croppy Biddy Magee, asking if she was his way inclined; he thought she could be, 'For I am thinking of the darling more than I might.'

It was a fair enough question, an honest desire, but an unreasonable hope. Tom Rankine was shaken by it. Not because Kale was fifty-three years old and Biddy Magee aged but nineteen. She was pretty enough for a king. Nor did he think about any difficulties for a young Irish woman living in the wild bush with an outlaw. Not if it was Kale.

Biddy Magee, camp follower, was passed round a circle of compliance since Clumpsy M'Carty saved her after the battle of Badajoz. No more than a girl, in grief at the loss of her protector, a grenadier; Clumpsy had found her with some other adventuring females in the same distressing condition. The sky was their canopy, the turf their pillow as they followed Wellington's army in Spain. They had travelled to England with Rankine and his thousand sheep, and afterwards come on to Botany Bay. Biddy was Clumpsy's charge on the *Melanthus* on their voyage out. When Clumpsy was arrested for horse stealing Biddy went on trial with him. Both became convicts. If it were not for Biddy bewitching the judge advocate, they might have hung.

The thorn in it now was Biddy's present whereabouts, as assigned convict servant in Tom Rankine's domestic arrangements at Parramatta. It was foggy and frosty in the creek hollow where Rankine had his cottage. The floorboards and the bed boards creaked. With Biddy to warm his bones, Rankine had, at that time, and for the best part of a year, no reason for believing his life would change in the respect of love, for the excuse that Biddy's passion was easy, she was willingly warm enough — only a little gentling was required, and sometimes a drink of wine while they laughed and joked, and so very nicely glued to his ribs she was then, that nothing much else was wanted, he believed, on his side of the bed, nor hers, than his enjoyment and pleasure.

Then he had a directing dream. A herd of sheep passed him in a clatter of hooves and from out of their swirling dust a face of beauty and pure longing turned to him with a human gaze. He woke with his heart still going out, even while his arms went around Biddy, and while he stirred against her and they even found each other, he was lost to that other one, who was, he knew, Meg Inchcape.

He recalled when it started. How could he ever forget? A crowd of bond women went up a road to get back inside the walls of the female factory before dark. When they broke from each other, one remained outside and Tom Rankine followed her with his eyes. It was his first sight of her. Fixed in his memory was her free style of walking along a road, a barefooted beauty floating with a gypsy woman's elastic step, her skirts swaying and her large breasts flouncing and her black hair flying out. He learned she was a free woman of convict blood, the famed recalcitrant Desmond Kale's daughter.

After his morning's dream Rankine went out looking for her in the real light of day. The part of his dream that was still ramping up his bones, thickening his blood with desire, roused the most extraordinarily brutal coarse desire unfettered by the idealism of his vision. It rubbed him against his breeches, that day, and he feared that if he didn't blister he would gratify himself on his horse with its skittering in the open road. Parramatta was not such a big town and it did not take very long until he came into sight of her. All he told himself was one word, 'Everything' — that everything depended on reaching her, and after he reached her, on discovering her, knowing her, asking her; but what? Hand in marriage? Heat of raging bed? There was that moment in her dreamed gaze — as it found him, when it smokily enclosed him — when the future was revealed to him as an entire sphere.

Meg carried a laundry bundle on one shoulder, held by a bare browned arm, the other arm swinging free. It was like a club was wielded on Rankine from the inside of him at the sight of her. She went along a dusty street and he rode alongside her, bidding good day from a dry mouth, and touching his cap. She stopped and stared at him indifferently. She took a step back. A sadness or reverie in the angled solemnity of her expression pleased him. In a voice rather ordinarily inflected and flat, she said, 'Where do you think you are going on that fine horse, trooper — forward, back front, or sideways? Let me go past. Have you no control of her?'

'Madame, you must be joking,' he heard himself say. He chose to be slighted! And so saying heeled his mount into a rearing cavalry stance, useful for decapitating Hindoos while wielding a cutlass, but otherwise open to question, and imaginably seeing his frightening horse reflected in her curved hazel eyes, its neck stretched, its teeth enormous, its front hooves raking the air and the whole entire tableau bespeaking idiocy out of proportion.

'Go by, there is your passage, ma'am!'

The horse sank to its four feet and Rankine found himself being laughed at.

There was bold contempt in the way Meg tucked her hair back into her bonnet while bending her head and reaching one hand up behind her bare neck, somehow strokingly. Then the second look back. It showed she was interested. Or so he thought as their encounter settled. The way she put the little finger of her right hand to her teeth and nipped the fingernail, while balancing her washing so adroitly. She had long elegant feet, fine strong toes sifting the dust of the road. Her workaday habit and physical bearing was an example of the power of those with nothing. How much humble suffering had gone into her making? She foretold a great serious-ness. Or a great continuing foolishness in him, whatever.

'Madame . . .'

That word, the address of a vapid charmer, not useful on washer-women unless despicably intended.

Oh, but the connecting gesture: the way she turned on her heel and walked off. Loping you might say, loping and the image of her long-legged high-breasted walk multiplying into the thunder of the herd. The way her long black hair streamed behind and her catching eyes stirred around her. It affirmed her importance, her power as she shifted her washing bundle from the left to the right shoulder. The ordinary civilities of love defeated him. His face took on a saturnine demeanour.

What Rankine thought was, in the interval of a few deep breaths and giddy notions: 'With this woman I shall spend the rest of my life. I shall forsake all others. Together we might do anything. Everything depends on reaching her, and after I reach her, on being raked from the throat to the belly stave.'

They went their separate directions.

And really as it ensued, she continued ignoring him: he was quite put out. Boxes of sugar candies he sent her (made by the master of caramelos) roused no response. When he saw her at the governor's washing lines she contrived to ignore him. He pursued his dangerous interest with Kale. For without his wool thriving Rankine had nothing to offer anyone, not even himself.

When he learned that Stanton was proposing to take over Meg's son, Warren Inchcape, as his tied apprentice, he was dumbfounded. When he learned that Meg, in a reversal of convict loyalties and trusted bonds, might negotiate conditions with Kale's flogger, he was dumbfounded more. When he realised he loved Meg regardless he was dumbfounded to the limit of his understanding.

Rankine rode on without stopping. In the night country it meant picking along slow, his horse stumbling and shying. It was something he'd done enough times in Spain in the interests of advantage, ridden all night, gone hungry until he was done.

Here there was danger of blacks; danger of getting lost; risk of straying from the only possible direction into ravines on the left and right; tumbling into dry riverbeds; going over cliffs. Fear of those who slept in the bush was another particular. Rankine damped that fear, his courage being all cultivated nonchalance. When he glanced groundwards in the radiant starlight and saw a figure in a blanket roll in the early hours, a pale round face under a woollen cap, there and then gone — like the moon on the floor of earth, where it didn't belong — he was alarmed, and spurred his horse on. It was said that the minister, Stanton, went out after dark and lay with the Devil. Such blatant superstitions made the Irish affectionate, yet Rankine had seen him.

Even so: in Spain there was worse — treachery, banditry, insurrection, and disease. There was never this profound stillness, this feeling of benign immensity hanging from the stars down into the treetops. A pair of horse's ears framed a universe of breathing trees and low fires burning on the ridges. If harm should come, it would arrive in the midst of unbroken satisfaction. There was a white sandy path formed by wild cattle. It shone in the starlight mile after mile. Stars came up behind, stars wheeled down ahead, bleary in smoke.

Then it was pink misty morning, the birds of this country all screaming, cackling, scraping, piping, whistling. There was never such a show. Doves, cockatoos, parrots, finches. How Kale named them! listing what he called 'that first man', George Marsh, the naturalist, had called them. In the misty gullies kangaroos stood watching in mobs of dozens as the horseman rode past. There was one remained longer, stocky as a man in a tight grey overcoat, with furred testicles hanging below.

By this hour Rankine was at the southerly boundary of occupied lands. He was at the farthest fling of Stanton's Laban Vale, broadly defined as all territory between where Rankine now stood — a smoky blue ridge visible from a hilltop near the minister's house — and a view from the same hilltop along in the other direction, towards far distant Parramatta. The western border was the biggest river, glimpsed metallically shining in a grey expanse; and rising from the far bank was the wrinkle-ridged, blind-canyoned, impassable blue and smirched gold Caemarthens, as Marsh had named them, that had spat him out.

Rankine climbed into the fork of a tree, took his telescope and looked back. Implanted in the trunk he found a rusted spike with ridges of bark grown around it. An earlier governor, having in mind to clip Stanton's terrain, had sent out a few settlers this way. Within months they were Stanton's church deacons, making long rides to the Laban Vale chapel, St Botolph's, for Sunday observance. Soon they were in his employment, to make ends meet. When their potato crops failed, their isolation drove them spare and they walked off their farms despondent. Stanton called them his poor strugglers. Claiming their land back for grazing, he petitioned the governor for many thousands of acres more: if the governor would not give it to him, he would sail to London, he publicly declared, and get it from the king.

'And I have met him, this great man,' mused Rankine, 'lying in the dirt, scratching his cods, and my horse's hooves kicking pebbles in his face, as he lay there and not speaking.'

Rankine rode on, splashing into duck marshes, no way around them. He watched two emus stalk through a chewed grassland on the other side. For a time he was lost. Then some familiar ridges reached down. 'Look for the ones like five fingers of a hand,' Kale had reminded, and Rankine was then able to follow particular kinds of tree, as Kale had instructed him, so far with the stringybarks, higher up with the boxes, all the rest of the way along into the ones called ash, then the woollybutts, growing wide apart enough for a bullock waggon to fit between comfortably, if it ever pushed through. Leaf tips glittered like mirrors in the winter light. Termite mounds, high as a horse, stood forward, looming like pale hoods of flagellants.

For many miles Rankine found himself travelling up what constituted a long, low hill, three days long, and to an estimated height of three thousand feet he went above sea level. The country was ever sandier, scrofulous, poor, but you might not think so from the varieties of hardy vegetation that grew there. Ferns, heath-flowers, and paper daisies growing in cold winter light, sometimes sheltered by large trees with an understorey of coarse, reedy grass, and hardy-foliaged types of shrubs that made no sort of feed for a horse. By the end of each day Rankine arrived where there was water. On the third day he watched for the signs of black smoke on a white tree, and of two saplings twisted into a hieroglyph where the first time they came along they located a blazed trail. (When Kale found that trail he knew he was right. It had been lying in the bush ten years growing over like a scar.) Here was the grassy flat by the clear stream that Kale remembered. It was named 'the duck mole reach' by Marsh. Sheoak trees with fine needles. Clear running water with platypus bills breaking the surface like small black floating sticks. Three axe blows in an arrowhead shape pointing a way: 'Go sixty degrees off the angle pointed for the true bearing.' These axe blows were grown into bark, and hard to find, but once found, most essential.

It was there that Rankine had turned back, and the others gone on ahead. Now he went on ahead to find them.

THE DAY OF THE ESCAPE they had run the few miles west from Mundowey, forded the biggest river, bidding good day to indentured farm hands watching them pass. It was there Kale lifted the long-haired dog by the hind legs, declared it unwanted, and would slit its yelping throat, he said, unless it was cast from them. Those hardened convicts at a word from Kale trampled over their tracks as best they could with the help of such cows, pigs, and horses as they were providentially tending. A boy took the dog and said he would look after it. Moreno was downcast at losing his heart's treasure. 'Or else he kills my dogs,' he said, explaining its fate to the dog itself, as he slobbered a kiss on its nostrils.

Kale directed them on. Rankine wore rags and took orders from Kale. He was the complete unknown, the willing accomplice incognito. When descriptions were made later he was not there among them.

On then to the western ramparts of broken, golden sandstone. Dry creeks smashed in tumbles of stone from an obscure plateau in a series of tangled gorges. After raking the sheep through thorn bushes they entered a double-walled runway of rock, in storm seasons a torrent, as testified by large tree trunks stranded high on the sides of the gorge. They drove the sheep fast up and around, leaving few scatters of dung as they cantered along, heading into dry rock terraces. They held the sheep penned restless in a cleft while Kale picked out one, a ram, slaughtered it, and dragged the entrails in a continuing direction. Then at a precipice off to one side (for thus the country angled, in every way mad as imaginable), when one sheep leaped, all leaped — the remaining three hundred and four of them clean away into a pool of water the colour of strong tea. Down those sheep went in a cascade of angled bellies, jostling rumps and alarmed heads and hit the water already swimming. They clambered shivering wet to the bank and gathering their instincts, went along afterwards quieter than before.

It had proved worthwhile . . . the jump into oblivion . . . as Rankine learned when he saw the tracker's report a week later, and heard the governor declaring a trail gone cold at the ramparts and for sure Kale was perished. Except Rankine knew everything otherwise: they had angled back east, then south, crossed the biggest river twice where it was smaller; muddled through broken country; climbed that long, rough hillslope, and come on south through many slow days, and were safe from anyone's harm, as far as they knew.

It was near dark when Rankine arrived at a promontory of rock overlooking a sheltered valley. Three fires appeared in the shape of a triangle on the dusky valley floor where nothing so unlikely was predictable in nature. Rankine fired a pistol shot. A faint shot answered. In half an hour he was down there far below with Kale and Moreno, his horses watering in a clear shallow stream.

Kale wore a cape made from sheep skins sewn together and tied at the neck with a leather thong. Moreno hung back from the firelight awaiting his turn for the greeting. Kale came at Rankine with that commandingly dissatisfied impulse in his greeting as was first experienced in a damp unlikely dungeon.

'Next time come sooner, Rankine, or I'll get tired of these capers.'

Rankine smiled, fairly exhausted, waiting for an encouraging word from a man who made no concessions. 'We have done it safe,' he said. 'It's all made to look invisible. After a hard long ride, anyway, I am here.'

Under his tattered grey hair Kale had a broad forehead, damp brown eyes, a flat nose and wide, deep-breathing nostrils; a long upper lip, plump lower lip slightly quivering with antagonistic humour: 'We have done nothing yet that would even stir the dust of this country.'

Kale's jutting jaw was made to attract a punch, and Rankine was tempted. Others had given Kale a taste of his own proud medicine, leaving scars. But Kale had a saving grace withal, a wise engagement in that contradictory air of stubbornness. It created the spell of the Irishman and the only one resisting it hereabouts was Moreno.

The Spaniard looked a fright under his narrow-brimmed, high-crowned hidalgo's black hat. In honour of Rankine he put on a red waistcoat fringed with black piping and gold thread. It was crumpled and dirty as he was. His flat dirty face was framed in tangled sidewhiskers; his features were pinched, small raisin-eyed. He sent Rankine a look of oblique resentment, unmistakably dismayed.

But still, the two men embraced, holding each other tightly and gladly kissing so many times on alternate cheeks that Kale said:

'It is to be a continental inamorato, then?'

They were doing their living from the inside out of Moreno's condemned rams. Rankine established his position by the fire, saddle and bedroll spread, and by the time he was ready there was food for him on a clean new dish. They started with a grill of intestines on a rack of sticks, lit by a tallow wick. As a side dish, Kale consumed the eyes — spearing them up from a mess of baked head. Those eyes broke in the mouth quite firm, without spraying their jelly over the teeth.

Still hungry after that first round they sat by the fire on skins eating foreleg shanks. Except for a heel of bread and cheese, Rankine had eaten nothing for two days. Moreno had a small skin that was almost pretty, with a waved, fine gloss that appeared like the richest watered tabby. 'It is a fine skin,' said Kale, 'but remember what I said, Payolo Moreno, your rams was no good, and the reason was their small size, and their colours with red in them.' Moreno sulked, warming himself on his prized Santiago's skin. They were down to the last ram out of five. There would be a lambing soon from the ewes mated before the escape, unwisely mated, as Kale so very needlessly said.

'Baby lambs poached in ewes' milk will be on our bill of fare soon.'

Rankine broke out the spirits. They toasted their enterprise in beakers of brandy. 'Here's to our honest start,' said Rankine. The brandy filled him with good cheer.

'Are they on to us, mate?' said Kale. He grinned like a raving banshee. His years of official torture had battered him far from his long lost Irish gentleman's niceness of complexion, white scars puckering an eyebrow, distorting a corner of his mouth; in his speech was a roughened burr from being grabbed around the windpipe and half throttled, in a prison-yard thrashing.

Rankine told him they were so far safe — how the chase was put aside, from the governor's lists, though not, it seemed, from the flogging parson's.

'Nay, I am glad to hear that,' said Kale. 'As long as he fumes, you can follow his smoke like the black fellow who knows everything before it happens.'

Kale did not think about Stanton constantly, the way Stanton thought about Kale. But he judged their connection precisely, as along the blade of a knife, having no doubt that when the last trump sounded, he would be in Stanton's sights.

Before they were too settled round the fire Kale made his next demand of Rankine. He wanted the parson's big-framed ram, Young Matchless, for his own. 'Work the animal free and walk him over,' he said, with a toss of his head. It was like a Sunday stroll was proposed, and Rankine out gathering the finest blooms. An earlier ram, Old Matchless, was originally bred by Kale, with many of the good points wanted in a sire. Kale had bred Old Matchless in happier times, but long since Stanton claimed the breed as his own. 'It is well past time to claim the breed back,' said Kale. Young Matchless was Old Matchless's direct descendant. 'A grandson of forceful impact, I want him for ourselves. It is the season for taking. We have the ewes for our purpose, and have the country spread before us.'

'You have something wrong,' said Rankine, looking at the way Kale sat protecting his back.

He found Kale had lumps under his armpits the size of duck eggs, from his infected flogging wounds, which Rankine bathed and dressed. Moreno might have done it, and nursed Kale, for he had the stomach to oblige — but not the courtesy to offer.

Rankine wrapped himself in his blanket and lay on the dusty

ground. Drifting in and out of sleep, as they yarned, he told of a load of trade goods, of which his saddlebags held particulars, goods that were conceivably to be diverted as far as the duck mole reach on a waggon — specially if they could be brought forward by the trader who owned them, in the name of certain profits, without Parson Stanton getting any hint of where they were bound.

At the start of the midnight watch Moreno found himself kicked awake. He took his orders from Kale: banked fires against warregal dogs that came in the dark and threatened ewes from under the lowest bars of the hurdles and then skipped over the top. The dogs' disagreeable yodelling cries taunted Rankine, causing the hair on the back of his neck to stand up; but the dogs hardly warned of their approach when they began to mean business. Their golden coats and slit orange eyes were for their own appreciation alone, as were their small, sharp teeth bared in grinning refinements of hunger, and their musty, excitable smells.

In the morning the warregals' footprints were visible in the sand under trees where the last putrid meat was hung. They found that a ewe was taken. Surveying the torn, dead ewe Kale blamed Moreno for dozing on watch, which Moreno denied, and so Rankine stood between two men only sullenly tolerant of each other. Their mutual dislike troubled Rankine who was devoted to both equally and for opposite reasons. It was the superb dedication of the one and the independent scorn and ridiculous royal elegance of the other that kept them balanced in his affections, but not to each other face to face.

The head of the valley where the sheep liked to gather in a preferred sheep camp was decided as a place for a better sort of camp for all. Frost and morning mists flowed downhill and they were sheltered from the worst of the cold southerly winds, but not the north-westerlies. Throughout that day and the next they built stone sleeping shelters from the wind, raised a wattle-stick palisade against dogs and thatched the shelters with boughs. Rankine had five days before he was expected at barracks. They constructed a sheepfold from rocks, gated it with hurdles, and years from now the stones would be discovered in the shape they gave them, and beyond their cooking fire would be unearthed the green broken necks and pebbled bottoms of the French brandy bottles they smashed when they emptied them. It would be wildly imagined how they must have roistered there for a good long time, but any walk up a joining ridge, and along to a jumbled peak, would have shown another sort of answer.

'It is a whole province for us to get around,' said Kale, pulling his cloak tightly around him, as he pointed out features to Rankine in the knifing cold wind. The satiny blue sky was clean of cloud. The winter sun was brilliant. Fold after fold of ranges spread south and east. Only to the west was there a flattening effect, as of a plain, but so far away it was surely a mirage in the blown haze. 'Here, it is greater than Kilkenny by a long straw, though not so green and plush, with duck mole reach on the northern limit making a depot, like you suggest, if a waggon is brought up. Each of them rocky ridges hides a valley, of which there are between six and twenty. A river goes through like a snake.'

'Something like a paradise all up,' suggested Rankine. 'Including the snake?'

'A very steep paradise with wild dogs too, and though we have not sighted any natives, we have seen their fires.'

Looking down, they watched Moreno moving sheep over a low ridge for their day's grazing, leading them down into a valley bottom where meagre watercourses trickled through prickly undergrowth but where the sheep would soon fan out, settle, and feed till their bellies dragged and spoiled the untouched kangaroo grasses for their own uses. Where it was precipitous going they never lost footing, although some bolted and rode down on their backsides tearing their rumps.

'Not yet a full paradise,' said Kale, looking back over his shoulder as if Moreno might be listening, though he was at least half a mile away. 'Attend to me, Rankine — if you get me the ram I want, Young Matchless, and the man I want, Clumpsy M'Carty, and bring me the girleen I want, Croppy Biddy Magee, it will be paradise enough until our shearing. He is a great man with the blades, your Moreno, and then I shall be happy to see the backside of his greasy arse.'

Rankine disliked giving Kale all his consideration without getting much more than some grumbles back. Kale sensed it, too, and stood leaning against a boulder, half turned away, half smiling. The more he asked of life, the more he thrived — though it never took away any suffering. This was incredible though.

'You could at least express some astonishment, Kale, at what I have done.'

'Oh, yes,' said Kale. 'Spoken with proper exasperation. My astonishment's in the sheep you gave me —'

'Not gave — gave over —'

'We shall argue that expression when they build back up to a thousand, as I think we agreed. Wait on their wool, Rankine, the astonishment in their wool is all the answer, to your niggling ways. Send me a packhorse drover in a month's time and I'll send in some woolpacks of finest fleece. They can be sent to England, for an opinion on their grade. I believe they shall amaze the bowels of the woolstapler who grades them. As for a drover and carrier, there is a good trusted one, John J. Tharpe, originally from Cavan. He knows how to dodge and weave.'

'I note the instruction,' said Rankine. 'But "niggling"? — I don't like that —'

'You'll need Tharpe's whole team. Don't say Kale asked for them. But say the fellow with the salt has an answer.'

'Whatever that means.'

'Whatsoever indeed,' said Kale. And then began singing half under his breath, as they walked back down to the valley floor.

TOM RANKINE KNEW ONLY ONE thing of Desmond Kale when they began in this: it was said by all that Kale was the inordinate man for a sheep, but was so tied down in chains, incorrigible with abuse, he was lost to men's ordinary ways. Whenever he stirred himself he was laid up with a flogging. Oh, and had a daughter — that handsomest damned washerwoman in the governor's laundry sheds. Yes, they had met. Yes, they had exchanged two words. And yes, just as soon as he found her, Rankine lost her in the very utterance of the two words spoken between them.

When his duties took Rankine into the gaolyard at Parramatta, all such matters were enlarged by intensified wonder.

Out of the prisoners crowded into the holding yard there was one who stood apart. A tense, measured manner attracted attention, in the man who hefted his chains, as if they were made of paper; and the slumbering, powerful gaze of a captive centurion was seen, as he turned his head and stared at Rankine.

'Who is that man over there?' said Rankine, already guessing. He was told it was the Irishman — a singular sort of reply: because of all the numbers present, Irish were in the predominance. Thus did Rankine gain his first lesson in the admiration of Desmond Kale, even from those who hated him.

There was no sunlight in the punishment cells. They were built half into the ground and smelled sourly of mould. Only in one room a narrow window admitted paltry light, and there Kale was returned after being counted.

Rankine took sight of Kale sitting in a corner of that rock-hewn cell with his chewed grey hair and sad, courageous features, his large-knuckled hands hanging between his knees, his head thrown back and singing.

'It is something about the singing,' he decided, 'that brings the guards running.'

'He is not allowed it,' said the superintendent.

'Let him go on with it.'

'He is testing you, captain,' warned the superintendent.

'Allow him,' said Rankine.

Doubtless the fellow would wrench Kale from his cell and take him along by the heels, back into the yard and deal him a few keen blows, if an officer was not present.

Light seemed to come on Kale as a marvellous privilege in the dank space.

'It is said that if the Irishman ever cries out on the punishment block, it shall be the end of them all.'

'That is interestingly thought,' said Rankine.

'It is their kind of superstition, expressed with holy fervour, but don't they see — it gets Kale flogged more.'

This said with relish.

At the time Kale was between severe floggings, his hide a ploughland of punishments. Before he received his next lot of lashes — following a brief spate of freedom — one man at least would make sure, from pity, it would be his last.

The encounter was barely a year after Rankine arrived in the colony with his bought commission and his Spanish sheep, when garrison duties held him in town and Moreno, out past Toongabbie, walked a wretched landscape watching their sheep do passingly well on stalks and sticks and stones. It was clear by then, that for all his excellence, Moreno might ruin the flock. The Spaniard pushed breeding ideas vainglorious to himself. They were sheep obtained in Spain in unsought violence and the answer against unsought violence came to Rankine as a recompense: it was to let Kale have the sheep and breed up their numbers. The justice would be in the freeing from justice of Kale, and the glorification of his freedom. It was to grant a life, where life was carelessly taken.

Rankine kept himself fairly sociable in town, among his fellow officers, listening to their rivalries about stock, not arguing their loud opinions back at them and rarely letting on he knew what was a lamb, a ewe, or a wether as distinct from a grub or a flea moving in the distance through the scanty trees around the edges of the settlement. It was not safety he craved in this subtle role, it was danger: truly hazardous fuel for interior justice. His instinct for risky dealing had brought him to the right place when he landed at Botany Bay and found, beyond the prison grid of barracks, stores, and stockades, a wideness of land vaster than oceans — and just about able to support sheep and an officer seeking a fortune in sheep if that officer was one who feinted, baulked, and dodged his way along. Except it had not been clear what to do, at the level of requital Rankine craved, with just a few hundred sheep, plus lambs, until the day he met Kale.

'Take me to him,' he said.

Rankine was led down a set of damp stairs with padlocks closed and iron bolts rammed shut behind him. According to orders he was slated to relieve the under-commandant of the dungeon, but disputed those duties as beyond his obligation. He soon got out of them, too, for there was a manner Tom Rankine had, a charming, airy easiness — something to do with his extremely pale blue eyes, so startling in a poxy face, that always seemed to be playing on matters he was best allowed freedom to follow. Something to do with his closeness with the governor, too, it was said. Both had been in Spain — Wilkie with the 88th Foot, later 1st Battalion Connaught Rangers, dubbed by General Picton 'The Devil's Own'. While that closeness was exaggerated, it could not be denied — you were a Sir Colin Wilkie favourite if you dined at government house one day a week, and Rankine sometimes went four. Because where else could you get blithering drunk on quite superior wines, and be witless with horseplay, and establish yourself? Where some others paid coin as a bribe, to get on, or equivalent value in rum in barrack room trade, Tom Rankine at least always started with engaged under-standing, charm. It saved his pocket, and if you thought it would take him nowhere in a colony of getting and gaining you did not know Botany Bay well enough. His deepest need, though, was tuned like a lampwick in daylight. It was not plainly seen.

Of course, a man was the same man all through. Know him better and stubbornness, laziness, and self serving might emerge from behind those keen pale eyes, and a bundle of other qualities, good and bad. There was a stepbrother in Yorkshire kept a resent-ful record of the worst of him, the two brothers being estranged. Wool was the stepbrother's expert trade. He'd been left nothing in Rankine's father's will except six silver quaffing cups and a box of ivory dominoes. Rankine gained Oak Farm. He had everything, you might think, yet his feeling of loss, after Spain, drove him to amends.

To nobody, not even himself, had Tom Rankine been able to say, 'I am dying to be rescued.'

Instead, he sailed to Botany Bay and rescued Kale.

He stood at the bars until let in. The guards left them alone. After Rankine introduced himself Kale spat at his feet.

'What is this all about?'

Moving his feet, as if a flea merely hopped over them, Rankine said: 'It is about wool, Desmond Kale.'

Kale's sour expression did not change until Rankine pulled from his pocket a fistful of wool staples. He laid them out on the stones, under the best available light. Then he waited.

'Are these any good?'

It was a long time before Kale answered, when he said, in a voice with the melody of his singing in it, and without any lilt of contempt:

'They are an angelic sepulchre away from the penetration of shite.'

I T WAS BLAISE HENRY CRIBB'S genius to examine fleeces shipped to a Yorkshire sorting floor from four corners of the world and make more sense of them than could be explained in words or read from their careful measurements. Consignments came from England, Scotland, Ireland, Wales; from thistly Argentina, snowy Vermont, from regimented Saxony, from painted France, and from golden parched Spain and then increasingly from one place in grisly particular farther flung than the rest — where Cribb was obliged to admit wools flourished supreme.

But each time the prison colony was listed Cribb cursed:

'Again?'

Botany Bay wools clipped tighter than concertinas (in ribbed dusty bundles) were slung from ships' holds, trolleyed to Thomas's wool hall and broken open at Cribb's convenience. He stood at a slatted table gathering their light tumbling splash. He interpreted milling needs between fisted samples, taking his time with thought, tapping his wide forehead with a pencil and wrapping his full, damp lips around its soft chewed end, or snapping a piece of chalk between his fingers, not to be disturbed — then strode along in the light of cobwebbed glass speaking orders to clerks and carters, receivers and handlers, as sailing ships unloaded and mills were supplied a portion of their wants.

Cribb's profession was woolstapler, a word meaning sorcerer or something like it when you looked under his hat. There was an effect quite uncanny on Cribb's sensibilities, a confusing magic to his touch around wool. The woolstapler's craft was ordinarily enough explained as bridging between the breeder of wools and the manufacturer of them. The woolstapler purchased the fleece and occasionally sold it in the same state, but oftener assorted it: dividing it into different parcels, according to degree of fineness principally, or the possession of some property fitting for a particular commodity, say for the hatter, the clothier, the hosier, for the maker of men's suits and coats or for women's airier stuffs. Was it Cribb's feel — his hand, his eye — or was it his heart involved mainly? Or was it more his passionate buffeted anger around the matter of wools, his roused intelligence that both frightened, and impressed?

Blaise Cribb was a stocky man of stumpy commanding figure; he was aged thirty-nine. He was French born, English raised after the age of four, with a large head, penetrating dark eyes, full shapely mouth and chin — strong-nosed, unruly dark-haired, wide-shouldered with a contained gunpowder energy. His impatience, resentment, and ferocious curiosity marked him out as more demonstrably Continental than phlegmatically English. Cribb had the look of an exiled commander in waiting and roused interest accordingly — a harbinger of empire whose time was to come — though when *would* it come? Blaise Cribb was always slightly out of place among his own . . . and yet, when he came into sight, striding down into his home village, his coarse-weave navy greatcoat sweeping the cobblestones, spattered with mud to the pockets, he seemed like the truest expression of what came best from that northern English farming soil, a disdainful servant of livestock's hard-worked perfection, where nothing worthwhile was gained without independent scorn. You would have to say — a Yorkshire-man complete, despite his Frenchified start.

Cribb was raised in wool's greasy service from lambing days to the plate of boiled mutton with blue potatoes, representing a feastly goodbye to a life lived out, whether of ram or ewe, while a collie dog loyalled at his feet or gnawed at a bone and Cribb sank pots of dark beer in the Inn of the Four Bound Sheaves before rolling home insensible.

It rained on Cribb emotionally that he was a blot on the name Rankine as he returned on many black nights up a byway path, to his stepbrother's farm. Ugly Tom Rankine's farm, as Cribb only half accurately called it, seeing as how the captain had no working part in it, being thankfully abroad, and Cribb lessee at a peppercorn rental through overdone consideration on Rankine's part — how dare he condescend so!

Needing no lantern, Cribb was drawn by a glow in his brain, to stumble around drunk and fuming, getting up hate for the moss on stones that once was his delight to peel, in a study of patterns of lace and continents, with faces of men in the moon.

Oak Farm was where Blaise Cribb had galloped a shaggy pony, roamed with flocks enjoying a childhood more carefree than any he knew except Tom Rankine's who took his place and favour. Ignorant of love's calculations Cribb had loved that boy six years his junior, carried him on his shoulders, shown him willingness and strength unmitigated by guile, had gone to work early on behalf of them all and learned breeding lore from the man who knew as much as anyone needed to know, his stepfather — the natural father of Ugly Tom, Sir Hugh Rankine.

A good acreage was promised — in a conversation Cribb never forgot, conducted with the stepfather at a high corner of a turnip field and a neighbour as witness — sworn indeed to be the youth Cribb's, upon old Sir Hugh's death; and later again, over a brimming glass, was pledged by the venerable liar to be where Cribb would raise his own boys (when he had them) under the moors and upon them, where they would learn something from their step-grandsire about flocks and heath, game and hawks, speckled fish, rich pastures and purplish turnips jumping from soil of dark crumbs scientifically rotated. So it had been intended, at least, if charity colours interpretation, but never does — through perfidy of will and testament. Something had gnawed in the old man's brain about the breeding of Cribb's own son being deficient.

Blaise Cribb in his early twenties had fathered a son on the distaff side, named Jonathan. The woman Cribb generated Jonathan upon, Peg Johnstone, was a deficient slut by country designation — seeing that all Johnstones were tinkers, thieves, and coin in the mouth jingling whores. It anyway justified theft of Cribb's inheritance as down the knife blade of desire came his legacy denied. He kept the boy for himself, since a baby — would not have him stolen by tinkers or anyone else. Nor did ardent uncaring Peggy's death soften Sir Hugh Rankine's antipathy. When Blaise Cribb, hostility alight, rampaged wilder, he was well cut out.

Cribb tried not thinking too much about his benefited step-brother, Ugly Tom, but was not always fortunate in putting him out of mind. He spoke Rankine's name as odious when reeling drunk; tried to avoid putting himself in any situation where he might be drawn into conversation about life in Botany Bay. But Cribb was born at a fated location — midway between Malmaison and Rambouillet, home to France's best wools — in the year of a glow in the sky, the time of a comet with a lanigerous or woolbearing tail. He was born to a studsman, Wade Cribb, and a woolcombing demoiselle, Yolande Rousillon, who, after the death of her husband (the natural father Cribb barely knew), went over the channel as Sir Hugh's mistress before her early death. In a passion of mourning her, Sir Hugh made Cribb his son. Then the squire married more equably, if more dully, and fathered Tom Rankine, whose charm finally broke an old man's promises, and whose core flock of Spanish sheep these some years later promised a breed unrivalled, in the climate of Botany Bay, while Cribb's apportionment in England all failed.

At the dockside Botany Bay spilled out its wools — not in great quantities, nor always consistently good, but quite stirring in potential. Something was going on there, you might say, like new stars being born into the darkest corner of the sky. Cribb was drawn back to these improving wools' traces wherever he turned.

The two breeders to watch, Cribb early decided, were 'M. Stanton' and 'D. Kale'. They were first seen some years ago as private exhibitors in two bundles of best samples, names on pasteboard tags. The very best samples Cribb paid for, but did not put up for sale — keeping them in boxes to be taken out from time to time and looked at in best lights, laid long upon a table, and there parted and eyed, not in any wish for sensation unless as a technical mark of comparison — but always leaving Cribb with an extreme dampness of mouth, an intense physical sensation, an experience of singular lust, or its near relative, abomination.

So Cribb found himself thinking about Botany Bay and its

wools more times than he liked. Without wanting a bar of it, he became the authority on them, and was sought out.

A contemptible lot would stop him short, send him back to the tables where prentices and foremen gathered and Cribb's voice thickened with bitter sarcasm — damnable stones in the matted material to give an example, they set him going — wool having crossed the wide oceans carrying scrapes of sour earth, links of shattered chain dumped in, torrents of sand where a sheepwash had failed, carcass of native dog found as makeweight.

But the 'M. Stantons' and the 'D. Kales'? They were the harbingers. Luminous when washed, the Kale was hardly bigger than an otter's pelt. It was raised by Kale and trusted by him to Marsh, when the naturalist returned to England, after which there were plenty of 'Stantons' but no more 'Kales'.

Cribb and George Marsh met under notable circumstances. It had been the first but not the last time Cribb was asked to make guesses about the breeding of New South Wales sheep and found himself paraded before ancient gentlemen wearing the silks and velvets of an earlier day and obsessed over wool. It was during the October Stuffs Balls for the encouragement of woollen manufactures in Leeds. Rankine at that time was newly gone soldiering. Jeremy Bramley, as he was then, later to be Lord Bramley, knew a man who knew a man, and so on. That man was Sir Joseph Banks, instrumental in having the merino sheep introduced into England where it was fated to fail. But Cribb did not know that yet, the degree of its undoing to come: he badly wanted some — and Rankine would gift it from Spain eventually, as if to illustrate the adage, beware what you wish lest it smother you in blessings.

Bramley and Cribb went by coach more than a hundred miles to meet Banks and learned from Marsh that Sir Joseph was in bed having a bad winter of gout and confinement. Bramley was at the beginning of his magnum opus, *The Shepherd's Sure Guide*, and was ushered in to Banks for the benefit of his wisdom. There was a great mess of papers in the house and Bramley was given the run of them for as long as he could spare. Cribb was taken by Marsh to a store-room and shown the bundle of wools that afterwards remained his disturbance when it came to deciding if New South Wales wools were any good. The small Kale fleece was a copper-burnished salmon leaped from a sullen stream into one's very own hands and then finding for all the seeking to follow there were, save for the interesting Stantons, only dull small fish left to do their growing. The character of the breeder? A convict shepherd, Marsh said, ever to remain unpedigreed, perhaps, except a piece of information was related by the botanist and the name sprang out. The house of Kale: a destroyed family of Ireland known to be good with fine wool sheep but politically overwrought and exiled into shame and destruction.

From then on Cribb had something positive to report about colonial wools when asked, by saying there was boundless poten-tial; but each year after his first evaluation he never saw as much improvement as he wanted. He looked for increased density and fineness, length of staple and brilliance. The Stanton lots, over the next few years, held to the initial standard with some variation. Stanton was the best supplier for what it was worth. Improvement here in staple, there in fineness, everywhere in length — except without leaping improvement overall. The glimmer, the shine, was missing. Of the wool of Kale, still no sighting to this very day.

Cribb's habit was to say, of the prison land: 'There was never any place in the world where a sheep was so keenly sought after improving, with so little knowledge of the art in doing so.'

What Marsh had pictured for Cribb was a place of dry sticks

under a pitiless sun where there was feed and water only scantily available, but where sheep oddly thrived or rather pushed out fine wool from their barely living skeletons if they survived drought and being speared by savages.

Now Rankine was gone to New South Wales with three hundred of his King of Spain's thousand brought down the Sierra Morena and shipped from Cadiz to Hull. It was the bonanza of sheep duffing that enthused the British officer corps into a fashionable frenzy upon Wellington's victories. The seven hundred gifted to Cribb by Rankine's derelict largesse because of not thriving were no sort of gift at all, and Cribb, having accepted them, having wanted them, found himself wasting them and not entirely irrationally blaming Rankine. When Rankine sailed on the *Melanthus* he took with him his remainder sheep; his lugubrious manservant, Moreno; his Irish footservant, M'Carty; and a young woman of M'Carty's pleasure, Magee. There were letters since then, but no history of the sheep.

The matter of Botany Bay wools and Rankine's sheep at the heart of them burned and fizzed with Cribb. Remedy was the whisky flask, carried at all times and replenished from a square bottle kept in a brown leather bag. Drink gave Cribb the feeling of glorious universal components flying free of his will. Though it soured his stomach, reddened his nose, bared his gums, it made him godlike and careless. Mentally, when he chased what mattered — the object of his deepest rage, betrayal by his closest adopted kin — he was more like the campaigning soldier he despised: Rankine himself, so hot-blooded with aim that even his own death might be irrelevant to the purpose of putting matters right in the warring heavens.

'ANYWAY...' SAID REVEREND MATTHEW STANTON, rather belatedly to his wife, as he emerged from his study where he never liked to be disturbed, through an amount of furious concentration needed for letter writing to the governor (rather than needed for his sermons, which came naturally spouting free):

'Anyway . . . my dear . . . all such matters concerning an escaped convict named Kale . . . that fellow George Marsh . . . governors . . . black boy . . . renegade sheep-breeding officers . . . Jews buying wool . . . convict connivance and superlative sheep — whatever, whatever — they all lead back to the decision to be made about a boy . . . Warren Inchcape . . . coming under our roof.'

'A decision you have made, my dear Matthew?' said Dolly, 'Come whatever I think?'

'Nay, the point I would make to you plain,' said Stanton, giving his wife's hand a squeeze and concluding his argument as if logically mapped, 'is that if I don't have a natural apprentice in my ram sheds, my Saxons won't *do*, and there is no better way of sealing the matter than binding the boy to our hearts. You see, when he is around sheep he is a paragon, and I wouldn't want to lose him to anyone who thinks they are better than me.'

The next day Stanton rode to Parramatta and examined Warren Inchcape's mother, Meg, as to her needs in life, about which he found her willing to talk, despite the possibility of some sort of confederacy lingering with Kale. He was interested to discover it by lifting up and looking under every one of her courtesies.

'I am beating my brains out,' he said, handing the woman a card embossed with a Gospel text, framing a rose of Sharon in a shade of crimson, as a token of good will, 'to remember where we have crossed paths before.' Except he remembered it very well. She was on Kale's arm when he fell over drunk in the mud, when she was a maid of sixteen, which was to say, at a ripe old age for a lass of convict blood to begin her romps.

As for her memories of Parson Matthew Stanton, they were not being investigated. You could only be fairly sure she knew him everywhere.

Showing him into her hut — the door a canvas flap — Meg Inchcape observed the finer points of etiquette, taking from Stanton's arms his riding crop, his big round hat, his satchel of tracts, and handing him a mug of water that only faintly tasted of clay, as it was drawn from a pitcher standing on a cool shelf, where the mud had settled thanks to the addition of a little ash. He could hardly turn around without brushing her elbow and feeling her warm breath upon him. She had him at a disadvantage with the look of her hazel eyes, only a little guarded like a hawk's and conniving to keep herself humble at his service. Whatever she felt for Kale she hid the feeling, in hopes for her son. Love was strongest when least sensible — Stanton knew — and Kale was a man involved in his own catastrophes, but she would want to save him from a hanging as far as she could. Safety was in doing what Stanton wanted: handing over her son.

It was an improvised boudoir Stanton found himself in, with an emphasis on a woman's shrewdest commodity in a sprig of wildflowers and a mirrored shawl draped over a rough bench, decorative invitations to the senses. Threadbare as they were, the adornments did not persuade Stanton that Mistress Inchcape was entirely virtuous in the struggle of life, trying for a little decency where she could. On the contrary, the dexterous muting of lechery was implied.

The rough bench doubled as a bed, a deeply comfortable one it appeared to be if a rail was removed and blankets unrolled over a corn-husk mattress with eyes of buttons sewn on. Short of asking for a show of its utility there was no possible way Stanton could position himself to guess whether upon lifting the cushions there was a hidden hinge, and the space under the bed would reveal an empty box or a full one. It was certainly large enough to hold a fugitive. So was a box room at the side of the house, more like a broom cupboard, which Meg told him was occupied by an old convict woman, Mother Hauser — servant to a servant, in a gradation of beggary the colony made possible through its glut of workable felons.

But if Kale were alive, returned from the back country and hidden in the room (a wild supposition to be sure), Meg Inchcape seemed in no hurry to rid herself of her visitor. She was skittish when it came to settling on a figure that would warm her to persuading her boy to come over to Stanton's ram sheds. She asked for the amount of twenty-four pounds a year, twice the figure Stanton paid out on a shepherd, and said with a wry inclination of her head:

'If I am to shepherd Warren, like you want, so that he always goes home to your fine house, that is the amount I will need to keep me from other resorts. He should come back to his mother on the Sabbath, too?'

The way she asked it, with a rising intonation of charm, sounded as fine a note of promise as Stanton had ever heard from a woman threatening moral backsliding.

'If I should let him,' Stanton cautioned.

'Only after church muster, without a doubt,' Meg Inchcape conceded, as Stanton was known to be soothed by numbers of heads visible in his congregations, better than any bribe of rum or kisses that would turn an ordinary man.

'Not every week, madam, Lord help me, it is too far a ride from my sheep station into this town.'

Thus Stanton tried to bargain her down, and while he waited each time for her answer (which was always no, she must have the twenty-four), he looked around the interior of her hut, and agreed that although there was a dish of blue delft, and a shiny knife and fork, and those enticing although threadbare declarations of the womanly sort, which made him wonder about a man spreading his limbs there, the place could do with more deserved fortune.

'How are you getting by? What are those "resorts" you might be thrown back on, apart from being our governor's leading washer-woman?'

'Only people's favours,' she said, with a foxly lift of her chin. She would do almost anything to avoid or postpone marriage, allowing her that freedom, if it came to anyone putting the question. The reason being that she still, in a part of her feelings barriered from change, suffered from a long-time heartache, stemming from a desertion and a hope of return.

Though her words, as Stanton interpreted them, went entirely another way: they gave the hint that she was a harlot outright under the pretence of poverty. Or was making the political point, that beggary was the lot of her class. She was native born, with faults of convict blood and habits of consorting with scum implied. Just think of her father. Just think of her mother, Patsy Inchcape, the wildest, most unmanageable screaming foul-mouthed slut that had ever been held down on the flagstones of the female factory to have her hair shorn off.

'In any case, bless you, you've won me,' he said. 'Twenty-four pounds it shall be, paid in portions of two each month, beginning after Warren has proved himself happy.

'No doubt Warren shall always be able to bring you a mutton haunch slung across the saddle, and whatever we might spare from our garden — hush, now I am going to boast to you, Meg Inchcape — we have plantains, loquats, guavas, mandarins, pomegranates and cherimoyas, a fruit from Peru.'

'Watch out, he will grow fat.'

With their business settled, Meg had the style to ask Stanton if he would take a splash of rum before his ride home.

'At your leisure,' he answered, taking position near the fireplace of cold ashes, a hearth almost big enough for him to step into, as he was not a tall man, more bulky sideways with a heavy chest and powerful sloping shoulders, a short neck, strong arms and bandy legs. He poked his interfering head in there, and was amused into being metaphorical when she asked him:

'What are you doing in my chimbley, father, getting yourself all so sooty?'

'Looking for one of those opossums that gets into narrow places, with a taste for nectar and sugared treats, so that an honest householder will never get rid of him, unless someone does the dirty work and gives him a sharp jab with a stick.'

COMING AWAY FROM MEG INCHCAPE'S row of huts built flat-faced onto the dismal road, Stanton found himself the object of hostile attention from urchins, layabouts, and various known molls passing their day in stupefaction of drink. It quite ruined the mood when a hurled clod passed uncomfortably close to his nose. It made him long for the unpeopled countryside of Laban Vale, where the worst thing to happen to a man was being swooped on by a magpie or bitten by an ant . . . worst thing if the man's name happened to be Matthew Stanton, that is.

'Stanton!'

It was indeed his name. He twisted in the saddle to see who called out — a man with a lurching limp and a deformed left arm, moving in the opposite direction, up and down in the receding dust like a bobbin. Then came the curse of the Irish:

'Stanton! You're the first, you horribilis cunt, and bugger my eyes if I don't get hanged for it.'

Only in his private diaries and never in his letters of complaint to various governors had Stanton recorded that curse. It was the pledge reserved for him specially — one heard often enough, however, to call it treasonably common as dust and flies.

This day it happened that a constable and a work party were approaching from behind some trees. Never before had a vilifier left himself so exposed.

'Seize that man!'

In a wild direction the man ran, with Stanton galloping after him. He jumped down from his horse. The constable raised his stick. They backed the man to his knees, while the work party, linked by chains, sat on a bank side.

'What is your name?' said Stanton.

'It's Patrick Lehane.'

'Well known as the useless and hopeless,' said the constable.

He was a miserable, skinny, wasted sort of a man of around thirty, with unshaven sunken cheeks, shifty eyes, and a craven, taunting manner. He had an earlobe stretched almost down to one shoulder, a hole in the middle and dangling from it a piece of shell from the South Sea islands.

'I never spoke. It was not me. Where was your witnesses, anyway?'

'Constable, did you hear this man say —'

'Say what when?' said Lehane.

Stanton could not bring himself to utter the phrase. But he took Lehane by the shirt and said close into his ear, 'Mr Lehane, within the hour, under statutes of punishments allowed me, I shall have you tied to the triangle and whipped your fifty lashes. And tomorrow I shall come on with another fifty again. And so on until we come to an understanding, and you tell me who minted those words.'

'Get me a drink,' said Lehane tersely. 'For I do have sumpthin to tell.'

Within the half hour Stanton sat with Lehane in a private cell in the Parramatta court house. Lehane was quite changed after his capture — companionable and expansive. His ruse in keeping an unruly reputation intact had worked so far, he explained. Stanton gave him a beaker of rum. Lehane offered himself as Stanton's agent.

Stanton made sure they would not be interrupted, by bolting the adjoining door.

'It is your confessional,' he said. 'So tell me, what is it you have, and what you wish in return. You took a great risk abusing me. You dared a flogging, you claim, in order to serve me?'

'As I say, I would rather break stones than be flogged. I almost would honestly rather hang, than feel them knots again.'

'You have my undertaking you shan't be flogged, not in my jurisdiction, good man.'

'In writing?'

'In writing,' said Stanton, after a long moment's hesitation. A promise had nothing to lose, through being made to a malcontent.

'It was an officer who plucked Kale,' said Lehane.

'I am already sure of it myself. You have his name?'

'Naw, but I seen him.'

'We are only equal so far,' said Stanton. 'I saw him myself.'

'In daylight?'

'That would be better,' admitted Stanton.

'It may be,' said Lehane, in a flash of pride, 'that you have heard of a bushranger who goes by the name of "the eye of reason"?'

'Here, there, bailing people up,' said Stanton, 'and giving out pamphlets addressing rights and wrongs relating to the Irish rebellion, where he was misrepresented, and betrayed, and so turned to the life of the highwayman, not through any fault of the authorities but through the ostracism of his own good people?'

'That's me, the very same one.'

'I have indeed heard of you, over the years, but I can't say a dispute between treasonous rogues leaves me with very much interest in your sympathies.'

'Be that so, you may have the same enemies as the eye of reason does. The same needs to settle a matter.'

'That might be better. Only I can't think without names.'

'Say their first is in king.'

'Ah, that's a good seditious start. Their next?'

'It would be in acclaim.'

'Go on.'

'Their third in landed, poor landed gent. Their fourth in extreme. Would that make you a name?'

'It does,' said Stanton. 'To the letter.'

'The *eye* has a hideout, a cave overhang in a wild place. It is a long way out.'

'Which direction?'

'That I can't say, but I *shall* say, when it's safe. It is hard by a popular ridge beloved by the dark people. Follow them, go with them, sleep in their camps — lie with their willing — and this country falls open to finding in ways you wouldn't believe in.'

'I am sure you are right, and just as inscrutable as they are you would need to be, in order to thrive with them.'

'It is through there a redcoat, a king's ranger comes and goes. So far, he's been a way off for personal naming. I couldn't catch up without being seen meself.'

'Then what is your point with me, Lehane?'

'Sooner or later that redcoat shall feel a pistol to his neck, and he shan't be asked the question, his money or his life, but asked to ransom his life to ye, sir.'

'Is that your proposition?'

'If I am on the loose and have my freedom, it is.'

'You possessed that freedom before you cursed me.'

'If the eye of reason is ever pulled in, he shan't be flogged at all?'

'He has his freedom before my court,' agreed Stanton, 'but be sure — if betrayed I shall have your eye of reason's spectacles on a string.'

'As long as he ain't flogged,' said Lehane, 'you can grill em in butter.'

They made an arrangement about meeting places in the woods beyond Laban Vale homestead. Stanton gave Lehane a purse of holey dollars, as a token of good faith. One through the front entrance of the court house left, the other through the rear walked free.

Continuing on his way the minister kept raising his hat in pretence of good feeling to this person or that, while keeping his mouth pulled down in defence of his inner character, which he was able to pass by the filthiest of arguments without any disturbance of steady feeling, as a rule.

It was still high noon. On a far corner, under the sandstone wall of the female factory, there was a milling of people at market, soldiers and hawkers, and a number of good wives with their baskets. Black people of the outer town bargained their trifles of spear and grinding stone, and among them Stanton saw Titus — or was pretty confused certain he did — taller than the rest.

'Holloa!'

'Holloa, my boy!'

Yes, it was Titus who stepped clear of the mob and waved to Stanton with lissome ease of his reedlike arms that he raised in a not particularly English way. It was Titus's day of manufactures, Stanton recalled with a frown, and probably as far as Mrs Stanton knew, the lad was at this moment closer to home, boiling up soap with shell lime and washing soda, common resin and mutton-fat potions, keeping them supplied with bars of sweet-smelling soap, some lengths of which he would have parlayed to market that morning, for a hide-bound certainty. He would not make a living but would take one, that was his boy.

Titus's delinquencies and strayings were a blotch on the surname of Stanton — it did not help he was given a stallion to ride, and would take to the ridges like the southerly wind — but there was still a sensation of amused pride to be had from his antics. Such pride was never in doubt, and Stanton was not so lost in lawful firmness as to forget his own heart (and he would like his quondam friend the governor and a few other grousing intimates to know it). Enough was plenty enough, however. There had been some brisk canings around Titus's legs and bottom but never a proper whipping as was fully deserved — now fancied by Stanton as delivering himself, in the good old bullocky style of Mick Tornley, no standing back but shaking the cat free of knots as was carefully done, and baring his teeth in a tight smile in that pause of pity before the lash came down. If it was not to be Lehane it would be this other.

Little doubt Titus would be home before the minister himself, by means of a cross-country flit, leaping logs and womback holes without falter in a flat gallop. Titus wore a white collarless shirt with pantaloon sleeves, tight blue military trousers with red piping, and laceless boots whipped of dust with a neckerchief. His hair was soft brown rather than wiry black like his tribal cousins' mops, tufty as a cobweb duster when he did not use pomade. Titus dear boy of noble reserved mien with such fantastical features, proud forehead only a little prominent, handsome fall of nose only a little flattened out, refined sneer of upper lip, liquid eyes rather un-fathomable, though not sad, only a little heartbreaking, and amused smile flaring only sometimes too hysterical in humour — dear fellow true prince of sable realms of old you are heading for a flogging.

On his long ride home, passing through scrublands and dry pastures on sandy tracks littered with clattering scrolls of bark from gum trees, accompanied by noisy calls of white cockatoos attack-ing poor settlers' Indian corn, Stanton spoke aloud of his accomplishments in this embittered land, of which only his horse could hear, so that he presumed it did not count as a sin to boast:

'Over the next low ridge we'll see to it, m'lad, the better soil I scratched my head about when it came into my hands, when I ran a few poor seasick Africanner sheep onto it, in the care of a sinner recovering his soul, and the sheep at least thrived. This while I tended to other sorts of flocks — to my eternal merit — in Parra-matta and the camp, as my first convict flocks called Sydney Town, as some still do — it was where they were tipped from their convict fleet and set up camp under tatters of canvas.'

The white mare's head pitched and rolled in a rhythm of movement that sent agreement into the whole of Stanton's body. Nothing pleased him more than countryside spiralling itself up through the fork of his legs. How he loved the strong neck of a horse and the dry hair of its mane rough in his fist when he grabbed it! 'So little attention was paid to ministers in those days,' he complained in a satisfying way, 'that religion was made to appear contemptible. I was brought out as a lamb to the slaughter, but as a sheep before her shearers is dumb, I was not dumb. Sometimes I preached in a convict hut, sometimes in a storehouse of corn. Sometimes I did not know where I was to perform on the Sabbath day, which made me quite uneasy and put me out of temper with both the place and the people. Then I came back to my small grant of land, and the shepherd I had there when I started.'

THE RETURNING THOUGHT OF WHO that shepherd was tensioned Stanton's knees; and his horse, taking it as a signal, ticked along faster in a rapid stitching trot.

'Kale was more contented then, a newly assigned fellow, green to the hard country, and I was busy as he was, weren't we two shepherds that thought, 'There is no more behind, but such a day tomorrow as today''?'

As still, after many years, it remained that day in Stanton's mood, because he believed he wasn't a miserable man, except in the way life grew out and made difficulties until it seemed he had flogged Kale back into his life without resolving their differences. Accounts were to be arranged and profit taken, according to a belief long held (that had already made Stanton rich): 'We cannot work unless we eat, and as the colony stands in need of everyone's help in getting meat and blankets, everyone should lend a helping hand towards the common support.'

Kale had worked flocks with superior natural understanding but hadn't a brain for getting himself quit of politics like others who walked the preferable path, and allied themselves with their betters, finally getting a grant of land. Stanton had allowed Kale to run a few sheep of his own with his flocks but not to mix their breeds, and making clear God would like to be thanked for bounty if the right words could be found upon a fellow's lips. Kale however had rather a habit of silent judgement based on interpreting his bond with Stanton: regarding him as no gentleman although Kale himself wore rags. This interior bias that Kale preferred to his chance of salvation was veritably Irish, and more aggravating than a torrent of words in Stanton's face, because it made an argument and amplified an accusation without committal to the letter of speech. 'Nothing said' was the clue to 'something found wanting' in the object of the warped silence.

Desmond Kale had been born Irish, protestant Irish but no less a man of dreams was he, and a wafter of words especially when drunk. After being assigned to George Marsh, the jumped-up weaver, Kale threw in his lot with radical Fenian Catholics arrived in a boat to inflame his thinking with slogans of Ireland above all. What Kale's original sentence had been was lost in documents never sent with the convict fleet. It was either small beer or large, Kale's pride had no opinion. One heard that troopers had burned hayricks and sacked dairies of Kale family lands, had blown turrets from gatehouses and driven a poor young gentleman to live in caves and make raids with a vicious band from the hills. There seemed no limit to the elaboration of legends around Kale if you listened to the talk of how he was wronged.

A great matter of annoyance with Stanton was the squeezing out of the particular sin of which Kale was convicted in the Kilkenny courts. When he asked Kale when they knew each other better (in their earlier times) Kale only smirked, as if of their two, Stanton was the lesser, because he carried no stain of tragic experience, only the soap to wash it out.

So if there was another source to the flogging Stanton had ordered Kale over the rake stole from his ram sheds, it was that smirk and that silence. It implied manure of some superior sort being raked from a ram stall, for which a choice ten-shilling rake and a sharpening stone and a shearing hook that was also missing, but was not laid on Kale, would do just fine.

Oh but another thing one Sabbath day in an earlier year, when Stanton had done preaching: Desmond Kale came up to him and insulted him in a most daring manner. Spirits had loosened his tongue and cracked open the bitterness of his heart. 'What a lamentable thing it is, that you cannot serve God, Matthew Stanton, and strive to be honest, with a twentieth part of the industry you exert and the trouble you take to recommend yourself to the Devil.'

At that time Kale was in a state of merrymaking almost constantly stoked. Stanton had taken charge of his sheep, the flock Kale had been allowed on his own (good doers they were: the ram Old Matchless a prize). The head constable, being present, Stanton asked to tackle Kale and take him before the magistrate, who was an officer of redcoats. Stanton immediately waited upon the magistrate and roared to him Kale's improper conduct, how riotous he had been among Stanton's flocks that day in taking down his trousers and making water on the ewes' backs, and singing Irish melodies instead of working. 'Have the goodness to confine this man until sober,' protested Stanton, 'to prevent any more disturbances on the Sabbath.' But the magistrate being in sympathy with the faction of rationalist officers (who had no love for the Irish, but hated righteousness more), instead of attending to Stanton's complaint, considered the complainant himself vexatious, treated Stanton in a manner unbecoming to a gentleman, and dismissed Kale in his state of intoxication.

Subsequent to this gross irritation, the Irish rebellion struck and was put down — men were walked to a gallows, others put in irons — but rebellions lasted in other ways, likewise their curses down the years. According to confessions the plotters had vowed the minister 'was to be first'. This was the dexterous acid now on the lips of the crawler, Lehane. It was hard to forget someone intended sticking you through with a pike. Lehane in their confessional confirmed it was Kale who'd framed the proposition to his bold confrères, Kale who'd spread venom in the streets, always something about Kale touching to the sourest pith. When a governor earlier than the present one asked Stanton would he become a magistrate, even though a man of God, Stanton had gladly agreed — it was wrong to refuse the wish. A reasonable feeling it was joining civil to holy power, giving flex to a moral, as when Moses hefted the tablets, or Jesus of Nazareth cast the money lenders from the temple.

The first time Stanton was asked to say prayers with men who were to hang next morning, they shocked him by having no contrition, but he blessed God who had made him to differ, having called him from a world that lay in wickedness.

As to the warmth of Meg Inchcape's welcome, and the agreement he won, it did not occur to Stanton that she might be more than a little afraid of him, as a magistrate whose judgement ran through the settlement just a little way aside from him, scaring up wildlife, scarring backs, pursuing Desmond Kale to the limit of imagination, and arriving home whimsically whimpering to have his head scratched.

Back at the homestead Dolly Stanton was more than usually annoyed in the arrangement of domestic rule. Dolly had a fine instinct of knowing when Stanton was pleased by another of her own sex. Titus — busy about his duties without his horse being rubbed down — had a pocketful of baby sugar possums which he employed to surprise guests at dusk, posting them above doors as the lamps were lit, sometimes scoring a hit when they flew into the soup. 'If you do not return them to the forest,' his mistress said, 'I shall drown them in a pail.'

In bed that night Stanton spoke inadvisably of Warren Inchcape as 'our new boy', as 'good as a son' — raw reminders of Dolly's failure to bear her husband a son, and signals of his authority. She gave off waves of injured feeling, and Matthew said, 'All in all, I would say he is ours when we want him.' Her small, pretty face thickened with unshed tears when he turned to snuff the candle. It was an old hurt, and Stanton had to admit a reluctance on his part in taking her into his arms as joyfully as he might. To loosen a thread of her pleasure was to unravel a garment of resentments. In their lovemaking mainly and mostly (though not every time!) she merely registered what she was there to do, holding back on welcome while urging his attainment, the sooner to be fretting over it all. There was only ever the one child, their darling Ivy, now aged fourteen, a lively spirit to say the least.

Dolly grumbled:

'Sheep and nothing but sheep, the meat on their bones, the wool on their backs, oh, and the tallow in their muscle too.'

'They are the currency of the colony,' said her husband, in a tone of pious regret, rinsing around in his mind a lingering impression of Meg Inchcape as they had discussed their various matters in her bark hut. When he thought of her there, he thought less of Kale. Then he thought of Kale's sheep — and whoever's — represented in the threads Joe Josephs gave him, which he wore now twined around his wrist and swore to wear, rain, hail, shine, and bath time, until Kale was found. He held his wrist to the light and fondled it. Keeping with Kale was not such a bad thing for those sheep if they thrived until he found them. How violently amusing to have Kale as his shepherd again.

After plumping his pillow and settling his head for sleep, Stanton went on thinking aloud: 'How good it will be — a boy with a knack for living in the wild, an observant, persistent, native-born stockman bound to his master by ties of obligation cutting deeper than those usually applying to the occupation of colonial shepherd — a practice in which many men, and a few strange women of horrible independence, customarily go mad by tearing their clothes off and coupling with snakes.'

As for his wife's thoughts, it was past the diplomatic time to ask them.

DOLLY STANTON HAD NEVER THOUGHT she would travel much past the local parish markets of Horsforth, Yorkshire, to enlarge her interests. They were always so very strong enough where she was born. As a passionate young woman she experienced confusing fires in her emotions and allowed herself fair latitude of behaviour under hedgerows and when the moon was throbbing full. Mere resentments against cloddish boys, such as Warren Inchcape, or passions for smoky young Calibans, such as her Titus, seemed like side plays to her experience of deceptions, stratagems, and getting to where she wanted to be each day of a flouted existence.

At eighteen she was engaged to marry a soldier away fighting the French, a connection that freed her flirtatiously to bestow kisses without too much worrying about entanglements. Her reasoning was that as she was spoken for, she stood outside the usual result of a young woman compromising herself during a summer evening's games. Amid Horsforth hedgerows whether it went further than games, she would (as a minister's wife in later years) rather not say. What she took in private was kept in private, and besides, what young girls liked gossiping about, it happened that the boys and men mostly kept secretive to their lived experience. And so she was not so much talked about in her small village of sharp tongues, except as a person of definite likes, a stubborn temper, and of a rebellious vanity that never allowed her to know when she was really beaten.

Dolly Pringle, as she then was, since a young girl had had an air of rightful indignation over her deserved luck. She felt distinctly ill-fitted to the low-doored cottage where she was raised, with its attic weaving loom and expectation that if she were to go upwards in life it would be by climbing the worn steps her mother had climbed, into the roof, to the spinning wheel under the attic window glass. Her father, a good, strong, simple man of unquestioning religious faith, was not ashamed to boast that he wore the clothes that had been manufactured by his wife and sister and daughters. But Dolly was like somebody in a story book who was described as unravelling at night all that she had woven in the day. It was expected she would marry her weaver, who might run twenty sheep, at best, in a stone-walled field of three or four acres when he returned from the continent of Europe a seasoned trooper.

Her persistent underhand admirer that summer was a short, square-built and large-headed young man named Blaise Henry Cribb. He travelled the district as woolstapler contracted to Thomas's Mill, of Rawden. His work required superior sense of touch and a quick eye as he divided fleeces into baskets with an accuracy that was never disputed. Cribb was above Dolly's station in life — of continental blood, through his French mother's line — and a friend of young Bramley, of Bramley Abbey. Cribb was passionately wanting Dolly and quite magnetic with his louring, furious-eyed certainty of getting his way. It was something to feel the power of Cribb's demand, beckoning with his gaze that stayed with her when he left the woolstapler's corner of the barn and went outside calling for a drink of new milk. She brought it to him in a canister and watched his ribbony flushed gullet swallowing it down. There was never any question of Cribb rescuing her from her engagement, and truthfully to say, she never sought any such escape. It was being not free made her free to try twisting her shackles. It was the very condition of being spoken for that made her dalliance with Blaise Cribb possible: an amusing interlude with none of the edge of a dangerous affair, which it should have had in other circumstances. The idea that she might brand Cribb for life with her love did not occur to her. If it had, mightn't it have been amusing?

In the evenings the milkmaids went out, carrying wooden pails and low stools, looking for their ewes to milk wherever they found them in the fields. Sometimes they delayed until almost dark when the ploughboys finished pulling their stated number of back loads of thistles. These swains and hopefuls pursued them in this opportunity of near dark and it was cleverly Cribb who got in her way under the willows where she liked to find her sheep. It was better drained ground and she thought the crossed-over roots were as good as flagstones to settle her stool on. Cribb dragged any reluctant ewe from a corner and held it by the jowls, while Dolly, getting behind the sheep, took as much milk as she could in the few minutes needed. Afterwards they wandered the slow way back, where few others went, going under a bridge and Dolly always arriving at the dairy alone, lugging her full bucket and considered unapproachable in her brash defensive manner with grass stains on her milking apron where she was kicked by a ewe, and grass stains down her back where she wasn't.

Blaise Henry Cribb was an intense and rather impossibly lovable person, in Dolly's eyes, a little older but not very much wiser fellow whose sin of pursuing a tinker woman and leaving a son had angered his stepfather a great deal. That stepfather was often a subject of Cribb's puzzled conversations, to which Dolly only half listened. The person who interested her to the extent that she never forgot her name, was Cribb's mother, Madame Rousillon. That Frenchwoman who died leaving a half-French boy to grow up in England in the care of a yeoman farmer who married and fathered a natural son and preferred him to Cribb.

A man who persisted in getting what he wanted was Dolly's definition of attachment, explaining why, of all the young apprentices around, it was the one who'd gone for soldiering she first chose; then Cribb; and a year later, when her soldier boy was dead, and she was contrite and all opposite to her inclinations, she would then accept the bow-legged young minister's hand because, of Matthew Stanton it was said, there was no earthly limit to his determination, nor any heavenly one that showed itself either: and so she pledged him her life.

In doing so she believed what a jump she made in changing herself; but her years in the colony disproved it on reflection. It was her habit when nodding off to linger her thoughts on this. How the means of being one's self changed on the opposite side of the world but the essence was hungry for appeasement. Realising that the colony offered the greatest change of all — raising the socially unequal, despite its prison aims — only brought back stronger how there was something unfair in that prenuptial interlude with Blaise Cribb. Unfair to her and the emotions that stirred her still: for she was more equal to them now, and to him — the idea of him, not so much his reality, as she hardly ever wondered what life had brought him, time and distance working their blank . . . except on this pillow when a memory of touch brought her turning into his strong arms — the fragrance of woollen oils that rose from his throat remembered as a mode of intoxication. Wool was an odour her husband brought to their bed, and then she thought, comparing their courtship antics in her feelings, how Blaise Cribb had a son even then, and Matthew Stanton never gave her one.

Of course, there was a limit to any running about in the open as the northern days shortened, elm leaves fell and the lanes clotted with gold, gusts of wind lifted rooks like scraps of charcoal in the sky, and rains came and the farmyards turned all sour in mud, white frost painted the hollows and clouds on the tops threatened snow. They turned their life indoors. They listened to the wind rattling the shutters and it was not always the wind, either, but sometimes it was Blaise Cribb wrapped in a dark coat, wearing a porringer hat pulled down to keep his ears warm, and carrying a bottle of whisky to warm himself as she would not. For she spurned Cribb that autumn of prayer meetings and hymn services, savouring the sweetness of doing so, quite as sweet, even, as the balm of forgiveness when she took herself to Christ, and wearing a white kirtle was welcomed as a minister's bride at the village altar.

Chorus of the Second Part

WHERE KALE LEADS FARTHER ON

WARREN INCHCAPE WAS ALONE in sheep yards one day, at Toongabbie where he'd spent much time since early boyhood as fetch and carry, pizzle wiper, shepherd and sheep shearer, dog feeder and mouse catcher. His mother had placed him young in the care of old Aaron Tait as a way of keeping him from orphan school, where fatherless children were sent and learned how to thieve and lie.

Heat lay over the settlement roofs, shingle and stringybark, rock shelter and hollow tree. Ticks rose in the dust as sheep scuffed through on yellow hooves, hard-cased insects urged to be swallowed on each intake of ovine breath, spindles of lick hanging down, leaves of ironbark trees rattling the tar-tipped wool of their backs. A shallow creek met their noses with a green porridge of slime, which they drank, or did not.

Warren was a thickset, muddy-eyed boy wearing a hat woven from the leaves of the cabbage tree, a loose shirt, and moleskin trousers originally several times too large, that had been supplied by his mother in preparation for a time of growth that had already started. His boots he kept supple with a little beeswax and mutton suet rubbed over the soles and past where the stitches were. To save on wear, he went barefoot when he could, and spent some of each day pulling thorns and small sticks from the callus of his heel.

At his work Warren looked lazy, which was the wrong impression to have, as he was only at his ease, and waited for the animals to declare their next move ahead without too much forcing them on. As he waited he dragged a stick on the ground, disturbing a gravelly ant bed as if there was all day to stare at what ants did, by helping each other in a rushed nervous way, or turned his head with his body following as birds flew round the bowl of the sky. A sheep that wanted its own way more than others he watched sidelong to be sure it was the trouble-making one. Then it was moved to another flock, from which there was no argument of return. This was a mob that Aaron Tait kept on the creekbank, close by the huts, where he dived among them with a long slitting knife, and strung their guts in trees. Around Tait's yards there were always creeping flies and waggoners using a switch of gum leaves to keep flies off as they prodded the sinew and fat, to give them a bargaining point.

Because Tait liked plenty of meat on a big-framed sheep, there was no toleration of smaller breeds of the finer-woolled kind that were favourites in the colony among officers and the few free men who were about making money from wool. Tait thought wool a scabrous interference upon the hide of a four-square meal — wool being worth less than mutton in his trade. But Warren thought wool over because it was in front of his eyes all the time; he woke with his nose in its pillow of crimps; he scooped bundles from dead sheep when Tait allowed him dead fleeces to pluck; and when he was sad, Warren wormed his fingers through the deep staples of the better-coated ewes and dreamed his fingers had the freedom of their own wriggling to go wherever they liked, say through clouds in the sky or under the earth like a womback badger or a bandicoot mole tunnelling.

A day he remembered: his father and grandfather walking together, a day blazed in memory when they tossed him in the air and he landed in mountains of wool . . . Since then Warren noticed wool's variety from sheep to sheep where other boys did not: to them they were animals to whack and despise. Warren made out in his own head what was carried from the ram to the ewe, or the ewe back to the ram lamb that was better or worse, depending on what was wanted in a breed. Just in the same way as Warren learned his words, by having a book he leafed through under a tree, in the furnace heat of day when the sheep stood with their heads packed in a circle — and went nowhere, they were so hot, and seemed to fan themselves by shuddering their fleeces — so wool became another way of his speech, and anyone who could speak it with him was his friend. The vanity that he was the one to decide about sheep grew in him thus and was one reason Aaron Tait said to his mother, 'Let him go to Stanton whatever the cost to our pride,' which Meg Inchcape was agreeable to, through their risky blend of needs. The less she said to Warren about her reasons the better, she decided, at least until he was taken in. His tendency to attachment was strong, it could be fully relied upon.

Nobody else was moving about as Warren hipped ewes against rails and tipped heads back to look into mouths. If one got away he ambled towards it without hurry, taking hold with a cupped hand under its jaw, stilling its fright. The only other movement came from birds on a branch, pecking into their chest feathers and upraised wings for lice. He looked up and was captivated by them, because birds were a token of Warren's sentimental attachment, a sign to his longing heart.

The rest he remembered of his father was around birds: being held up to a stump of wood to see the dishwasher bird making semicircular motions, spreading its tail and making a loud noise, as if it were scrubbing a pot. He remembered the white cockatoo his father had, called Car'away, which he took with him to England, and then to Barbados where he went after that, and then back to England once more as far as his letters told — which was not too much as they contradicted each other in what they promised. Car'away was a bone-white bird with a sulphur crest that had raised in alarm like a shearing hook if anyone came near Warren, who lay on his back at the age of four or five and reached up with his fingers making a rough tearing noise against the direction of the feathers.

These birds that he watched here today were choughs. Black satin wings with white understrokes and red eyes, and almost as big as crows. He knew a chough was a kidnapper, waiting until a chick from another brood was a useful age, and taking it in its beak over to its other camp, where it was used to help raise their own young ones. That was a habit boys knew about, in a prison colony where every hand was upon the throat of another, and taking over men and beasts was the theme of duty and gain. But choughs were a family-living sort of a bird, all brothers and sisters together in noisy chattiness of flocks between six and ten. They had mud nests in the trees the size of pudding bowls, so well made they might have come from a potter's wheel, and when the birds flew off it was never in wild alarm, but with a sociable planing flight, those at the rear gliding over the ones at the front in a graceful curve, the abducted newcomers no different from the old hands.

A face appeared through the leaves as it had on other days,

almost to the hour, round and red under a wide white straw hat, a man in white trousers, white shirt, the trousers held up by a brown waistcloth, so that a resemblance to a round mushroom was complete. Warren spun around and caught Parson Stanton's eye.

'Good day, sir.'

'Hello to you, Warren Inchcape. Those are the sheep of a reprobate and a ragged bunch too.'

'If you would let Mr Tait have Young Matchless, to put over his ewes, they'd be finer next spring.'

'Well, he can have a ram,' said Stanton, 'but not that one. What are you thinking? If you want to make him a parting gift come over to my place, and take a pick of my big-framed culls.'

Warren thanked him and supposed the old ones still had a bit of spunk in them.

'You'd be right about that,' said Stanton.

There were matters Stanton wanted to understand lest the Trojan horse of offence was in Warren Inchcape.

'What do you know of your father?'

'Less than that,' said Warren, displaying the bare palm of his hand, streaked with dust. It was believed Warren's father was an officer who left the country without his regiment and returned to England, unable to face down Kale.

'Is he in England?'

'I don't know.'

'But you resent him?'

'I don't know.'

'But you might love him?'

Warren wiped his hand on his trouser leg.

'Warren?'

'What?'

'Concerning your grandfather — we must be candid about this, or never get on — do you bear me a grudge for sentencing Kale? For you must know, boy, I had Kale deservedly punished, and I think there has been no stealing since, from the Irish gangs. Do you feel much for Kale?'

Warren lowered a hurdle and allowed the ewes to fan out over a knobbly pasture of tree roots and weeds persistently growing in bare dirt.

'You are the one that says Kale all the time.'

The sheep disliked straying far from the boy, Stanton noticed with a smile. He was a pied piper of lambs and a St Francis of the woollybutts, unless Stanton was very wrong.

'Well, Warren, shall you live in my house?'

'What does my mother say?' said Warren, wheedling a bit, just to remind himself, in his precocious independence, that he was fifteen years old, and had nothing to bargain except a mother's love.

'You had best ask her.'

The answer came a few days later, as Stanton had prepared it, when Warren appeared at the farmhouse door with his belongings in a sack.

'It is no longer needed to prove,' boasted Stanton at a religious gathering, in the whitewashed slab church of Saint Botolph's he called his poor temple, 'that the children of concubines and rascals can rise above their parentage to the highest degree of attainment. It has been shown a few times, by an almost natural law — which only needs the application of Christian example for it to thrive.'

Another week passed and it felt like Warren had always been with them. At work among Stanton's sheep he was a plump attraction, dry-lipped, always rubbing his doughy nose and scratching himself under hungry ribs, always thinking a few steps ahead of the flock. When counting them out or standing in the yards to marshal them up he seemed to do nothing much, letting the sheep do their thinking, but when it mattered looked over his shoulder, leapt sideways, threw his arms wide like springs:

'Hey, hoo, hurrup, get back, stay, worry them around, Squire!'

The words were addressed to a shaggy part-collie dog that was covered in blue sores on its hairless patches, that worked with its nose grovelling to the ground, pointing towards a leading sheep, meantime an eye rolling back in the direction of Warren. It was known that Desmond Kale never used a dog — not unusual, as great shepherds, there were, in the annals of depasturing who never used one at all. But Warren was opposite from that. His future was flocks in sheets and oceans of rippling movement by the number, so many sheep that the irregularities of the land would come up through their legs creating gullies and hollows of movement. He would need only to point, and raise an eyebrow, and the whole direction of the country would change. Thanks to dogs.

'Where did you get such a glorious dog?' Stanton asked him.

'From a boy at Emu Plains.'

A bell was rung to muster the convicts and it was agreed the afternoon tolling marked Warren's freedom if he could be spared each day. There was a tan waterhole in the creek where he kept a lump of soap in the cleft of a tree, and strung his clean shirt on a bush and shook it clear of dragonflies and caterpillars after bathing.

Hair wet and face washed clean, except for a trace of clay behind the ears, Warren showed flecks of green in the murky brown of his eyes, sandy lids apparently lashless, scrubbed skin giving him the look of a frog, a frog prince may be too, but not yet anyway that earthly prince that Stanton spoke about to his wife, as an argument of persuasion to get a prodigy hooked in his wool staples.

Warren at least had the wonderful certainty beardless boys have, that whatever they understand of the world is the best of wisdom. Stanton marvelled at his daily work and his lack of resentment.

SEEING WARREN COMING OVER THE paddocks young
Ivy Stanton called, 'At last!' She ran from the finished part
of their house, jumped over beams of sawn timber,
skipped twice in the air and took Warren by the arm and called
him brother. Walking him around the garden with enthusiastic
jerks of interest she pushed him past where builders laboured
with a scowling stone-breaking gang making blocks for house
enlargements and fitted flagstones for a covered way. 'I have my
sturdy boy,' she seemed to throw, to the grown men who peeled
her helpless with their eyes. A better sort of assigned convict —
whom Ivy fondly greeted, for they were a better class of sinner as
well, the forgers, defrauders, counterfeiters — tended those
grapes, figs, and vegetables of every name that were the pride of
her father, who had had the rare zeal to assign a patrol of gardeners to the task of picking off grubs and smashing locusts and
shooting rainbow parrots with small shot. When it was dark, a
nightwatchman went around scaring rat kangaroos and other
marsupial pests that emerged from the ground, making free with
supplies.

At the end of the garden wall Titus appeared with a bat, to try Warren at cricket, and Warren squared up to the ball, swinging out and lofting it high over the paddocks, where Titus went scampering with a whoop, his arm extended into the air as he ran backwards lifting his skinny knees high, and caught the ball neatly. 'Out.'

They went inside among the mirrors and old furniture brought out from England in sailing ships. Ivy liked showing Warren everything good in the house, there being never any end to the treasure they had, and she liked whispering which servants were preferred by which others in lovemaking, and where he was to have his room when the house building was finished (at the end of the hall off the shady verandah, was the sworn stipulation for a brother, she said). Warren slid to a halt under the cuckoo clock and waited, listening to the muffled lurch of the cuckoo wanting to come out. He drew sharp breath timed to the movements of the small wooden bird with eyes like punch holes. Never in his life had he seen anything like it, and he loved that bird.

When they went in for dinner, table manners had to be grafted on Warren, though he had a few, Stanton saying he'd learnt them from his dearest mother, had he not? Gnawing on a bone and splashing into a bowl of gravy, he kept himself neat enough, except that he must never hold his spoon in a fist, but crook the handle across thumb and forefinger just so, said Dolly Stanton. Now he had two mothers, said Stanton, placing his hand on his wife's wrist. 'He is the luckiest boy in the world.'

At their meals, when he wasn't being taught manners and watching how much he piled on his fork so it didn't fall off, and resisting licking his knife with a curl of his fleshy tongue, which his born mother never minded, Warren stared at the painting the Stantons had over their fireplace. It was a battle piece with a drummer boy and men scaling a heap of rubble with the Union Jack lit by burning timber fallen from a ruined castle. It seemed to Warren that the cuckoo clock and this picture of the Spanish wars made being taken to the Stantons' worthwhile just for the wonder they stirred, and when he added Ivy and the amusement she made from everything he almost cracked his cheeks grinning, and they most likely thought he was mad.

Though Warren had never met the captain, he was told by a convict in their barrack sheds, the old soldier, Clumpsy M'Carty, about the adventures Clumpsy and Ugly Tom had had in Spain — and it was like that picture showed, he said, with a lot more blood and guts.

One day, when Stanton asked Warren if he knew of any demons and rogues among the king's rangers ('boys being like to go dashing between soldiers' legs on the parade ground, as do cavorting stray dogs, and both knowing good from bad by their smell'), Warren innocently answered: 'I know of some bad sorts, but from all I've heard, Ugly Tom Rankine's their prime candidate for a hanging.'

'You are honest,' said Stanton. 'And from what I've heard he's a dandy picnicker and a governor's prime crawler, and would not know a lambkin from a duckling. No more substantial than that.'

Warren was quartered with Titus in the garden hut that was the original house where the Stantons had camped, all three of them when they came out from Parramatta, in the early days before Titus was added to their family to make a fourth.

It was small, dark, but quite a clean smart box, constructed from split slabs of the derrobarry ironbark tree, lathed, plastered and whitewashed. Warren's bunk was down one side wall, a canvas stretcher between two stringybark rails, covered with a possum-skin rug. Titus's bunk matched it on the other wall, with a table and a fireplace between, and a small room off to the side, low-ceilinged and narrow, that had once been Ivy Stanton's nursery. It still had a wooden cradle in it, and a plaster doll with a lace cap, where Ivy had left off playing with it, since it lost its arms and nose.

While they made themselves ready for sleep, Titus would recline with the side of his head resting on one hand, leaving the other arm free to scratch himself on the back of his head as he listened to Warren, or to wave, palm flat, fingers spread wide in the air emphasising his exclamations of delight in the friendship he had going with Warren.

'They put me in there with Ivy,' Titus gestured to the little side room, 'when I was a grub, they put us in one bed.'

'I think they's planning to do that when I come over to the big house,' said Warren, 'they love me so much. Parson Stanton, he's goin to breed me up to her.'

'You can be sure of that,' said Titus, to scratchy laughter from the other dim bunk. 'It is the Lord's plan. Breedin is the best sport. She better be ready, cause which way you gunna do it? By the powder method like she thinks it's done, that's what she told me when we seen a hen and a rooster makin dust.'

'I'll do it in the good old way like a shearling ram tupping the gimmer hogs and ewe hogs hard as he can,' said Warren in the argot of Aaron Tait who'd brought it from Yorkshire when he came over in chains, and imparted to Warren between sucks of his clay pipe. 'Gettin a good look in and goin over the theaves and double-toothed tegs and up from that the two shears, the three shears, up to the six tooths till they bleat something bad and drop down dead, that's how I'll do that job of work for Stanton's swell mob.'

'That's how you'll gib it for sure, Warrie inch-long boy. Like some goanna up a tree, wavin its tail, you'll go inter her.'

Warren did not tell Titus how in the afternoons, when he was finished washing and changing his clothes, he stood at the edge of the trees along the creek and waited for a very long spell with his heart prisoned in his chest cavity tender as a captive bird. He saw Ivy in her sun hat coming along the garden wall, a freckled hand shaded over her eyes peering into the bright paddocks looking for movement. Warren launched himself from the trees of the creek so she would keep a hold of him with those eyes of hers that so mocked him, so stirred him up, and not go back inside again, nor round the back to charm Titus silly or tease the convict men. He ran, she ran, he wanted Ivy just to himself as the other half of their pigeon pair, all because of their few cheerful games around the garden, and because of being shown everything great in their house (which was all stale news to Titus, because he had grown up with it), and because of what Stanton said, that he was one of them now.

Sleep was in his eyes, a sandy grit. When Warren woke much later Titus was down on the hearth where they kept a log smouldering. He was hooked up on the beaten earth floor, knees under his chin, his nightshirt struggled off, his weskit in one place, his button trousers in another, both neatly folded the way an officer's valet would fold them.

Other nights it was Titus led the way in friendship talks, driving words like mobs over the rises and gullies to the places where the sheep of Parson Stanton sometimes led Warren on a good few days' shepherding. Warren listened agreeably to Titus's low mumble, like running water over stones, with its many wandering diversions, Warren sitting with his arms folded around his knees, tickling a tuft of possum-fur rug into his nostrils, a habit from when he was a baby and used a cockatoo quill, in his quiver of satisfactions, which made him feel like a floating dust mote inside his own head, until he sneezed.

There was a forest where the trunks of trees glistened gobs of sap from their smooth bark, like blood from under armpits. One tree stood behind another, one tree to either side of them, more pale trees behind those taking up the clear spaces until it was like being in a room slabbed in timber trunks. Yet through that wall of wood a horse could gallop free. Or a waggon loaded with prisoners — yes, they said Kale had gone like that. Into the trees.

And if you stood stiff as a grasstree spear and waited, never cracking a twig under your foot, the first grey kangaroo would come up to the ridge, look around, twitch its ears, scratch its chest like a man with pleasurable intention, and then other ones would come up and they all would pass through the trees in a file between them, crouched low coming in, springing high going out of the grey berryergro box trees, until you ran out of numbers to count them. It was a place where fire came down the bank of the biggest river, rolling and pouring through the great trees, where the honey bees liked nesting, and the eaglehawk circled up, white palls of smoke driving bunches of sheep ahead, the mob being turned by fire and driven back home with burned twigs and ash in their wool.

One afternoon when Ivy was not to be seen, and the servants were all snoring loud in the afternoon heat, Warren crept down the hall of the Stantons' house feeling himself tighten in the belly until the strike of the hour came on. It happened that a day couldn't go by without his coming to stand under the clock and experience the surprise. The spring in the cuckoo machinery unwinding tick by whir, he could feel it loosening inside himself until the burst of it would be the release of him and he would go rolling outside laughing and making the cuckoo noise up in the back of his throat. Meantime he stood coarsely breathing until the hour struck and the bird shot out. But soon he was aware of another rough breath in the house, closer than where the servants lolled with their fingers on the necks of bottles and on each other's waists and inside legs.

There had been an argument between Stanton and his wife. In those arguments it was always Mrs Stanton who won. It was expected they were riding to a neighbour's that afternoon, as she loved her horseflesh and wanted canters. But they were in their rooms, which were cool between thick walls of beaten earth, complaining about the boys they had, first Titus, then Warren! Mrs Stanton said in Warren's hearing, 'How can he sleep in it, when he will be over there?' — which information Warren did not understand, except it was about the room saved for him in the part of the house they were still building. The language of her expression made no sense unless he was to remain a plain hut-dweller with Titus, though there was another and wilder idea, which lifted a stopper on his feelings. It came to him after the cuckoo chirped and he was outside rolling his belly around in the dry sticks, laughing. Namely that when they took their voyage to England, which they talked about completing as a family, when a ship was ready (if it ever would be, at the governor's leisure), they would take Warren with them. Their parents in the old country were getting on, and they wanted to bless them before they died. So there would be nobody sleeping in the room that was still open to the stars, still to be roofed, ceilinged and plastered, and fitted with a bed, a boot box, and a mutton-oil lamp. Then indeed Mrs Dolly Stanton might truly have meant, How could he sleep in that room, when he would be over in the old country being taken about?

OVER IN STANTON'S SHEEP YARDS as the weeks went by, it was all the same with Stanton's fine sheep as it was with Tait's rough flocks. Halt, hydropic tumours, green wool rot, evils deformed and foul, hoarse coughs, Warren Inchcape found them out.

But Stanton, he learned, was reluctant to admit them, and quieted Warren down, keeping it as an arrangement between them, which argued that while Stanton's worst animals had a few rotten diseases, they were nothing as compared with the guts griping, dirty rotten livers, wheezing lungs and bladders full of imposthume that his rivals' sheep carried to him many miles across the dry hills of the Cumberland plain. The effect of this agreement, or conspiracy of truth, was not to turn Warren against his new master but to make him stand taller into the shape Stanton wanted him to fit. Warren did the foulest of jobs in good spirits, paring rotten hooves the stink of which beggared description, being suggestive of bad teeth decayed in the jaw, and of something worse, that Clumpsy M'Carty, their old soldier from the Spanish wars, told him, 'after they won the battle of Ciudad Rodrigo', was like the stink of death.

Soon Warren could relate the pedigree of the Saxon rams without any prompting, and know by the turn of their faces one ewe from another, and describe their temperaments as mothers: lavish or neglectful, flighty or persistent.

The bond stockmen who were Stanton's sheep hands were sparing of effort, working the government stroke. A bunch of them were the same ones who after being flogged with Kale had now found themselves assigned to their flogger. They resented Warren only a little as the one playing up to the parson magistrate in all his talk about sheep. On the good side of their judgement they had an insane fondness for the boy. He was their crown prince of the crackling meadows and only needed a test to confirm his kinship to their legendary ways of thought. Of his descent from Kale, they knew every glorious and disappointed detail.

One day a decision was made: they broke a small rule of close confederacy and did so cannily, releasing what they whispered was a banded tale and told it to Warren, to see what reaction might come from Stanton if it alighted in his ear and came back to them like the turtle dove. It said blackarsed Titus took a wether, cut its throat and gave it to his black people who came along the creek and spoke to him in their heathen lingo. It would mean Titus would get a hiding and that was all right. But that tittletat bird might wait until it snowed at Christmas to harm Titus, because Warren Inchcape had the honour of the colonial born, which was to say, he was of that newborn race on the face of the earth of whom it was one of the worst reproaches to be a crawler.

None of the bond convicts dared talk about Kale within earshot of authority — their cuts were too deep and his escape too perilously insolent — but they trod a light measure around the name at other times in their enjoyment of the man who was free in the bush.

One of them, James Moroney, was a poet: a dazed, daft sort of youngish man with fair hair and cobalt eyes, who had been transported from Ireland for some figment of wrongdoing involving political priests, and who could never address a direct word to anyone without a susurrant stutter. It was Moroney who picked up from the empty air the first verses of a ballad, brought the words down to the surface of his furred tongue, and vibrated their repetitions in his narrow voice box. There was no stutter when he sang and the words went in low excitement among the stock hands, telling of where a man breaking his shackles might aim, of what he might do when he struck out making free with his livestock. Oh, he'd break through the sandstone ramparts, he would, and fly to where gorges opened to a stock route so fine. Inland pastures they would unroll greener than Kilkenny sheepwalks under his toes, according to the ballad that was spun by James Moroney, poet.

It was all in Irish, so Clumpsy M'Carty worded it and whispered the English back into Warren's ear.

One day Clumpsy, who had been a Kilkenny woolstapler's boy before he was in General Craufurd's army in Spain, spoke of the sheep husbandry of the Messrs Nowland of Kilkenny, who had six hundred pure merinos in their charge.

Clumpsy was a big, handsome, soft-faced man of about thirty-five, given to hot flushes and overpowering fevers that according to several accounts was owing to having his testicle glands crushed in a rock quarry by banditos in Spain, or in another explanation from having the soap of his ripest manhood creamed to excess by the powerful energies of one Croppy Biddy Magee.

Clumpsy said:

'During the green Irish summer they were pastured, those six hundred fine white woollies, on a farm of gross natural herbage improved by grass seeds and clover. In the bleak heart of winter they were housed in the day during wet weather or allowed to forage in the snow. They were all under the charge of the one young man,' said Clumpsy with muted significance, looking around at his fellows — those scarred, disgruntled lags, each one sitting to his own stump of wood, which he was ferocious if anyone else took hold of, each with a clay pipe clenched in his gums, and a bushy beard extending over his coarse shirt front. 'For certain, the one young man it was that you mean,' they said, keeping their eyes around but not upon Warren, which only emphasised it to Warren's mind, that information of a kind he resented receiving was being heaped upon him for purposes disliked by him. Although it was only five weeks since Kale was elevated to oblivion, the event had the feeling of something happening long ago. His own life was too exciting and heaped with too much experience in that time for him to celebrate, inconveniently, the vaunted honour of Desmond Kale.

'At the sound of the horn all the sheep flocked around the young man if he stopped, and followed him if he moved along. Well, it was a grand sight, it was magic, but he had a little trick, and I'd recommend you play this one, Master Warren, if you can loot the briny. Salt was the medium by which this docility was chiefly produced.'

'Salt? Given how?'

'Trickled out of a hole in his pocket.'

'What, in this whole great place, Laban Vale, I am to carry a bag big enough for Mr Stanton's thousands of head?'

'All I know, young fella, is you would have to see how that one young man done it. Because he was the one.'

'Without a doubt the one,' echoed the others, though without too much energy in the matter, as too much recent experience had beaten their spirits down, so that sometimes when Warren came upon one, he was more like a carcase of a man in the bits of throw-off clothing he wore that were little better than rags.

'So I waits for a man with salt,' thought Warren, 'and an attachment of trumpets made from a ram's horn melted straight, as Reverend Stanton says was made by the Hebrew priests, in a small fire of ashes in sand. Oh, my sainted aunt!'

'On your feet,' said Clumpsy. 'Here comes the croppies' friend. Are you busy, Mr Stanton?' he brayed up the last sentence, as the shadow of a horseman fell across his face.

'What a question, Clumpsy M'Carty,' said Stanton as he was helped down from his mare. He was jovial with the Irishman, an entirely false state of affairs, as in principle the grinning caponed hypocrite was not to be tolerated.

'I'm on the level, sir.'

'There's nothing level in your cursed nature but direct villainy, soldier.'

'Ah, reverend father, sir —'

'Call me whatever you wish, whatever cultivates your respect,' said Stanton with jaunty disdain. 'But "father" is an Anglican title on its own, without the "reverend" added in.'

'You see, that's what we don't know,' said Clumpsy with egregious enthusiasm, 'and have to ask you to find out. What does the Holy Writ say of dogs, are they much favoured?'

'Dogs?'

Clumpsy winked sidelong. 'Dogs' was code for a man who never used dogs, but called the sheep to him, and fanned them away, by other strategies of shepherding.

The question was quite delicious and Stanton was unable to carry on with being remote. He loved having answers and here, look, Warren had started going among the sheep, Warren and his dog, Squire, who had a trick of jumping the rails and running along them a few giddy paces before dropping down ahead of the flock.

'Glory, what a sight!' Stanton enthused, puffing out his chest and dancing a little jig on his square feet as if he himself was the next for work, and sure would be if he wasn't so restrained on the leash of a Higher Master, who had better toil for him to do than rushing out showing up old lags.

'That particular dog, for example,' insisted Clumpsy, 'she's a great one of God's creatures, though with loads of gravel in the back, and cold palsies, bad as any sheep, when she's finished working and lies down fit to die.'

'I am working on your answer, for you see, as far as I can recollect, there is nothing in the scriptures favourable to dogs at all.'

'Oh, no, that cannot be true. I'd be very upset to find that out. That's in your protestant scriptures or in the other?'

'There is only one word of God, and if you were educated in anything but bayonetry, pillage, tall tales and criminal horse coping, you'd know it.'

'Sure, sure, so tell me.'

'In former times it must be supposed, the dog was a common pest and destroyer, only good as a warning or guard against wild beasts. We have had the whole history of mankind since Eden to make our improvements, by the grace of God.'

'How many years is that?'

'Five thousand, four hundred and ninety-seven, I believe. Some say quadruple that number for an upper limit, by ill-informed calculation.'

'Phew! That's a lot, so the doggy has come a long way.'

'Man not so far,' said Stanton complacently.

'Look at Warren, will you,' said Clumpsy.

The two men turned to the pleasure of watching a specialist born to the task so fittingly, that they were surely justified in thinking their interference a fault.

'The sheep hear his voice,' said Stanton, 'it is pleasant — there's no hurry in him — he works as if there are years ahead of him — which of course there are — and so, being patient, his work gets done much sooner — he is all in it — dreaming in it — playing in it, for he's still a boy —'

'Aye, we should watch out for when his cods fatten, and all the agreeable bits of him go wild, and he's lookin out for a draught of wimmin to cool the fever without his knowin what it is, till he finds a trollop and nails her.'

There was sour, lost envy in the flabby man's words.

'Clumpsy M'Carty,' said Stanton quietly, 'if you don't bury that filth I'll strike you.'

'I fergit meself,' the man dropped his head.

'Stand aside from me. Get working cleaning the stalls, and by jolly when you bring the tools in be sure they are counted and locked away.'

Clumpsy M'Carty went off. It was suspected, but never could be proved, that he was in with Kale quite deep and was the one who tossed him the rake the day it was stolen — that thankless metal-toothed T that every day Kale wasn't found now acquired the lustre of a royal sceptre, the way men handled it, passing it one to another, begging for a turn. At least they got more work done — that was a benefit. But Stanton regretted having it repaired.

Dust and harrowing blasts of sunshine gave back the sight of Warren Inchcape bringing the sheep to their fold with the help of his parlous and devoted dog.

Without Clumpsy M'Carty to bother him, in this sight before him Stanton experienced an emotion akin to the satisfaction of seeing a paddock of fine pasture, just after rain, take care of future frets. Something like it was needed in a dry country. There was going to be fortune in this boy, and favours to bloodlines of tups going down generations.

That evening Stanton boasted to his wife: 'I believe we made a superlative choice, already he's strong as an ox, reliable as sunrise, steady as a tree, and loves us both.'

Except it was not both who sent love back beaming the other way. Sad indeed it was to have to talk about it so soon, but Dolly Stanton was never one to keep her emotions hidden under a bushel, even on the Lord's Day. One of them loved Warren less. That was the score between them.

'Warren's qualities have a big hint of contempt,' Dolly said, after observing his ease of manner on wandering into their house and listening to the cuckoo clock. 'Free as a tom wrapping its tail around our bed legs, he is rather too presumed.'

'He cannot presume what is offered him on a plate,' answered her husband, rather too priestly for her temper.

The next morning, Sunday, Stanton worked on getting his sweaty Geneva collar unstuck from around the wattles of his neck, where it set up a red itch the moment it touched him, and putting on his cassock, under which he wore nothing, not even an undershirt, only a pair of white duck breeks cinched with a greenhide thong.

Dolly had a prideful habit of frankness. There was no escaping it. She reminded Stanton how she had kept mostly silent during the bargaining for Warren's services with Aaron Tait and back and forth to Meg Inchcape.

'My husband shall do as he must, but that boy's presence under our roof remains a case of too much ease of acceptance, without a hint of humble pie — mongrel convict vigour being coddled where emigrant refinement' — which was to say her own breeding capacity — 'has failed.'

'Never again, please never again say that, my sweet piccalilli lemon,' said Stanton, in the aggravating way he had around terms of endearment, which seemed not fashioned for her feminine pleasure so much, as applicable either to a donkey baulking its harness or a pet cockatoo in a cage, if it shrieked too much.

Really, without anyone knowing what had come to pass, Dolly appointed herself Warren's enemy in the house. It was a check to Stanton's needs. Facing her husband square was a regular requirement in Dolly's life. But too often was tiresome, more from the energy expended in perspiration wearing him down than from lack of inspiration to bother.

A matter that Dolly did not raise with her husband yet, because it was not shadowed over into becoming a fault, but might be quite underhand useful if it ever did go wrong, was the puppy love Warren had for Ivy. Dolly directed its jealousy towards Titus, looking for opportunities to inflame any feeling.

When he came looking for her, she said:

'Where is Ivy, you ask? Oh, Warrie, I gave her a picnic to take along the creek, and sent Titus to carry the baskets for her. I am not sure which direction they took, but if you hurry down where the old log is fallen, you might catch them before they gobble the yeast cakes.'

All the time knowing they had taken the direction of the flat rock.

AFTER MORNING PRAYERS IN ST BOTOLPH'S pit-sawn timbered chapel, Warren was given his first day's liberty to visit his mother since coming over from Aaron Tait's. Word had been sent to his mother during the week, that he was to be expected.

'You are somewhat as good as a son,' said Stanton, farewelling Warren out of earshot of his wife. 'For sure you'll have fine horses and flocks of your own one day, you'll be Warren Inchcape keeper of your own stud rams, broad acres and you know a farmstead with a tight shingle roof and a lick of smoke rising up from a well-made chimney place, to welcome your dear mother in, in her deserved old age, which is a long way off from her good self yet, to be sure.'

The promises sounded like Warren was the luckiest of their three; and Warren with the wind in his earth-coloured hair, cantering off on the pony Stanton allowed him, almost pitied the minister for the great generosity he bestowed, because if Stanton gave away any more he would be left begging.

As Warren trotted in to Parramatta past noon he turned his head and heard a noise of music coming through the trees — fifes and a towrow of kettle drums. Although he was late kicking his pony to his mother's hut he followed the sound where it led.

It was a company of foot, marching to the fifes, returning from church parade in a scour of dust with a lean captain and a portly sergeant major attached to the side, the pair of them on wide swings lengthening their pace keeping tempo, shortening their snappy steps upon the inside turn. The drill held Warren rapt as the soldiers came together in closed ranks, sounding their dusty boots on the stones of the barracks' ground, every foot awaiting the order to halt and be dismissed. Watching, the boy was aware that the captain stared in his direction for moments longer than was entitled. It was as if he knew Warren, or was warned of him in some way, or just wanted to be sure the watcher understood what a fine fellow he the captain was, and what a show Warren was given by a company of redcoats, all on his own, at no cost for entertainment except the time spent.

'That will be Captain Tom Rankine,' said Warren, 'Ugly Tom, who fought at the battle of Ciudad Rodrigo with our old soldier, Clumpsy M'Carty, who said his bold captain was like a devil's hoof was planted in his face, from gunshot wounds, and his ears were the shape of wood fungus, from being chewed by a mastiff while being held down, not to mention from having the pox, but he was brave as any man born, and the kindest, too.'

When the troops broke off and went to their barracks, Warren sauntered along with an arm around his pony's neck. He tried keeping step with the animal, skipping his feet the way the captain corrected his nimble gait, as if being out of step was the greatest part of being in step, because then you could do something showy with your toes. He was in a dream as he went the next hundred yards, he was in the Spanish wars — those earsplitting fifes and drums Clumpsy talked about, that roused a frightened soldier's blood, made boys into men, brass bugles sounding the charge, drifting gunpowder smoke peppered with shot like little birds whizzing over the hills. Clumpsy swore every detail in the Stantons' painting over their fireplace was faithful, except brains spattered on rocks that Clumpsy said was like scrampled eggs the Spaniards pushed in their faces.

Because of these thoughts Warren missed noticing the captain chasing up behind him, the buttons of his dress jacket undone, a hot searching look in his long twisted face when Warren swung around.

'Warren Inchcape! Is that who you are, boy?'

'What if I am?'

'Have the goodness to haul up under a tree. Or are you too touched by the sun to enjoy a spell of shade?' replied the over-heated officer, who introduced himself by name and rank and shook Warren's hand. He was not as ugly as Clumpsy said, only from being pitted with the pox, and more like his character was all a matter of finer expression, with his face going up one side, down on the other, and his pale eyes like ash in the morning's fire, as he urged himself upon a person.

'I am in a hurry to get to my mother's place,' Warren answered, puffing his chest cockalorum style. The show of inflated manliness made the officer smile, as without any ceremony he tugged Warren's horse over (and Warren obediently following) to where a large white gum tree grew its lower branches onto the ground, making benches for travellers, which they had polished with their trouser bottoms and carved with their names and marks.

Before any further explanation the officer pulled a lump of confectionery from his inside pocket, examined it for dust and grit sticking to the sugar glue, and raised his arm to smash it against the smooth tree trunk, holding out a clean result of crumbly insides for Warren to pick through.

'Take any piece,' he invited.

Warren did so, and the next moment his tongue was following a lump of sweetmeat around inside his cheek, causing him to reflect that a gift he had in one part of his day — Stanton's promises and praise so honestly sworn — followed him through into the rest, and there was still his mother's kitchen to be eaten up before dark. He took another piece of rock candy while he had the offer, and held it ready while eating the first.

'Is it good, or not?'

'Is goob,' he said, sucking until he was almost cross-eyed, extracting a smooth tarry flavour.

'It has an imported syrup of wines and spices boiled in molasses,' said Rankine. 'My servant made it, and I always carry a portion in my saddle bag — so that whenever we meet, Warren Inchcape, I'll have something to throw your way. The governor's wife says, when she eats my rock, that if she closes her eyes she is in Scotland still, on Princes Street, where she liked to shop for the best candy rock — except there's no writing down the middle of mine, telling us where we are. I laugh, and tell her she's more like in Spain, and the rascal who boiled her sweets can no more read than write.'

At this hint of the officer's closeness with the governor's camp Warren contracted his mouth in imitation of the crafty way the officer himself did it, because by that rather charming twist you showed you doubted something without being too unfriendly.

Any mention of the governor's camp in the Stanton household made the dogs under the table yellow their fangs, and Warren was now with those dogs on the matter, having fairly quickly acquired

Stanton's views all and some, on the politics of the colony. They were all in his feelings, but if asked, Warren would not have been able to explain what those politics were, how he fitted them, except to say that people of the convict stamp were not to be treated equal to those from birth unbranded, but always kept lower to be fair to the free. The thought made a conundrum of Warren himself, close blood relation of a hated, flogged criminal, henceforth to be raised as a cuckoo'd shepherd in a free man's habitation.

'You have a question?' said Rankine, as he waited for a certain irresolution in the boy's face to clarify.

'Does Clumsy M'Carty lie?' said Warren.

'What about?' said Rankine, rather sharply as since the escape every last question thrown his way came double edged.

'The stories he tells about you — cause if only one of them is true, you've seen some sights together.'

'Clumpsy don't lie, except to speak better of others than he does of himself. For my part, I'm glad to be out of the wars and seeking my fortune in New South Wales.'

'In spirits, sheep or horses would that be?' said Warren quite smartly, as it was said there were no pursuits more precious to officers than rum, flocks, and getting their mares in foal to the newest-arrived stallion from Calcutta. But if it was flocks, Warren had, like Stanton, and anybody else, never heard of a Captain Tom Rankine's having any.

Rankine gave Warren a long considering stare, wondering what he knew of Mundowey forest and the movement of pedigree flocks under the control of a difficult Irishman. He would love, in the name of love, to tell Warren everything. To test him with trust and have him pass it to Meg. To so warm Meg that way, in the absence of any other way — any more sure close warm touching way —

that they would be almost physically bonded even if they never even barely touched. The only compensation of this suspenseful courtship was in the nature of courtship itself, that it was a hopeful venture, and reduced Rankine on many days to waves of pure longing, in which he forgot himself.

Already rumour was so rich around Kale. But so mythical were the details (while staying accurately rough) that nobody believed in them as fact except the poetic believers of utterance itself. The exercise had been kept tight for almost eight and a half weeks now. In it, now, the chief actor in the affair apart from Kale was a remote station keeper with just a few particulars varying from the usual, such as that nobody must be told where his land was located, what livestock was on it, who his stock hands were, or anything else.

But when an answer came to Warren's question whether it was cattle, horses or sheep he was in, Rankine heard himself saying, for the first time to anyone outside his tightest inner circle:

'I am in flocks. That old ram of Parson Stanton's, Young Matchless, is he a sheep to interest me?'

'You know the one?' said Warren.

A gesture of airiness took over.

'Yes, I may. I happened to be riding through your district and saw the said object a way off. I went over and had a feel of his jaws. He's a true English sheep the size of a small pony with shanks of choice meat and coat of coarse blanket consistency.'

'You must be in mutton, then, if all you cares about is size and coarse wools.'

'Nay, I'm in the other. Fleeces.'

There was a long implication in the word fleeces, that would tell Warren almost all there was to know: that Rankine was born to hang — only it was not the way it played out.

'Would he do me, Warren Inchcape? Come on and tell me true. I want your smartest opinion, as the one who knows.'

Warren, squatting to the ground, rocked on his heels, holding the reins slack, cabbage-tree hat pulled down over his eyes, pursing his lips into the round thinking shape favoured by stock dealers as they stretched negotiations along — forgetting for the time being that Stanton was the master decider in the matters. It was Stanton who said Young Matchless was a good-to-great wool breeder, and Warren who looked at the wool and thought it was even better than that.

'Only if you are a butcher,' said Warren importantly, 'would you talk that way, not if you wanted him for wool.'

'But his frame for wool is what I would want, to put over smaller ewes, and so, in time, to bring back some wonderful big rams, like Young Matchless himself, only shaken out with a good quality of fleece, as if they wore a greatcoat of long hairs, and their fibres were roosted down into their girdles all over, and thick compressed together . . .'

He was quoting Kale, to see the effect of the words in Warren's dreamy eyes.

'You'd have him there,' said Warren in admiration of such a vision for a sheep, which he was afterwards to remember as a way of thinking, until somebody better taught him more. Still, it made no difference what anyone thought or wanted, because —

'He is not for sale, that ram, not this year, nor next.'

'I am in more of a hurry than that. I am putting flocks together for a wide move. You see, I am just at my start.'

'I thought you might be,' said Warren, everything being suddenly explained. Rankine was playing him along. He had no stock at all. 'Seeing as I have not heard nothing about your flocks, Captain Tom.'

'True, they don't exist this side of paradise,' said Rankine, with shy relief over being extricated from where things stood, and not quite having to lie about it, either. 'Only I have great hopes.'

'All I know is that everyone nowadays is in the way of putting their flocks together, if they wear epaulettes and carry swords, because they say being a redcoat is better than working a plough, or an axe, in getting this colony covered over with livestock.'

'Very true. Except every faction of officers has another faction against it, and each two factions are feuding up against a third which they deal with by making consuming alliances. So all they have time for is to count their head of stock, in a race of competition, and boast about numbers, without considering the advantage of the material they have, which those of a different mettle may do on the quiet, if they are so inclined.'

'What breed of small ewes is it you want?'

'I dream of the Spanish — so much so, that a few of the more beauteous shall have to wear black lace and dance the tarantella, and rattle chestnuts tied with string, while they go through their paces.' As he spoke, the captain shone with a curious madness in his unusually light eyes, from which Warren guessed he was not so much describing a sheep, as trying to confuse him with fancies, for whatever reasons of charm.

'Oh, yeah, and whose flock would you get them from?' said Warren with an almost jeer, because there were only a few breeders of Spaniards known in the colony, according to Parson Stanton, and they had extremely disreputable claims to authentic blood, being Spaniards gathered from abroad via ports of call where Stanton said they had been jumped upon by rams no better than Arabian goats, and had not originated in Spain at all. There were *none* that had, scorned Stanton: but if there were, it was but one rumoured band of them, that had been brought into the colony without being announced in the broadsheets, nor paraded in the dusty streets, nor boasted about in the grog shops, nor at officers' dinners. Nor had they been speared by blacks for which crime the natives would be made to pay with a life or two, as practised to keep the peace until sheep overran their grounds and they saw the justice of it. If so they would have been heard of, too.

'So these are the ones you want — that don't exist,' said Warren with finality.

'Well proven,' said Rankine. 'But if I find them, and when they're pinned down, shall you come and look them over, and tell me if they're any good, Warren my boy?'

Warren promised he would. He felt taller even than when he started the day. But why all the charm was explained away when they went their separate directions:

'Give my warmest admiration to your sweet mother,' Captain Tom Rankine called back, when he was good way off.

THERE WAS A COMMOTION DOWN at the huts as a small boy came running to announce that Warren was seen at the end of their road.

Meg Inchcape stepped into the dust with a dishcloth twisted in her hands, keeping her eyes on Warren and his pony the last fifty yards. 'Here's my proud boy,' she said to a neighbour, as above her head the dishcloth snapped into a flag of welcome and then dropped down and was bundled into her fingers again. Without offering any more greeting she stepped back inside the hut to her kitchen fire, and Warren might have wondered what was up with her, except there was always a reserve in their greetings that doubled their intensity, as the more wanted the occasion, the less likely they showed their emotions.

Two small underfed boys who thought Warren a great man came running up to his horse and fought each other for the privilege of leading the pony round the back until neither boy was much use to him, and they squabbled — one left squirming in the dust with a bloody nose and the other running home bellowing with a sore fist. Warren wondered what surprises his mother had for him — what gift prepared, what favourite dish, what special tidings saved for the day, which even if they were trivial or stale tellings she would manage to relate with interest. He remembered he had a few red-flowering twigs in his pocket, and took them out before he went inside, arranging them into a dry sort of posy.

His eyes were unused to the interior shade after the bright sunlight as they embraced; she held him off, she whispered his name, she took him to her arms until his head was crushed against her breastbone and he said:

'Ma,' in a small voice of objection.

Everything was set out on the table. He could see the trouble she'd taken with the help of old Mother Hauser who came in and gave Warren a pungent kiss on the mouth while he tried to avoid looking at the goitre on her neck. There was a dish of wet devil, made of slices of fried salt meat with a thick peppery gravy, which was put back on the fire where it bubbled.

As for his lateness, he blamed the tactics of an impetuous officer for delaying him. It meant the soup had gone cold and was reheated and burnt, as Meg had imagined he wasn't coming at all — that Stanton had gone back on his word, but if he had, what could she do about it? Warren saw how every time his mother turned back to him there were tears.

'Old Stanton,' he said, 'ain't all bad on his own home ground, it's only rogues in Parramatta get him worked up . . . What's wrong, Ma?'

'Love tears,' she called them, whatever, they were about with her. There seemed more of them than ever before — the bright darts in her smile that came from every angle when she raised her head after kissing him, all over the cheeks and turning his face wet.

'Ma, what is it, some person done you wrong? I'll run them through, I have a dagger,' and he showed her, the handle grip black with dried blood scented of animal deaths.

'Put that away. It has been too many weeks since you went,' she said. 'They've been two months, Warren.'

'Shoulda I come sooner?' he said, thinking of those interesting weeks in a new place, when he never worried about getting away, but played as the speaker of Stanton's great part in the sheep yards.

She smiled and dabbed her cheeks. 'I only wonder where my haunch of mutton is, that the parson promised you would bring over in a bag.'

'I clean forgot to ask, and he never reminded me. He's like that unless you give him a kick, his plans and promises are too big for his pocket when it comes to putting his hand in.'

'They killed an old ewe, and the stockmen ate it yesterday, seeing they have a right to the culls or anything that's too sick to walk. On a Saturday afternoon, when they finish early at three, they are allowed to cook it up.'

'You must be carrying some in your belly, along with that sugar you ate.' She patted where a dusting of confectionery crumbs remained, the discovery interesting her as she touched her fingertip on her tongue, in apparent recognition of the substance.

'I eat better than them convict shepherds,' Warren boasted, 'and go back for seconds whenever I like, out into a kitchen that's bigger than this whole house.'

Warren did not immediately name his delayer as Captain Rankine, because the greeting given by the officer for carrying to his mother worked against his affection for the uglified man, making him feel that he was only being used as a love messenger after all their talk about sheep. It was not the first time either with an officer, that Warren had been used, as Meg was not the kind they just made a motion to if she shook their fancy. They mounted campaigns, being struck by her looks and mettle — and she would award victories according to how much they excited her enjoyment and laughter, and cut them off, or invite them back in, just as it pleased. Some of Warren's earliest years were spent crawling between their polished boots while Meg laughed outright. He wondered who it was now — there were always numbers of them around, officers or men, and if they annoyed him, there were some he liked very much, and all of them he granted had the best judgement for liking her. How could they not?

As he sat at the table and Meg served him, Warren talked himself up, wanting to prove to his mother that he was whooshing up in the world, all true to what she hoped by his move to Laban Vale.

'You have no count of the information I keep about rams and ewes, all in a ledger that the parson reads down the columns one week at a time, right through to their first lambing and culls, and he ain't yet found fault.'

'I am sure he could not, Warrie, even if he tried.'

There was some mood of sadness in her today that he wanted to dispel. He was a little put out that his arrival had not cheered her as much as it should, except when he spoke of the officer who waylaid him.

'Our walls must look shabby to you,' Meg said, 'after what you have in your grand establishment.'

'Every single stick of furniture they bring up the river from Sydney, and rope onto a waggon and take out to their sheep station, twenty-four miles.'

'And we poor women chase after it, feasting with our eyes.'

'Nay, but my mind is here,' said Warren, 'always at the last minute when I go to sleep.'

Meg reached over and touched Warren's hand. 'Last thing at night's when I say my prayers for you, so that we are never really apart, Warrie.'

'I am just sick of them hinting around Kale all the time, as if the worse he is, the better I am for everybody.'

Meg leaned back, removed a cloth cover from a plate of meat, and waved her hand across it to keep the flies away until Warren was ready make his choice of vittles.

'Your mysterious interfering officer too, did he mention "that man"?'

'No, Ma.'

'The officer was "ugly"?' she said, with a faint smile. 'And greased his favour by feeding you sugar candy and parting with a dose of prettying up, by saying he passed on his respects?'

'Yes, Ma. Admiration,' he said.

Warren drained back the last of his soup without bothering with a spoon, and speared a piece of salt meat, chewing it trenchantly before asking:

'Why ain't I ever to get angry about Kale being whipped?'

'Can that wait until after your pudding?'

'It always has to, and then you say there is too much for me to know, and we are a thousand puddings later. But I am started in the world, and we have a woolly-head black boy at our place, Titus, who whenever they talks about floggings the tears roll down his black cheeks, his heart is so sympathetic soft, and he asks me what them Stantons don't like talking about — not even their Ivy, who's quick — even though they's Christians down deep as the well goes.'

'What is it your Titus asks, that they don't like saying?'

'How can I have the cold soul to understand that my grandfather was flogged to the underskin and wished for dead by the man who loves me like a son.'

'What is your answer to that?' said Meg, after a long silence, and now they went into the catechism of their lives, and even Warren, who would eat the horse and the whole pack team before he would say his belly was full, waited with the fat going glistening cold on his lips until they dealt with the recital.

'I let them think what they likes. Or I say, "I'm not the one who goes on about Kale all the time, and why don't they shut their gobs."'

'I love you, Warren, but you must not cry, just yet. What is your next answer, that is always the one between you and me, and I asked you to remember it, though I think you've forgotten?'

'I never have, because Desmond Kale was so hated, so beaten, so worked over, that it became too hard to bear and even my grandmother, Patsy Inchcape, was taken and had her hair shaved off, in the female factory, so that everyone would know she was depraved and disorderlied with Kale. The law went after Kale like a warregal bush dog, but we was lucky. We had over us a fear so strong, a hatred so deep, that we went into the ground like the anteating porcupine, or the womback showing its arse end up, with a slap of hairy armour plate, until nobody could harm us. Ma, I was born into this country a native, but I had no leather hide nor quills either.'

'Love came out with you,' said Meg. 'That was your great protection. Every bastard child in the colony is ransomed to charity, a cold dish that can only be warmed by guile. Lately, when Stanton's shadow came over us again — by sentencing Kale for that metal rake, which he stole to garden my mother's grave — praise be to blessed Anthony, patron saint of gravediggers and herdsmen — I considered the resolution, that fear and hatred could build a shell of safety for their objects, even in the parsonage where they was fomented. That is now your position in life, until such a time as we are safe.'

'Does that mean,' Warren dared, broaching the next step of their recital, which always risked her fury, 'when my father returns to Botany Bay?'

THIS TIME INSTEAD OF THROWING plates Meg went to a small wooden box, that had once been a sea captain's letter case, and was left in her safekeeping by George Marsh, whose arrived letters she kept inside it, tight pressed under a brick of glassy quartz that Marsh had brought back from beyond the cataract of Carrung Gurrung, and presented to her like it was a diamond from the mountain of light.

'I do not know what to say, or what to have you believe, but I have always given you the best picture I can, about your father's plan of coming back to Botany Bay under better circumstances than when he left.'

'I have never waited for him, anyway,' said Warren. 'Though I practised my alphabets writing him letters and drawing a likeness of five kookaburras roosting on a cold winter's night. His letters back was always overjoyed and promised me the world, under particulars that in the next mail we received was always changed, because he never made his promises the same way twice, just like he never told you there was already a Mrs Marsh, after he promised he loved you.'

'Enough of that anyway,' Meg wiped away a tear. Over the whole time since Marsh sailed off she had kept him as a monument to fidelity inside herself. It had not prevented her from a few heated dalliances, hurried excursions in love — but when it came to irreversible pledges she had been immovable, and the reason was loyalty to Warren having a father at all, in a country where orphans and illegitimates were the order of the day. 'Warren's father is a man of principle,' she maintained, giving nothing out, which was evidence to some he was an officer, if they believed in honour, and an argument to others he was an officer, if Meg was being ironical. Through this time her notion of George Marsh was more and more like a statue, inside of which the light of a candle could be seen moving around as if the man was in the edifice somewhere, crawling about on his patched knees, looking for a way out.

'Well, I cannot remember last time he bothered to remember I was born at all,' said Warren

'That is over,' said Meg.

'Good for it,' said the boy.

Meg often asked herself: How regretful that a boy full of feeling, racked by loyalties and affectionate dreams, felt coldness towards the man who fathered him — found no excuses for Marsh's blithe lapses the way Meg herself did, over the whole seven years since Marsh upped and left, when what she always tried was to make him look good and paint the boy's memory in, unless she started throwing plates. Their relation to Marsh was the closest sealed secret of most of what they shared when they kissed goodnight or goodbye. And the reason first was Kale's — for if Kale had ever found Marsh took her at sixteen and was her user from then, under Kale's bonded nose, Marsh exulting in her bound silence, her half-prisoned but willing girl's yielding, there would have been murder afoot. So she was always resolved to wait until Marsh was dead to tell Kale it was not an officer that had taken liberties with her in the dark of one night, but Kale's own nuggety master on their march to Aleppo Mere and into the Caemarthen Mountains, and not over one night either but through a whole year's count of assignations, until she came to term with a boy. The second reason was over the promise Marsh demanded of her himself, in all his dark-browed, homespun vanity, when they parted on the shores of Sydney Cove and he sailed off with his crates of specimens. 'She was not to make light with the reputation of one who aspired to fame, and was legally married to Mrs Marsh' — and pressed blossom that she was, with a boy in her charge, she had long obeyed him.

Meg unfolded a letter from the box. 'Now for the news I have been waiting to tell you when you had your day of rest, which I can hardly bear to speak out. I want you to study this piece of parchment, Warren, that has just come from England.'

'Is it to brag how great he's come?' said Warren, sneering at the green pickle he was about to bite, as if appetite was the last thing he would offer a plain pickle, but would stoop to its need despite that reluctance, if only to spite that not quite gentleman, his father.

'No, the opposite is true. He is dead.'

Warren waited for feeling to strike him.

'Dead?' he repeated flatly, observing his improper reaction mirrored in his mother's eyes, but wanting to live in the frozen moment longer, where he would not have to feel anything. 'What has he left me, because there was talk about that, and you thought it would save me.'

'Small hopes that I had — won't you hold my hand, Warrie, and say a prayer that you're sorry?'

'No,' he bargained. 'Not yet, I won't. What is it, his clothes, hats, and boots?'

Warren looked hopeful.

'If earthly possessions is what concerns you most, your inheritance is not finery at all — a few books and maps, they are in a chest held by an attorney in London, "that you may collect at any time according to your convenience,"' she read to him, through her tears, which had been flooding for every reason the whole afternoon.

'That will be easy, then, I will do it when I get there,' said Warren, lifting his chin not quite as satirically as he sounded, in the light of what was hinted behind thick walls of the Stanton house about them taking themselves to the Yorkshire county seat they sprang from, and ever so humbly in the East Riding of that place, living it up there as returned improvers with their tales of flocks and victories won converting heathen Tituses.

'He is buried in the churchyard of St George's, Hanover Square, near Connaught Place, with another Botany Bay traveller, Captain Flinders. God rest his busy soul.'

Meg folded the paper. Warren sat forward and looked at his mother, the things that were said sinking in. The list of vexations. The pall of sadness over them. His father's greatness in his father's own mind more important than any convict girl's happiness and her boy's well-being in the dust of New South Wales.

Warren felt more alive because Marsh was dead, that was the truth of it. Pretty much ready to burst his buttons. Here they were, working up their fortunes out from Parramatta, and Marsh lay rotting dead in London. They would not have to tread so carefully around Marsh's name any more; it would not be Kale who warned their sensitivities quite as much, on that point. They had waited, and made their lives better, while Marsh's that promised more had slipped away. So Warren felt brave and pugnacious — the elation of the survivor; he was the ember become a flame that was the last heat of the dead man. Meg saw Marsh's tarnished vanity in Warren's muddy gold eyes. Finery. He was left some finery of penmanship and map marks. They must be valuable because the letter said they could only be collected in person, over the signature of one Warren Inchcape, boy, of Botany Bay. A precious thought from one gone, who'd remembered his son at the end.

Warren went to Meg's side, kicking his stool back, and stood holding her in a way that was more like she was holding him for the grief he was too stubborn to speak, and swaying as she told him while referring again to the document in her hand:

'The worst thing is that his wife, poor Mrs Marsh, died before him, and there was nobody to bury him except this kindly old lawyer, Alexander Ritchie, who writes that George Marsh had no stock of worldly goods, but out of such as he had, his first desire was to provide for one he meant to take to him, when he was flushed with rewards from his patron. That is to tell you, Warrie, he was waiting on his master, Sir Joseph Banks, who was ill almost the whole time from when your father arrived in the colony. Did you know, that waiting for his benefaction for the space of many years, Georgie never had a single letter from Banks? He returned to England with all his collections, his maps, his loyal black servant, Mun'mow, his cockatoo, and the wool samples you remember, as each one he took, another was put to the side and saved for you to study when you were old enough to understand their names and uses.'

'I was always old enough to understand their names and uses,' said Warren thickly, reluctant to credit anybody for his earliest bleatings around sheep unless it was Desmond Kale, and that name he'd swallowed so long from habit, that even talking with his mother he let it pass by, like the full moon shrouded in storm-clouds, or a hearse under a black cloth containing a breathing corpse.

'Please don't be cold, Warren. Your father Georgie Marsh was proud, and vain, but never was mean, and I honestly loved him with all my heart for his bold independence and passion of feeling. Also for his murky eyes which are qualities you have in you, when you look at me like that.'

Warren took the page of paper over to the light of the door, where he studied its details with the aid of his index finger running along each curlicued line and spelling out the words.

'Now here is the parrot as well, which is mine too, it says, cold and alone without its feathers in London, *callow*, is the word they use, at age estimated twenty years — that same bird,' said Warren, amazed, 'as used to cry out its own name, Cara'way.'

'What is wrong with you, Warren?'

For in speaking the name, 'Cara'way', Warren's voice caught in his throat. Choked there and burst his flood of tears.

When Warren's tears were done his mother put his head on her lap and stroked his dusty hair.

'Remember him,' she soothed. 'Remember the man your father.'

And it was definite that he did, because there on the day Marsh sailed, had he not carried him on his shoulders while the parrot sat on Marsh's right arm digging in its claws? It was a day when Warren rode above heads, smelling southern breezes and tar — a small boy torn from impressions while the next lot were forming like new clouds in the racing sky.

He was lifted down from Marsh's shoulders and placed on the stones of the street — left there with the bird staring at him from its wet leather eyes while two men talked, Marsh and Desmond Kale. The stones were greasy and stank. Mud splashed in his face. The rows of Sydney Town houses looked down on him from above one another's rooves. The stones echoed the sound of boots, the iron wheels of carriers and the sound of Cara'way scratching his feathers and making music with his small chain that kept him captive, then throwing his head back and screeching, while his bright yellow crest rose alarmed.

Marsh washed Warren's muddy face in a horse trough, which made him pull back his lips. He did not like being touched even gently in the face, even by his mother. Up on those shoulders again — Marsh happy and singing while Kale took charge of the cockatoo.

'You wore a green jacket with a spray of honeysuckles,' his mother said — and he was held out over water! — the sailing lighters loaded with planks of new sawn timber aiming straight at the docks, slapping up waves, veering away at the last moment as their sides met the wharf and sailors threw ropes.

Marsh was beckoned by Kale, Warren was carried between them: they climbed a flight of stairs above the dark decks of the wharves, in one of those sandstone buildings that Warren thought, once he saw them in sunlight, were built of butter blocks. His toes never touched the steps, one man clutching either hand. The bird ran before them. It was tied to a railing as they went in.

The place was the wool room of a merchant where Kale went around pulling tufts of fleece from bundles and Marsh behind him wrote their parcels on cards. They were for taking back to England and making an advertisement of them to Sir Joseph Banks and the manufacturers J. and W. Thompson of 'Park Mill', Rawden, Yorkshire. It was all recorded in the slip case Warren was left, and which he took out sometimes and studied by candlelight. The best and choicest parts were called the picklock, the next most excellent the prime. There were the choice, the super, the down, the head, and the downrights. Warren believed he always knew the main differences between wools because he was born to them. But knowledge had started there in that room, as very likely his memory of important existence had, the day George Marsh sailed off. Warren looked from one man to the other as if he had gone to sleep for the rest of his life with his dull-coloured eyes half open, his pale lashes blurring what he saw in a golden pile of bins as the two men moved from one to the next.

Nothing in the greatness of living would ever escape Warren from then on. A good grab of wool could be bunched into a staple hardly bigger than a fist. That same portion could be spun into a piece of cloth and cut to a pattern and worn. Combing wools weighed up on a scale, a pound's weight of fleece sold for two shillings while in Saxony the best weight of Saxon merino fleece was said to fetch six shillings more.

George Marsh took Warren and held him high with a deep laughing conviction of greatness, and threw him even higher in the air, catching him in a low swoop so easy that up he went again. Next they stepped away from under him, and he found himself falling through the air into a pile of wool, sinking down like a louse tumbling in the forest of a sheep's back.

That light of pearly fleeces was the light in the darkened room with the door held only half open. Kale reached in and smeared wool's greasy yolk under Warren's poky nose.

W HAT WAS TOM RANKINE TO do, he asked himself, without a Biddy Magee to clean his house, cook his salt pork stews and mutton roasts, polish his belt buckles and brass buttons, blanco his webbing, undo his scarlet uniform jacket with nimble fingers and strip him of his riding trousers when he came home too drunk to do his own fumbling?

If Desmond Kale was honestly to have her, how was it to fall out? Nothing was too much trouble nor too far removed for Biddy's willing compliance. That was decided. She was one of life's plucky ones, with a sweet warm kiss and a swathe of green leaf poultices and potheen remedies keeping her from trouble in case of expecting. But like a traded filly was she simply to be pitched in a stall and teased to another's want? When it came to the mark it proved impossible for Rankine to ask Biddy anything of the sort, impossible even to think it. As for Tom Rankine in himself — he in some ways loved her enough to resent the reach of casual permission, that he had once used to house her for his own. It was what he told himself, at least — to both his own two faces.

Rankine was jealous of Biddy's compliance even as he enjoyed it, yet all the time brooded over Meg. He even blamed Meg Inchcape in his imagination for the confabulation over Biddy, through telling himself that if she were warmer in response to his overtures, he would be finished with Biddy Magee weeks past.

Matters changed when Biddy came to him with a distressed problem, and he asked what the trouble was.

'The man is ill,' she said.

'And so?' he pretended to not quite understand.

'He is sick to die.'

'There you have me, Bid — who?'

'The Irishman.'

'Well, fancy that. Was it posted in the Sydney *Gazette*?'

'It was in a song I heard.' She lowered her eyes.

'A ballad?'

'It was.'

'Oh, Jesus,' said Rankine. 'Has it gone as far?'

'But can't I please go out there,' said Biddy, 'to wherever it is, and nurse him back to health with some mashed turnips and broth?'

Rankine went around knocking over chairs and slamming doors. It was in a song she heard. It had gone as far. There had been a visit from Clumpsy M'Carty, witness in a case being heard in the township, Clumpsy being allowed by a Parramatta magistrate's largesse to wander an hour before being hauled back to Laban Vale. The pair of them, Clumpsy and Biddy, had gone swinging along the creekbank with their arms around each other. Rankine and Clumpsy had spoken — enough said to serve Kale's cause — but it seemed a good deal too much information about Kale moved through the Irishry independent of Rankine's caution.

'I've never seen such a temper,' said Biddy. She began gathering up mint leaves, geranium flowers, nettles, and making up small packets of mustard, linseed meal, soda bicarbonate, special clay for poultices, cloths for hot foments, and busied herself filling precious small bottles with volatile oils, mild vinegars, and searching out, in the markets, a particular honey as grainy as gravel, that was favoured against the ravages of the cat, if smeared on thickly enough.

The fact of it was, that while Rankine wanted the duo of Kale and Moreno as tight as a knot if the plan was to work, the knot was now loosened too far. He thought of the knot that might hang him when the rest came in. In that event, his friend, the governor, autocrat by decree, would show him another side. Then Rankine thought, at least in the shadows of the scaffold Biddy writes her own ticket of leave. And things take their own course — once set in train.

In the course of that year Biddy had covered Rankine's absences by saying, 'He is off on his duties' — which indeed saved him so far. It was the truth as she saw it. She had no idea of his adventures with Kale. When taking leave of his barracks' room colonel, Rankine only needed to say he was riding out for a week for it to be wisely nodded that he was doing the governor's will in some wriggly fashion — and no great particulars entered in the regimental record, if anyone did ask. The governor himself conversely believed, when Rankine was afield, that he was on regimental officers' business, which was all about gaining and getting, and good luck to him. Fortune could not be deserved by a nimbler buck than Ugly Tom, and if he did gain his bawbees without livestock, as he seemed set upon trying (having disposed of the Bengali fat-tails he arrived with) — more luck to him still. As a trained army surveyor, he would have a good eye for pegging out land.

Doubtless one day soon he would want his grant of acres, like the rest of them, asking Wilkie to petition the king.

That wise assumption could soon wear thin, however. For at their next dinner Sir Colin said, 'There's a new ballad, Tom — see if you can't find an auld rogue to come in and sing it for his supper. I promise him a jug of blockade. The authentic peat juice. The glory of it is, nobody shall understand but me, and while the singer might tremble, he shan't be called on to pay.' Sir Colin Wilkie was a veritable folkways gatherer in this regard, just as it seemed Tom Rankine was, at his end of the equation, through his sheep and his live bodies tied to the improvement of sheep by every refractory sentiment.

A week later, it was a Monday morning, Rankine left Parramatta before first light, barefoot Biddy — with red colour in her cheeks and a parakeet feather in her hair — astride a fine prancing pony, and Rankine with his black mare and packhorse loaded heavy. Biddy was excited at going to meet up with a wild man. They went a long way round to the sou'-sou'-east, where small settlers were trickling along where the authorities hardly bothered them. In that rumpled low country Biddy was chirpy. It seemed to her so pleasant and so reassuringly populated, the Parramatta bush. 'We are not in the deep bush yet,' Rankine cautioned her. Settlers were along dry creeks and up crumbling gullies where they planted a pear tree and built a clay chimney place, and kept a good few secrets, you can be sure, clutched to their hungry bones and behind their flogged, scarred old backs of old. They asked few questions of the officer and the Irish girl, only gave them their crumbs of earnest hospitality. One of them they met was John J. Tharpe with his team of packhorse geldings. Rankine had a word with Tharpe, 'about a young man with salt', and was treated to Tharpe's acceptance — a promise to be led, come shearing time, wherever.

From a high ridge, in the far distance, they saw the sea. Then they turned inland to the south-west. Somewhere thereabouts was the cataract of Carrung Gurrung, that George Marsh had found and lost.

Biddy jumped down into Rankine's arms as soon as it was dark, and if there was any rustling sound in the night, she said, 'Something wants to bite my brain!' and she buried herself in his blankets, scared of opossums and native cats and whatever else with teeth.

It was new country where they came the next day and nobody following them that far. But somehow Rankine missed finding the ridges like five fingers and the variety of trees, and so missed, farther up, the blazed trees with their axe marks grown over. Birds were scared up in flocks of raucous white cockatoos, and of funereal yellow-tailed black cockatoos, and dusty grey-pink galahs screeching a thousandfold across a sky of smoked glass and lightning-crazed dry hills. Goannas with tails patterned like chain mail clambered up tree trunks, just out of reach, and hefty wombacks grazed at evening, brown lumps of earth. 'Look,' said Rankine, getting down from his horse: there was a lonesome anteater porcupine waddling through the bush and tossing up dried dead leaves. Biddy laughed and screamed at the hilarity of the little bloke. Rankine walked the fellow along for a while, soft as he could. Its dark quills were yellow tipped, its snout went into the ground like a leather punch taking food up from nests. When Rankine stood closer it baulked and churned digging into the hardest of ground, closing down its quills and tossing up lumps of loosened soil teeming with ants. Bigger trees showed treads axed by natives looking for honey combs but Rankine told Biddy, without being too sure of it himself, how there were few signs natives lived in the territory still, or that anyone had passed through in a recent month of Sundays.

In this he was wrong. Because not far from where they stood was a camp, where a stalky figure stirred by a cold daytime fire, annoyed himself, then lay down again. His face was blackened by unwashed smoke, he was filthy, dirty tangle-haired — he was a white man. 'Where are those bastids taken off?' Patrick Lehane said. 'They promised me another wife, a young one. I could do with one of their boys, I'm that fecking voracious, you know.'

He placed an arm over his eyes to shade the sun, and missed seeing the riders not far off.

'I don't like it,' said Biddy. 'Where is Kale?'

Rankine said nothing. How could he tell her they were lost?

'Anyway,' he continued to himself, 'it is good having no blacks in a district when you bring in sheep. One has no wish to disturb anyone's hunting grounds, to have speared sheep on one's hands and the need to warn off natives with a firearm discharged in their direction. Pleased anyway to avoid killing a man to preserve a sheep.'

'Listen, is it bleating?' said Biddy.

It wasn't. It was Lehane bellowing for his share of bush companionship. If he'd looked around, instead of just yelling, he might have found someone closer than he dreamed, and finished this whole thing off.

The sun rose late over high stony bluffs and set early into purple hills behind them. Down the centre of a valley after passing through narrow walls a main stream took wide meanders and trickled, pooled, filtered away to nothing under dry mucus-covered stones and only reappeared a few hundred yards farther along if it had a good mind to. They doubled back and found another way.

It was a place Rankine liked for its soulful pity — an old riverbed to the west of the present one. It formed a semicircular wall that looked as if it had been pushed up by a giant earthworm and trees grew over it. Almost vertical bare earth showed between the trees, giving Rankine an impression of looking down from above and of floating over what mattered; a scrofulous scraped area like a red diseased scalp.

'Are you all right?' Biddy yelled at him.

No, because the baked dry but flourishing bushes and desiccated stones banking the shallow watercourse reminded him of Spain. That was the pull of it. Spain and the trouble it caused, for which the prized flock of merinos was both blame and recompense. Talk about killing a man to preserve a sheep — no need to look around here — just look back to Spain and ask for the Spanish thousand.

And so they went up a ridge, side by side, dolefully.

Biddy was scratched by thorn bushes and burnt by the sun. Rankine realised as the trees thinned that it was possible to take a bearing, and that no more doubling back would be needed. Over in the hazy south-west he saw aligned the ridges like five fingers, and after another day's hard going they came to the first of them, and ascended. It was another three days of jumbled slow going, matched to Biddy's idling pace, before they attained the duck mole reach, where Biddy, bush-broken better, was captivated by a green ledge of grass shaded by sheoak needles. She bathed in the clear stream and dried her coppery hair in a spill of late winter sunlight.

'Are we safe?' said Biddy.

'We are.'

'How come we are safe?'

'It is all in the distances involved, too far for anyone to follow.'

'We've had no trouble,' agreed Biddy with pride. 'Hardly any at all, except where a hellish thicket gets in the way.'

'Others are not as good as we are in pushing matter aside. They start off confident enough. They lose their puff, fall into ravines, double back, drop their compasses, go bush mad, and that has been the way since the colony was framed, when a line was drawn, and everyone stayed inside it. In the main, they still do. It is such a vast ocean of land, they cannot imagine it, and when they do try, do not get far.'

'Are we the first to break out?'

'More or less, in this direction. I believe we are.'

'How come so?'

'Because of the gentleman — Kale.'

'I knew you would say that. I could live right here,' said Biddy, with her smile of irresistible bounce, and Rankine, who was drinking rum, sauntered over to where she sat on her blanket wearing very little after her bath except a coarse hemp undershirt against which her bare skin glowed. Carefully settling his pannikin in the grass, where it would be safe for him afterwards, he took Biddy's hand and held it down to her side, and pushed her a little roughly falling backwards across the blanket. She was ready for him and not too perturbed.

'Dear little Biddy,' he said.

'Why are you sad?' she touched his face.

'Nay, I'm not, I want you.' He ran a hand up over her pale, plate-like breasts, while with his other hand unbuckled his trousers.

'So here I am,' said Biddy, with her inviting giggle messed in with her warmest kiss. Just as Rankine pushed her down harder, and she obliged him by deftly arranging her knees to his purpose, she said closely into his ear: 'Hold me, won't you, don't ever disgrace me, Tom.'

He did not like her, ever, using his name, Tom. If he asked himself why, he would not like the answer. She was his servant, that was all, and at his service even as she spoke.

Not until afterwards, sitting alone and apart on a square rock, drinking his rum getting himself drunker than he wished, while Biddy sang and coaxed the fire under their gruel, did Rankine fully consider what she said. Disgrace her? How could he not?

'MOVE EM ON, YE BASTIDS!'

It was Kale, striding down a gully behind his sheep. First get the sheep in, then make your salutations to those who'd battled nearly a whole week to reach your honour. Not to mention what else.

Rankine and Biddy jumped out of the way as the sheep came clattering towards them. It was as if the sheep, not the man, were the gladdest. The sheep went into their circle of stones and lay down peaceably from newly formed habit. Moreno and Kale tied the hurdles and checked the palisades against warregal dogs.

'There has been no more depredation since you left,' Kale said to Rankine. 'But there is too much grass getting eaten for too little result.'

'Everywhere's green as it ever looked.'

'You can't eat green. Not on its own, captain, without bulk sustenance combined. It is a scathing compliment to this country, that it is very responsive after rains. At the first lick of hot wind, she wilts. We are in late winter, soon to be spring, with summer fast on her boil. Then it's a long dry penance, and the real character of the place comes over it.'

'May be it's true of this valley, but what about the next one over, the six or seven of them you boasted a province, Kale, wider than Kilkenny?'

'I said not as green.'

At the sheep camp they unloaded the supplies and hobbled the horses. Their horses needed rest but would not get very long.

Kale showed courtly good manners around Biddy, sending Rankine blithering glances as if he could not believe his prize.

Biddy, to Rankine's complacency, curtsied to the man when he asked her about the hardships of their ride.

'Those hardships were pretty awful easy, Desmond Kale. Captain Rankine was good to me.'

When the civilities were done Biddy stayed at Rankine's side, shy and uncertain, wondering what next. Moreno went around the camp packing his gear ready for the morning. He was riding back with Rankine. Biddy sorted her medicines and Kale pulled up his shirt to show the progress of his sores. They were improved lower down, but under his left shoulder was a raw mess.

'Does it hurt?'

'It is painful,' admitted Kale. 'It has been, too long.'

'He doan tell me that,' said Moreno.

'How are you, Payolo?' said Biddy.

'Very appy, Missus Magee,' said Moreno. And he was. That was plain as his sonorous moon face, clean shaved and dashed with reeking toilet water. His hair was razor cut in a fringe fallen square across his forehead. His eyes were red.

Only one thing to mind, though — this from the master of caramelos, when he looked admiringly, but resentfully, at Rankine:

'Please to remember that without Moreno there is no sheeps, no deception, no getaway. *Acuerdate que si mi no existirian las obejas, ni exito, ni escape.*' They talked out of earshot of the others. 'No sheeps gods without me, either. There cannot be two gods with sheeps because each shepherd he markers his own creatures. It is the breedings principle. With you, Rankine, it is hunger for the daughter, Meg Inchcapes, draws you to Kales and love of fleeces. I marched Kales through the forest, I broke his chains for hims. Doan forget being put to death is more than a servant pledges a master unless in the infernos of wars.'

'It's a sheep's war we're fighting,' said Rankine.

'Do you like it here, Biddy?' said Kale.

'I'm a bit frightened.'

'There is no need.'

'Well, I like it well enough,' said Biddy, with her hands warming to the fire as she looked about her. Was there ever a body farther flung from Ireland?

Kale lay on his side on a bed of brush. 'You don't have to like it, dear. No, not at all. There is better for you somewhere, I smell it.'

'She's game,' said Rankine, coming back to the fire. 'Oh, but you are, Biddy.'

Rankine was not disposed to suffer any more baulking from her.

Biddy prepared a bread poultice and placed it over Kale's wound. 'There, there,' she said.

'Just this cool touch of your fingertips would cure me, Biddy Magee.'

'Will you shoosh.'

The stone shelters had been improved. The largest was raftered with wattle posts and roofed with bark. It was a veritable cottage, except you had to crawl to get in.

Kale crawled in there, fumbled in a sack, and when he came out presented Biddy with a pair of skin slippers made in honour of her arrival.

'These are wonderful warm,' said Biddy, touching them to her cheeks. She tried them on. Then she looked at Kale, and at Rankine, with a tight configured frown. 'How did you know I'd come?' It might have been better all round, if Biddy had been stupid.

'Our Kale is a queer one,' said Rankine, rather emphasised.

'Aye, I'm a bit touched,' said Kale. 'I had a great feeling in my bones, that you would come to me here. It is all right, dearie, don't you mind too much whatever you feel, as we are gathering up our flocks and making a ways off to somewhere better.'

They were eating their mutton stews and it took Rankine a minute to understand what Kale said.

'Kale, did I hear you right? You can't think of leaving this place and risking even shorter rations when lambing is near as it is. The sheep must go on biting harder and so thrive their wool.'

'Is that an order?' said Kale disdainfully. 'Of course we stay for the lambing, and the shearing, whichever comes last, then it's best to pick up.'

'Keep them here, Kale, in these valleys. Their wool goes the next step and shall densify as is noticed in rocky ground.'

'Only possibly for the number we have,' admitted Kale, 'but when they drop lambs they'll have dirt to eat and the valleys will be a wasteland. It shall be like the Arabs who can never get ahead because their flocks eat down the place of their encampment so quick they are obliged to herd them onwards too often; very destructive to their flocks' improvement on account of the young ones too weak to follow.'

'All right,' said Rankine, 'but mightn't the valley make a good headquarters for a station even if you push on? A great advantage of the route is its secrecy against being followed by the traps. It is in all respects a deep hidden collection of canyons.'

'We have our own commissioned captain of rangers with us, a veritable trap himself, as the best antidote against the bastids,' said Kale.

'I am sorry, Kale. It's a dreadful ride this far. You cannot expect me to keep coming up — if you are God knows where.'

'We are "God knows where" already. Here is the man advising all about sheep,' Kale turned to Biddy, took her hand and played with it in the firelight, addressing his sarcasm to Rankine all the while. 'Here is the man leads the mob in Mundowey forest, risks his neck saving us, and brings us safely forth for the dream of their wools' government.'

'I don't understand,' said Biddy.

'Haven't ye been told it?' said Kale.

'Told. What?'

She turned to Rankine.

'Told what?'

'You covered for me the whole time,' he said.

Then Biddy understood. All the household mystery of the past three months was clear to her in a word. She stared at Rankine. 'It was to save the man?'

'Payolo was the great one,' said Rankine.

'Well, it is the greatest thing,' said Biddy.

'You've been very discreet with her,' said Kale, raising his pannikin of rum. 'If things are as tight in Parramatta as ye pigeon pair, they'll never pin it at all.'

'I gave her my trust. Without knowing why, she kept it.'

'Nothing is changed,' said Biddy.

'Something is changed,' Kale said roughly. 'The reason, you see, poor Biddy, is that Rankine just wants us to stay here, delay, prevaricate, hold. He wants to bring Meg Inchcape down and build a hut from the stones and clay muds of the valley, roosting it with beams from the sheoak trees that grow on the stream banks and sift the wind through their sad needles.'

'You are mad,' said Rankine.

Biddy covered her mouth with her hand, sick with a sudden rush of humiliation and outright disgrace. 'Meg Inchcape?'

'Aye, me daughter, the officers' sport,' said Kale. 'For which I don't blame her weakness, only her pride, and them officers for their fatuous child-getting upon her.'

Biddy drew in against Kale and stared at Rankine.

'That is the truth. They only play-act with feelings.'

Rankine had nothing to say now, except to condescendingly declare: 'I love you Biddy, but if I love Meg it wasn't chosen by me.'

'That's an easy lie.'

'Biddy . . . Biddy . . .' He reached out.

'Don't come near me.'

Kale said:

'I have in mind an arid moor of salty grey-blue foliage waist-high rolling to the horizon where you might run a million million sheep this side of an admittedly imagined river. I shall flog meself down to the bone to gain there, now that I have the means, my stretch of freedom, good breeding livestock, Biddy to look after me and hopefully a top breeding ram, Young Matchless, by all rights me own.'

'What are you talking about, Kale?'

'There is a place. It's past where I went with Marsh, while he stayed in a camp by some kind of bidgee river, botanised and bird-watched, drew maps and stirred the wallaby stew. I went a month's hard riding farther out for the gross whopping hell of it. Marsh was grandly pissed off when I returned. 'There's a great place for you,' I said. It would have made his name, for you see, away out there it's a native contenong, whole kingdoms and divisions of em, thrashingly magnificent people. Tall men, fine-looking women, happy little children plump as Biddy Magee; and acres of a blue bush, which is no use to them but I brought some fronds of it back with me, and fed to a sheep, because of a feeling I had, about the salt it contained. The sheep ate every bit of it, and licked up the shreds. They did so thrive.'

In the night Rankine heard Biddy crying.

'Biddy, come over here,' he said.

When she made no movement or reply he got up, and went to her blanket roll. He found her enfolded into a ball, tight as that anteater porcupine bunched into itself, and just as skilled at squeez-ing in closer when he touched her, and as prickly when she flinched. 'Go away.'

In the morning she was nowhere to be seen. Rankine and Moreno were packed ready to go, with a light frost still on the ground. 'Leave her be,' said Kale. 'Have some mercy.'

Rankine went through the scrub surrounding their camp beating bushes with a long stick. He saw her ahead of him crouched, and then running. He chased her in a wide circle until she ended back at the camp. When he called goodbye she was clinging to Kale, and that was how it was then, with Biddy Magee.

IT WAS SPRING OR WHAT passed for spring in that country — a thump of heat, a few rainstorms, howling westerly winds, colour crashing out of the mangled forests, wattle blossom shining heavy gold before turning gold brown, producing brittle seed pods that withered in the shape of twisted horns.

Convict gangs marched out and marched back in to Parramatta and Toongabbie. Stone cutting, wood cutting, road making, field ploughing, stump burning. The punishment rosters were filled to the craw of justice. On a gibbet, a hanged man swivelled in the wind and baked in the sun, a warning to nefarious meddlers to be wise to themselves. The governor ordered him stay up a while longer.

Rankine and Moreno rode back towards the settled district. The way was dusty and hot as they rode between trees, around boulders, into dislocated dry creeks and over such long miles of rough stony ground that their horses stepped tenderly sore.

When they saw a snake they killed it, beautiful creature that it was. There was something about a snake insisted on having itself skinned, the skin salted and kept wrapped damp in oilskin until such a time as it could be preserved in glycerine and pure alcohol.

It beat tanning with such soft living suppleness imparted that you looked for the fangs.

Moreno went off and found a shearing gang.

Back in Parramatta Rankine bound his letter case in the skin of a five-foot king brown. He took out this venomous satchel to draft demands of the governor, thinking of the hanged man, of Kale, and of what else, when he got the words and the thinking right:

Sir, As an officer in your service and as your chosen friend, who knows you are not a designing man likely to prey on the poverty of your charges, I ask what are you doing this term of yours to better so horrid a system as can be witnessed daily in the king's name where people die, some by the bayonet, some by the halter, some by the lash delivered by righteous hypocrites, some by hard labour and starvation or confinement in rotten cells for their principles.

The page was a mess of splintery nib strokes as Rankine bit his lip concentrating, drawing blood. Was he so serious a governmental dissenter to question authorised rule in a traceable letter, when words were a crime to men of law, more dangerous than snakes? Only in his mind, for now, and on that besplattered page, did he appeal to his friend General Wilkie, a hungry spirited man of close acquaintance who could never see a dog or a cat harmed without shedding a tear. The system was not made by Wilkie but was minded by him and didn't the one with clay in his hands have the power of shaping? With a feeling clearly defined in his emotions, along the lines of compulsion, of being drawn to yet another accomplished act, Rankine would one day deliver a bundle of these buckramed pages to the governor's desk, and the governor, amazed or otherwise at the man he thought of as so much merrymaking champagne froth, would bring down his sword, or otherwise consider.

Already there was a feeling around the settlement that while Desmond Kale was far and away free as a bird, the one who'd sprung his catch might soon be snared. He might soon swing on that gibbet himself, shadowing over the seeds and weeds of the byway.

There were said to be agents watching; a narrowing-in of trust. At government house Sir Colin examined the epileptical blazing-eyed misfit James Moroney, who recited his piece in Irish. Moroney was vain of inspiration and presented his fragment as allegorical, bardworthy, lofty, apostolical, rippling his voice like a bagpipe chanter. Sir Colin found the almost mythical details of the narrative almost mythically elevating, but not quite, not quite . . . and decided there was something in the words needed looking into, as upon a real or imagined survey of inland parts. That libel Parson Stanton made on the officer corps — he remembered — claiming an officer was involved in the affair at Mundowey:

'Mayn't there be something in it?'

For the ballad resplendently said:

A man went west in a vision, into the sunset flaring in the red tips of the gum trees — around his neck was slung a ram. Under each arm he carried a ewe. In his hair was a nest of purlambs and gimmerlambs. Between his teeth was a long stick hewn from the hardest known of Botany Bay woods, the hickory wattle, with a curved natural growing elbow for a crook. In a haversack of softest lambskin was carried a salted ham of mutton, a stub of sour sheep's cheese, a bottle of French brandy. From rock to rock the man leaped, confounding his pursuers. Oh, you can be sure how

the traps found a rattle of sheep shit across disturbed leaves, and
a string of wool caught in the beak of a crow as they chased him.
A piece of the wool was brought back and made into a thread that
the Devil wore on his wrist. You can be sure the traps had a good
mystifying time of it out there, where they turned around finally,
and came back without him, blistered on lip and heel, scabs of their
falls bleeding from their shaking knees and torn fingertips.

Sir Colin sent an invitation to Tom Rankine to come join him at his table. He was overdue there, missed. Rankine he considered well able to assist him in a matter. Easy mannered, plausible, Rankine was formerly of the survey corps in Craufurd's Spanish army, with a quick tongue and a fondness for inscrutable ditties. As far as was recently known, Rankine kept an Irish girl for his bed, and was fond of the race, as the governor himself was fond, within limits. 'In recent times,' the governor asked his secretary, 'who among my officers is seen — by their store records — to have drawn warrants on French brandy, a good scarce quantity of that high-grade spirit? And might not the same deceiver wear a twist of wool around his wrist, may be?'

The governor's letter lay on Rankine's dresser, asking his reasons for scorning the vice-regal table, and saying, if he did not show his face soon, Sir Colin would have him brought in wearing shackles. It was an affectionate jape, could be naught else, but caused Rankine to quake, and look to making amends.

Thickets of boronia and wattle blossom scented the air. Next day Tom Rankine brought Meg Inchcape native flowers picked from the wayside. He was back to his start with her, whatever he grandly hoped. He was back to the ordinary civilities of love, without much expectancy. He'd not stopped loving her since his first vision of her. But greatness was not very bold, mightiness a mere grain of sand. Somebody wrote that somewhere. All came to dust and he told himself, yes, he was a monk, an ascetic, a mulligrub in the universal scheme of fame. He woke each morning with a thumping head, resolving, each morning, that although there were sorrows he needed to drown, it was not quite as thoroughly needed as drinking half the night. Biddy's absence made him pine for her touch but not a great deal. One night he cried into his pillow but only a little. When his dream of the thundering herd with the face of unearthly beauty tempted, he sat straight up in bed, wide awake.

The wildflowers grew on unlikely thorny shrubs with profusion of colour, knurled miniature blossoms of bacon and egg, fugitive crimsons and golds, hard as wire. They dried without losing any colour for weeks, or else came in vines frothing up trees with white or purple blooms that wilted almost before Rankine could rush them into Meg's hands and say look.

It was not the first time he'd brought her flowers, leaving them at her door, on some days piling them into the arms of the withered crone, Mother Hauser . . . Never before finding as he did this day that Meg herself stood at the door, and smiling.

'Hello . . .' he said, a stone in his throat. 'Allow me . . . I don't mean to disturb you . . .' It was not very well put. An officer did not always command.

'It is our Captain Rankine! . . . Where is your leaping horse?' There was a knuckle of amusement above the bridge of Meg's nose that he rather liked, that lovely long nose being pronouncedly Romany.

Her glossy dark hair was thrown back from her forehead, tied with a piece of string, her strong eyebrows smudged with flour, her cheeks freckled — he'd not known it — never been as close! — and were high-boned — wide, hazel eyes, slightly upturned, shining with energetic delight; lips hovering a half smile when she looked at him with a gaze so honestly strong it seemed to sense his truth better than he ever could — and upon the bare curve of her neck Rankine, given the chance, would swear a thousand fidelities.

'For you,' he said, putting the blooms in her arms. He was candidly surprised that his persistence had some sort of result — that she stood there at all.

'All mine?'

'They seemed to belong to you, Meg Inchcape, at least, when I saw them, I thought of you — as I gathered them up. By the wayside.'

She held the bundle and ran her fingers through the top of them, like a mother caressing her child's hair, lightly but passionately.

'They are beautiful ones.'

'Watch out for thorns . . .'

With his finger and thumb he unpicked a stem from her sleeve. In the moment of the action he heard her breathing, saw the strong pulse in her neck, and felt the warmth of her breath on the back of his hand. There was definitely heard the harsh snick of each thorn breaking free.

'Won't you please come in?' she said, when this odd intimacy was over, lifting aside the canvas flap, on the outer side of which old Mother Hauser had recently kept Rankine shifting from one foot to the other for a full ten minutes while he was sure Meg fumed inside, for whatever reasons of state.

'Into your house?' he masked disbelief.

'Humble as it is, you are welcome.'

The earth floor was brushed clean and a busy contingent of blowflies circled looking for scraps from table or shelf to lay their eggs upon, but were unlikely to find some. There was a shape on the floor like a bundle of rags: a little old figurine unfolded from there, nut-brown faced and sparrow-hawk featured. She crouched, feeding sticks to the fire. 'Mother Hauser sleeps in the wood box against my shack wall and keeps out intruders, as a rule,' said Meg.

The smell of baking made Rankine hope that his welcome was going to get better. It looked as though their cordiality was going to meet a celebration, at least, an idea only slightly dented when Meg said she was expecting Warren, all this was for him.

'Sit down,' she invited, as she prepared the kettle and set about making tea and finding a precious pat of butter that was melting in the fire's heat.

In the fireplace the diminutive crone deftly swung a pot crane holding a hot-water fountain, a griddle, a camp oven and all of them cooking away, while at the same time she worked, with bare toes on the handles, a set of bellows to bring up the flame just right.

There was a coarse rug on the corn-husk mattress that served as both couch and bed. There Rankine sat, his hands on his knees, his back straight. Folded on the top of that rug was the same piece of cloth embroidered with mirrors and a scrap of silk material that had caused Parson Stanton to decide that Meg Inchcape was pretty much a damned clever whore.

Rankine, by contrast, and to his eternal merit — if time would allow tell — saw everything around him as wifely in a manner of ways, womanly and great-hearted, settled and showing devotion to the smallest of threadbare domestic touches of the household arts . . . When Meg Inchcape pledged herself to him, that would be, and stopped disturbing his dreams. The moment he set eyes on her again, he was drunk with her again.

While he gathered his thoughts and sorted his impressions, another part of his mind raced along preparing his answers. Before his mind was ready, though, his tongue wagged:

'Biddy Magee was raised in a sod house,' he said expansively, 'where any place above a bed of earth was fit for a king. She was amazed when she came to my cottage, to find a bed of straw, a chair, and a table made available to her — in her own quarters — as well as cooking pots and always a tub of best potatoes.'

'What are you trying to say to me, captain?'

'That Biddy had her own little cubby out the back of my house, she had somewhere of her own and possibly as comfortable as your own little nook, Mother Hauser, do you hear?'

'She is deaf,' said Meg, setting a place for two at her table. 'Probably lucky for you.'

'Why?'

'Your dalliance with a maidservant has been known around the settlement for twelve months at least, and people don't even bother telling me this any more — that my greatly persistent soldier admirer, who tried to run me down with a horse, and brought me flowers all through it, and sugary sweets, was double dealing with a nineteen-year-old girl, although some would admit she is pretty enough.'

'That is over,' said Rankine, humbled, cut, shrinking and dropping his head.

He watched as Mother Hauser took the lid from the cast-iron oven and with a wooden spoon lifted an arrangement of small pies onto a plate.

Meg leaned with her elbows on the table, not six inches from Rankine's face. He caught her living breath and felt the fullness of her existence in the warmth rising up from between her freckled breasts. 'You have given your maidservant her leave?'

'She is gone,' he agreed while looking around, not wanting to say where.

'It is what I heard, but wanted to hear you say it.'

Meg poured his tea into a cracked blue cup and they smiled pleasantly at each other, except Meg's lips had something more serious coming upon them.

'WHEN I WAS VERY SMALL,' said Meg, 'my mother had bad luck and she suffered terribly. She was a nurserymaid in a gentleman's family and was able to have me there in the day if I made no fuss.'

'Where was it?' said Rankine.

'At Emu Plains barracks, but I barely remember where it was, nor how cruel, except it was my place and I was happy, and my mother was with me all the time. Sometimes she would be struck on the back, or slapped in the face, if she paid me too much attention; for my love, she was punished by her masters! Hard choices pressed her down. She dressed in clean rags but was declared by her mistress to have plenty of clothes of her own, and was given only a gown by her and received neither wages nor clothes in all the time we were there.'

'Where was your father, Kale?' said Rankine.

'Where was my father, Kale? Away with sheep, was what I was told, although whether he was, or in irons, for his politics and pride you might guess.'

'I would guess in irons.'

'We had plenty to eat and drink and were strictly kept to the house, except at night, when I was taken from the nursery and put into a room where the other maids were. I slept with my mother. She was vexed and angered at her treatment. Never suppose that a servant is merely a chattel without heart of feeling nor brains to think.'

'Never again,' Rankine, abashed, took his cue, and certainly meant it.

'There was a freewoman kept in the house. She had a bed and a bedstead and my mother's bed was kept on the floor. It was only the floor and I woke each morning with soil in my mouth, from breathing it in. The freewoman had sheets but we had none. My mother was proud, she made a decision about who she was to obey, and set it down as a principle with herself. She matched her pride to my father's proud temper. She was English born, from Dorset. When our master's mother-in-law came to stay, and gave orders, she refused to obey her. There were no charges of misconduct preferred against her but she was returned to the service of the Crown.'

'That was bad,' said Rankine.

'I should say so!'

Meg thought he wasn't listening or paying attention, but it was something else. In the same room as her, Rankine had the uncertain feeling of missing her, still longing for her. When their eyes connected the part of her that stirred him most was absent, ungraspable, or always only hers. He was in love with her immortal and ephemeral life and also with her bodily self down to imagining her entwined with an officer betrayer — father of Warren — who in his fancy was a goat, lacking every refinement.

'Are you listening to me, at all, Tom Rankine?'

'I am. Your mother was returned to the service of the Crown. That must have been bad luck, seeing as how some of the people we know are assigned to their husbands or vice versa, making for cosy arrangements.'

'She was lucky at least,' said Meg, 'that she was not taken and put into chains quite yet, like my father whenever he opened his mouth. For we came down here just across from where we are now. See, where the smoke is going up, where that charcoal heap lies.' Rankine peered out through the doorway. 'They who we came to are still there and worn into themselves with toil. The mistress a prisoner holding no indulgence and the master a blacksmith. There was another child there, a boy my age, he died poor thing. My mother in that situation might do as she liked, and that was her undoing as she was allowed to drink and go to the public house, and stayed out all night if she pleased. Where was my father at the time, you would still like to ask? Now he was in that cell block where you found him, fomenting rebellion, now in another, lying in chains. This was after the paddy's rebellion and he was lucky he was not hung. Or unfortunate he was not hung, considering his suffering and the way heaven is always painted better. He loved my mother extremely but this was the end of them. If my mother asked for anything in her situation she was told they were too poor to give it to her, telling her she could get it for herself provided she did not trouble them.'

'What did that mean?'

'What that means I am too ashamed to tell you although you might guess, and anyway I was too young to understand when she — when she sold — all right, I shall say it — when she sold herself. Mother Hauser was her broken-down maid when she was there in a place of prostitution.'

Rankine waited as the pies cooled in their dish and Meg gathered herself and continued:

'She remained in the situation six months and then fled. What for her was a miserable escape, for me was a wonderful time. We lay on the riverbank and made shapes out of clouds, collected wildflowers in our arms . . . and like the blacks we slept in a hollow tree and a very fine house it proved.

'My father was assigned at the time word of our plight reached him, and he was prevented from coming away.

'Now to the worst part. The man who ordered it over my mother's objections — to have her beautiful hair shorn off — was his master.'

'It was the *parson* who put her back down?' said Rankine.

Meg said that he was the one. 'But if I let my hatred rule, there will be no victory and no benefit to Warren or ability for Warren to become better than those who brought him into this world.'

When she made this strong statement, worthy of a reigning queen, Rankine squeezed around the table, leaned to her and put his arms closely around her. She turned awkwardly from him, not wanting a lover's embrace, which was an unfair judgement on him, to say the least. For at the moment his desire was progressed past self-interested ways even at the level where it was instinctive, an occurrence that charmed his idea of himself immeasurably, though it could not last possibly past another few minutes.

'It was not only my mother that day,' said Meg, getting busy with the teapot, a bit flustered, 'but a huge congregation of unhappy women in the prison yard. One of them was Mother Hauser here, taken along as a companion in suffering. They collected a heap of stones, and when the minister and the gaolers entered the area they threw the stones as fast as they possibly could at the whole of them. My mother screamed the most violently. She swore that no one should cut off her hair, and she was screaming, swearing, and jumping about the place bereft of her reason. When the minister approached her, to calm her, and so control her, she took a pair of scissors in her hand and commenced cutting off her own hair. Then she ran wilder. Coming before the windows of the dispensary she thrust her fist through three panes of glass in a row. With a bucket she broke some more panes of glass and the bottom sash of the window frame.'

'The minister avenged himself over Desmond Kale,' said Rankine, 'his shepherd gone to the bad, by defeating Kale's wife, your mother?'

'Something in Kale was unconsumed. After she died and her grave was only tended by me, and a storm came down from the top of the gully and washed away all the stones — when Kale was released and wanted a rake to tidy it up, he went out of his way to find one and bring it over to Parramatta and do the job.'

'It is going to be finished,' said Rankine, taking Meg's hand. 'It has already well begun.'

'How can you say "well begun"? My fierce mother impoverished, abused, imprisoned, insane, ill, dead — unrestfully dead in a pauper's graveyard, a gravel pit.' Her grip tightened in Rankine's hand. He felt the sharpness of her fingernails cutting before she let him go. 'My outrageous father proud, blaming, striding it out wearing a tuft of hogget's wool in his ears, his thoughts bent by men using him. Who are they, anyhow? Does anybody know?'

'Nobody seems to know,' said Rankine truthfully, though only up to a point.

'"Well begun"?'

'You don't know me.'

RANKINE TIPPED BACK HIS HEAD on the slab wall and looked at her. 'You don't know *me*,' he repeated. Meg looked slightly up at him from the other side of the table, in the chinked tan light of her one-roomed house.

'I don't know *you*?' she said. 'I would say I don't. Something gets in the way every time we meet. Do you always look at the world through a fringe of lashes? Quivering, almost shut like half-lowered blinds. What's going on behind them?'

Rankine took a slow breath and decided.

'Sometimes it's tears,' he admitted; then, in no great hurry, he confessed it all — the escape in the forest, the trusting of Kale, the Spanish thousand of blood-money sheep reduced to two hundred and gifted to Kale, made three hundred with increase of lambs; the unwanted rams, the stone gullies where the sheep went up, the jump they made down, the wool flying in shreds and the prized sheep driven, then how driven they were until the duck mole reach was taken and a fair way beyond was achieved by Kale, where he now lingered, the sheep roughly grazing.

'Dear God save us and Mary too,' said Meg, her hand over her mouth.

Rankine's revelation included vignettes to soften the hardships: pale peaceful forests and birdsong, clearings with smoke twisting up, sleepy afternoons in the saddle. Telling it to Meg, he made rough country into a series of rooms — places of fanciful safety leaving out mention of thorns, insect stingers, sunstroke, thirst, leaving out trackers, troopers, search parties with swords, guns, iron rings, and men bearing oiled and knotted whips. He omitted signs of native bands, clutching their bundles of spears. He omitted the endless turnings around and going backwardses, as Biddy Magee called them, nor did he raise topics of brown snakes, black snakes, tiger snakes, typical of sandy-bottomed country as they sought a straight way on. He omitted mention of Biddy Magee herself, as a morsel for Kale's delight. He did not leave out, however, the murmurous suspicions lapping him higher and closer each day in Parramatta.

At the end of it Meg stood up and stepped back, using as much force to get clear of him, in the small space available, as she had used in leaning over him — her mouth corners tense white, her eyes flickering around him unsettled, alarmed, and quite defenselessly afraid:

'I had no idea.'

'You've heard none of it?' said Rankine.

'Not a whisper.'

'You've not heard a song in chorus, in Irish, mentioning Kale?'

After all the rumours, it seemed fairly likely she had.

'Nay, I hate that tongue. When I hear it, I go deaf. The same happens with harping on Kale, the way some do.'

Rankine, having harped on Kale, wondered where he stood. As far as it looked, still badly.

'Don't tell me any more,' said Meg. 'The knowledge is far too dangerous.'

She stepped outside and searched up and down the road. 'So this is the end of it,' thought Rankine, and stood to go. Then, as he ducked under the low ceiling, he cracked his head on a crosspiece. He moved his fingers wonderingly from his scalp to the brim of his hat, and Mother Hauser looked at the ceiling as if to thank it for being so strong.

When Meg came back inside she asked the old mother for a drink of water, a dish to wash her face and arms, and for a piece of scrubbing cloth. Rankine awaited his dismissal. It did not come. The expression on Meg's face was changed, the fear was gone as though when she went outside she saw something there that removed her fear.

She nipped her fingernail in the distrait way he'd seen her doing, that so moved him as she loped along.

'I saw a crow, a dog, and a dust devil. That's all. I was expecting Warren all this time.'

She gazed at him from eyes that were softer, considering.

For there was Tom Rankine in front of her. All changed in front of her. She had never known defiance so real, so certain of its right. A captain of rangers with close-cropped steely grey hair, pale lingering eyes, an adventurer's half smile and a twisty curl at the corner of his mouth — he was defiance brought into the light of day, not defiance ground away futile in a prison cell, its hair shorn off, holding fistfuls of broken glass, bleeding across its back, or fifty lashes one day, fifty the next.

'Oh, dear me,' said Meg. She laughed briefly, amazedly, letting out something long kept in. Rankine was the answer to a question she seemed to have been asking herself, without knowing it, before her heart was ready.

Then, with apparent carelessness, she leaned forward and reached to her shins and bunched her skirts in her hands, paused and looked at Rankine over her shoulder, her hair falling loose like a thundercloud.

Rankine's voice ran dry. 'Look at you, Meg.'

In Rankine's eyes, she was acting bold — the same as in his fancies, except making it somehow dislikeable towards him, or at least unnoticing. It was quite as if he were not in the room at all. Or in some totally opposite way, just there for one purpose, which was for him to have her when she was ready and be done with it. But he could not have her yet, she seemed to warn.

'She has no modesty for her own protection,' decided Rankine of the daughter of Patsy Inchcape and of Desmond Kale, that pair whose love was split, compromised, ruined, but never quite utterly defeated. How could she not help being strange, he thought; it was her guaranty of freedom in a prison place; and for that reason, and some others, how could he not help loving her?

Meg brought her calico dress up over her head with a harsh rustling sound and passed it to her servant. Standing bare before Rankine she bathed herself in all her beauty and worn lines, her tawny breasts purple-tipped, her strong thighs shining as she washed herself, he did not know why so candidly, with such apparently absent-minded impunity, except it was truthful to her, and in that vision his love was stamped.

As was hers, in his watching, if only he knew it. But more cautiously, less expectantly, more unconsciously timed. Watching her Rankine certainly had the feeling of being in a dream. He was compelled by strangeness the way a dream compelled. As in a dream, no action of his would deflect her from what she decided. This in time would prove her greatness to him.

When Meg was done, dressed in a clean plain shift, she swept up her hair. With dexterous twists she tied a bandana, from which a few dark curls escaped. She held out her hand to Tom Rankine. 'Here is a ribbon,' she said. Her hands were rough-scaled from washing-sodas, scented from wool oils, lanolins that she used to improve their smoothness. He loved her for the imperfection and the used quality of her life.

Not understanding it, he just stood there. Then he tied that crimson ribbon around her neck with trembling fingers.

'If we are seen together,' she said, 'it might save you.'

'I don't understand,' he persisted.

'Christ, Tom, they won't see past me.'

Past me to Kale.

They emerged into the fresh daylight and walked the dusty road to the same creek hollow where Rankine had taken Warren. They sat on the same white low-hanging branch of the gum tree that was called the croppies' parliament. Initials were carved inside love hearts, slogans were scored with nails and scratched out.

'People are watching,' said Meg.

He understood better. They were to be a couple in the eyes of the village now. It was decided putting an arm around her, pulling her from the waist towards him. She lifted her face to him, as some fellow officers and their ladies walked past in the near distance: and Rankine lost no time getting her kissed. Busily public and practical, unexpected, agreeable and novel it was, involving soft lips and someone's biting, nipping manner — that soon had a flame in it, a torching shock of love, which they were just both gasping from, before falling to it a second time, when they fell off the tree backwards, landing in the dust.

(Word came back to Tom Rankine within a day, as good as a governor's signed reprieve, stating that Ugly Tom Rankine's name was confederated to Desmond Kale's for the single and very obvious reason of Kale's splendiferous daughter being his lover. By this means gossip concerning an officer traitor took a holiday, giving run to gossip of the roistering kind, of an officer struck to the cods by a washerwoman's flaunty pouch. The governor was seen rubbing his crotch and making the sign of the index finger poking through the rounded finger and thumb of the other hand: 'Tom Rankine is in rut,' he said at his men's table. So the imminent danger to Rankine withdrew, as Meg understood it would, except may be — as the governor went on to say — there was danger to Rankine's pride, for Mistress Inchcape was known to be restive and untameable.)

On the ground she reared over him, her hands on his shoulders pushing his back to the gravel. 'This will be good,' thought Rankine, 'so very, very beautiful and good.' The sun was sharp through the gum leaves overhead as he made out the tent of her hair colliding around him. 'This will be very good,' he thought, lifting his head to find her lips as she found his again: but was mistaken.

A tear splashed on him. 'Meg?'

He sat up beside her.

The next moment he was awash with her tears, salted and streaked by them, as he touched her face, drew her hair back, and she sobbed into his shoulder, and he offered his best handkerchief (last laundered by Biddy Magee) in which Meg buried her face.

'Why?' came her muffled question. 'Only tell me why.'

Rankine answered from back in the dirt somewhere, with as much of his why as he knew, as much of his why as he understood, which was not very much.

Chorus of the Third Part

WHERE KALE IS NOT QUITE FORGOTTEN

*A*S A SPANIARD I FEEL *much more able to supply the wants of my Nation, and as an individual the loss of my property by Tiranny is no less painful; but if there is no remedy I should nevertheless find alleviation of my troubles if thou, Capitan Rankine, should permit me to buy of ye a certain quantity of Fire Arms at thy disposition (the Magazine under your guards) in consideration of my kings merinos which I have ready for ye Keeping in a certain playce, eating of freshly herbs. Goodsir, since I cannot insure my Flocks here in Spain I shall have at least the pleasure of being useful to the Cause, altho I have not been so to the Commerce National — (signed) Yncan, Manuel.*

Why Rankine had been chosen, in that time and country, to receive this curious letter he certainly knew: it was musketry in a stone coop desired by two rival bands.

Every night brigands had crept around trying to get past the sentries and by day employed all manner of dissimulation and eager friendship to get their hands on powder, shot, and bayonetry. Don Manuel Yncan then was the broker between these guerillas, a landholder with his castles in ruin and doubtful politics his only bargain. For his purposes Yncan had obtained, and held in a safe place, one thousand of his Spaniard king's best sheep.

The brigands were a swarm of flies getting stickier by the day. As Rankine hotly wanted this king's sheep, whichever of the two bands was most favoured by Yncan was a matter of no great opinion to him. The arms were needed to strengthen competing positions over fellow Spaniards and to use against the retreating French (they were captured French arms) now that winter was coming on, and the French were shrinking, like a blue stain bleeding red at the edges, towards the Pyrenees.

'If Yncan sells those arms on to the highest bidder then the very best of good fortune to him' — was Rankine's not very deeply thought-out but deeply self-serving opinion. The arms were feasibly Rankine's own to sell, not registered yet to the quartermaster as spoils. Only let it be done soon, as the people were hungrier than ever, in a land where dry crust was a banquet. British troops and their camp followers were hungry, birds were falling from the sky, the mice, the rats, except those on the battlefield, where they fattened on corpses, were all scant ribcages on four spindly legs — every living thing was skeletonised bar lice and bedbugs plump as blisters.

There was already the debacle, fresh in Rankine's mind, of a sheep-chasing murderous roasting of finest-woolled flocks, when companies of the 95th regiment took up position in a wood of oak and cork. As soon as their arms had been piled, a ferocious attack was made on two hundred of the best breed of sheep. Fires were lit and livers and kidneys grilled while slippery warm and the hearts still pulsing. It was seen some parts were even savaged raw. Private Leonard Knags was selected out by their colonel to be representatively punished, and although Rankine had seen many men flogged and ordered punishments himself it was hurtful to see Knags, an obliging, tireless, cheerful, and lumpy young soul, so roughly handled by the drummers who both administered floggings and beat time to the lash. He was stripped and tied to a gun carriage in the middle of a hollow square formed by Rankine's unit of men. Knags suffered like a piece of raw meat thrown on the rack, there softened near to death while Rankine stood by sick and silent, obedient to orders. Such looting of livestock, he agreed, caused hostility among the Spaniards whose cause they were fighting for; and to some it seemed that with the common enemy, the French, in retreat, the British would be next foe in line.

As soon as he could Rankine went on with his men, Leonard Knags foremost among the best of them.

A rocky canyon stood between Rankine and the mountain pastures where the thousand sheep were held by a doughty shepherd, Moreno, nephew of the black priest Moreno — he who was forced into hiding and emerged transformed with a troop of three hundred horsemen, and a great deal of terrible fame after shooting four French prisoners to every Spaniard executed. Any male of Moreno surname then, female of the same name, or child caught by French regulars was tortured and put to death. Fear was in the dry cold air of the sierras. Rankine had given his word he would take young Moreno with him and carry him safe to England, as part of his contract for sheep, but first had to reach him. Sides changed slippery as cloud shadows ascending the bare rocky upland. The friend of yesterday became the enemy of today, and so in a stone quarry came a volley of shots, distantly drawing them on, and then at close range men stood up from behind rocks showing their intentions as plain as their dirty faces.

Horses were cut down, men fell, a rabble descended yodelling hatred of betrayers — for Yncan had done the dirty and traded the arms to their dearest rivals and they would therefore kill the source of them, Capitan Rankine.

But Rankine and his company adopted defensive positions back to back inflicting more damage than they took — but oh, the damage that they did take!

Honest stone-cutters from the quarry watched the transaction from vantage points and afterwards helped bury five young men in hard ground. They chiselled their names into a square boulder under Rankine's tearful direction — to give them such honour as their service demanded, which hardly acknowledged what Rankine owed. Their names were Henry Gale, Richard Haywood, Timothy Wolfe, Leonard Knags, and Robson Crosby. In his worst times to come, Rankine would bring those names to his lips, and recite them, a litany of sentries blocking him from heaven's gates, holders of life's best hopes and bravery fallen victim to cupidity over sheep.

At the last, when it seemed all heads were counted and his remaining men were safe, a groaning was heard and they found Clumpsy M'Carty lying with his legs writhing and his breach bloody. Two stones had been used to crush his stones between them.

'We dance according to our own legs' — an old Estremaduran proverb. 'Our hearts are our secret wonders' — that was another saying of shepherds wandering lonely in the high sierras. It applied to Moreno's love of Rankine. Snows turned into torrential streams and wildflowers came out from crevices in stone as Moreno chained them and wore them in a garland on his head. *Dios todo poderoso*. Rankine said he looked like a young bull and he would fight him. Bogs sank their sheep to the bellies, crevasses threatened, dark nights without end and lightning storms bewildered the brain. Bargains were made with sheep gods. Their hearts were their secret wonders in the revelation of deeds of which they were capable: theft, escape, loss. It was all prefigured there in Spain.

'Within a month of reaching England, my hair turned grey,' said Rankine, 'as it used to be quite dark.'

'I am sorry to hear it,' said Meg, 'although I have to say, it agrees with you.'

Rankine walked Meg back to his cottage that first day of their closeness. They did not touch as they walked, but could not stop turning to look at each other with shy eagerness. There was nothing more to be kept from each other, Rankine believed. She told him how the father of Warren was George Marsh, dead in London, but that if she'd had officer lovers — as Kale fumed — they were not worthy to stand beside Rankine, even the highest of them, because of what he had done. ('Does that get me into your bed?' thought Rankine. 'No.')

The eyes of Parramatta were upon them — a gentleman captain of rangers and an available washerwoman. They were a delight to the respectable. It was barely ten days since the rattle of bed boards was heard with Biddy Magee squealing for all her worth about fifty yards in both directions.

Meg said:

'If you love me, Tom, I will send Mother Hauser across in the morning to clean your house and wash your bed linen. Look where the swallows are nesting, making a mess. You have spiderwebs in the corners. Leaves blown in. So much neglect . . .'

'If I love you?' Rankine echoed.

She turned and touched a finger to his throat.

'If you love me.'

A rush of heat blew clean through the house with doors open at either end of a passage. Meg's capacity for springing surprises was infinite, Rankine's hunger for giving what she asked was absolute. It was the strangest thing, and remembered to his dying day — how deeply bone-satisfied he was with Meg from that moment. They were not yet lovers. She strongly resisted his intentions, in that regard, not by any word or gesture but by principle of the very power in their love itself. The fever of wanting her that previously sprang on him as a four-footed beast came as a deeper desire run into the peacefulness of the settled herd. They touched fingers. They looked and they sighed. Any fiercer lovemaking could wait . . . and so Rankine went on with his account of himself:

'Starting in the high country of Almaden, coming down from the snows, crossing the bare plains pursued by banditos and wolves, I had myself a bunch of the very most extremely well-bred animals in the history of the world, a royal flock, and a shepherd and sheep shearer named Moreno, descended from the Moors who shipped their north African doers into Spain in the year one thousand.

'For they go back that far, and they were mine, understand, no longer the King of Spain's, they were paid for in blood of brave soldiers of my own fierce company, of which only a few were left, and Clumpsy M'Carty was one.

'Then I had my Spanish one thousand in England for a while, but ask them to thrive there and all they did was cough their lungs into the grass and mince around on pustulated feet, while extruding a wool the weakness of worms. As my Frenchified stepbrother said, when he still liked me, and thought as highly as I did of those sheep, "*Il devient citoyen du lieu qu'il habite*" — they become natives of the place they inhabit. I gave him seven hundred to make the peace between us. A reckless gesture: it was the wrong country for them. They are made for growing their legs long, browsing on rough herbs, going for miles and getting into all sorts of byways where they find they will do, and the harder they go the better they shall do in a hot country, like the ox whose number of teeth they share, and their secret is the glorious beauty on their backs.'

'And that is your "why"?' said Meg.

Rankine nodded the truth of it. 'As much as I know.'

R ANKINE, HEEDING THE GOVERNOR'S LETTER requesting his company at table, put on his red mess jacket, white trousers, campaign medals, and high black boots, conscious of dressing for some last high battle to be fought with overtopping nonchalance.

As he left the house he filled a small sack with candies in the shape of piglets and starfish, treasure chests and kneeling bulls. They were the best of caramelos saved to soothe a sweet tooth, a biting tooth. He thrust the sack in a side pocket.

Rankine reported to Sir Colin Wilkie's house at his officers' dinner that started at four in the afternoon and went on until four in the morning.

A cheer went up when Rankine walked in. Tin cups were banged on the bench and his name loudly chanted.

'Ugly Tom! Ugly Tom!'

Various other opinions were essayed.

'When the Irishman hears an officer's got his daughter pinned, hoots he'll roar!'

'Like a maddened dog in a bear pit, he shall!'

'Rankine shall smoke Kale out, carry him over, bring him in, and then he'll be sorely beaten!'

'With a ten-shilling rake in his hand for Rankine's raking, no less!'

As the governor made the sign of the promiscuous finger Rankine looked blankly secretive, which was to say suitably stupefied by contentment. He grasped the sack of treats in his pocket to hand to the governor but swore when the sack broke open and half filled his pocket with sugar. Left whole was a pig that the governor crunched between his teeth in a moment, making pink spittle at the side of his mouth as he chewed.

They sat down a dozen men each side of the long bench and ate rock oysters, snapper fish, roast goose, turkey, wild duck with pellets of lead shot still in them, boiled pork, fowls, a round of beef, mutton, pork chops and all washed down by buckets of Cape wine. Most of the company drank Cape wine, that is to say, but Rankine as best and loyalest prodigal son was offered Sir Colin Wilkie's good Madeira from the governor's own jug.

A great deal of wildness prevailed after toasts were raised to various eminences starting high as the king — as the governor began to see, after dusk, lurching majors and flushed lieutenants disappearing into the bushes and most of them returning, only some few lying sick asleep until they awoke hours later, staggering up with dew upon them, and coming into the house hardly missed at all. When Rankine disappeared Wilkie smiled craftily. He'd be having wild Meg in the laundry sheds between courses, nae doot, as the governor (without fanfare) had tried to enjoy her a couple of times himself, in earlier days — Mistress Inchcape's skirts hiked up and her head turned aside resisting his hoarse breath and rapid attentions, asking him to please behave and be quick about it. Cold, he called her. He seemed to remember resentfully mumbling something about risking his skin and fortune for the sake of her touch but as she never showed she knew what he meant, by any gesture of good, he decided against her improvement, and left her alone.

Wilkie was known as 'auld scratch', a man of sixty keeping on the button. Having fathered two children with convict domestics he liked the in-and-out game too much. Born on the island of Harris and Lewis he'd never seen a coach nor heard much English spoken until the age of fourteen when a kindly dominie took him away to improve him. He was classically educated in Edinburgh but remained a son of the peat bogs and herring baskets who broke bread with dirty fingernails among the diplomats of Europe, and at Botany Bay urged table companions do likewise. Hunger unchecked in the slabbed halls of despotism fitted him best. Who was to tell a governor he was wrong? Who dared? Only the king, but the king was a long way off.

Except one man dared: Parson Magistrate Stanton slandering him to the point of saying he allowed black masses to be sung by atheist Gaelic priests, had congress with goats, drank the blood of slippery eels, and would rather have convicts at table than anyone higher.

In the wee small hours now, look how well it went! Rankine came back in, groaning and holding his head but charging his beaker with wine. Here was Tom Rankine up with the best, playing horsey to the governor's rider around the table legs, while fellow officers wagered the race and hardly bothered asking where Ugly Tom was gone these many hours past — 'Asleep under a tree, with a fuzzy head,' said the governor, rousing a chortle. 'But who with?' he baited. 'Hee haw.'

Rankine's authentic horse might have given him away if it could only complain of being ridden so hard. It was in a terrible foam of sweat, salt greasy and damp and badly used, standing out in the yard after a wild gallop of many miles, to Laban Vale and back. For a sheep was taken from the Stanton flocks that night. A sheep and a ram.

At dawn, the alarm was raised by hutkeepers along a line of woods, east of the biggest river, to tell Parson Stanton quick fast and get him down there to look at the blood and entrails on the ground before the ants and flies ate them. It was the worst place troubled by warregal dogs. Only the feed was good at that time of year, which was why sheep were shepherded there.

Stanton came riding up with Warren behind him, on his busy important pony, and Titus on foot. Titus was followed by the old man, Mr Moon. Titus and Mr Moon walked along, the rest of them following, the old black man scanning the tracks of the marauding invaders of sheep and sometimes laughing with a bare parting of his gums, as if it was all too easy for him — making Stanton grumble — while pulling his opossum-fur cloak tighter around his shoulders, sometimes frowning and making a sucking whoosh out of his mouth. There were scattered guts and blood to be seen, a gullet was looped on a branch, kidneys were under a bush like a pair of blue jewels, but whether it was the ram that was missing or just a poor sacrificial ewe destroyed for deception was beyond telling, unless somebody found a torn handful of wool to examine, and then Stanton's eyes would light up at the find. Then he would know if it was Young Matchless's torn fleece scattered on the ground or strung on a bush, revealed by its fine, dense staples welded on a supple hide from where any wild dog might have taken it, like a ripped piece of uphol-stery from a sag-bellied chair. But there was no wool anywhere of the sort. No wool meant no dogs. No dogs meant the ram alive somewhere in the hands of his enemies.

The words the old man spoke ran evenly coming from nowhere and going nowhere except into Titus's ear and out the other side.

'What is he saying? Confound him,' said Stanton. 'Speak up, Titus, like a good Christian boy and tell me straight — what is the old debbil saying about my ram last night, murder and mayhem, or as I verily believe, a piece of plotting that I shall flog to discover.'

Stanton swung accusingly round on his shepherd and raised an arm like the judgement unanswerable of Yahweh. Clumpsy M'Carty lowered his head contritely, and said, 'It was the warregals what done it, coming in awful quiet on their padded feet' — which Titus underlined by speaking for the old man:

'Mr Moon sees one big doggy come down, he stands about there and looks around, big red tongue licking his chops for a decent supper, warregal goes round teasing quiet as he can. He flies in and takes one by the froat. Wait a minute now. He says two of them now, they carry the sheepy between them.'

'Dogs could not do that, for it would take men to carry that wonderful sheep, he weighs a hundred pounds bare shorn. You are all a bunch of liars.'

They stared at him expressionless.

'Liars from birth.'

Towards dark Titus led Warren back to the place where the ram disappeared.

'Clumpsy was here,' said Titus.

'Clumpsy was here when it happened?' said Warren, talking in a low whisper, feeling his legs shake, beginning to understand that the convict stockmen of Stanton's were not just former thieves all sitting around smoking their pipes in rum-drinking befuddlement, cured of bad deeds done before they were lagged, but were Stanton's present thieves messing his paddocks between them, nothing in their bent natures cured. Was there never to be any peace in the world?

'Lookit, pop your eyes out,' said Titus. 'See where our Clumpsy come round this way, a long way, from way over in the trees with a warregal dog.'

'So there really was a dog who made the attack, like Mr Moon says?' Warren was pleased to think so, anyway.

'No, like I says,' corrected Titus, giving Warren a cuff on the ear, 'Clumpsy brung one to make it look good. Keeps it on a rope with a broken leg at his hutkeeper's hut. That bad man puts the sheep on his back, pluddy heavy, here's where he hoists it up off the ground, here's where somebody gib him a push.'

'Two of them now? Who is the other one?' said Warren, the drama of the night pictured in a few worn scratches in the ground, a scuffle of twigs, the imprint of what it took to lift Stanton's good ram, the dust a little more weighted and unweighted in places.

Titus roved his head from side to side and looked over the ground, not directly under his feet but always a perch or a pole ahead, where the light glinted more on irregular bumps and stirrings of dry sticks. He was just as good as Mr Moon at this.

'That is where that first sheep come in,' he pointed, 'the dead one, they want to make it look good, so the parson don't flog, and don't they want to have good fun! They tie a sheepy's front legs together and then his back legs, and they stretch him on his back, and they rip up his belly. They scoop up the guts and they tear them guts from the carcase, and with the other hand they stir the blood that comes from the belly. So they makes a good story to gammon the parson, and a big ram for breedin and nothin is wasted. Didden

I tell you, that breedin is the best sport, Warrie inch-long boy. They want him for his quick jump.'

Warren squatted on the ground, his stomach hurting from the bad excitement of the day, and asked Titus what he didn't want to know:

'Titus, who is the other one, that gives the sheep a lift onto Clumpsy's back?'

'That is the pox face,' said Titus, scratching the dust with his bare toe, and glancing curiously at Warren, who turned quite pale at the information. 'I asked that old fella, Mr Moon — he's my uncle — why he wrinkles his nose too much. He's smellim sweet-meats when we come down inter the hollow.'

'What are you talking about?' said Warren, afraid.

'The pink sugar, the white sugar, that was all mixed up in the sheep shit for him. You seen that old man wrinkle his nostrils and smile? You seen him! You seen him bendin over double and lookin down? Talkin about bush honey? But he never meant bush honey, Warrie, he meant them sugar treats, it was the smell of them sugar treats hangin about in the air or in someone's pocket tuck. They ain't faint smells to old Mr Moon who can stink a little lizard pissin no bigger than your inch-long-nail prick while he's up on a gallo-pin horse.'

Warren went over to the least-disturbed piece of ground. He took a stick and with scratching fury drew a circle around a soft footprint, and called Titus over to look.

'Is this his boot with his mark on him?'

Almost immediately as Titus looked, Warren started scuffing the bootmarks out.

And Titus nodded:

'He's the one they's goin to hang, Warrie.'

JOHN J. THARPE, DROVER AND packhorse driver, formerly of Cavan, transported for sheep stealing and having long avoided the noose, found himself back practising his original pilfering craft at the direction of Desmond Kale, through the graces of an English officer whom he barely knew, and heartily mistrusted on the evidence of his nation laying waste to Ireland. But the check on Tharpe's mistrust was that password of their dealing: salt.

'The young fellow with the salt has an answer,' Ugly Tom Rankine had said, and so pulled Tharpe in for his stint of exclusive droving at the behest of Desmond Kale.

After the ram taking, Tharpe made his rendezvous with Young Matchless at a pit where the ram was tethered well back in the woods awaiting his next ownership — horned as a spiral staircase and stamping his jointed forefeet with pettiness to be gone. Tharpe took him up with care, and some difficulty, holding the big animal in a canvas sack tied at the neck, bolstered with a bedroll, its belly draped over his packhorse's back (hoisted there by a rope thrown across the branch of a tree), its hind parts only occasionally hiking out. Thus, he got away from the parson's lands as fast as he could.

Tharpe had deeply set bruised-blue eye sockets, a beaked nose, high-crested hair the sheen of Dublin stout. On his lead horse he crouched forward, his long legs dangling and his packhorse coming along behind. They proceeded all day fairly quiet, making frequent stops while Tharpe walked the ram about on a lead, then put him back in his bag again — they were finding a routine — but towards evening the ram became disturbed. When it kicked one too many times the packhorse broke free and jollied ahead of Tharpe, which was how it came through a rough camp, a mile farther on, scattering Patrick Lehane's fire and all his cooking pots, giving Lehane the sight of a bucking horse with a bagged sheep as jockey.

Ten minutes later, when Tharpe appeared in pursuit, the campfire's owner was nowhere to be seen — but Lehane saw Tharpe well enough, from his hiding place in a cave mouth: Tharpe's horse scuffing soda bread from the coals and landing it in a hundred ashy pieces some distance in Lehane's direction.

'If that is not John J. Tharpe transporting a stolen sheep to the likes of an outlaw,' said Lehane, 'I am an elf in green satin.'

Patrick Lehane stayed huddled away until dark. He well knew that during the paddy's rebellion, Tharpe had stabbed an informer, leaving him out in the bush for the meat ants and warregal dogs to consider. Call it political need, Lehane called it joyful murder, branding Tharpe as a man who carried a filleting knife in a hairy goatskin sheath and sharpened for pleasure any time. Lehane might be next, seeing as how old resentments smouldered. It would not matter to the condition of Tharpe's immortal soul if he circled back and finished him. One murder was good as a dozen for a man pledged to hell. The eye of reason spent the night imagining ram bleats as a sign of Tharpe camped close, creeping about on his toothpick legs. For two nights afterwards Lehane slept in several hollows of familiar ground, like a womback did, then in sandstone overhangs until he was certain the immediate interest was gone from him.

It was another two weeks of idling in his camp until his black friends appeared after a stint of wandering. Lehane was only too glad to see them — Billy, Mary, Pegleg and Crouch, and several else of them, strangers who came and went from other bands.

Their naked shadows appeared first between sandstone outcrops and then their dusty bodies appeared through the gaps as they came on talking and laughing. From them Lehane learned of this and that. They'd been visiting their wise old man of the creekbanks, Mun'mow, who told them about a ram (horns spiralled) being taken one night from the flogging parson. So this confirmed it — Mun'mow it was who'd been brought to the parson's sheep hurdles at first light soon after it happened, to study the disturbed earth and read the sheepy signs of which Lehane for one had no doubt: it was the parson's ram on Tharpe's horseback — being taken to the outlaw, Kale. Lehane could already see the pearly sweat on the parson's face when he told him.

Getting on with their tale Lehane's blacks gusted with laughter and staggered around in dumbshow. They plucked their cheeks with their fingernails, to denote a poxy face; they threw ash in their scalps, to show grey hair; and they minced around with a high-stepping gait to mimic an officer of redcoats — a pox-faced, grey-bristle-headed captain of rangers they called Tumbankin.

'Now I have a name, just as the parson wanted,' said Lehane, catching his horse. 'I have two names, certainly — the great deceiver's and his moiderous sidekick's. I shall make my way to Parramatta via Stanton's Laban Vale, give him the intelligence, accept my flogger's pardon, and live out my days as a respectable tame paddy with my pardon as good as the pope's own absolution, carried in my pocket to show anyone who doubts, for he promised it in writing.'

Playing a tin whistle through trees beside a purling upland river, John J. Tharpe swayed along hopeful looking for Kale.

Except for signs blazed on trees he easily believed he was lost. He came out where pale tussocks grew, some as big as sheep lying down with their heads lolling in dewy grass. The white ram — now walking tame — disappeared into the mist until Tharpe found him lumpy against cloud banks. Tharpe waited then in a prettier place, the duck mole reach, he gathered it was, from descriptions Rankine gave, sheoak-shaded if he had the locale right; and lit a fire to warm himself. The ram he kept tied up for its misdeeds, lying on its side snorting snot.

'It is a good enough place for a shebeen,' decided Tharpe, uncorking his whisky, 'to be called the duck mole's retreat or the fat lamb's rest even better — J.J. Tharpe, licensee. Here's to ye, my lad!'

The silence echoed his name. When his droving days were done he'd be a tavern keeper. There'd be people out here by then. They would be after following Kale.

Tharpe climbed the eastern hill to watch the sunset and enjoy the throw of the land. 'It is all open grazing to the far west, bestowed by God as far as the eye can see, and awaiting occupation by the deserving poor.'

Tharpe had opinions on who they were, however. Not who you might think, but a gentlemanly sort of Irish poor. It was the gentleman in Kale appealed to him, not the rebel. The whole of the closer country back near Parramatta was busy with convict settlers felling trees and hefting dry rocks and knowing nothing of farming but quite pleased with their grants of forty to two hundred and eighty acres and unwisely believing they would get rich scratching in seeds. It was a vast and puerile labour they were about, converting Botany Bay into a semblance of fields where seasons failed by rote, cockatoos descended by the fives of thousands, and whatever stood up green was knocked down by kangaroos. Tharpe was contemptuous of any sort of farming getting on. There was no life for a sheep in his judgement of a country unless the landscape had cloud shadows dappling its hugeness and men had freedom to come and go where a good drover served them. He believed Kale knew the same. Small settlers were little better than beasts of the field. Their huts were bark strips and their digging sticks were made of wood. They stole each other's steel axes to cut wood for the axe handles their neighbours stole back from them. Ants and moths ate their hoard of seed. If they had a cow it was milked until it bled, and they beat its bones until it died.

So far as Tharpe had come there was a silence of axes in the forests, an absence of beans and corn wilting in the sun, it was all pushing forward and parting branches. The way was returned to the wheezing of a tender-hooved ram and the crickety noisy bigness of the woods, where lengths of dry bark dangled from the forks of white gum trees, hanging down to the ground like madwoman's hair.

When Kale joined him, next morning, there was no warning crackle of sticks. But a presence before the fact of him.

Tharpe looked around. There he was, Kale, bulky on his pony, the king of all serious nonsense: his lower lip protruding like a sulky boy's, his eyes soggy like an understanding idiot's, his long silver hair tied back in a queue like the prince of tides'. Tharpe doffed his hat and before he knew it, bowed from the waist. Kale carried a tight bundle of wool on a packhorse and rode with the girleen of Botany Bay, Biddy Magee, sitting close up behind him on his speckled grey pony, her arms around his waist, her rosy cheek resting on his shoulder.

'Kale, a very good day, and to you, missy, the same.'

After looking over the ram and expressing fascination on its good points — horns, nose, mouth, teeth, neck, rump, belly, and all its better points of wool, for which he claimed credit through Young Matchless's well-chosen forebear, Old Matchless — Kale began in with a complaint. Kale had been known to shear a sheep himself but disliked it, he said. That bastard Payolo Moreno was the expert bladesman but hadn't returned up country as promised, to get the wool off. Kale carped about why as he explained his riddles of wool to Tharpe, that he'd shorn himself, and they'd spilled rippled to his feet like brass shavings. It was not the full total he wished for, but a good enough sample at 150 pounds approx. From its hidden core of greatness, when it reached the other side, it would strike up amazement enough. It would be seen as a fine answer to resentment.

'It shall resound honour to the fallen house of Kale,' said Tharpe.

'It shall be known as mine if it gets into the right hands,' agreed Kale.

Then Tharpe said doubtfully:

'Sent under your name would be a glorious touch. But will the traps allow it to leave Sydney, marked Kale?'

'I don't think so.'

'What am I to do? Ship it marked Rankine, a redcoat's consignment, when he's underhand thick with Desmond Kale? Is Rankine to be trusted with ye, Kale?'

'Look, without Tom Rankine I'd be rattling my dags in a dungeon, disbelieving in hope, festering. You are my right arm and he is my left, John Tharpe. Put your name to the bundle — J.J. Tharpe.'

'Were you seen coming out?' said Biddy.

'The packhorse was,' said Tharpe. 'It was the scrag, Lehane. The horse went through his camp and ruined his supper. He'd have seen the ram, at least, if he didn't see meself following soon after. He ran away. He's a snake.'

'Don't mention snakes,' said Biddy.

'Are you frightened of snakes, Biddy?'

'I pretty much am, Mr Tharpe.'

'You mustn't be now.'

Tharpe had little time for women, except to resentfully take one when needed. They were a race of which he adored few but his sainted mother, yet was jealous of Kale in this. Biddy was put to commonplace use, supremely young and raised from her blanket each morning fresh as cream curds and pretty as a lambkin, with a laughing spirit and a good kindly question as to everyone's well being, including that of Tharpe.

Kale showed him the woolpack.

'To make sure the wool gets through without meddling I have composed a bundle of two divisions. Top drawer is old ram's wool but before you get much deeper, there's skin of a slain womback.'

'Phew! There's something in there all right.'

Kale went to the ram and faced him, countering that sheep's wary head buttings with head lowerings of his own. Kale made a swift movement in behind the horns, upending the ram and asking Biddy to fetch him his blades. Working slowly, almost tediously, he shore Young Matchless and thrust the parcel of warm fleece into the very centre of the malodorous bundle.

Tharpe strapped the woolpack on his second horse. 'The main thing,' said Kale, 'is to cozen the parson if he gets his hands on it before any gets shipped to England. He'll be outwitted when it gets there. If you are showing round samples, here are some portions, make free.'

Kale pulled fistfuls of loose wool from a sack.

'What is it?'

'Dead ram's wool, not a bad sort, but inferior to the ewe. It is common currency in the colony and might have been bred by anyone, except may be for the reddish brown tinge it carries, favoured by simmering Spaniards.'

'Kale was a gentleman in Ireland,' said Tharpe, turning back to Biddy. 'Don't let it be forgotten. When he is settled I shall personally bring him a barrow load of St Patrick's turf that's been delivered in Sydney from Ireland as a proof against snakes. I can see Kale now, settled in his house away over the country, perfectly content, thanks to me and the turf I have in mind sowing down around him. His turf and his great ram grazing till kingdom come.'

WHEN THARPE RETURNED TO PARRAMATTA he complained to Rankine how it was all too arduously done — that Kale had the parson's ram in his keeping and was putting him over his ewes by now; but that he, Tharpe, never wanted to undertake such a crazed hot scratchy ride again with a ram in a sack. He told about stumbling on a bush camp, scattering pots, pans and ashes. 'If I catch Lehane I'll skewer him,' he said. 'There'll be none of that,' said Rankine. But Tharpe's sleek black hair was awry and his eye sockets pitted in dust. His horse had cuts in its flanks and limped from a stone bruise. He would do whatever he chose when he came to it.

'Did Kale give you wool?'

'He did,' said Tharpe, pulling samples Kale gave him from his pockets. 'It's a greasy stuff, but he makes a lot of it. I'd do it again for Kale. There's a bundle he wants consigned to England under a third party's name — me own, since you're asking. When I get the report I'll let you know.'

'Very well,' said Rankine, having worked out with Kale that neither of them was to be named in shipments but the wool was to get there somehow. 'Mark it for Thomas's Mill in Yorkshire.' Notwithstanding this arrangement Rankine resented Tharpe's possessiveness.

'What a great slap of country it is,' said Tharpe. 'All right when you get there. I have a whim to be settled down that way, when it's brought closer by people who'd like a drink and some company. The duck mole reach is a pretty enough place, but it's awfully lonely so far, till the word gets out.'

Rankine said nothing, only thought, 'I'll be down there before anyone.'

This was the week when Rankine took delivery of a three-roomed canvas house in a style new to the colony of New South Wales.

He rode out seeking Joe Josephs, to ask more space in his load for the cartage of prepared uprights and patent slotted boards. They were shipped from a manufacturer of portable houses in Bristol — a compact apparatus of crossbars, brass screws, bolts and hinges to be collected from a riverside landing stage. A lightning rod with a barbed point was supplied. Bundles of canvas forming roof and walls were conveyed from Sydney Town. The equipment was to be home as Rankine and Meg forayed out, slow as they liked, supposing they fended off blacks, found a way across gorges, cleared tracks through fallen trees and made their way towards Kale and his ram-bucking pastures. One month here, two months there until they were beyond the duck mole reach, settled in. It was how Rankine pictured it to Meg, always in the same cadences, making light of vast troubles and not even asking if she wanted it, he was so convinced of the expedition in himself.

Rankine had ordered the tent house before he left England. He wasn't so aware then of a resource of trees for the taking —

saplings for uprights, bark for roofing, shingles falling free to the axe blade prolific as morning sunlight on gum tips. Yet he considered it would please Meg to have something better than a roughly hewn shelter. There was even a design of porch.

The first difficulty of the matter was in locating Joe somewhere on the Cumberland Plain, the second in getting Meg happier being commanded over a matter of porched canvas cottages than she liked.

Leave was requested from Rankine's colonel of rangers; a note sent to the governor. Rankine's openly expressed intention countered suspicion but he played a trembling hand. *I am decided on a piece of country in the problematic south.* ('That phrase has a ring,' said Wilkie, approving Rankine's petition while pressing a finger to his temple and making a few cloudy resolutions around his friend.)

Because Rankine was decided on Meg's part in the arrangements before she knew about them, she bridled at his air of ownership. Of a sudden this tent house and her place in it were all Rankine could talk about in a colony of rock shelters, drab huts and miserable hovels. 'How clever we are to carry a house on our backs, like the South Seas turtle,' he said. But Meg was not as persuaded as he wanted her to be.

He's tyrannical, was her summation.

She's not grateful, was Rankine's opinion.

Meg rode out with Rankine on several days. Rankine was set on getting her used to the mode of travel after too much time in town. 'Feeling out the country,' Rankine called it, chasing after Joe to get his consignment loaded and to satisfy possible government agents with open intent. Meg had never travelled much past the boundaries of Parramatta before. It was her *terra incognita*, the Cumberland Plain, all dust devils and heat mirages — those blank erupting distances whence Warren emerged, on his sturdy pony, when he came to call. The farthest she'd been across the dry forested sheep-ridden expanse was Emu Plains barracks, on the biggest river, and that was in her blighted infancy, when she was hauled along in the dust by her unhappy mother.

So far then it proved a not very successful introduction to a better life in a disgruntled week. Meg was new to a horse. The hot dry distances tried her. But more, there was the fretting about something not right between her and Rankine. More than the tent house bothered her. It was their struggle of wills over the next elevation of their love — this before their first excitements of love were even rolled in silk.

Rankine had no doubts, since his dream of Meg's gaze, that he loved Meg unto his death, but he was rubbed raw with questions over these next steps now. He wanted her in his bed, close as could be. Why wasn't she ready?

Meg was guarded since being broken to an oversupply of promises from men of rule. She was stubborn with her needs of protection with the next risky man, no matter that she loved him best. 'One step at a time,' said the same warning finger to Rankine's lips that had promised, so beautifully, 'if he loved her'. The two were badly out of tune with each other despite smilingly looking into each other's eyes as they rode side by side, or lying pressed in each other's arms on a horse blanket when they stopped for tea, suffering ant bites and prickle burrs for the sake of renewing their first supremely matched understanding. 'If it was ever understanding, at all,' muttered Rankine, his mouth twisted quite unlikeable when he got up, and turning his back to Meg hitching his crotch where his prong was stuck in the warp of his trousers.

Trees showed in a dense blurred line along creekbanks but thinned on approach to a bark-strewn shadelessness. If a stranger appeared Meg was convinced they were being followed. She was not to lose this nervousness in her life with Tom Rankine for a good long time.

It was mid-December and full summer upon them. Creeks proved dry when they came to them, wearing a chain of muddy ponds. Rankine took mistaken directions, missed the trader where he was supposed to be set up, and rather than several nights' sleeping under the stars (in preparation for their longer journey south) it was an exhausted saddle-sore Meg and a petulantly disappointed Rankine who returned to Parramatta on each of successive days without Rankine's arrangements being properly worked out, and Cupid's darts all dented.

The following week Meg begged off coming on yet another ride. She gave her reasons, while between them her deepest resistance remained unspoken.

Rankine asked what was wrong with himself. He'd been an assured lover in his previous amours (where, he acknowledged, something less than prophecy was at stake). Now, he feared, he was in danger of getting cast in the role of *sympathique* — a helpful weakling in love. Old Mother Hauser did not let up from regarding him derisively as an officer and a man. She cleaned his house of dust, mopped, scrubbed, laundered and cooked as Meg efficiently directed — but to what end, Rankine began to wonder, as she stoked a fire under Meg's bath, and scuttled around cadging scented soaps from Stanton's boy Titus. Was the tremendous foretelling of their love just another of the illustrious pranks attraction played, in bringing a man to his knees? Like the day she'd flaunted her nakedness and slowly, ceremoniously washed: what did that mean, when the visionary element left him with just the vision, except to leave him coarse with wanting? They were regarded as a hot collation, the pair of them, by gossips from the governor down, but don't whisper this too loud around Parramatta: Meg Inchcape had not yet shared Tom Rankine's bed in any one of the salacious variations gossips thrust in. To Rankine, at least, it was getting too puzzling why. It had saved him with the governor but he could possibly die of this. Unrequited lust was the yoke of a man's duration in the suffering of civilised forms. Here Rankine was, scrubbing a beautiful woman's back and adoring the damn tendrils of lovely hair slicked to her sunburned neck, while she pleasurably sighed, and after rubbing her hair blazingly dry in proximity to her lips, was given another scorching kiss to get along with, replete with a sensation of 'enough'.

There was an explanation of her baulked consent. What it was, was not yet quite clear to Tom Rankine. It would have to be torn out of him — that he might recognise it, instead of denying it. Knowing Meg awaited some further sign from him, he could not just take her in the rough (his preferred style of satisfaction). She had a way of taking charge, ever so gently but skilled, over a man born to command. Though confirmed consent had never been a question with the likes of Biddy Magee, Rankine was in irons when it came to touching Meg. It was the power of someone with nothing but beauty and pride.

Hadn't he held her in his arms and counted aloud the thousand ways he loved her? Let her show her proofs. He would happily count ten thousand more and still not exhaust ways of loving her.

Rankine did not see what was being signalled in front of him. He buffeted around his cottage like the rutter the governor said. All right. How to get on with this and slake himself to a pulp? It was in his power to show a sign, though God knew what — he'd only show it if he knew it. Meg had formerly used plenty of guile to get on, in her life of bare-bone survival, not excluding the granting of sexual favours to previous officers and one known explorer, deceased: why now was it up to him somehow to take the step, to bring her further along where she wanted? Wasn't he enough? She suffered convict inferiority, and was proud not showing it. What else?

He was not too aware that his class position was written all over him, that in his easy charm was always the command to kneel. Why, think: even Kale the intractable obeyed when he called on him, in that rock-hewn cell. But not Meg. She was half Kale pride, half Inchcape wildness. One half bewildered the other. While their love was profound, may be, a history was yet to be written of two in one.

But their needs were to be fused before they knew it, in a throw of cards.

RANKINE WENT OUT OVERNIGHT ON his next try at finalising Joe's loading. Without too much trouble this time he located the trader. Joe was not as far off as he'd thought, only stacking corn at a place by the river, near the landing stage where the tent and boards were bundled ready. They greeted each other with boisterous pleasure. Joe was immune to neither risk nor the promise of profit. With Rankine, friendship tipped the scales both ways.

To Joe, Rankine was the man who wanted his waggonload of station goods carried farther into unknown country than anyone else. There was decisiveness and good humour in the officer, and — what spoke as strongly to Joe — a willingness to pay holey dollars in advance, which Joe had used to secure his bullocky, Mick, for the entire coming season. Joe had no idea that Martha, his exquisite forger wielding pens and inks, was also tangled in Rankine's interests. Nor was Martha aware, when she did her best, what was intended to fall out. Six months ago she fabricated versions of military warrants used to spring Kale from Mundowey forest. Martha's 'His Majesty's loyal servants' and her 'trooper Browns' were a curlicue specialist's delight of purple inks on parchment packets. She was well paid, and bought a bolt of splendid black satin fabric to reward herself. She made it into a fortune-teller's dress.

To go deeper in Rankine's direction, tonight, was Martha's purpose in a set of cards she kept in a camphorwood box. She had dealt them over Rankine after their first scare, the day Stanton came into their camp after Rankine rode off with an armload of quart pots. The cards told her, then, they were safe with him, because Rankine showed in the cards particularly strong as the man with rays of goodness shining from his heart. (Devils were banished to shadows, wearing chains, when she drew cards over Stanton.)

Rankine sat by lamplight on a patterned rug, under the Josephs's loaded waggon, and was invited to concentrate, if he would, on questions of his own importance. The pack was tattered and worn. It was experienced in prediction down to its old-country stains and rips from Bohemia. It pictured skeins of silver creeks winding through meadows, glittering icy mountains, pewter cups overflowing with black wine, stars in the winter sky, bejewelled caskets, flocks of long-necked geese, ships in full sail, fire streaming back from a woman's hair. The ace of spades was a soldier dancing, the king of diamonds a rabbi, the queen of clubs a blackamoor, the jack of hearts was ringleted twins, a boy and a girl. Each numbered card from ten down was a contrasted picture of life.

That day was the longest day of the year. Twilight lingered.

Meg, missing Rankine's attentions with a twisty pain in her heart, went along walking with old Mother Hauser to a garden plot on the western road.

She asked after a man named Cahill, who lived in the back, in a small hut with a path well trodden to the door. Cahill was very quiet about his vocation. He preferred being visited at night. Having been transported to Botany Bay under guise of being plain Kevin Cahill, poacher, he was below the authorities' notice as a priest (though not as a bond convict gardener). If you were raised in the faith, as Meg was by her mother, you needed such a man from Ireland; you confessed your sins to him and were given absolution, and if it was the blessed sacrament of marriage you craved, you were prepared in it by him, and made holy up to and surpassing the expectations of your husband to be.

'Must he be a Catholic, though?' she said to the priest.

'It's best he is, though in this country there's a lot of pious wishing to be done, and few rewards in that direction. Put it this way. There's nothing doing unless he loves and respects your religion near close as he does love you. Does he love you, Meg?'

Cahill seemed to think she could judge on this, so highly did he regard her among abandoned women.

'I believe he does. Better than any man ever.'

'Can he be trusted with my calling?'

'Entirely.'

'Bring him over to see me, then.'

Meantime under the Josephs's waggon there came the rather wily suggestion from Martha that Rankine examine his cards in light of the question he was resisting. 'I don't have a question. It's she who's giving me trouble,' said Rankine, without too much grace.

Martha fanned the pack before Rankine's crossed legs.

'Pick one out.'

'I don't have a question.'

'Say if you did.'

It seemed, then, that he did. It was there in the vexed annoyance of his expression. Remaining silent, he hesitated, then turned up a card. It was a goose girl catching a golden ring. Sceptically pensive, Rankine twisted the card between his fingers before letting it fall.

'What is she doing, captain?'

'It's a piece of nonsense. A goose girl chasing a hoopstick,' he said, putting the card face up in front of him, and turning the next card over. 'Who is this, then — a woodcutter?'

'Yes. But what's that coming to him through the clouds?'

'Another hoopstick again.'

'You are the stubbornest man.'

'Let me try for a third,' said Rankine, warming to a thought and turning up a card, narrowing his eyes to see better in the dusk. 'Thought so — that confounded hoopstick again, what does it want of me? — with a waterspout coming up through the middle and a smaller waterspout on the left and three more waterspouts on the right.'

'Are you convinced?' said Martha. 'Mightn't you need an heye-glass to see?'

Her waving a hand in front of him and leering provocatively hinted that nothing was quite how it looked. Rankine snapped to attention.

'Oh, it's a hand,' he said. 'A woman's hand. Wearing a ring.'

'Hurrah.'

Martha was friendly with Meg Inchcape in Parramatta. Rankine knew that, but was unaware — not understanding women as much as he thought — that she knew of their trouble, understood it better than he did, and was able to see in a splendid love what wasn't right, but how it was triumphantly fixed by a lucky draw.

Of course, true luck was in a person's playing odds with confidence — otherwise there might be a rule, that you could not make your own luck from shreds and tatters.

Martha fanned the gilded deck, and Rankine more seriously continued his choice of cards, laying them out in front of him, face down. There was no more talk of hoopsticks. Turning the cards over, he drew the seven of hearts, a turreted castle; the four of diamonds, a carriage; the nine of clubs, a bouquet. Each time the circlet of rough twigs appeared he was barely able to understand how he'd missed seeing it before — a ring of gold inside the outer covering. In truth, there was no outside covering: because what he'd taken for twigs bound in a circle of willow wands were brushstrokes of gold paint worn through on the burnishing of symbolical gold rings.

It so happened that Joe had a gold ring, in a kidskin bag of jewels. It was on the market at a fair price, with only a little haggling involved.

And that was how, in a dusty glade of trees, next night of the full moon (which was as soon as the following Sunday) Tom Rankine and Meg Inchcape were married.

The ceremony took place a few miles from the river, out under trees, where Joe stopped their waggon. Those who attended were advised to leave the main tracks and follow a set of deep gouged ruts where a rag was tied to a bush, then to follow a lighter impression of tracks through dry grass. 'Be there by nightfall,' was the word. '*Come*,' was sent to Warren, but was a message equivocally mangled en route; anyway, he did not come. As many of Meg's friends from Parramatta came as could find their way, which was a good number, but from among Rankine's fellow officers there came not one.

Meg had nothing more beautiful to wear than Martha's gypsy woman's costume worn for fortune-telling. Tightened at the waist, where Meg was slenderer, lowered in the hem, where she was taller, it accomplished on her a ravishing sweep of black satin, its dark folds shimmering blue as a cock bowerbird's plumage in naked lights. The dress had an orange silk embroidered collar and cuffs, in a pattern of flower-de-luces. A trader's treasure box was rifled to find jewels and perfumes. Over her long combed hair, which fell in a ripple to her waist, Meg wore a black lace mantilla saved by Rankine — he did not know what for, until he took it out for his wedding day — from a box of mementos of Spain. Her face was pale and serious when she caught Rankine's gaze. She was the paleness of bleached dry leaves in the dry grass.

Storm clouds travelled along the western horizon. They pounded the rocky ramparts beyond the biggest river. Sheets of rumbling white lightning played behind the tallest trees. The priest, a bony man with large knotted fingers, arrived on dark and hurried them into a gathering. Mick Tornley lit two bonfires, one either side of the clearing. It was Mother Hauser gave Meg away. Rankine heard Meg and a dozen others obediently chanting Latin, saw them crossing themselves as the priest scuttled between them fingering wafers onto their poor tongues. Then the priest called to Rankine, and whispered his questions: did he love Meg's Church; would he never stand in its way?

'As I do love her,' said Rankine.

'You are bold, impartial, regardful, allegiant, and known as a friend,' said the priest, making a sign. Joe Josephs wrenched his head aside on seeing that sign.

Before Rankine knew, Meg was given as his wife, and he was taken as her husband — and they could hardly believe it, the fountaining of joy, the renewal of hope, the corrective of disruption. They could not remember what the troubled questions were between them. They were all gone away. Rankine was the proudest glad fool in Christendom — Meg the conqueror of his life. The lack of civil papers in their form of marriage made no difference to their pledges. Papers would be obtained in time: Rankine wanted to see the governor's face when he told him. A washerwoman taken as bride. Do not just stand there gaping. Pray sign the declaration.

Placing the chamfered gold ring on Meg's finger, Rankine lifted his eyes to Meg's — her hazel eyes almost reluctantly lifted to his. Overhead the moonlit sky was glassy clear; Meg's face was lit by intermittent strokes of lightning. Rankine's parched hungry eyes were on fire gazing at her.

All bowed their heads when the convict priest said so, raised their heads when he said so, and cried into their blessed handkerchiefs as he gave the benediction.

Afterwards, Leah Josephs served sweet plumcakes, Joe served rum from a cask, Arthur Josephs played his violin and Father Cahill tipsily recited a ballad, which nobody understood, except that in some lines he looked at Rankine in a measured, knowing way, and struck a hand to his knee, with a rhythmic crack. Mother Hauser took Mick Tornley by the arm and they danced until both fell over. The drinking, dancing, and toast making were accelerated because of the coming storm. A rush of wind came through the tops of the trees, then died away.

Before too long Rankine went around these friends saying good night and then he came to Meg. Taking her by the waist he lifted her onto his horse. She was a dreamer in a dream of contentment. Climbing up behind her, he held her around the waist and everyone gathered in and farewelled them.

Trees formed an archway of trunks and branches. Moonlight slipped bars of shadow across their backs as the mare stepped through bars of shadow in front of them. There was not far to go. Meg tipped back her head while Rankine kissed the fledged hairs of her neck. Coming up behind them were piled silvered towers of cloud threatening the moon. They rode towards a dim light coming low through the trees. As they grew closer to that light Meg made guesses of what it was. There was the fuzzy glow of lamps and the shadowy outline, enlarged, of a three-legged stool. Somehow it seemed the moon had broken off part of itself and crashed through the trees until it took on a shape of a house and a room. It had glowing walls with lanterns lit inside.

'Under the porch with you,' said Rankine to his mare. He got down first. As he set Meg down, she slipped through his arms like a ribbon of moonlight. Rankine hobbled the mare. He turned back to see Meg with the palms of her hands brushing the canvas walls. She was quite absorbed in the motion. He could have stood there watching her for an age, but the sound of the canvas on the bare skin of her palms was the whisper of sand sifting through an hourglass. A drumming whisper of touch. Love a connection of moonlight condensing hope down through thin walls. After tonight Rankine was ready to throw the tent away and told Meg so. 'You mustn't, ever,' she said. This made him smile, and he did remember their differences. They stood awkwardly at the threshold until Rankine remembered his duty and carried her over the log that made the front step. (Rankine was not to tell Meg it was a bastard to rig up. He was never to complain about it. It had taken two days. There were the boards needed to make a portion of floor, newly sawn gum wood, sticky scented yellow boxwood planks — and then ask him how the bedding required all the plucked widgeon feathers from a dozen miles around Parramatta, and three layers of rare silk. Not to mention the pillows. The time Mother Hauser spent scrounging them. The time Martha spent embroidering them — all for this night of storm.)

A rattle of heavy raindrops went over the roof. There was the smell of damp dust before rain, the clatter of twigs, the pungent oil of gum leaves released by stormy dampness. Rankine steered Meg into the side division forming the bedroom. The walls were guyed taut, timber and rope braced. Meg sat on a stool while Rankine checked the rigging. The legs of the rough bush stool had scabs of bark on them. When Rankine came back he knelt on the floor and unlaced Meg's boots. Undoing his shirt he placed the bare sole of her foot against his heart. Their eyes met, Meg laughed and pushed him away. But when Rankine stood, Meg turned mutely accepting, as he undid the hooks at the back of her dress, wrenching where they resisted. His fingers were fat from wanting, his cheeks and his lung passages congested with drawn blood. He pressed hard against her, feeling for her givingness. 'Tom,' she chided, lest he rip the precious material. Satin hung loosely from her shoulders. She guided his hands. He tugged the material from the waist, leaving it slumped at her feet. Then she was ivory lit, resplendent in every curve and hollow turning in his arms. He drew her back against him and stroked her belly. She sidled around, accepting, waiting, breathing. The closeness of her body gusted with heat and pungent Eastern perfumes sampled from Martha Josephs's jars and pots.

The moment was upon them, it was Rankine's choice how the moment was played. Her fingertips traced an electric pattern on his skin. He dropped his arms slack, as if he was already done, while his arousal said otherwise. Meg stepped clear of the dress, collecting it in folds. It was her first act of housekeeping under their roof. She took the mantilla and drew it across the foot of the bed. Quite openly, then, to his gaze, she scrambled across the bedclothes and turned offering herself to him, lying back on the downy bedroll. Rankine doused the lanterns. 'Tom,' she called to him. Racing cloud-shadows whited moonlight inside the tent and darkened it by turns. Lightning sizzled, cracked, exploded fairly close, may be a tree went up, dazzling the eyes but they had the lightning rod. It was barbed over the cap of the tent house. Only a part of Rankine's awareness checked the progress of the storm. The other storm was in their lovemaking.

NEXT TIME THE JOSEPHS WERE found, their party was picketed inside boundaries of Laban Vale, some miles from the parson's homestead, with orange sparks of a campfire flying up in the first dark. It was a week since the wedding. A plan had been made for Rankine and Meg to ride out and join them on their way. They would continue together from there as far as they could. But someone else arrived first.

The supper pots were all to one side when Patrick Lehane got down from his horse. Two of them had blankets spread on the ground and were smoking their pipes — Josephs father and son. They had muskets beside them which they only fingered lightly, when they saw it was just one man, and a white one. Either they had never heard of the eye of reason or did not believe in the eye as a threat; whichever way, no credit to them. Their horses stood in the trees hobbled and their bullocks were hobbled in the sand of a dry creek, pulling at whatever they could find of fodder and breathing sternly in the quiet as they munched noisy clusters of growth, staring their wide dark horned heads through the reeds by the campfire's throw of light. The wife and two younger children had a lantern and were settled under the high floor of the dray, their legs crossed on a patterned rug unrolled on the ground. They stood out to acknowledge their visitor. The wife was dumpy as a beehive; the daughter, of an age to be eyed, with a strong figure and a fringe of black hair across a white forehead — and so Lehane consumed her with his stare until she damned his ogling by turning aside. The boy of about nine or ten had a head as big as a pumpkin, and Lehane wanted to kick it to smithereens, just for the heck of it. The good wife beamed out a welcome that Lehane would like to rub in her shining face. It was all too comfortable, too cheerfully loving and complete except for the bugs and moths bothering them, diving into their light and sizzling in the flame.

'Who is it, Joe?' said the wife.

'A passerby.'

'Do you have any baccy?' said Lehane, thrusting a hand deep in a pocket as if he had coins there, stirring his fingers around conspicuously to be sure it was known he intended to pay.

'I do have baccy,' said the trader, 'as it happens, and plenty of it, but it is all high up and bundled, can't ye wait for it?'

'Not if I want to keep on my way,' said Lehane.

Joe Josephs offered his own pouch then.

'Take a good fist of niggerhead, and consider yourself in debt to Joe Josephs's friendship, sir. This here's my eldest boy, Arthur, and over by our house on six wheels is my Martha and the two younger ones, Leah and Solly. No doubt I shall learn to know you better, if you join our fire. So far I am wondering if you have a name at all. This gentleman soundly snoring is Mick Tornley, the bullocky.'

They looked across at the lumpy shadow on the dirt.

'I have heard of Mick Tornley,' said Lehane, turning pale: Tornley stood for no nonsense, and he'd not counted him into the equation of a bail-up. So he'd better hurry.

'Oh, and the next thing you are going to say,' said Joe Josephs, lowering his reedy voice, 'at least from the warning look on your wise count'nance, is you know Mick Tornley will kill two or three bullocks at ten guineas a head in twelvemonth's driving unless he gets a sovereng every full moon, and I better have my geld ready because it is a wide country we are in.'

'Something like that, matey,' said Lehane, reaching around to his backbone and releasing his pistol. 'Now if you would all step forward, and get in a line, I shan't bother you long. You can get back to tormenting our saviour with your evil spells. I am Patrick Lehane, the eye of reason. I would ask the young lady to collect everything shining silver or gold. Go to your father's pockets, dear.'

Chinking coins were passed to Lehane. The girl limped back into line.

'Five holey dollars, is that all? You shall have to move faster. What is wrong with you?'

'She is lame,' said her little brother, which the girl did not like hearing.

'Now would you answer me, Joe, where is your gold?'

'Leah,' said Joe, 'look in the trunk. You know the pearly one?'

'I'll do it,' said Solly.

'Run along and hurry,' agreed Lehane.

The boy went under the waggon and dropped from sight on the other side. They waited for him to reappear. Lehane levelled his pistol on Joe. There was an unnatural quietness everywhere.

'Where is the boy?'

'He is directly behind you, sir.'

Lehane felt a tickling at his waist, like a mouse escaping from his trousers. When he turned around it was to find the boy holding a cocked pistol pointing at his heart. The trader and the older son scooped up their firearms and Lehane was completely covered and done.

'Thank you, Solly,' said the trader, as the bullocky stirred from his blankets, blinked awake, assessed the need and without a word too many set about finding greenhide straps to bind Lehane's wrists and ankles until morning.

'What is my crime?' said Lehane. 'I am only a victim of temptation, which is a very human thing.'

'We shall let the parson magistrate decide on you,' said Joe.

'Too bloody right,' said Mick Tornley. 'And whatever else you've done can be flogged out of you, you thieving bastard.'

'Have mercy,' whined Lehane. 'I would rather face anyone than him.' Complaining, he seemed oddly satisfied though.

Parson Stanton was unaware how sincerely and passionately the governor was trying to find him a ship to England to get rid of him. If he'd known the effort being made he might not have wished as much to go, leaving matters to ripen in his absence to his hopeful advantage.

Writing to the governor over his stolen ram, Stanton said he was doing everything he could to cover the many evils in the removal of his prime stock, short of having his own shepherds arrested, tried, flogged, hung on the gallows tree and manacled, thrown on a ship, taken to Hell's Gate in Van Diemen's Land, wherefrom if they ever returned it would be as broken souls, in no way usefully productive. This he said in defence of his reputation as a charitable man.

Lifting his head from the ink-spattered page Stanton looked through his garden into a thin line of distant trees, out into the morning's boiling heat, great whack of summer, where a horseman was appointed to be met by him, week by week. When would he come? Where was Lehane with his promised information? It had been too many weeks and Stanton felt gulled. Why, the minister, through charity, would consider every unlikely story he was told and give to each its credibility before moving on to the next claimed event and the next, until he arrived at the truth finally, which he would know when he took Lehane by the throat and damnably throttled him. There would be the Devil's own tussle to come out when he came in.

Stanton struck out his letter and started again. It was not really the governor he wanted to address directly, it was the king. Only a voyage to England, it was decided, and a further grant of land would complete the justice pilgrimage begun with a few poor fat-tailed sheep and continued, now, between high ambition and undermining conspiracies of purebreds. Had a rural parson ever risen as far, only to be bothered by mute opposition? Sometimes it seemed to Stanton that Kale himself had elevated him by the very scathingness of his challenge; that he would have been nobody without Kale. And this only drove him more, to define himself crowningly.

Their voyage was the topic of the household when it wasn't the taken ram. Dolly wished to take Titus. Stanton intended they take Warren. So they would take them both, with Ivy, he declared; and the pair of them, husband and wife, smiled reconciled enjoying a picture of Titus swanning it in London with reports being sent back to the governor of the impression a black boy made on their lordships as a missionary example in cravat and split tails. The only picture Stanton held against it (in private imagination) was of Titus being licked by the clunking cat wielded by Stanton himself — studs in the fronds like cherries. The black race could very well be dealt with — hounded, banished, if not converted — but as for the rest, Stanton would like to say to the king, when he gained his audience:

'Your Majesty, you have made a prison colony of Botany Bay, but the very scoundrels it was founded to keep, do range its immensities with an expression in their heads, that it is the prisoners' country now, and by what rights do free men graze there?'

Somebody else was in the room. Ivy with her back to her father flattened her nose on the precious window glass, where fairy water splashed, hesitated and sped in beads, swelled and joined.

'Why is Warren so sad?' she said.

Warren's dogs, maggoty half-bred biters, fell away from his knees and ankles. In the driving rain he was slicked with cold, his freckled skin white and his eyelids blinking water away from his lashes.

'He is missing our ram, Young Matchless, and blaming himself all the time,' said Stanton.

Ivy turned from the window and asked her father, with the freedom of address allowed her, 'Is Warren always to be such a drudge?'

Stanton sighed, set down his quill and shaped his hands into an attitude of prayer, resting his pink dimpled roughly shaved chin on his fingertips.

'He is my apprentice, m'dear, that's the nature of the bond, not slavery or unwilling assignment but the arcane wizardry of sheep-craft. You should hear us at the shearing discussing points. Then you wouldn't call him sad — he raises his voice and shouts at me, laughs, all fired up with sheeply imagination, and we box each other over the ears with arguments, some of which he wins.'

'I long to hear you at the shearing discussing points,' said the girl, not having the least idea what was meant, but always wanting to be out in the world doubling, quadrupling the experience she was allowed, enthusing and pleading to the limit of her need, and a fair distance beyond.

Her father argued:

'If there be no rogues and villains always around in my fields that I am supporting, through love of God and no other reason, believe me, all prodding and swearing at each other, and with dark ideas in their heads, some one of them stealing my Young Matchless — for sheep murderers they are, barely restrained by fear of the cat, scoundrels wanting their tickets of leave via cunning, who wouldn't respect you, no, not at all with their dirty ways, and,' Stanton relented diplomatically, 'if it was not always so dusty or wet, sweetest dumpling — I would have you over there in my men's yards in a flash.'

'It is hardly ever wet. Some of the old men are the dearest things. They love me and if they ever lift anything, they know they'll get whipped. You are trying to confuse me, Papa,' said Ivy. 'I wish you wouldn't so much.' She had impatience to know something she didn't — to experience whatever it was she could not — and hated his soft talking around her. But she was trying to confuse him as well, for when he was not present on the farm she went wherever she liked, even into the yards.

Stanton asked her to come and stand close to him. He fondled her fingers and tucked a loose strand of fiery hair behind her ear, then drew her to his side with lubberly warmth. It was their way together.

'Are there any birds in the trees?' she eventually asked in the thin voice that assured him she was his.

In answer, he whistled the song of the thrush that was her calming enjoyment since infancy, a trick he had with his malleable, large lips, bringing them to a puckered aperture like a ring of dough. So much for the fearlessness of the wild colonial lass, Stanton thought to himself, who dreamed of riding a great black horse, uncontrollable except by her — a mere splinter in the saddle — driving at fallen tree trunks with as much spirit as she might kill a red-bellied black snake, or fight wildfire with gum-tree branches, or take a poker to a thief who might want to kiss her lips (as she only thought), before he swept the family candlesticks into a sack.

Ivy had a small eager face, pinched pretty like her mother's but brighter, fiercer — a thinnish-lipped version, her mouth slightly knurly through a birth difference to give her a look of natural scorn that was really quite a feature. Her mother considered her a handful of jumping jacks and hardly saw how the two of them were alike. Stanton himself had brought her into the world twice over, first by begetting her upon his wife and second by being the lone attendant in his wife's sea cabin when she was born, during their voyage through the roaring forties on their way to the colony. After her umbilical cord was cut, Stanton had nuzzled her little chump's face still bloody with mess — then a great wave came in through the skylight and half drowned them all. If the minister had not been holding her she would have washed out. Stanton still regarded her as a child, despite his wife's forthright information, recently announced, that she was now a young woman, having her time of the month arrived upon her in tears and defiance.

'I will tell you what, we have almost finished building the wool hall to store the fleeces,' said her father, 'and to lock up my rams. We are ready to dedicate the wool hall with songs and games, country dances. I have heard someone is coming through with a waggonload of goods, we shall time it for then, and they might have something we like.'

'If it is Joe Josephs and Martha and them, they will have ribbons and stuffs.'

'They certainly will,' said her father. 'I am expecting them any day. I'll send Warren to hurry them in.'

'We'll dress up the walls and tables,' said Ivy, excited at the thought of Leah Josephs coming, the girl she longed most to see, with Leah's brother Arthur playing music on his fiddle.

'Splendid,' said her father. 'Remember the song for the shearing?'

'You start it.'

'Jog on, jog on, the footpath way,' sang Stanton, 'and merrily hent the stile, a merry heart goes all the day, your sad heart tires in a mile.'

'That is peculiar. You are peculiar, Papa, and you are too fat, you are —'

'What is the word you are trying to say?' Stanton affectionately encouraged her.

'*Horribilis!*' she cried.

'WHERE DID YOU HEAR THAT word?' said Stanton, with sudden unnatural calm.

'From our Titus, he is a great mimic, you know that. "Papa, you horribilis crumpet," he heard people say, which probably is not very nice, but I told him, with butter and after being toasted on the end of a fork, you *are* very nice, Papa.'

Ivy jumped up and kissed her father on the top of the head, then ran from the room. Stanton resumed his correspondence with a cold trembling hand, pulling down a clean page of parchment. Refreshing his quill in a dish of purple ink he condensed his correspondence down to a ten of angry stabs:

1. *It is hard grind funnelling the vastness of God down the necks of a convict plantation and converting the heathen.*
2. *The native race has no wants, lives free and independent, has little more thought of tomorrow than the fowls of the air or the beasts of the field, putting no value upon the comforts of civilised life. Yet I do try and am tried sorely. If they cannot be saved, what is to be done with them?*

3.   'Put everything in four feet,' I was advised on gaining the colony. I am vilified for it. But sheep are better than redcoats in taking a country over. Some of my money goes on printing up tracts and some is portioned to pay for a missionary sent to the Bay of Islands. Some goes to the native heathen. I have not gained one convert (only half a one, the boy Titus). The rest goes on sheep.

4.   Nothing is put aside to pay for my family's passage on a voyage to England because I have the king's guaranty as a government chaplain to pay for it — when you as governor tell me that a vessel is found.

5.   Find me a ship, sir, to take me and my family to England (in comfort)!

6.   Remember the treasury is to pay for it (formerly agreed).

7.   Remember the money I have spent. It will grow while I am gone, not all to my benefit.

8.   Pray that their lordships in London remain aware that my sheep are thriving. The true Saxon breed of merino is in the hands of one who turns his mind to improvement. Let claims be made about wools on the other side of the law. Do not listen to any of them. Should their wools thrive in my absence, they are mine, by descent of my ram, Young Matchless.

9.   My fine sheep are raised in country away from Parramatta towards the biggest river, hotter, drier, dustier, hillier, a combination of acreages that nobody wanted except a struggling chaplain of His Majesty's established Church, no object of envy to begin.

10. I want ten thousand acres more.

Stanton pulled on his hat and walked out into the paddocks away from the house until he found a wide-spreading pale-trunked berryergro box tree. The morning was bellows hot after the thundery shower. The leaves of the box tree stood hanging down like shavings of steaming tin. Stanton kicked hot stones at the base of the tree expecting, at the least, a message — a ball of paper to roll out. The eye of reason was a bookish complainer, but no writing was there.

Back at the house Dolly had his coffee ready. Stanton liked it from a tin pannikin hot enough to burn his tongue, three cups at a sitting. The only other drink he liked as well was wine, which he swilled when the mood was upon him with a darkening thirst and met the Devil in a quandary of mutual wrestling, remembered next day in prayers and a bad head.

The Stantons kept a good store of coffee beans after living through a shortage some years before, when they were forced to drink a concoction of roasted chaff and eat mouldy corn and womback hams accompanied by pot herbs of *Atriplex halimus*. Barrilla. Botany Bay greens.

The time husband and wife shared over the hot kettle was a good part of their friendship on busy days.

'Warren was seen with an officer,' said Dolly, handing Stanton his cup, 'talking under the tree at Parramatta they call the croppies' parliament, which gives the only shade for a long way around. Anyone coming up to it can be seen from the open ground, but by the time interested parties get close, their topics of conversation are always innocent, while their faces burst with holding it in. Only this time, Warren punched and pushed and didn't care. It was said he shouted the name of your ram, Young Matchless.'

'Who was it he attacked?'

'Captain Tom Rankine.'

'That name again,' said Stanton complacently. 'Warren does take on sides! It is a glory to him (seeing he takes mine). The craze among officers is to breed wool. Our boy is known as good in wool, but he is sad, he misses our ram and blames himself — while officers — such as this Rankine — know less than nothing and half their flocks have tongue blain and thrush. Though I believe Rankine has no flocks, but lives day to day in the governor's pouch.'

'The governor's pouch is not the only pouch where he lives,' said Dolly, restraining her triumph, but not very well, 'because Captain Rankine is the one, or the main one, that is messing up your Mistress Inchcape's bedclothes lately. I believe they are gone on each other as far as that goes. Watch out he doesn't want the boy for his own, as some men do, to snare the woman in further.'

She had Stanton there in his jealousy of where he stood commanding the Inchcape dame, for he said nothing, only coloured spottedly and swelled a little before letting out his breath. He knew that Dolly could hardly even glance in Warren's direction any more, having developed a dislike towards the boy of the kind she often whimmed through her passionate logic against persons, dogs, or sheep. But then he was flattered by her jealousy when she said:

'Matthew?'

'What, darling pie?'

'There is something I have never told you.'

'It is our time for talk. Pray tell.'

'I had a suitor before you. I left him passionate with hopeless longing, which I don't remember why — I never told you before.'

'You were too ashamed?' he condescended. It was seventeen years gone, at least.

'I was not ashamed. No doubt he always remembers me, while I hardly think of him at all. Anyway, his name was Blaise Cribb, of Thomas's Mill, in Rawden.'

'I can't say I ever went to Rawden,' said Stanton, with a startled look, 'though I remember an alnager and wool sorter of that name, Cribb, who came to Leeds.'

'Blaise Cribb?'

'Indeed, Blaise Cribb. He is the one who writes to me about my wool, each time I send consignments.'

'You seem angry with him,' said Dolly, rather pleased if it was stirred-up jealousy.

'I have a quarrel with him as he never praises my wool well enough. There is a feeling around of someone better in Botany Bay — I am mystified who.'

'Then it is Kale,' said Dolly.

'It cannot be Kale — you cannot breed sheep while wearing irons. That is fairly well established in the rule of law.'

'Then it cannot be Kale. Obviously.'

There was a chewed, fraught silence before Stanton continued.

'Cribb writes that to meet a standard, my wool — that could hardly be bettered in the whole world — needs to come "up". Where is this "up" to be compared? Where is its nonpareil, "up"?'

'*I* cannot tell you, Matthew,' said Dolly, drawing back.

'Did Cribb get so far,' said Stanton, leaning forward, 'as to make you a proposal, Dolly, did you say?'

'Not as far as you.'

'I am thankful for that.'

Stanton needed no reminder that his marriage invitation to Dolly all those years ago remained a thorn between them. His proposal had not been passionately expressed — that was the quarrel — rather put forward as an offer of convenience, based on the practical Christian principle that two might go out and missionise the world better than one, and would she come along and helpmeet him, as the Good Book urged, until death did them part? With reasonable alacrity she accepted and donned the white kirtle. It was not without fiery love, either, that proposition when he made it and when she answered in the bridal bed. Just it had seemed more heavenly a statement, at the time, than falling to his knees, chewing her frugal lace petticoats and howling with want (which was how he'd inwardly churned at the sight of her). There was no guessing a woman's mind. Whichever way it went, he was the one left looking foolish most.

'You rejected a saint,' said Stanton. 'I remember there was a martyr, Blasius, or Blaise, a hermit of the old days living in a cave.'

'What happened to him, your Blasius of old?'

'St Blaise the patron saint of woolcombers he was made, by the early popes. He was put to death tormented by iron combs. He was scourged, and seven women anointed themselves with his blood; this sounds like your Blaise, don't you think?'

'All the maids sighed over him,' she agreed.

'Whereupon their flesh was raked and their wounds ran nothing but milk, their flesh was whiter than snow.'

'But that is terrible.'

'In any event, angels visibly came and healed the women's wounds as fast as they were made and when they were put into the fire, it would not consume them. Though after the miracle of milk and being burned they had their heads cut off.'

'Clean cut off?'

'Off.'

The finality of the statement, with its unanswerable judgement upon women, had the effect of numbing Dolly into silence and leaving Stanton complacently satisfied.

Except she looked out the window and said:

'Who is that over there?'

Stanton went to the doorway. He shaded his eyes against the bleached outside light.

'Where?'

'In the woods across the way, on the far side of the track, where you sneak around, Matthew, when you think nobody is watching. There is a bullocky under the trees.'

'A bullocky?' he peered.

'A bullocky, a bullock, and a man waiting.'

Stanton lost no time in getting across there, rocking from side to side on his bandy legs and fanning his hot face with his floppy hat the whole three hundred yards. He expected Mick Tornley on the evidence of a brindle bullock with cocked horns, but had given up on Lehane and was surprised to find him too — and tied by leather thongs knotted at the wrists, lashed at the ankles and sunk at the foot of the message tree.

'What have we here?'

'The eye of bullshit dipped in malarkey,' said Mick Tornley, red-brown of face, coming forward holding his sweating coiled whip.

Lehane was not quite entirely melted in the shade.

'I am a victim,' he struggled to his feet, 'of Jews.'

'What? More of that thundering?' said Tornley, pulling a dirty spotted cloth from his pocket. 'Do you want your gag back on?' He turned to Stanton. 'We are witnesses to a bail-up, one of us Christians, the other five being the Josephs, man, woman and children offended against by a streak of crawling maggot.'

'Are they safe, those good people?'

'Unhurt, but inflamed to the gizzards by having their goodness repulsed. Seeing as how they welcomed Lehane to their fire, gave him baccy, and would have fed him, too, if he hadn't drawn a bead on them. They have a mind to seek justice. They know what justice is, or should know, anyhow, from their taste of irons. Joe speaks highly of you, he does, as his very particular friend. They shall lay it at your feet, anyway, and be coming through tomorrow. With your permission we shall camp on your flats till Lehane is tried and sentenced for his nuisance. He deserves a flogging, at least.'

'That is for me to decide.'

'With all the facts laid before you,' agreed Mick Tornley.

Lehane fixed his eyes doggily on Stanton, licked his grey lips, dropped his narrowly boned head to such an extent that Stanton was not surprised when he sidled against him, almost rubbing affectionately, like a kangaroo hound, and said, out of earshot of the bullocky:

'The one you want is Tumbankin.'

Or so it sounded like.

'Come along now,' said Stanton. 'I am taking you in.'

'I *sharn't* be flogged,' baulked Lehane, a boast more than a plea. If Tornley had one good reason for wanting to flay him, Stanton had a good few more. He disliked being put to a test. It enraged him being held to a promise. Lehane's duty of informing caught him in a tangle, replete with hooks. There would be thinking to do around it, a letter to the governor by express rider, may be, along the lines of: 'The traitor in your midst is called . . . "*Tumbankin*"?'

'Come along quietly,' he said. 'We have a cell in our barracks' sheds, with a straw-filled mattress. No more nonsense for the moment.'

'Are there biting fleas?' sneered Lehane.

'Just a friendly one or two,' said Stanton, understanding what Lehane meant. More like cruising sharks with sharp-toothed grins, his countrymen, he thought. He would keep Lehane under lock and key until the matter was sorted between them.

'You will be safer there,' he whispered. 'Do you understand?'

'I am a seized bushranger,' Lehane boasted. 'Your villains shall applaud me, when they hear.'

'Something like it,' said Stanton. The preferable possibility was they would tear him limb from limb.

He walked with a hand on Lehane's shoulder, a gesture of consolation in captivity. Mick Tornley thought it as decent a show of shepherding as a bestial charlatan ever deserved from a flogging chaplain, and followed along to see what was done. He walked with his bullock led by the nose-ring past the homestead garden, past St Botolph's chapel, past the wool hall with its half shingled roof, belltower, and sheep yards ready for the week's shearing; and so down another dusty two hundred yards to the convict bond men's barracks on the Mundowey track, where Stanton's convict workers lived, under their overseer, Galvin.

The bullock bellowed and swayed. Tornley smacked its side with a whip handle. Lehane was led to the safety of the solitary punishment cell. The bond men were out mustering for the sheep-wash and did not see him come in. Only the sergeant of convicts, Galvin, saw him secured. Galvin and a newly arrived shearer, Paul Lorenze, camped under a tree with a blanket, a quart pot, and awaiting the rest of his gang, who last time he saw them were washing their clothes in a mud puddle, and spreading them out on a banksia tree to dry.

Gaunt, ugly and exposed, a low shameless building with vent holes and narrow windows barred with iron, the barracks' sheds positioning gave a clear line of sight from the homestead direction, if there was ever a revolt.

At the sound of a heavy key being turned and Lehane kicking the walls and swearing, Mick Tornley was satisfied justice was begun and climbed up on his bullock, riding him forward on the shoulders. Galvin returned to his office. Stanton peered in at Lehane through the bars.

'Here we are, then,' he said.

'**I** WANT MY WRITTEN RELEASE,' Lehane peered back at Stanton through the bars. 'As promised.'

'You have made it too difficult for me.'

'I've given yer the name.'

'Thank you for that, as now instead of having to satisfy you, in all your glory, I must satisfy those you've wronged. One cancels the other out.'

'Well, I've given you the name,' sulked Lehane.

'Tumbankin. Sounds like a native,' said Stanton.

'Not when you say it slowly, it don't. It puts on trousers and a lobster's red coat, its face pockmarks all over in little pitted rings, it grows grizzly grey hair and looks out from sad eyes like burnt paper, it says, "I'm the governor's friend. Tumbankin."'

Lehane giggled tiredly.

Stanton said the name slowly, and laughed. Not possible. *Tumbankin.*

Then he thought it over, and his mood changed. That someone riding past in the night. That someone stooped half asleep in the saddle. That military campaigner crossing miles. That man who comes and goes, and each time is seen closer to the heart of a matter — that man getting his chest thumped by Warren Inchcape under the old gum tree while Young Matchless's name is shouted, and then makes his way to Kale's daughter's bed. That man of subtle fame who Stanton had never so far met.

Stanton asked Lehane for as many precise details as he knew: 'Dates said officer enters rampart of southern ranges, dates comes out. Times of travel, day and night. Names of native informants, your friends.'

'Billy, Mary, Pegleg and Crouch. You won't get *them* in court.'

'It is all very strange.'

'There's more. I seen your ram being carried past.'

'By the same Tumbankin?'

'Only by a horse.'

'A horse?' said Stanton dryly.

'Aye, he was tied to its back, and the horse bolting.'

'Whose horse, then?'

'It never stopped to say.'

Bidding farewell to Lehane with a warning he should be flogged to the gristle if he was lying — only possibly saved if not — Stanton stumbled through his garden scattering flower heads, scaring up birds, annoying his gardeners and, without a word to his wife, only a hiss commanding silence, hurried along the flagstoned verandah and entered his study and slammed the door. Dolly knew better than to insist with questions, while the house servants fell to their scrubbing and rubbing and their surreptitious sidelong winking: 'The reverend's a thrashin around again.'

Stanton addressed the governor in a hurried script:

All is revealed. The traitor in your midst is Captain Tom Rankine. My informant is held. There are natives keeping watch.

The night of Thursday last, when my ram was took, where was he then? The day of the Mundowey ruse involving Kale, where was he, pray? — on duty, was he, then?

The more Stanton wrote in this captious vein the more certain he was of Rankine's role at the centre of the plot. But the eye of reason was a blathering witness unproven at law. There were details lacking, sufficient to dissuade a partial governor from making a move against one of his own. To get this carried, hot-blooded conviction was needed from the minister himself, directed straight up — strong as when he preached — REVELATION his source of knowledge in the molten fountain of FAITH.

Stanton called for his horse and rode to Parramatta, and that same evening delivered his letters to the governor's secretary and refused to leave government house until he gained an interview with Sir Colin Wilkie.

Stanton was kept waiting in an antechamber until after eight. But he was well acknowledged. Candles were lit. A servant brought a plate of bread and cheese, a bowl of mussel broth, a mug of Cape wine. Stanton leaped up when the governor entered from dining, still wearing a stained bib and holding a hammer from smashing crab shells, with Stanton's letters stuffed in his breast pocket and all of them sprayed with oily sauce after being read.

Stanton made his accusations — he thought in reasonable tones — but was told to restrain himself, to sit down, to spell them out sensibly, to lower his voice and get himself composed. The governor called for brandy and ever so softly and superciliously said, while running his oiled fingers back through his thatch of knotty gold hair:

'It is Tom Rankine, you say, who took your ram?'

'You seem less than alarmed, and I wonder why,' said Stanton, 'as we are both equally endangered by disorder in this outpost of moral conquest.'

'Then be assured in the matter, and feel safe from your best protectors, whom you seem intent on vilifying. I have been through my officers' lists. On Thursday last, when your ram was took, Tom Rankine was with me the whole night.'

Stanton bowed his head, mortified. Yet clenched his teeth, and lifted his head in jerky movements until he met the governor's eye once more.

'Didn't I tell you, sir, of my belief that an officer with sheep broke Kale of his irons, in the Mundowey forest, on the king's birthday last ninth of June?'

'You did propose it, Reverend Stanton, and I listened very closely indeed when you named the N.S. Wales rangers.'

'Well?'

'It seemed a grand idea to me then, as it does now — a loyal regiment in collusion against their king.'

'One conjectured officer of that regiment might not be such a fancy, a man besotted with Irish politics holding views in private. I could not name the Mundowey one before, now I can.'

'Your informant gave you it, as well?'

'No,' admitted Stanton with strangled reluctance. 'It is more this time it came through sheep.'

'Oh, it is sheep, then, above Pat Lehane?'

'I make a deduction based on sheep — based on who travels the night country with treasonous purpose, wrapped in a military cloak. The mystery of Mundowey is sheep. Whoever aided Kale picked up sheep. That is known. Rankine is not known for sheep, but I believe he acquired a superior flock and fooled us with them.'

'You are right in that, he acquired a flock.'

'What?' said Stanton, rather more than surprised. Thrilled, he would say rather.

'Rankine arrived with sheep when he came to the colony. They were fat-tailed mutton breeders carried on the *Melanthus* under Captain Quayle.'

'Nobody has fat-tails any more,' said Stanton. 'The breed is discounted. The only blood of the fats anyone needs is a tiny percentage, invisible except to the expert eye, as a builder of frame. As wool breeders, they grow something like nests of wire.'

'Please be assured they were fully described in Rankine's manifest of shipments via Calcutta.'

'I heard of a flock in the wilds, that grew fine wool, better than any. Since Mundowey they disappeared from the face of the earth.'

'They were his fat-tails, then?'

'You must know your sheep, sir,' said Stanton with caustic brevity.

'Now you listen to me, reverend magistrate. I love this Ugly Tom, but I love my duty more. The things you say do worry me. You have your agents, I have mine.'

'What have you learned?'

'That the worst devil wears a twist of wool around his wrist.'

Stanton felt his heart lurch, his mouth go dry. He covered his left wrist with his right hand, tugged at his coatsleeves, and took another draught of wine.

'It's what my Gaelic tells me. That Kale is gone so far into the outlands he's sure to perish before he can ever be found. The land itself is a punishment.'

'It is why it was settled,' said Stanton, who wanted more of it nevertheless. 'The *gahlic*, as you enounce this word, gave you this?'

'Aye,' admitted Wilkie, 'through a poem, a ballad.'

'Oh, it is poetry, then, above intelligence?'

'Look ye. Tom Rankine is no more political than a pinch of snuff. There's nae politics between bedsheets, and very little morality asked of a woman's consent.'

'My sheepcraft apprentice's mother . . .' Stanton said, with a look of mottled contemplation coming over his face as he remembered a half dream of morning: she drew him to her with a tired consent, raised her hands like two deep bowls, and out from her shift shrugged her large bouncy breasts, peerless ivory, mulberry tipped, with goose-bumped buds. The stocky man Matthew Stanton ran forward with his tongue drizzling lick and bleated his want —

'Her bedsheets, you say?'

'She is our queen of laundry sheds and look no further, now, for it's there she answers to Tom Rankine on every one of your suspicions. He's made some sort of hedgerow form of marriage, my people tell me, to keep her tamed. I do not blame Rankine for making a fool of himself on Meg Inchcape's account — she is a grand composition of parts — nor you on her account.'

'Nor me?' said Stanton.

'Aye, for making a fool of yourself on her account also.'

'How?' said Stanton in a higher pitch, and reddening.

'Her son, Warren Inchcape, is your sheepcraft apprentice. That's cosy enough.'

'Warren is Kale's grandson, with all Kale's genius but none of his trespass.'

'Then aren't you thicker with Kale than anyone, on this score, reverend? Doesn't that boy put you closer to Kale than is Rankine?'

Wilkie held Stanton's eye as he spoke, and Stanton looked back at him, caught. 'I thank you for your time,' he said. 'You have been more than gracious.'

There was little left for them to say to each other then. Stanton had a better idea of their equality in controlling disorder. The man of impractical government and the practical man of God. See who won of the two of them, in the game of prominence.

'We shall part our separate ways, and do our separate deeds,' said Wilkie, 'and if we cannae wake each other to our separate purposes we shall be like the rest of the world in feeling justified.'

'To say the least,' said Stanton. But *he* would be going to England, he wanted to crow to the governor, when a ship was found. And after his time in England he would return to the colony blessed by the king with more land to his name, more information to his call, more power to his wristband of wool than could be imagined. The governor, conversely, would complete his duties and never return to Botany Bay again. From the mutterings that were enlarging around him, as the convicts' friend, he might even be recalled before his term was complete.

The governor took Stanton's letters from his pocket and smoothed them on his knee.

'Young Warren shall travel to England with you, I agree, when you have your ship.'

'Oh,' said Stanton, with querulous gratitude. 'Our ship. And he'll return to New South Wales improved, if the place ain't always preferred for convicts and rogues.'

THERE WERE SIX OF THEM all told in their close crew when Warren met them for the first time — the father, the mother, the older son, the daughter, the younger son, their bullock driver, and spare horses hobbled with relief bullocks that numbered a round dozen. They were on their way out of civilisation's reach but had not yet come very far, having only just reached the inside boundaries of Laban Vale. Stanton had sent him to welcome them with condolences for being bailed up. The boys, he would learn, were the horse tailers, and also the girl was handy on an old nag, wheeling around to bring back stragglers or chase a rogue bullock across a clay flat, as Warren would see her do one day, when he came to know her better, and got up on a horse to follow her as far as he could.

From closer in Warren shielded his eyes from firelight as he walked into their camp. It was bright, their blazing fire, until those around the flame dissolved from dazzle and took back their details of shirt and trouser button and shining eye. He stated his name and was made welcome when they saw it was just a stout boy striding into their camp with legs like sticks a-cracking. It was a matter of pride to them to welcome strangers even after their clash with Lehane. Their ire was roused but their charity remained undimmed.

Warren shook hands with each of them. Mick Tornley, the bullocky, he knew as the finest of that slouching breed of experts known. Joe Josephs, Warren saw, was not to be judged by the gold threads in his weskit as being too fine for everyday use, or by the vainly perky top hat he wore tipped back on his head, that would never stop any sun, and his gold teeth dangerously boasting the wealth he carried in his smile. He was a shadowed, thin, sharpish crook of a man, but a cheerful and apparently kindly fellow well met. Tornley, the man they paid in gold coin to guide them through the bush, sat on a stump drinking tea and telling their story of being bailed up by Lehane. When it was told, Warren said:

'Before I left, I looked in and seen him. He's a sorry sight.'

Warren looked around at the waggon standing stolid and still against the stars, the high load of store goods in the dark which represented, in his mind, uncountable riches and mysterious desir-ables. The wife and her younger children had a lantern and were settled under the high floor of the waggon playing knucklebones, with much argument, their legs crossed on a patterned rug unrolled on the ground.

'Do you have any cuckoo clocks?' Warren wanted to ask, but didn't, from shyness of desire. Instead he said:

'I have heard my master say, Mr Joe, that you always have what he wants, and he enjoys wrestling you down to his buying price to get it.'

'If there is gain in it for both,' agreed the trader, 'I do bring a cove what he wants from wherever it comes — Birmingham, Egypt, China or America, I don't hardly care — and meet him for what he gives in price with dungaree cotton, steel knifes, tobacco for chewing, black tea in a lump that would stop the toothache, it is so packed into itself, and porcylain so fine it floats on the breath of a baby.'

He turned to his son:

'Arfur, our friend here don't have no blanket, will you shake one out like a good boy and make a place for him nearby?'

'This one is mighty clean,' said Arthur, as he dusted a blanket of fleas. He was a handsome boy of about seventeen, with thick dark eyebrows, a considerable sidelong way of looking a person over, and a greatly hooked nose that got in the way of his prominent dark eyeballs. He had long fingers and knobbly wrists. There was a violin case on the ground and Warren imagined he'd heard tunes being played on a fiddle earlier, the sounds carrying on the breezes as he came down the last half hour of track through Mundowey forest, where owls hooted back and forth and there was the ghost of nefarious doings behind every tree.

From the corner of his eye as Arthur made ready the blanket, Warren saw Joe flick a canvas to the ground and cover what lay there. It was a quick action but not quick enough. There was not much time to look, and the ground was dim shadowed in the direction Warren had not looked before, but a branch flared and showed him. It seemed like an array of stoneworker's or blacksmith's tools lying ready that weren't to be noticed by strangers — the knob of a driving hammer, a twisted pair of tongs, and a steel chisel-point. Then they were covered. If the hammer was incised with the government's broad arrow you could be sure the rest were, too. And so they were dangerous goods, for a certainty.

Joe put his arm around Warren's shoulders and walked him to the other side of the fire.

'Does this little nest please you, here by our blaze?' he said, wrinkling his eyes and puckering his mouth into a smile of concentrated pleasure that almost shrank into a dark tight sugarplum. It stayed there for a few seconds until he next spoke. 'Arfur, get them quart pots bubbling and offer our friend a swallow of tea. Ask your mother and sister out to sit with the stranger till it's time for bed.'

'Thanks for your baccy, and your offer of tea,' said Warren, 'but I am asked to make you welcome to Laban Vale, then I am to keep on walking, otherwise I'll be in the wrong place for tomorrow's sheepwash, that starts before seven, not counting the time it takes to get them yarded, which might be a long time. It is a mucky job, sheepwashing, and we never have enough hands.'

Warren was given his mug of scalding tea anyway, as refusals weren't counted by the Josephs, and passed a fistful of sweet bread, which was like damper bread being cooked in the ashes without leavening, only softer and deliciously made with sugar and eggs. Being delayed was all right with Warren then, and there were those others under the waggon he wanted to meet before he left.

'Arfur will nip along with you and help with your sheepwash,' said Joe. 'Won't you, boy?'

Before Arthur could answer, Warren said:

'What, and stand up to his waist in mucky water and push an animal under till it wants to drown, an do it all day until when he gets out he's wrinkled white as a peach, all for a shilling for a whole day, oh, and a tot of rum when he gets them rheumaticks from cold, even on a hot day too?'

'Arfur needs a shilling, don't you, lad? And if you force him to swallow it down, he'll take rum for his rheumaticks. Our other boy, Solly, and my girl, Leah, will take over, and tail them horses on his behalf, and with a good will, and so he's yours and the parson's for the pleasure of your need till he's all wrung out.'

Arthur seemed to accept whatever his father wanted for him. At the same time, Warren rather sadly guessed that this family had a way of understanding each other, not quite by hand signals, never exactly by looks, hardly even by codes of speech but somehow easily done. It might be by agreement of love — that's what it might be — but say whatever it was, Warren was quite outside the circle of its easy grip while wanting to come in. He had never seen a keener look on the face of a young man, to do what was suggested in the way of skipping off with a new mate and getting an eyeful of filthy water he knew nothing about, except what Warren had already sketched to discourage him.

'Sure I'll come,' Arthur said, snatching up his blanket, tying a string to his fiddle case and throwing it across his back, looking around for his hat. 'And if you teach me what you know about wool, I'll drown as many sheep as you want.'

Warren saw the affection of a glance passing to his father, who nodded slowly like a sage, so deep a rejoinder you had to be wise yourself to see it.

'That's what I like about him,' said Joe. 'Ain't nobody more willing than Arf. We all agree, me and my boy and my wifey who is coming out to meet you in a minute or I'll say she's rude — that Joe Josephs is your flash expert on silver plate and whether your diamonds is glass, but I have been gulled by wool experts. On our last foray into the bush that was way beyond the coal river, fighting floods and fires and thieving jackasses, I come back with a golden load of trash, for when it was examined and weighed they told me it was only good for stuffing in the roof of a house. They would not let it leave the country, even on a empty ship, of which there was never a one, thanks to this here wool rush that is on. Whether it is my eyesight or what, but I would say I was in the wrong country by bad choice, except I have my son to depend on for fleeces now, and it might get better.'

Joe startled with a yell — 'Marfa!'

A short wide woman jumped out from a rumple of firelight and acknowledged her husband with a passing scowl:

'Choice. That's a good word. We was never anywhere by *choice*, Joe.' She turned to Warren. 'He is the one that got me lagged for him, when he was already in irons on the filthy Thames, making me his fence without me knowing it, by having passed into my hands, by his cronies, a load of argentry, candlesticks, candelabra, and ancestral plate — not that the judge believed me, love, though I rouged meself scarlet and wiggled my little finger at him, like I seen others done, to get meself a better man than the one that'd led me astray.'

As she spoke, Martha Josephs looked up at Warren from a humorous brown face fringed by greying brown curly hair. She was like a stout pot with a stone on its lid, that gave intense rattles with steam shooting out, every time she spoke. She was the one who gave Arthur his nose, you might say, from hers that was like a jug handle. The excitement of her conversation hit Warren direct, as she thrust her forehead to get against his, to get a hearing from him, and grabbed hard to his elbow and fingered his funny bone, and stepped on his toes as well. Then she grabbed both his cheeks and pinched them hard, muttering 'luffly boy' before spitting over her shoulder. As he reeled back from her aim, almost to the edge of the fire, she followed him and broke off her attention, bending over and juggling quart pots, sweating over the fierce hot bed of coals as if she had an argument with them for doing what they were wanted to do, throwing up heat. 'We was both transported — what a lovely voyage we had, on two different ships, me with two of me children,

Arthur and Leah. Our little Solly was the one that was native born because when we arrived, look who was already here waiting on the dockside to fold me in the arms of love — my avid trader with the scabs of ankle irons still on his narrer leg bones — poor creature, me loving Joe Josephs. Seeing as he can't lie straight in bed, we took to this life of sleeping on the ground, to make ourselves a better reputation.'

'I takes off me hat to her,' said Joe.

'And what is this now?' Martha Josephs shrilly demanded to know of her son. 'Where are you going to, Artie?'

'Not far at all, most likely?' said the boy, with a glance at Warren, who said:

'To the sheep yards of Laban Vale. There's a long walk in it, but we shall make it sooner if we stride off early. We'll grab a few hours' sleep on the floor of our hut. It is not a bad sort of a bed, the beaten earth. Our cook will wake us with tea and cold mutton chops enough to make us sink in the sheepwash, and we won't be hungry till noon.'

'Three shillings,' said Arthur, turning to his father, 'is the last of my debt. When it is paid,' he turned back to Warren, 'and he gives me what he is holding for me, which if it ain't broken in its box of straw, and there is enough sheep to wash for my money, you will be the most amazed sheep handler that ever drew greasy breath to hear it sing.'

'What is it?'

'That would be bad luck to tell, in case the waggon tips. I don't even hardly dare express it in my dreams. But it's —'

'A harmonica,' said his mother.

'Ma, I wish you wouldn't say,' said Arthur.

'I have heard a harmonica,' said Warren, 'played by an Irish man and all the best tunes played he pulled with his lungs making the notes. It was like a honeycomb, played along his tongue. We cried tears for old Erin as he sucked and blew.'

Though what old Erin was, Warren had little idea, except it was easy to cry for.

'That shows what you know,' said Joe's mother, 'because this harmonica of Art's ain't no mouth organ — it is a model made in Bohemia, by a relative of ours, Herr Josip, and it don't look like notting you could put in your mouth, young man, unless you was a glass-eating dragon. It is a hinstrument consisting of a row of emispherical glasses fitted on an haxis turned by a treadle and dipping into a trough of water, played by the happlication of a finger. It is so delicate the glasses are likely to break.'

'Thank you, Ma,' said Arthur, who even though he was the one who saved the shillings to pay for what had been sent across the seas, he was not allowed to keep the pleasure of telling all to himself until the right moment. His pride was great but his mother's pride in him was greater, though she seemed she might consume him on the way to expressing it, and have nothing left of him to boast about.

'We are all walking on feathers for you, Art,' said a voice from over the way.

Warren saw the girl emerge from under the waggon, straighten herself and stand with her back erect against a high waggon wheel. She placed her hands on the small of her back and eased her pain from crouching by leaning back and thrusting her chin at the sky. He expected her to come closer, and she came a few paces, but they were as close to the fire as she seemed to want to come, over there in the starlight. She had a disguised difficulty to her walk, something she wanted to hide, a lurch and it seemed to be that lameness holding her back. She drew a shawl over her head against the night air, pulled it down to her chin, fingered it getting the folds over her throat. In the firelight her eyes shone dark in Warren's direction without any movement in them, just a long, soft, shining stare like the pull of the moon when it was already way down.

'Leah, this is our new chum, Warren Inchcape, of Laban Vale,' said Joe.

'Pleased to meet with you, new chum,' said Leah.

'Hello,' croaked Warren, feeling very small.

Leah glanced away and called to her youngest brother to come on out from under their waggon. This was Solly, aged nine, a splinter of Arthur in the appearance of agile energy waiting to unspring, but more like his sister, being the other one who was darker skinned. Indeed both were bronzed olive, and shone duskily in the firelight, like strangers from another place, and not of this family. Or may be it was they belonged here more, on the dry earth, and the others were the visitors in passing. Anyway it was like when Warren watched the family of choughs, with their mud nests like pudding bowls and their low looping habit of flying through the lower branches of trees, when he longed for this one or that one in their flock, the birds mingled and called to each other until they unlocked his heart. Then he remembered the kookaburras he drew for his father: there were five of them, and his heart was full.

The Southern Cross turned over in the sky when Warren and Arthur made their farewells from the camp. The Milky Way shone bright, making shadows. Arthur breathed hard as Warren led him fast along and the violin case thumped against his back, sounding stringy twangs against its inner green-baize lining. Nightbirds called in the raggedy trees, scrapping magpies played notes, flew up, attacked each other, settled back on their favourite branches and tucked their beaks into their wings and dozed. In a thorny scrub a rufous fantail bird sang loud and long, and the two boys stopped and listened. It was such a strong, cheery, noisy babble in the night, it hurt the ears.

IF TWO STICKS FELL ON the ground in the shape of a cross, Joe Josephs shuddered. The smell of roasting pig on a spit pan turned his stomach. When he saw the Irish of Laban Vale crossing themselves he spat sideways, muttering a phrase of protection. Even at Rankine's wedding there were moments when he'd wished he were somewhere else.

Joe was raised by costermongers and goldsmiths among London gangs who never deprived themselves of philosophic debate even when hungry. There were so many through history nailed to one sort of cross or other, he learned, that were built on the shapes of X, Y and Z, or else they were stoned, defiled, murdered, raped or burned in their houses. It would never come up in Joe's conversation unless there was severe aggravation. As when it was said Jews nailed God to the cross. As Joe worshipped God he was offended, and Lehane might have got away with their coinage free, except for his expression in that regard, against persons.

Joe looked in through the bars and confirmed to Stanton that although the man who sneered from the corner of the cell was less than a man, he was the same one who bailed them up. Stanton said he would hold court after the shearing. When Joe asked why they needed to wait, before getting rid of that shame, Stanton was evasive.

'Shall we go somewhere and talk?' he said, leading Joe to his garden. Stanton was excitable and busy minded.

'Do not judge the fruit by its skin, but break it open and enjoy the juices.'

He handed Joe a withered, wrinkled orange.

'What now?' said Joe.

Stanton said it was an opportunity for them to take their ease while the sheep were being herded by Warren and his parlous and devoted dog. It was the day of sheepwashing. It was all going well. Warren and Titus had the help of Arthur and Solly, and of the cup-shotten Irish, who, if they were not drunk at breakfast, gave a good impression of being so, and certainly were by dinner. There was no need to ask where the liquor came from, but because Stanton was out to please Joe he made no objection to Joe drawing rum from the barrels he carried at the side of his waggon and selling it off at a tidy sum. A certain level of drunkenness made a useful worker of a man who stood all day in water up to his chest pushing sheep. And the other point was, that the man who spent his wages one day presented for work the next.

Neither man was good at pretending he knew what it was to be idle, it was not their style. Both were hard-working mortals in their own striving fashion, leaving it to wives and daughters to lend an unhurried quality to time, if they so wished. Joe stared at his orange and cracked into it with his thumb, tearing down one side and pulling it open, before trying a portion in his mouth. He found the fruit oily and sour but persisted in eating from courtesy. Meat, potatoes, and a plump hen were his preferred fare, as the parson very well knew, and if he couldn't get a young hen, the nearest old rooster would do very well, specially if boiled in a broth with onion, nettles, salt and dumplings.

They admired the banana trees that were pride of the Laban Vale orchards which Stanton boasted were getting as well known as his sheep. The minister took a pointed stick and jabbed the trunk of one, causing a plume of water to spurt out. No bananas had yet appeared on the tree, and he thought depriving it of nourishment might force it on. 'The principle works with my Saxons, by alarming the diet and driving the animal to cover itself.'

'Difficulty encourages attainment is a very wise saw,' said Joe, whose actual experience of life put the matter the other way around most emphatically.

'I expect every day to see the purple bud.'

'I have never seen one, nor eaten a banana.'

Suddenly it was annoyance that made Stanton stab the sterile trunk so much — a wish to advance his aims without any more frustration and convey a message to Joe without compromising words. There was never a more amorally understanding man on the face of the planet. Stanton believed Joe understood what was wanted of him through a process of inhalation, made possible by ancient wisdom leavened through present-day cunning. He only lacked eyes for wool. In pursuing the matter of Kale it was best not to name names but have it deep fathomed through wool. They had agreed on that from the start. The idea had come ripe, *now*, in Stanton's brain, of Kale raising his sheep in the outlands and being left to multiply breeders while Stanton awaited his time. In London (pray for a ship) Stanton would seek George Marsh's maps; he would return with better information than he had here; and if Lehane could be frightened quite out of his wits he might still be useful. Then there was the matter of the quantity of trade goods Joe carried, enough to establish a veritable sheep station. How excellent to have it transported without paying, to exactly where he wanted it, without having to bother himself in deciding where that choice location might be!

The minister and the trader walked farther in under the apple trees, the olives, the pomegranates and the cherimoya fruits from Peru, and every time a bond servant came past pushing a wooden barrow filled with stones, or struggled with wooden buckets to dampen the ground, or weeded on all fours around the tomato vines and beans, Stanton placed his hand on Joe's shoulder and made a boast about how well his produce was doing despite the bugs, rat bandicoots, and afflictions of hot, drying winds. Then as the bond servants moved away, with ever mistrustful glances lingering behind them, he resumed his purpose. He said he had a gift for Joe.

'It is my favour to you. It is the guide in wools you asked. I have prepared samples of the pretty good to the rather good. You can use them as your beau ideal.

'Do not let them out of your hands, keep them clean, rolled up, protected in a soft lambskin. Whenever you think you are shown better you should quibble and subtract. Mostly, the woolgrowers of the colony are men of ignorance. They follow fashions in livestock, today sheep, tomorrow turkeys. Their sworn labels on bundles of wool tell no more than they need when it comes to truth — so and so Smith's by the One Tree Hill, or the O'Keefe's by the Kangaroo Flat. The rest is long wool when it's short wool, fine when it's not, best wool for dead wool and so on. Only a woolstapler knows the difference. I can't think what the combers and carders of my home village make of claims from The Wombat Badger Hole and Past Half Mile Hollow Rock By Burnt Tree. The colonial-experience style is a galloping consumption of mock humility. It doffs its hat to no man, putting on airs via the republic of the bark hut. It is Irishry boiled down to a pitch of botheration. Everyone is scarred by chains — no personal offence, sir. I know you have served your sentence and made your peace with wrongdoing. You enhance, you don't degrade the progress of the place. Then of course you are English born.'

'Within sound of Bow Bells,' said Joe.

'We are getting complaints from our agents in the home country that Botany Bay wools are arrogant. The definition of quality seems to be, if it is from New South Wales, it is good enough. You and I differ, Joe, we stand apart.'

'I have always tried to fit in.'

'That is only your destiny as a Jew.'

'I'm seen as good as the next one, till I names me price. Then I'm back to being a Jew, with gold in the bedroll.'

'Nail a supply of exceptional wool and you will tie your fortune to a superior star. You'll come close to grace, and understand what I mean when I talk about being saved. The purest wools under heaven are a sign of God's bounty. Jesus was called the Lamb of God.'

'Was he?'

Joe wiggled a finger in his waxy ear until Stanton continued with his advice, and Joe started listening again:

'There is such high confidence about wool because it is based on the sheep's liking of New South Wales for its dust, herbs, and wide open spaces. For its dry going they are believed to pay out in gold, just for the asking. But small minds on small holdings make large claims, which are not provable in the fleece unless it is given some care. They must be understood to be shepherded to perfection.'

Stanton moved closer to expressing his need to Joe, when he said:

'It is far beyond the smaller establishments you must go, where there are no borders to runs, where there are no runs, where there is "nobody" — and yet the requirement for supplies is unbounded. Are you heading south?'

'I don't like to say,' said Joe, with the air of shrewdness that Stanton liked in him so very much.

'Before you get too far, sniff the wind. Go where it comes up coldest. You'll need your boys to fell trees: I've learned as much from the cur, Lehane — once you're down at the foot of the ranges, and begin your ascent, keep going. If it wasn't for my call elsewhere I would join you. Imagine us arguing the scriptures on top of a load, with tree branches parting the blessed hairs of our heads.'

Joe Josephs imagined it, with maybe a shudder, and said as enigmatically as he could:

'We shall go as far as maffematically calculated recipes for increased profit allow, rated by the number of turns in a dray wheel.'

'When you find the best wool I shall need to know fairly exactly where it was raised. Make maps and see they are kept private. Write them in Hebrew hieroglyphics in case they fall into wrong hands and I shall use my old Cambridge syllabi to puzzle them out.'

'Speaking of eyeroglippiks,' said Joe, warming to a mood of close conspiracy, 'I have a gift to make in return for the one you promise me.'

'Not so fast!' laughed Stanton, hardly knowing what to expect as Joe guided him to a nook in the garden wall, where earlier the trader had rested a canvas roll holding heavy, lumpy objects. Presumably something to sell.

'As a trader, I have many irons in the fire,' said Joe. 'I am like the busy blacksmith, who runs the danger of some metal burning and some getting cold.'

'Ah hah, blacksmiths,' said Stanton, aware that Joe had recently moved through the Mundowey forest where there was a fifty-pound reward posted for hammers and tongs — those precious tools of the blacksmith's trade long missing from government stores and used to make a runaway's irons crack wide. In Joe's way of thinking the closer he supported discovery the farther from suspicion anyone's part in the business would be.

Joe flicked back the canvas and there they were, ashy and charred from a forest fire. Just the knobs and the irons, not the wooden parts, of course, they were all burned up.

'Clever man.'

Stanton scratched the items with his fingernails and rubbed the scales of scorch, bringing up the broad-arrow insignia. These finds would not be returned to the governor's care just yet.

'Did you stumble on them by chance, or persistently rake the forest refuse, with the energy of a tinker?'

'We was only just moving on, hardly believing what was done in broad daylight by Lehane, when our little Solly slips down a pit, up to his chin in a hole of ash near a burned-out tree. This is what he fished up. What now?'

'I shall advance you the government reward,' said Stanton, 'and save you a ride back into Parramatta to claim the posted amount.'

'Some recompense for Solly falling in a frightful pit would be welcome. He is like his older brother, always in debt to his pa for material goods. There is a knife I am holding, that folds its blade down into itself and sits in a leather pouch no fatter than your thumb. Good for picking stones from a hoof or for throwing some distance into the trunk of a tree, as boys like to do when they's idle.'

'These tools,' said Stanton, 'are instruments perfectly suited to a job I need doing on my horned rams. There is a foreigner among our shearers, a sheepworking Spaniard, named Lorenze. He is a type they breed in that country to wrestle bulls, a fine glowering fellow, I like him very much — there he is over by the creek side with Warren's dog who loves him, a great sign in a man — and I shall ask him to do the job for me when the rams are brought in. It will be a theatre of amazement for whichever of my men is in league with the man who escaped through use of these tools. Pray look into their faces when we bring the irons out. Look for the one who shakes when we lop the twisted horn.'

TOWARDS EVENING STANTON FETCHED AN
armload of wool from a sack and went over to the
Josephs's camp, passing a portion to Joe to study.

'I think my son will be good on this,' said Joe hopefully, pulling
a few strands apart. 'We are as unlike as two can be from each other
in the matter of brains.'

'Leave it, Pa,' said Arthur, who was pinched cold after standing
in the creek for hours, prodding sheep through, and wore a blanket
around his shoulders despite the evening warmth.

Stanton performed what looked like a conjuror's trick, pulling a
scroll of cardboard from an inside pocket and flattening it on a tree
stump. He was watched by Joe and his son, and by the new man,
Paul Lorenze. Last to join them was Warren, along with his parlous
dog, who sat on his skinny haunches and gazed at Paul Lorenze
expectantly, while Warren scratched him between the ears.

Holding the card down with an elbow Stanton stretched strands
of wool along its length and tied their roots across the top with a
band of thread. Above each example he pencilled a description.

'There are but seven divisions in wool — the picklocks, the

primes, the choices, the supers, the downs, the heads and the down-rights. We remember the seven deadly sins, they are all too easy to recall to our fingertips — why not the seven virtues of fleeces, and their God-given glories?'

'It is all terribly hard,' said Joe.

'I am listening,' said Arthur.

'Please don't underestimate yourself, Joe. The principles of breeding are the same whether with sheep or oxen. You may know nothing about sheep, but cattle are more familiar, I believe?'

'We looks at their backs all day,' allowed Joe. 'Some days we gets down and walks beside them, and Artie plays the fiddle.'

'Ask Mick Tornley for a few ideas as you roll out, or when you sit around your campfire yarning. When Mick is home from the track he selects and breeds oxen to have his replacements all bellowing by the time he circles back. The same rules apply to any species. He will tell you that the first rule is to breed from the best, but that rule has its limitations and restrictions. One man will scour the whole country to snatch the best ram, or to kidnap a few prize gimmers.'

Stanton could not help himself. As soon as he said 'best ram' his belly rumbled, and he looked sidelong at Warren.

'There is a sort who will select the most promising sire, thinking to insure better alliances for his flocks. He comes along the road one day and tries to weasel a ram out of my boy who will have nothing of it. He must have a set of mongrels, if he has sheep at all. Some distant impurity of breed manifests itself; some tendencies far back in the pedigree of the race awaiting correction — I have not seen that man's flock, but you can be sure they will show signs of indiscriminate and injudicious dabbling. Fat-tails, no better than a joke. Yes?'

The question stabbed. Joe was mystified and Warren quite afraid at the audacity of Stanton's speech. Since learning that Tom Rankine masterminded the ram theft he'd felt nothing but sullen fear. What was Stanton trying to say, in his taunting, sarcastic fashion — that he guessed what Warren knew? Was he trying to console him with the talk of a scrappy Rankine flock, or to alarm him with derision?

From another pocket Stanton took a handful of figs. They came from the far end of the homestead garden, where he was proudest of his trees. It was early summer and the first crop. Although they were bird-pecked a few survived, split, sticky with fruit jam cooked by the sun, flecked with strands of wool and dusty, but Stanton passed them around and they all made a feast of them.

'Another man,' said Stanton, wiping his lips in two long damp sidestrokes and resuming his instruction, 'who is better acquainted with the rules that regulate vitalism, takes a flock, and having selected the best, he takes only those which he knows to be of the same breed. Notice I say *knows* and say *takes*. There may not be any legal niceties involved, if this man is a particular one I have in mind.'

'Is good fruits,' said Lorenze, with a short gasping laugh, a fig cupped in his hand and salivating over it, before scooping it into his mouth.

'Nevertheless,' said Stanton, 'he goes on steadily aiming at giving breadth to the animal and quality to its wool. Listen to me carefully now, Joe, as I am going to finish this passage with a *nevertheless.*'

'I am all ears, like the flaming donkey that waggeth his ears to show that he knows it all.'

'This other man knows that the sheep, in order to thrive, must have a large lymphatic system. He must have a capacious chest and loins, and a frame on which to secrete fat, with lightness of offal. A man takes those qualities which show a tendency to pervade, in one uniform direction, the whole of the flock; and this he takes to mend his own.'

'To mend his own,' echoed Joe, nodding with understanding of self advancement, at least.

'By this means all are a little improved in the direction he requires; and all keeping alike in their general contour, there is a kind of permanency and uniformity in the main features of the improvement. In terms of wool it will be a staple with length, fineness and density. A simple enough formula, if you know how to look, but desperately perplexing otherwise. Am I making complete sense, Joe? Lift up your head and look.'

'Give me your "nevertheless",' said Joe.

'The man I conjecture shall first have a flock of ewes the great quality of which I doubt exists in this country, but second he shall have my ram Young Matchless, and this is where I say my "nevertheless".'

'I think I am getting it now,' said Joe. 'Your nevertheless is, that if there ain't the matching ewes, the breeding is a waste, and so it ain't your bloke and there won't be no wonder wools. But if there's wonder wools, it's him.'

'Is good the red colours, just a leedle,' said Lorenze, throwing his arms out, apparently pointing to the dust behind the wool hall, thrown up at evening by sheep and so crimsoning the sun.

'Away past where anyone has ever gone,' resumed Stanton, draping an arm around Joe's shoulder, and whispering lusciously into his ear, 'there is my breed of man who puts himself above the rest by being vain about wool. He may use one of those names — "Smith", "O'Keefe", or whatever.'

The two men walked away from the others.

'A man he is, who responds to a little speculation about breeding without being able to help himself.'

'There he will have me stuffed.'

'No, not at all, dear friend, just take hold of his swatch of wool when he presents his sample for trade. Look at it hard. Remember my lesson? Say you believe it is not of the best, even if you think it is, whatever it is in terms of breed he posits. Even if you don't know what you are talking about.'

'You are askink me to lie?' Joe raised an ironical eyebrow.

'Though you will enrage him, possibly, by your unfathomable shrewdness, there is no lie involved, on the grounds that improvement is the Lord's will, and though we have glimpsed perfection in our promise of heaven, and may do so every day in our meditations, there is always more better to be had down here out of Eden. I believe even the Old Testament says nothing less, and so we are surely agreed.'

'Now you have found me out. That's my method, or should I say, reverend, was my method before I corrected the error of my friends and went straight as you find me in front of you now, in this here colony of forced improvers. You are saying, so to speak, the vanity of man is bottomless, if we only know how to make the appeal?'

'Entirely.'

SHADE TREES HUNG OVER THE waggoners' camp near the creek but the camping place offered nowhere to bathe, as the creek was mostly dry and its few pools were made filthy after the sheepwash and the bullock wallow. The Josephs carted water to their camp from the well in the homestead garden. Stanton spoke of the Josephs as his guests, to Dolly, but on the quiet. To have them openly talked about as guests compromised his politics of keeping separation between free and convict and convict-emancipist stock. Yet he loved them as Warren did, now, and bettered his imagination deciding what measures to take against Lehane on behalf of their innocence.

Little from the traders' waggon was yet for sale — because the greater distance travelled, the higher percentage profits cut in — only tobacco and rum, both commanding a good price from those who were needy and deprived, which was pretty well all the profligate stockmen Stanton had under his rule but not always under his thumb.

Joe heard Stanton's voice carrying over the paddocks from the wool hall, where he berated his builders to finish their work.

The wool hall was made of wattle and daub, a one-floored slab-sided shed of small cathedral size — a colonial triumph, it was, and sure to be famous. A shuttered belltower was capped with tea-tree thatching. The wool hall sat on an open sweep of dust down from the house, above the banks of the intermittently ponding, sometimes flowing, flat-bedded sandy creek overhung with paperbark trees and old Yarros or bastard gums and Tarundeas or great black-butted gums so called. The hall had verandahs and covered walks, the walks being for sheep and joined to a slatted shearing floor and a set of post-and-rail stringybark yards — all built of materials that were cut, adzed and carried from not very far, leaving a low breakage of tree stumps looking ugly, where it was recently pretty near the picnickers' flat rock.

On the other side of the hall, downwind, the four thousand sheep that had been washed over three days were yarded for shearing with their fleeces shaken out bright, being rid of their dirt. It made a humid, downcast picture of lumpy weariness in white. Bunches of sheep were deliberately sweated standing close together and getting each other hot, losing the crustiness on their fleeces as their wool yolk melted. Lorenze decreed it was good for the skin to sweat and nearly as good as washing to get the wool soft for cutting. Stanton found himself deferring to Lorenze in his opinions. The two men built up respect through mutual understanding of what was good for a sheep. It was evident to Joe that the minister, while full of arguments reckoned as soundly constructed, worked almost completely out of his emotions and made passionate attachments as swiftly as he declared his hates.

Moving about the yards getting up sheep that wanted to lie down and die (but didn't), the reverend magistrate looked as bona fide crude as any true Botany Bay farmer ought — which was to say, one who only crowed when it rained holey dollars. How he spoke like one, thought like one, and judged like one resounding his Yorkshire complaints over a recalcitrant half-paralysed leg-twitcher ewe, which was to say as well, he was unfeeling and coarsely joyous in a way that intrigued those who remembered he was a minister of God.

Joe came at him sideways with questions. Were there to be sheep in heaven?

'Most likely so.'

Stanton's prophet was called 'Door of Sheep', 'Shepherd', 'Lamb of God'. His own Church was called 'Sheep', 'Lamb's Wife', 'Flock of God' and 'Fold of Christ'. Sheep were Stanton's tie between this world and the next. The fields of heaven were soft and green, endlessly rolling and droning with honey bees and the belling of doves all mustered by angels . . . Joe did not like this picture, but liked the next one: perfection of earth as a sign of expectation, not of completion. It answered both to his trade and his prayers. But then the next one after that he hated — 'We only need to remember it all *to be saved.*'

By a rough count there were hundreds of references to sheep in the Old Testament, said Stanton, and that was leaving out their keeping needs: the sheepcotes, sheepfolds, sheep gates, sheep markets, sheep masters, shepherds, wool and shearers that were all spoken about, including Laban, the first shearer, in Genesis, the first book.

So it all went back and back . . . Mutton and goat meat were the favoured meals of prophets; their nourishment was divine. Unless it was an ass's neck well seasoned and well roasted these boisterous biblical giants were like Stanton in taste, they liked a leg or shoulder of sucking lamb.

'Joe?'

'What, sir?'

'It sometimes vexes me, in deciding how far I might have to go, to fight the Devil with the Devil's own devices. Must I wear the Devil's red clothes, drink his hot drinks, flash his forked tail?'

Stanton fondled the band of wool on his wrist.

Joe took hold of the threads. Peering close, he said he saw red in them.

'You are getting your eye in,' said the minister.

The sheep were in the arena of ground kept untouched for the purpose of keeping their wool clean. No sooner was the shearing started than the forecourt of the hall was piled with rolled fleeces. All hands were called on to help. The floor was slippery with threads. Warren and Titus kept the sheep up — woe betide Titus if he slacked and there wasn't one ready. Clumpsy M'Carty carried the tar bucket. The shearers ferociously knelt over their sheep, blasphemously protective of their craft and slicing their blades through the wool and moving fast. They looked up from under dark sweaty brows but the Spaniard's demeanour was the most festering. When Clumpsy caught sight of him for the first time here (he'd been out in his mustering camp, and was only just come in with his mob), Lorenze slipped his shearing blades from their oiled kangaroo-skin pouch and held them under Clumpsy's nose.

'Whoa,' said Clumpsy, reeling back, 'who in the name of forking merriment is tiss?'

Dark eyes behind thick lashes met his and told him to silence.

He was not to say, unless he wanted trouble, that they knew each other well. There was no helping it, either. Any Spaniard was a bad

Spaniard since a man had his cods banged between stones, held, torn and crushed. So Clumpsy kept his distance, unless he wanted trouble. There were all those Spanioloes running around the hill-sides in Spain, and they were in the business of changing sides.

There was sometimes a busy click in the air as the blades opened and shut and sometimes a whispering silence as the blades were held at a flat angle to the skin and pushed through like knives. Stanton noted who made cuts and would pay those shearers less. Clumpsy was busy around them stemming blood with his tar bucket. Lorenze made no cuts. There were three black women working on the floor and in the silences you could hear their giggling laughter. When the wool was cut smoothly along the pink skin it left serrations of tufts as the shears travelled without stopping in sweeping slices called blows. In the slatted shade of the wool hall they carved the wool into piles.

BRINGING UP YOUNG MATCHLESS, KALE gathered the flock behind him, forded the sheep through a braided cold torrent, counted them over and lost none.

They spread along a way as Biddy watched them. So many white rustling daisies advanced all at once in a field of moving wonder.

There were hardly ever any pastoral scenes recollecting Kale's earlier life in this country but this was one of them. The woman on the hillside shading her brow with her forearm. The flocks nibbling along in their serene flow made up of rips, startles, thrusts and jabs. How many lives, in one life, was a man to be granted?

Kale went to a hill, cleared a view of saplings with his short-handled axe, watched and was sure they were not followed. It was away in country so changed from the places where they began it was past all civilised knowledge.

In New South Wales despite the many dangers and now with a hanging crime on his head, Kale felt better placed than he had in Ireland. It was certainly better to have nothing, than to have something and see it reduced to nothing. Sometimes Kale knuckled a fist to his forehead and worked it all out. Other times his life was a tumble of fragments, and how one piece fitted to another beat him. He mostly felt he was not getting any younger, yet in all his capacities felt fit as he did at thirty. Since the arrival of Biddy his stricken back was entirely healed.

Kale rode on ahead. Biddy rode along behind. Young Matchless waddled rather than walked, but did so at a good pace, with womback stalwartness, hooves like little boxes, and when his wide horns bothered him by getting caught in a bush, he backed and sidestepped, stamped and shook, and stubbornly worked his way free of the tangle.

'He is like you, Desmond Kale, a truly square individual' — which Kale liked very much, being compared with a sheep, though anything Biddy said quite charmed him.

The next way along was a natural limestone ramp leading halfway up a higher wooded hill. The path narrowly admitted two sheep at a time between overhanging rocks before a coarse reedy meadow unfolded on the other side and the sky opened again. They could not get a single sheep through that passage until the leaders were persuaded to go on, and so the rest followed with every single one of them leaping in the same place as if there was a gate to jump over. The horses needed to lower their necks and be urged under the overhanging rock while their riders crouched before them and tugged at the reins swearing. Boulders dislodged and crashed into the stream far below, striking sparks and gunpowder smoke as they fell. It was all wondrous new to Biddy Magee with many fears to be overcome thanks to Kale, who told her of the impossibility of being followed, past a certain point, by anyone in authority save the one in authority in league with them. She believed him, having no choice because the alternatives gave out no hope. They would move along, breeding up the sheep, stopping here and there, until Rankine caught up with them. They would make an alliance with natives, if they could, otherwise their flock's survival was in question. Kale cursed for not seeking his man living in the bush camp, whose name was Mun'mow. If they had him with them it would be easier up ahead getting themselves understood, although Kale had no doubt he'd be remembered by one or two of those natives who never forgot a face.

'That is your fame for you again,' said Biddy.

With the ram running in the flock they moved up and over to more open country, dropping through tangled forests of tall trees, ferns, prickly shrubs, jumbled rocks and rubble landslips. High open country was a vision before them. The sheep spilling forward went like fish in the sea, their backs shining foamy curved as they leapt. How they crashed and bolted along! From the flanks of long ridges it was possible to view out many miles over dappled grasslands where lines of trees followed watercourses into the far distance. West now and westwards the way ran. Cloud shadows passed like columns of armies on the move. Native fires burned, sending up smoke, and it was reckoned their arrival was noted and might be opposed. Kale fingered his musket and Biddy the pistol he gave her. She knew how to shoot, he found, from her protection among grenadiers since the age of fifteen. Kale checked their powder. Kale went along felling saplings and Biddy raised hurdles against the bare bank of streams where they forced the sheep tight and lit fires at either end against dogs. The sun set with blazing heat but in the hills behind them the shadows were long and cool. Biddy trusted herself absolutely to Kale — her heart and her hand together.

———————

Judging by the clean smell of water in a rushing river Kale declared it was descended from snows. He declared it was the bidgee sort of a river found by Marsh and his black man. So they made a camp. Kale said it would do for a while. In the last light Kale took out his maps, that he had not let Rankine see but showed Biddy. They were hand drawn from Marsh's old maps, showing landmarks of a high-domed hill, a narrow-sided stream, and a wide sandy flat. And this was only the first unfolding of the concertina package Kale carried.

They sat around the fire smoking their clay pipes. Kale loved seeing Biddy puffing away satisfied. She was a keen little kitty-cat woman with cheeks red from the brisk weather. She had lovely refracting green eyes and a contented way of wrapping her sheep-skin around her, and refusing to go to bed until Kale yawned and said it was time.

Kale talked of right and wrong in the animals. There was a reddish hue in the wool of some of the sheep that Kale disliked and wanted bred out of them now that he had them. It was a mark of the breed seeing how the first brown moor, *moreno*, or *benimerine* had carried the first of them into Grenada. It was a red or fawn, buff or satiny feature visible in the wool in good lights. Kale said it had to go. 'It was put there by the scoundrel, Moreno,' he said.

Moreno insisted it belonged with the breed as of right. Because of this, Rankine, whose eye for a sheep was good enough, had seen ruin coming and that was the first reason he gave the sheep over to Kale.

'Moreno's feelings were justly hurt,' said Biddy.

'Agreed, and he is no longer trustworthy,' said Kale. 'Has he ever touched you, Biddy?'

'No.'

'And you knew him from Spain?'

'I did. We weren't bad friends either, me and Payolo. But he doesn't like white hens. From his first day of coming ashore he dwelled in the bush more than anyone except the natives that were already there. While away shepherding he found himself a black woman bought by craving of drink from the husband of one. Smoke of their fires was rubbed in his skin, ash and charcoal pitted. Boy, did he reek! When washing he bared his arse and splashed his fork in muddy water, streaked his beard with clay, pulled back his hair with fingers greased from wool oils. Burning sun bronzed him black as them poor souls. Nobody knew who he was. He is a free man of beaten pride and bound to Rankine through love and the promise of sheep. But it will be like Payolo has agreed to have his limbs torn off from love. He won't do what Rankine wants now. He will be raising some money for himself, to start again. He will want to come after you, to get his flock returned.'

'There's nothing to be done about that, but to make the flock better. Moreno wishes he was back in his own country, but Spain is a smoking ruin. He would be wrapped in his cloak by a fire at this hour, if he could be found there, listening to the wolves, and starving.'

'You are making me shiver. I never liked it. Rankine would be sitting in the door of his thatch waiting for Clumpsy to boil the water for his shave. Clumpsy would strop the razor, swipe it through the boiling water, soap the brush, lather Rankine's cheeks, and shave him. Then they would have their breakfast which Clumpsy would cook, scrampled eggs with onions. You have no idea, with the stink of death over everything. Out here's the only place where I feel I am rid of it.'

'What was the name of your soldier?'

'Donal Conroy, can we not speak of him?'

'Come over here, then.'

Kale sat propped with his back to a tree. Biddy tucked herself into his warmth. She fitted between his legs. They were exactly snug. He put his arm around her. The night was chilly on their noses and there was not a breath of wind. If Kale could have died then, he would have been content, except he had no wish to abandon her, and so his life would have to be very long.

What Biddy told Kale about sheep as their days went by surprised him into discovering that while at his head of the flock he saw plenty, it was at their rear, and coming around their sides, that she gathered much knowledge.

'They are quiet with you,' he said.

'They are very amiable grooming each other. It is all in their licking spittle, what they like — as they nibble, lick, and when they rub. They rub and they carry on. The next one along gets a feel of it, and all stay together. When we first come to somewhere new they circle around and explore. They go in single tracks following each other.'

'Have you never watched sheep as close before, sweetheart?'

'Never at all. We was so poor, at home, that if we caught a rabbit, we were kings over a spoon of its stew. All we wanted was our own goat, and a little cart to follow. I could not live there, so I left.'

'Following your grenadier?'

'Leave that alone, I said.'

'All right, my dear.'

'Why do their tracks make a weaving pattern, not a straight line?'

'Can you tell?'

'I think it may be the result of the lead animal trying to see the animals behind, and having to turn around to see behind their heads, like we do.'

'You'll begin to notice some sheep are more alert and wary than others. They are the ones to watch.'

'That would be Molly, Evelyn, and Bonnie.'

'How now, ewes have names?'

'They are the flock leaders, so why not? Is only a ram to be christened? I hear them when they cry out, Molly calls to the younger one telling her where she is. The younger one bleats when she wants to be found. It is a stronger sort of bleat, as clear as a word. I have seen them with a snake, going all rigid and freezing before I come up to them, so I am not as afraid of snakes as I was. I have new friends. As we watch them, they tell us what we want to know.'

'That is the way of shepherding. It is never the same with dogs.' Kale looked at her through his sheep man's eyes. 'Sheep are peaceful, not like people. They have their conflicts but they carry on. They don't like showing pain. The dominance of one sheep over another is not absolute.'

'They say that Parson Stanton makes your life a misery, Desmond Kale.'

'It is hard for anyone to make my life a misery, dearie. After my first experience of tyrants, no more. You see, I won't allow them. No matter if I face the solitary dungeon, feel the lash, nor when I wear the iron collar and a great heavy log on my toes.'

'You are free of weights anyhow.'

'Their punishments are my reply. The harder they come the louder is my answer. They cannot tolerate how their worst punishments come back at them. For they hand me my best answer, which is defiance.'

'Rankine stood up for you.'

'With Rankine, it's all changed,' agreed Kale.

'As for your daughter, you will have to forgive her as I have tried.'

'Must I do everything you ask me?'

Biddy remembered his reputation for enlarging slights and felt her power over him.

'Yes, that's the way,' she said.

He grumbled and swore. 'It's the officer corps, they had her when they wanted. They turned her proud among them. God knows what it's done to my grandson, a boy with wool up his nose.'

'You must mind it a lot, having him apprenticed so.'

'What he learns there, he'll take away. He'll keep a tally book in his brain bringing Stanton forward or pushing him back according to how he stands among sheep.'

'In Parramatta they say the parson never shuts up about you. But I have never once heard you speak his name, until now.'

'I don't even think about him.'

'Except you would like him defeated in his wools.'

She had him there. 'I would,' he said.

Over his rum that evening Kale recited lines famed for their sadness:

The harp that once through Tara's halls the soul of music shed,
now hangs as mute on Tara's walls as if that soul were fled.

THROUGH THE EXPERIENCE OF STANDING in water up to his waist and grabbing stubborn wet sheep, wrenching them upstream out of the muddy flow of the wash, and up onto a bank where they stood wet and dripping sadder than ever, Artie Josephs earned his remaining shillings and contracted catarrh. There was also a lumpy red rash that his mother fussed over with powders. Then there were the yolk boils.

Sheep after washing were like sheep lying dead in snow, everywhere white and lumpy wet, and none seeming to breathe as they lay down defeated awaiting their time to get up and be sweated, and then to be shorn. Poke them and prod them and nothing happened. They sloshed, buckets of guts. Turn your back and up they jumped alive oh.

Each night Artie moved his blanket to the men's fire and stretched himself out being entertained by the boasts and ballads of the men and warming his bones with a few chokes of rum which ran like lizards into his loins.

Lorenze watched from the other side of the fire. The green-eyed lunatic Moroney recited his words. A ballad could be put either for or against, but nobody would ever find Kale and beat him with just a ballad. You needed a sheep to beat Kale. If you wanted a sheep to beat Kale just ask Paul Lorenze.

He was up on the whole rampage. His anger was right up under his ribcage. At night by the leaping flames behind Stanton's sheds he was next, and he drew deep breath and sang of sheep numbered in their millions. They were divided into flocks, each under the care of a mayoral. At the head of all mayorals was the mayoral-in-chief walking ahead, who directed the length and speed of their journey, others with dogs followed, they flanked the cavalcade, collected stragglers, kept off wolves who followed and migrated with the flocks. A surge of mild beasts crossed the sierras. How it translated from the Spanish:

We are a singular race of men
Attached to our profession
Rarely quitting, never marrying
Always fighting, always drinking.
In winter we sleep in huts
In summer we lie on the ground.
Our food is bread and oil
We like best of all dripping
Washed down by strong wine —
Nuestro favorito la grasa de carne
con una fuerte copa de vino.

Three of them understood what the rest only felt. From his mother, Artie had learned his Ladino, the dialect of Spain spoken by Jews. Lorenze's music was all low f's and g's. Clumpsy was the other one. He'd learned his pig Spanish in Spain and called it a pig language spoken by pigs, and that was how he showed his hatred and fear of the pig man, Lorenze.

After sitting around the fire the boys moved to their hut in the Stantons' yard and Artie came too. He wrapped himself in his blanket and instead of staying on the dirt floor as he had been first invited he arranged himself top to tail on Warren's bed. Before sleep felled them the boys made yawning talk for as long as they could. Warren asked the same questions Stanton asked of the Josephs and the answers from Artie were as hopeful and vague as they were from his father:

'If it don't rain, bogging the waggon, if my pa don't forget to gild our bullocky, Mick, on the night of every full moon, we shall grab the miles better than anyone before. They say it's the best country, but it's been ignored, on account of reports saying it was all tumbled and broken like smashed crockery, and getting along was like walking on rooftops. But we hear it's not true. There are river gorges to cross, where our waggon gets carried over, and rebuilt on the other side. But then we are free.'

'You are a bold mob,' said Warren, thinking of the eyes of the one of them, Leah, towards whom his fledgling heart leaped adventuring. 'You love the trackless wastes, and under your waggon is space for the most comfortable kind of humpy you could ever fit up.'

'Until it rains,' agreed Artie. 'Then we all gets out and digs trenches, and the next day can't go nowheres till it fines up and the ground dries. We hang our carpets in the wind like washing.'

'When does it rain?' said Warren with sour sincerity, as this past year he remembered dry thunderstorms whipping licks of dust and raindrops trying to nail them down. When they were lucky the wet lasted a few hours — he went around with the corner of a sack peaked on his head, feeling admirable with his dogs.

'What about wild savages, ain't you afeared?' said Titus, may be forgetting he was born one — or out of need not to be taken for one. There was a story out: that when the moon became as large as the sun wild blacks would commence a work of desolation, and kill all the whites before them. It was warned by Lehane in the puddle of darkness at the back of his cell. But it must be taken care of before it happened. Two had been shot for trampling a field of corn ripening to harvest. Titus trembled saying they were very bad men, and deserved to be shot. The whole countryside was back into peace before trouble even started, and if the slaughtered natives had walked around the corn instead of running over it they would have been saved. Warren saw Titus weep and knew those people were kin.

'To be dealt with as they come,' said Artie with easy confidence. 'My pa's met worse in back lanes of Cheapside, or, depending if you prefer, back lanes of Parramatta.' Then Artie remembered and gave Titus some consideration: 'Them's wild convict savages he means, o'course, not your heathen blacks with spears and waddy dongers.'

Next morning two old men were told to go and dig a ditch for the operation on the rams' horns. Joe Josephs spat in the dust and muttered spells when he heard Stanton ordering the ditch be matched at one end by another ditch running across it and the two ditches together to make the shape of a cross.

With the word 'cross' on his lips the parson sermonised, saying how the rams were being crucified for their horns by a Spaniard, and did Joe know that tribes of Spain were descended from Roman soldiers who travelled there straight after the birth of Christ? Quite possibly indeed the one who speared Christ on the cross, to be sure he was dead, travelled then to Spain and raised sheep in his complacently misguided misbegotten pagan old age.

Instruction rained on Joe from the mouth of his friend. Was he never to be cured of this and that? But at least today it was Romans who crucified Christ, which Joe would remember and remind Stanton of, when next he blamed it otherwise.

Titus walked around picking up fleeces and bringing up sheep to the shearers. The three black women working on the floor sat to one side with ewes in their laps and the sheep sensed they would not be harmed, for they were floppy with approval of the service they were rendered by these gentle savages wearing calico dresses to cover their immodesty. Dolly Stanton supplied the garments at some expense and made them wear them before appearing before men. No sheep jumped up from their grasp and ran around scampering their hooves and slipping sideways until caught shivering, as they did with the men. Instead they slumbered like dozy babes. The women picked burrs and other foreign material from the wool, lanced cysts in feet and dressed sores in skin, and when they took up the shears they certainly proved themselves better shearers than the men, except for Lorenze, who was the master.

Stanton said these handy women, and their tatterdemalion males too misguided to work his sheep, had come in for his protection after the settlers on the biggest river had shot and chased some off. They were frightened people, although in the minister's opinion prone to exaggeration through a theatrical mistrust of white men and what they could do. As if to prove him correct, a deputation of whites reported that not nearly as many were killed as those that said too many were killed the day they were shot. Stanton said the blacks could stay on Laban Vale soil longer than the shearing if they accepted the steps of conversion, then they would truly have nothing to fear for the rest of their days. But if they resisted the blessings of Christ he would lose his patience after the shearing and dismiss them.

Stanton turned back to his other task of worldly education. He told Artie Josephs he followed a plan of sorting everything into four parcels. He boasted of being alone the woolgrower in the colony bothering with the division of four in his consignments, and planned to follow his consignments all the way through to England, he and his family on the selfsame sailing ship as his wool. 'As soon as the governor is pleased to consent to our passage,' he hedged.

They watched a shearer peeling a fleece with his blades. The first lot was picklock wool from the withers to the back; the next finest was from the belly to the quarters and thighs down to the stifle joint; then came the wool of the third quality from the head, throat, lower part of the neck, shoulders, and terminating at the elbow; finally there was the wool yielded by the legs, reaching from the stifle to a little below the hock. A small quantity of very inferior wool was taken from the tuft growing on the forehead and cheeks, also from the tail, and from the legs below the hocks. It was all bundled in for eventual pricing and sale at the best bargained rates on the other side of the world.

'Here is a kind of sheep you will learn to look out for,' said Stanton, in the next and hopefully last part of his lesson, when they went outside and the minister selected a fatigued ewe from the unshorn number, pulling her around and holding her against a post while his hairy hands walked over every part and Artie and Joe watched.

'She is a good Saxon merino, but I see you might be thinking not so good at all. But this is how they are. Some call them grown-out rats or miserable doggy sheep or drowned unrespectables but

I shall never decry what they carry on their backs. Thrust your fingers into the wool noting the fineness of the fleece and the blood in the skin like a pencil line when the fleece is parted. The wool lies closer and thicker over the body than in most other breeds. It is abundant in yolk and is covered with a dirty crust, often full of cracks. Black gold, it is called by the Spaniards, gum or jar by English farmers, and if you ask our Senyor Paul Lorenze over there, he will doubtless oblige you by agreeing it is wonderful stuff. But do not interrupt his shearing or he might slash you, he is such a rogue buccaneer.'

Stanton reached down fondly, lifted a leg as if to make the sheep curtsy, allowed its hoof to dangle while gripping the foreleg bone, and said:

'The legs are long, yet small in the bone like yours, Artie Josephs — if you don't mind me saying so, you are a skinny-shanked piece of work. Yet they will take both you and she a long way. The breast and the back are narrow, the foreshoulders and bezooms are heavy, but too much weight is carried on the coarser parts to please me. I do not worry overly on that point, however, I only dislike these folds of skin coming pendulously down under the throat. They are like a gluttonous old king's dewlap who only eats to satisfy his greed. Not our present Majesty, I most hastily add. The merino has a voracious appetite which yields no adequate return of condition, and although they taste good, mutton farmers hate them for they have no aptitude to fatten.'

Stanton put the leg down and straightened his back with a small sound of ouch, then came around behind the sheep and straddled it without needing to widen his legs, as they were bowed ready for sheepwork from birth. This way he was able to display the front of the sheep by holding up its head and without getting his hand fouled by sticky drivel. He spoke from between its ears that were almost buried in wool:

'I am an Englishman in my prejudice against these folds under the throat which are difficult to shear and wasteful. We oppose the superstition that the folds are good, showing a tendency both to wool and a heavy fleece. I am with Lord Somerville on the matter — Lord Somerville being the greatest sheep man in England after Sir Joseph Banks — he says a throaty sheep is not good in its skin, with no hurry to fatten. It is one matter on which I disagree with our new friend, Lorenze.'

Stanton let the sheep go and dusted his hands. He wiped them down the seams of his grimy moleskin trousers. He spied Warren moving sheep up, and said to Artie:

'Here is what makes me proud. Did you know, apropos of the scriptures, that the Church of God is called "adopted sons" in Galatians? Just a thought I have at the present. A passing thought.'

'I don't know Glayshens,' said Artie.

There was a commotion of dog, boy and sheep galloping from under the fringe of trees along the creek, where the afternoon light was so harsh that even the nearby trees were drawn away tiredly into a haze of headachy distance.

'Look at the young horned rams Warren is bringing in to the yards to have their horns cut. These are the pick of them, what's left after Young Matchless.'

Stanton and Artie ran over and grabbed a ram from either side. It bucked and made the horn threat jerk, twisted its neck, head shaking strongly and only when there was nowhere it could go, did it quiet itself down. This was a ram, by name of Slumberous, normally so naturally quiet that when Warren and Titus tried getting it to play butting games they had to throw rotten fruit in its direction before it became enraged.

Stanton stroked the horns as a demonstration, first one and then the other, following the ridgy, yellowed matter down and up and around and down to a point. Slumberous was a handsome sheep. The shape of his horns was like a spiralled E in good penmanship standing out from the cheeks and nose and a matching E on the other side drawn by a perfectionist's nib. It seemed a shame to cut the horns off from their living beauty, but they caused grief for the rams in thickets and in their fights, and as the grazing closer to the homestead yards was eaten away the rams were taken farther out into a low corrugation of spiny hills where the green pick was good but the vegetation wild and grabby. Joe Josephs asked if he could have the horns when they were cut. Stanton conceded, 'Save for one of the pairs, which I want to set over the doors of the wool hall to greet all comers.'

The eye of Stanton's best Saxon ram (after Young Matchless) was almost feminine, softly dark and drawn back almondish. May be Slumberous liked to be groomed because he was already cozy for it; his nostrils were a V making a silver snot line down to his mouth, that wore, when it was closed with the lips tight sealed as a vacuum jar, a pert little ladyish smile.

'Take your last look at how large, curved, drawn out in a spiral these horns are,' said Stanton stroking them over. 'Tomorrow they will be cut off clean. The head is large but the forehead rather low. It is made for butting so watch out for Slumberous when we release him. My boys seem to think I don't know how they tease him into ram fights, but it is all fine boyish fun, and I let them do it, because it keeps up a ram's mettle. I don't mind they throw rotten fruit to get him teased. But don't tell my boys I am on to their tricks or they'll say I'm a fond old fool. I am afraid here endeth my lesson because my wife is calling me from the house to attend to the small part left of my day. Have you a picture of the race of merino, Artie Josephs?'

'I think I would know one anywhere,' said Artie.

Chorus of the Fourth Part

WHERE KALE IS SAVED IN SHOW

DURING THE AFTERNOON A MESSENGER came to Laban Vale bringing a long-awaited letter from the governor. The man rode in from the east through the pall of dust raised in the sheep yards and after being fed a slab of corned meat and old potatoes, and drinking off a gallon of tea, he rode back in the same direction before Stanton knew he was there.

The letter was addressed to Parson Magistrate Matthew Stanton, *On His Majesty's Service*, but Dolly Stanton knew what was in the letter by the time her husband joined her.

The seal was seemingly intact although the folds where the letter opened were damp on a day that was dry and in no way humid. Stanton was charitable towards his wife's passionate curiosities and from the fluttery grin turning the corners of her dear mouth white it seemed they might have got their way with a ship. May be, thought Stanton, to be fully charitable at home, the post rider's horse sweated into the letter pouch and that was all. But may be too, Dolly had put a kettle on the stove and banished the servants from the kitchen to search for cobwebs and to track invasions of red ants in the rooms at the other end of the house, so that their nests could be found and destroyed while she applied heat around the seal and forced the letter open.

Stanton talked a little about ants to tease Dolly with expectation of what she already knew, while she squirmed and twisted on her stool and waited perforce. Ants were her fixation since the new parts of the house were built and there were crowds of them pumping from every crack and crevice. They had mistakenly built on ant beds, although when they looked, ant beds were everywhere on Laban Vale with a tally of types numbering many dozens, and that was not even to begin on the termites, whose mounds were as big as shepherd's huts. Termites were secretive within the earth and able to eat a whole house from the inside without announcing their presence until the meal was complete down to the last woody snack; they could have a new house eaten at one end before its building was completed at the other. There were the red ants and the small black harmless-looking ants that leaped and stung like embers. There were those all jointed like a string of blisters and tiger-striped, with legs of busy wire. These did not bite so much as race into everything including one's underdrawers and sugar bins. There were the ones called bull ants needing no introduction, except their bite was hideous. Then there were the ones that gathered under the window ledges like an army of seething black pins in the last of the light on a hot afternoon and unfolded glassy wings, flying up into the house and dying into the lamps, burrowing into hair, entering mouths every time breath was drawn. One of these crawled into the letter now and laced all over the words while Stanton read them.

'Well, well, well, and another well — we have it, our ship,' he said from the corner of his mouth, fielding a flying ant that bothered him. 'The *Edinburgh Castle*, she is called, with enough room in her holds for our entire wool clip and the product of a good few other sheep stations besides. This governor is not a bad sort of scoundrel hielander. I might almost be inclined to join him for an officers' dinner if he ever condescends to invite me, and my wife of course — darling, pretty Dolly?'

Something was going on with her. She was off her stool and falling on his front. Stanton knew his wife felt pleasure at the news, but suddenly, to his immense surprise, Dolly ground herself against him, and sobbed while embracing and kissing his throat with hot delight.

'My dear, my darling, my woddly doodly bride,' said Stanton, a little amazed and taking a moment to get into her swing of enthusiasm. It was not too common, this picture she made in his arms. He wanted to savour it a while. A buzzing insect under the table performed a bitter complaint as Stanton remembered lines he disliked remembering at all, from a play he used to carry in his pocket, when he was a youth dabbling in romantic shepherding and more poetically minded, lines of which always came to him when lust's possibility of slaking was dangled before him after drought: how three crabbed months had soured themselves to death, ere he could make her open her white hand, and clap herself his love. Dolly's attentions went on grabbing, and despite Stanton having a sorry headache it was stirring to a high degree as he shifted the palm of his hand down her waist and around to her buttocks to explore bringing her hips in closer. When she sensed that her husband was aroused she went with swift consent to their cool darkened bedroom. Stanton briskly followed on naked feet, holding his boots in his arms. He informed the servants they would be napping. With the door wedged closed and the distant animal noises of the stockyards in their ears, they forgot who they were for ten minutes. The cuckoo clock chimed but there was a surety their Warren Inchcape was elsewhere, occupied with the shearing, or he would hear them getting up their cry. When they were done with gratification they lay back, smiling in the half dark of the all too aware house, and imagined the cool breezes and excitements of their sailing ship putting about to pass between the heads of Port Jackson.

This *post coitum triste* moment of airy calm and maritime floating was disturbed when Stanton informed Dolly that he had found himself a sheepmaster to take the place of Warren Inchcape so that Warren could be brought along on their voyage.

'It is harder to find a good free man in this colony than it is to pass a kangaroo through the eye of a fish bone, but I think I have found one. Nor is he Irish, either. It is our very own Senyor Lorenze.'

Stanton rolled from the marriage bed, stood upright and stretched his arms to the tips of his fingers and, cracking his knuckles one, two, and three, felt calmly satisfied as he climbed back into his work-stained trousers. He was fully in command of his wife after taking her to him for once. He was out of that bedroom door before she could expostulate his smugness.

'Matthew?' she cried unheard, heaving herself back on the bed among the disturbed linen, stuffing her mouth with lace to be quiet about it. It was no good any more going over the same arguments with him. Oh, she was going to have to revise her thinking on the double-shifting stubborn deep qualities in that Christian man her husband. They drove her to weep and regret her extremes of gifted love at moments of high heaven. The same qualities were also the foundations of their prosperity. That is what she needed to remember too. Keep her mind on that and she might get what she wanted without great fuss. Pray for it, indeed — harmonious success as perfect as their wool might be one day. There was no doubt that mixing with sheep and wool made people less Christian, not more, in this colony, and her husband was having to walk several narrow planks at the same time. What of the rules he was pledged to maintain when he kissed the Bible at his ordination? Vows that were so beautifully apt to their parts of England, that was the riddle — the moors and valleys of the East Riding, and the walks and byways of flat Cambridgeshire that they strolled with their evangelical friends and would do so again, under a soft sky that always seemed gently stirred by God's fingers. But there in dear old England all the soils were good, compared with the colony's, and upon the episcopal vine evangelical passion grew healthy. When it took hold it gripped without sliding too much. Not so much here because, as Matthew often said, God loves a green field, but in New South Wales there was a fair bit of rough and everything was dry sticks.

So if Dolly liked the luxury of fine linen and sea voyages as much as she admired her husband's rugged sermonising in the pulpits of the colony at fifty-two Sundays per year and Good Fridays and Christmases, she resolved she had better learn to shift with the winds of morality as he did, and sup with the Devil. He did it with his whips. She would do it with her silences. So she dried her tears and resolved. If Matthew wanted Warren on their passenger manifest, along with Titus, they would take them both, but she would make of the lumpen boy a meal of her own.

IVY STANTON CUT PAPER CONCERTINAS with scissors
of Sheffield steel and made fabric flowers from scraps of
hoarded cotton, in a household where every piece of service-
able stuff was used many times over, and even the tornest of rags
had a price.

Late in the day when it was hazy, hot and dull, the two girls, Ivy
and Leah Josephs, dressed themselves like boys in baggy shirts and
trousers and went out into the paddocks to look for dry daisies, and
found a good few. They meandered along the creek with twigs
and dried gum leaves crackling underfoot. 'Hurry up, Leah!' 'I'm
coming!' The sadness in Leah's eyes was some kind of accident of
looks. Her voice was never sad at all, only soft, dreamy, and deeply
feeling. The pain she felt in her lame left leg she never complained
about. When she was tired she stopped and found something interesting to talk about until she was ready to go on again. Every step
she took she dragged a toe, gave an ankle flick, and sailed
forwards. Ivy had altogether whispered to Titus to come and find
them, and after that, because they were dressed as boys, to lead
them the back way, along a defile of the creek, around to the wool

hall. They would watch the shearing and help roll wool and be mistook for boys till dark.

When they had stowed their flowers and climbed up into the fork of a tree, Ivy pulling Leah up after her, the girls held hands and fancied each other's hair and competed to boast which of the two had the palest inside forearms. It was Ivy and not Leah. She was up on the bullocky's waggon so much, and out on a ribby horse tailing livestock under the burning sun, though she buttoned herself down to the wrists and had a big wide floppy hat tied tight under her chin so it wouldn't fly off.

'We are up in the trees with the birds!' Ivy kept announcing. Every time she did so the birds flew off with a squawk. Leah felt a bit too hurriedly led by her younger friend into something she wondered about. But the feeling only brushed her as she went along with it. The sun blazed lower but slowly. In the heat, lengths of smooth bark cracked themselves from the trunks, started at the tops and slithered down rolling over with a clattering collapse on the ground. Scrolls and strips lay around like neck scarves made from terra cotta. There was life in everything, a dry breathing expanding sort of life where if something was too tight around a growing thing or person it was popped right off. It was what Leah always noticed, may be because she was lame. But could not believe she would always be lame because there was another way to be born out of this condition. There had to be — a way above restrictions, and that was the attraction of Ivy, who was definitely the most outbursting young girl of good family Leah Josephs had ever met. Ivy did not seem to consider that around her parents and the Christian Bible they thumped upon her, was a picket fence of rules to keep her in. She jumped it over, and the first place where she landed was in her mind, after which it was easy for her main part to follow. Leah was the other way around — certainly her bodily self had no trouble jumping into her mind, and in there she was freer. But only in there. Of the two, Ivy was the luckier, though not the safer, through being equipped by good health to run wherever she wanted, and be two persons at once if she wanted to be, until something bigger than herself stopped her, which she had certainly not met with yet. This reminded Leah of what she didn't want to know, that one person was one person most likely for ever.

Across in the sand below them a snake flicked into sight and drew itself along weaving its thumbthick head from side to side. It was a black snake with coral-red undersides and was claimed by their glances to be nearly ten feet long. Both girls knew it was pretty near deadly but neither allowed their thrill of fear to take hold because they were not shriekers aloud. A snake was able to come anywhere, even up a tree and along a branch sinuously persistent. But they only said, 'Hmm, a snake, it must be after a frog in the mud hole.' Most important around their calm reaction was their status as colonial-experience originals of an exceptional warp, with a sworn intent never to cry out betraying their brave disguise. It was certainly true, that Leah from horseback or up on the bullock waggon, and Ivy from a secret passion for climbing out along tree branches and entwining herself against forks with Titus, had both seen plenty of snakes without worry. In New South Wales you could walk all day and never see a snake but as soon as you got up on a horse or up in a tree you saw one. Nor was it just the red-bellied black ones that were poisonous, but the copperheads, the king browns, and the tiger snakes that were so deadly nobody lived longer than a few hours after being bitten by one. Except that few were bitten, only those who tormented them — such as a convict man who found one in a net on their fig trees, at the end of the last year, and tried to take it by reaching his arm in. He died in their barracks' air sheds the same night. But even to be afraid of tigers was a show of feebleness. Leah said she wanted a tree python as a pet, to carry along in the waggon, and Ivy said Titus would easily get her one. But to watch out he didn't throw it on the fire, because he had a liking for snake meat steamed in hot coals.

'You are lucky to have good brothers,' said Leah.

'Good? You could call them that. Everything they are put to is work. My brother Titus is the most amusing. Everything with Titus is a game. Then there is Warren,' said Ivy with an honest stare from those cold clear eyes, set in her pale small animal face. 'I like it when the rosehiller parrots peck bran from his lips, it leaves flecks of blood and he winces, but he stays still because I am watching. He is always trudging from one to another, dogs, cows, sheep, hens, guns, bluestone, turpentine, sheep tar, knife honing, kangaroo meat for dogs. He never slows down nor speeds up.'

'He watched me,' thought Leah, remembering a strong stare in the moonlight which she answered with her own. She was some-times watched by men with a such a strong look, there was something about her that drew them, but she felt with a boy, not a man, that she could ask him what he wanted and not just be answered with the gesture of the sort they gave round here that she could hardly interpret into detail, but quite understood, when men gave it.

'My father loves him,' said Ivy, 'and as far as it goes with him, which is a long way, he is kind to him.'

'Your father . . .' began Leah, sounding it as a question.

'How dare it if Leah says what she thinks,' thought Ivy. People were not wanted even to try, not even admired friends. If anyone was going to stand up against her father it was Ivy herself because she alone was equal to the strength of him, through the love that bound them. That story of him holding her by one hand above the waves that crashed into their cabin and swirled around their necks, the day she was born — that story was vivid in her mind, it was a memory. She rolled herself over on the strong square palm of his hand, and bellowed the waves to retreat, and so saved him the day he saved her.

But it was all right because Leah could not even come close to saying what she thought. 'If I did,' said Leah to herself, 'it would be about Parson Stanton's power to strike fear. That almost merry, fussy, farmer missionary parson magistrate, with a round face like a dented pewter teapot, I have seen his reflection in the eyes of my dear father so fiercely threatening as to be always obeyed.'

Ivy peeled bark and took a sharp stick, and started scratching her name on the delicate greyish-green parchment of wet sappy tree surface revealed under her hand. 'I wish Titus would hurry and come,' she said.

Leah saw Titus first. He loped along through the trees pretty certain of which great tree the girls were in. They had already climbed higher. When Titus saw the snake moving he slithered around it and then came on with a soft call of cooee. Ivy dropped her twig on his head and he swung himself up with nimble enthusiasm, laughing as he came level to Ivy's toes and then her fingers and then her eyes. He was so pleased to see her he took her hand in his and held it to his cheek. Leah did not know what to say, as Ivy squealed, 'You're a snake! I'm a frog!' — or where to look, except it was lovely enough to witness if every thought she had about a white girl having her fingers nipped by a black boy was lovely. She'd had some thoughts sometimes, that almost were, in her speculations of everything in the world, possible: and 'lissome' was a word coming to mind as they played innocently enough. They were brother and sister. But then disgust was another feeling too — of a kind saying how could Ivy dare in front of me. How could she carry on ignoring me. Is it because I am lame?

Leah turned aside and wondered if she was going to need help to get down. She had made drawings in her journal of the year, which she kept of every day they travelled. She went back to observing detail. Titus with his shirt open to the waist, his handsome laughing smile, his tufty brown hair. With his trousers like his name, low on his hips, and higher than his ankles.

Ivy's chin rested on Titus's shoulder as she looked at Leah from behind his back. 'My brother,' she said with exasperated pride.

Titus laughed, 'Yes please!' as she scratched and pulled his hair.

U P AT THE WOOL HALL there was commotion as one shearer and another found himself without a sheep when he let his shorn one go and looked around for the next to be brought along. The shearers were cantankerous, hot, over-worked and rum-thirstily disinclined to go wandering out to the forcing pen and begin hoisting one over the rails and dragging it back losing time. They were paid for the count of what they shore, not for their time spent fetching. They were paid little enough considering the fortune in fleeces the reverend sir was rolling from their indispensable contribution.

Over at the house still tucking his shirt tails in, Stanton heard Warren bellowing for Titus. He knew straightaway that Titus was missing from his station, where he was needed to bring up the sheep. 'Tap the glass, read the lightning, bring on the storm, by jolly,' said the minister, coming as close to blasphemy as his temper ever allowed. It was often around Titus and his inability to be Christianised. There was no other explanation for the ruckus but Titus sowing disorder. It was a complication from the issue of sheets and Stanton's absence from sheepwork for an hour upon them. But he was not going to whip himself — he that'd had his wife and got his ship all in a day. He was going to whip Titus.

Oh, and was it too much to ask of Titus to spend more than two hours following at any regular post? The reason he was present all morning working sheep, and part way into the afternoon, was that Stanton had been there to urge him cleave.

Stanton stayed controlled cool and detached at every moment of justice done. Rage was never part of his judicial means, no, not least as he pictured himself in the impromptu courts he held in settlers' huts and in various convict barracks and some time even under a tree or in a rock shelter smoked by the fires of centuries. It was true what the governor said, he was detachedly able to throw a sentence out over his shoulder as he departed his courts. But to criticise that was the wrong insinuation over a correct situation. When he journeyed back to England it would be to take a picture of order with him.

But as Stanton paced around the back of the wool sheds rage came to him and he wanted to taste what it was without restraint. The feeling was of a rasping tongue craving the food of cannibals. He grew hotter inside himself and denser with certainty over his task. Was rage not a tool of action sharper than hooks, if wielded upon the nap of mortal boys with skilful intent? Now he was going to make his first great excellence of hands' upon rage and make it openly, knowingly, and zestfully. It was a breathy feeling of sails filling with wind, bearing his destiny onwards and securing something distant by the close attention of the moment. Now he would come almost close to inner delight as a public lesson. It would be his second lustful outburst of the day, and the way he was feeling, might eclipse the other in its torrent of lava.

Stanton stalked past the Josephs's bulky waggon, where Martha Joseph called and asked if there was something from her kitchen he would like to refresh himself. He made no reply, merely issued a garbled denunciation of black boys, but then doubled back and saw, looped on a peg of the waggon, Mick Tornley's bull whip gone cold these past few days. Tornley paid no rent but lingered fattening his beasts on Stanton's pasturage and having Stanton's convict black-smiths mend his metal wheel-rims in Laban Vale's workshops. There was no question that reaching for Tornley's whip was his right. 'Needs warming up,' Stanton rationalised, pulling the sweaty dark leather handle across the palm of his hand and admiring the diamond-weave leather plaiting of the make. Before even the long length of whip was looped round his elbow Stanton ran along his way coiling it into his fingers. The latter part of it dragged in the dirt following him like a hurrying worm.

'There you are, come over,' Stanton called softly on sighting Titus hiding behind a tree. The minister braced himself with a leg forward, a leg propping himself back, angled his shoulders, gasped breath, heaved, and spun the whip out, not very skilfully, but accurately enough, as proved by Titus jumping this way, then that, to escape its stinging tip. Stanton was aware of onlookers to the rear of him but was blind to their importance and deaf to their calls for mercy. The listeners he wanted were in missionary halls in London: there to boast of black converts. The word went quickly around, that the parson had gone a little loco.

The first strike encouraged Titus back to the far side of the tree where he thought he was safest but he was not allowing for the whip to pin him there. It was a paperbark tree from which Titus tore strips of bark as rags to mop tears in his frustration. The lash came from one side and then from the other looping across his back as

Stanton advanced. The tip stung Titus's cheek and drew blood. Stanton with a breathy growl stepped closer shortening the lash each step he took. It was interesting to observe that the lash's thinningly tipped power touched more accurately each hop. The first voice he heard distinct from his own words babbling inside his head was Titus's crying out, 'I am sorry, Father, I am sorry, Father, forgive me.'

'Which — father — is — that — hmm? — that you mean?' Stanton cried out almost with joy to elevate the stakes of the battering. Being close now upon the sandy terrace around the tree he found Titus within the range of a mere few feet of weapon. He wished for an assistant to hand him an even shorter thong, appreciating the judicial craft of flogging better after this excursion along the dry part of the creekbed. It was hard for one man to do well with so many tangling coils.

'It is you, my heavenly father,' said Titus with confused sincerity, and a racking sob.

'Know before whom thou doth stand,' said Stanton, underscoring each word with a sharp short hit across Titus's narrow shoulders with the stock of the whip. He was in a good position to vary the emphasis, and did so, but was suddenly jolted from balance by a succession of blows on his back.

From the relentless pattering of the attack on him, Stanton thought it was a tree branch being wielded on him, but it was small fists raining on him. 'Horribilis crumpet,' said a voice in his ear, rising to a scream as he shook himself, and a strange boy he recognised as his daughter fell to the ground from being draped round his shoulders, there to gather herself and stare at him red-eyed with fury kicking her arms and legs in the air like a suffering insect, and then to get up and run to Titus and throw her arms around him so that she was imposed between him and her father and the whip.

Stanton put his hand on her shoulder to peel her away from Titus like the shell from a crab but could not quite do so. She was far too skilled at clinging to that boy. Now Titus was making a confession, his cheek on the tree bark's papery smoothness and his pewter eyes seeking Stanton's beseechingly.

'Lord bejesus save me from me sins, look down on me Lord bejesus, here where I lie, sorry, I'm too sorry, make me love you Lord bejesus, amen to God and the angels, doan whip me, Father, I'm hurtin enough. I'm saved now, I truly honestly am saved too.'

'Is this call saying you don't want to be hurt?'

'It is,' Titus began.

'Say no,' said Ivy against Titus's ear. 'Say it is cause you want to be saved.'

'Cause I love Jesus,' Titus nodded, diverting his poor arguments and Stanton relented, drew breath, and spat from his mouth a rubbery wad of spit.

His anger was not entirely appeased, but it was fed. He had a little more wisdom now than when he started, but not much. There was now a method to be followed, at least. Each day he would bring Titus forward a little more into faith and do it with the whip. This had not been properly tried as an effort. They would find themselves a private place and get down to it. He would acquire a short one and a very short one, riding crops, and carry the scourges with him and the Bible and have Titus point to passages and recite them. If it was the truth with pain it was doubly the truth, the goad of salvation.

'Bring him to the house. Wear my coat,' as most graciously, and with heartfelt consideration, and with a bout of steady breathing bringing himself back under control, Stanton removed the smock he wore for sheepwork and Ivy draped it over Titus's shoulders. His poor shirt was spotted with blood but not very badly.

'Hold my hand,' said Ivy, with a sob, and Titus, with his shoulders twitching and hanging his head, groaning as if some sort of true dramatic tragedy had befallen him rather than what he deserved, went off alongside her and Stanton followed.

'Titus is sorry,' said Stanton with a nodding smile as he walked past each little group of onlookers. 'Titus is very sorry for neglecting sheep. Back to your stations at once. Titus is very sorry indeed.' This he told each and every one of them and looked them in the eye, native women, shearers, the Spaniard, the bond stockmen and Warren Inchcape looking over the sheep hurdles from a face as pale as dusted flour. The shearers hardly cared who was flayed as long as they were handed their sheep and not flogged themselves. They had an imperious power of skill but no warranties of safety from whips, except they had been told before coming to Laban Vale — now to their utmost surprise — that Parson Magistrate Stanton never flogged his own staff nor attended a flogging in person.

Warren Inchcape looked on blankly longer than the rest, and then broke off, heading back to his work. He was the staunchest boy imaginable and more like a function of nature than a movable emotional being. Stanton called to him: 'Warren, take your tea break with the men. Sleep in the wool hall on the fleeces. I will come visit you there, and Warren?'

'What?'

'This is nothing and all to the good.'

'There are still four hundred sheep waiting,' said Warren, listing the tally, 'and nearly all those will have to be brought back in the morning.'

'So be it,' said Stanton.

Why those two girls were dressed as boys was another matter. It would all be winkled out smelling of gross disobedience and cant. A small hint of it came:

'Sir?'

It was Joe Josephs's daughter with tears in her lovely eyes tugging at his sleeve.

'Please do not punish Ivy,' she said. 'It is my fault. I honestly blame myself.'

'Whatever for?' said Stanton with a pale smile. 'What have the two of you done that is wrong, except diminish your sex by wearing trousers?'

'Tempted Titus,' said Leah, lowering those eyes that were deep pools of anguish in her face.

'Titus is a dish for temptation,' said Stanton.

'I writhed and wriggled, whistled and made bird calls, and drew him away from his work. I was bad.'

'You? I don't think so. You are a trembling innocent. Titus wouldn't have come if Ivy hadn't. You see, she is touched by the Devil and the reason you don't see it is that Jews don't have devils and hells to worry them. It all falls on Christians.'

THERE WAS A LOOK ON the girl's face of something like double-faced truth. A fear so great it resembled loyalty, perhaps. Whatever, Stanton could certainly make use of it on this day of days for gathering in waverers.

'Dear,' he caught Leah Josephs by the arm near the garden wall, guiding her shoulder away from the house and pointing her towards her waggon home across the flat, where her parents awaited her, no doubt dismayed over the shenanigans and wanting to quit this place. 'No harm shall come to you.'

'Or to my father?' the clever young girl came immediately to her point. The sheltering instinct and passionate adherence of her sex to principles based in feeling were things that Stanton understood.

'Far from it. I am his protector,' said Stanton. Then he thought for a moment and said: 'As Ivy's close friend you will make me stronger still, so better for all our interests. How can that be done? You shall write to her, sweetheart, she has so little care for books, but loves a gossipy letter very much, shall you make her your confidante?'

'If you don't whip her.'

'You have a bracing cheek and not just a faltering foot on you, my girl,' said Stanton. 'Not whip her? That is something I doubt you should ask of a Christian, if he is father to the child. But you have asked me, and I will tell you, a beating will make no difference to that determined, wilful soul. So there you have my vow: no beatings.'

'Then I shall keep my diary and will copy her pages every day.'

'She will learn from that, at least,' concluded Stanton, giving the girl's shoulder a squeeze. 'Now run along. We have had our argument and we have our agreement. Be sure you keep it or something bad will befall. I have not finished with Titus, but do not be alarmed on his account any more, I have put away my whips. Or shall do,' he added, realising that he still carried Mick Tornley's whip around his elbow.

'Let me take it,' said the girl.

'Hang it on the waggon peg.'

'I know where it is,' she said.

Limping the wide flat ground between the garden wall and the waggon, aching in heart and hip and toe, Leah Josephs felt creeping disgust at the feel of the whip. If required to handle a snake she would do so, with composure and courage. But a whip? It offended her.

'We are allies, that lame girl, her father, and I,' Stanton said to himself, as he went through the stone-wall gate and entered the back end of the garden. 'Her letters will keep me in touch, as I will ask Ivy to read them out to me and show me their drawings. These letters will be a check on wily Joe, for one thing, but only one resort of the several I have. Country cunning supports me. Do not put all your ewes to one ram.'

As Stanton went along under the trees he picked an armload of fruit and took it to the hut. Anything to avoid facing Ivy just yet, or his wife or Titus again or anyone irksome, nor anything to tire him when he was already drained weak to trembling from whipping and shouting and following along on his feet, through the heavy sand of the creek. Equal to seeing Titus at court with the king, done up in lace, he would like to see the back of that boy running into the bush. There was a fairly sure hope that Ivy, faced with the model of her English cousins — milkmaids, sheep herders, weavers, and hard-working woolstaplers all — would cast off her sharp colonial manners and come right. He would honestly rather wrestle with God and the angels than face Ivy again for a while. His texts and cajolings had little effect on the sense of rightness she gave out. He would join the Devil's camp before hurting another hair of her tossing head.

Over the great news of their finding a ship, he was holding back, although no doubt Dolly was spilling it around to soak up tears. The first one he wanted to tell was Warren. He so liked picturing the world through that boy's eyes as a way of getting away from himself that he looked forward to seeing the reaction on Warren's face.

Seating himself for a few minutes of calm on the bench outside Warren and Titus's hut, Stanton let the details of the voyage come on. The setting of sail, the farewelling of the pilot, the busy interest of shipboard life, the watch bells! A call at the Bay of Islands (where there were missionaries to be helped) and then the floating islands of the Pacific! Their lagoons and cannibals' grins at a boathook's length! The roaring forties and a skimming over the southern oceans like a leaf! The rounding of Cape Horn in peril!

The beat up the Atlantic via Rio! And then the Thames, and London! Most of all Stanton saw the two of them, stout man and stout boy, getting out in London and making their way through the crowds to Garraway's coffee house in Cornhill. Warren getting his land legs and wondering: Sir, what was there in a Change Alley coffee house apart from coffee? Oh, boy, wait until you see beyond this door. Wool. Displayed by the light of a guttering candle. Wool. The sale of wool occupying a crowded hour. All bids for wool to be in by the time the candle burned down to the next inch mark. The chosen bale knifed open and a fist of staple pulled out. The wondrously bright shine of perfection in which all this mess of today plays its part.

The fruit Stanton picked was all bird-pecked and some bad grubs looking out but that would be no worry to Titus. There was no cause for the boy to go hungry during the next part of his lesson when he was locked in the hut with the door bolted, and a bucket provided for personal needs. That was if Stanton could wrench him away from Dolly who was busy soothing him.

Let her take her time. Let Ivy go to bed and be asleep by the time Stanton looked at her again. Then Stanton would make an entrance to his house, take the boy by the bones of his neck from where he was coddled, lift him off his feet, ride him along and hurl him through the doorway of his hut so strong he'd fly over against the opposite wall but not to break it.

It was expected that celebrations of the shearing would be cancelled and the inauguration of the wool hall happen some other happier time, after the shambles of the afternoon left its wreckage of hopes.

But those who thought so did not know their minister as well as Matthew Stanton knew his olden-day pastorals and songs and dances of an earlier time. Nor did they realise that for every break Stanton made to the smooth skein of existence, there was a healing sap held in reserve to spread forgetfulness over his actions.

In his days as a Yorkshire sheep boy the shearing was a season of special rejoicing. Not in the sense of the bad old heathen pleasures of getting wenches with child, wronging the ancientry, stealing, fighting — God preserve him from those that could be avoided within the bounds of his own propriety at shearing time. But celebrations of a sacred, even a sacrificial touch. They were not just permitted but required. Dances, but with a formal purpose of decorating thanks and making praise. Toasts of a sacramental nature making wise as well as glad the hearts of the labourers after their wool harvest. Let there be an amount of largesse thrown around, for did not Cecrops, founder of the kingdom of Athens about the time of Moses, ordain that the master of every family should after harvest make a feast for his servants, and eat together with those who had taken pains with him in pulling the fleeces off?

True, although the flaying of Titus seemed more like a prelude to the account given in Second Samuel:

And it came to pass that Absalom had sheep shearers in Baal-hazor, and Absalom invited all the king's sons, and Absalom commanded his servants, saying, When Amnon's heart is merry with wine, then kill him.

It was only how Stanton felt. It was not what he would do. What he would do was something better. He would pull the knife back, and instead of dripping with blood it would shine with butter.

It was late when he went in to Ivy expecting she would be asleep. Dolly told him to go quietly as the girl showed signs of a fever. When Stanton shone a candle through the partly open door, illuminating Ivy's narrow face, she sat up in bed and yelled at him that she did not know him.

'I would say her fever has taken hold,' he nodded to his wife.

One who expected the shearing celebrations to be cancelled was Warren, who after bedding himself down in the wool piles and looking at the stars through gaps in the roof, cried and felt woefully sorry for Titus going to play when there was work to be done, for going off when he knew Stanton watched him closer than he watched them all, and if there was going to be an example first it would always be made on Titus.

Warren had started the sore events himself by bellowing for Titus and drawing the parson out. Warren felt like wringing Titus's neck at the same time as he loved him and wished he could be free like him, just by answering his own heart whenever it called. But there was an urge in Warren to do what was asked of him, and help run the country over with sheep.

Warren was never so strong on misery at Laban Vale until tonight. He wished he had never been pushed in the way of it by his mother and Warren Tait, wished he had never heard of Parson Stanton and fine-woolled sheep although, at the same time, the sticky soothing odour of grease in the fleeces filled his nostrils and gladdened him into dozing.

When Warren woke again the stars had barely moved. Boards creaked and a lantern moved through the sheds.

'Over here,' he called, and Stanton came and sank down beside him.

'Look what I have for you, Warren.'

On the flat of Stanton's hand was a sheet of sticky paper holding striped sweets, bonbons and comfits. They glistened in the smoky light of the tallow lamp.

'These are made by our newcomer, Paul Lorenze,' said Stanton, pointing them out with a square-tipped finger. 'Which is it strikes your fancy? Take one.'

In the first suck Warren had of a bullseye, a rule came to him: that if a man was a Spaniard he was apparently a maker of confectionery as well as a master of sheep. All day Clumpsy M'Carty had sent looks at him trying to convey something about Lorenze, and this must have been what the leering, tongue poking-outs and implying by fingers all meant, telling him to watch Lorenze for an advantage. The advantage that Stanton himself now delivered on a sheet of tacky paper? Warren admired Lorenze for his strangeness and strength — the man was like a panther in the careful way he fascinated a sheep and then had her cover off quick as a cat mauled a bird.

'Warren,' whispered Stanton. 'London! There is a ship being loaded with wool. It will take us.'

'All of us?'

'Sitting on top of the wool and holding on to the yard arms.'

'And Titus?' said Warren.

'This is Titus's night for feeling sorry and you are not to go to the hut, forbidden, do you hear? Not even to hear him digging under the wainscot and weeping like a native mouse to burrow through dirt and scamper away. The difference between you and Titus is that I never have to make any promises around you, boy.'

Your presence is guaranteed to me where you are wanted and that is a boon. After London we shall go up to Yorkshire and visit the mills that lie in narrow ravines and project their chimneys up into the moors. You will understand more by watching their noise in an hour than I can explain to you in a year about combing, carding, felting and all those other words we throw around to justify our yield.'

'I told my mother I should be chosen to go there, and she only smiled.'

'Dear fond mother that you have.'

Warren's eyes shone. 'There is a bird without many feathers reckoned still alive, that I would like to bring back. Its name is Car'away.'

'What are you talking about? That is only the native name of the bird, *Kakatoe galerita*, the white cockatoo. They belong in Botany Bay, not London.'

'There is an old lawyer keeps my inheritance under lock and key, the bird on a perch, in London.'

'What is this talk?'

'My father had a cockatoo.'

'George Marsh had a cockatoo, that attacked my whippets, when we all lived at Parramatta, when Ivy was a baby.'

Warren looked shiningly at the parson, preening himself and dusting sugar flour from his chest:

'George Marsh was my father.'

'Great heavens, Marsh your father, not an officer, as is held?'

'No.'

'I heard that he died. I am sorry.'

'I am to have his finery.'

'Where is it kept?'

'In a cabinet.'

'It won't be "finery", Warren,' Stanton mildly scoffed. 'It won't be coats with gold buttons, knee buckles and silk stockings and periwigs, don't get your hopes up, or rather your vanities, as I remember George Marsh as a rough plain man whose rigging was always ripped torn and muddied.'

'It is "finery" of some sort,' said Warren, hating to have his father reduced by anyone but himself now that his life was getting larger inside him in death. 'Say finery of the pen?'

'That is a plausible use of the word, I suppose. Well go on. It is curious enough.'

'Curlicues and wiggles. Drawn maps, copied documents, proper letters and printed books. Prob'ly a whole trunk full. So finery I say as I likes the word and will say it again.'

'May be we can look at your finery together,' said Stanton, 'when we get there' — not pushing the point too hard, but wild at the thought of looking into Marsh's dossier. 'I am always interested in the discoveries of our early men.'

'You can help me find my way,' said Warren, 'as from what I've heard, London is a jumble of streets and lanes made for getting lost in.'

'I think I've told you that. It will be my delight to guide you where I can, and you shall need me,' said Stanton eagerly.

'You'll need *me* more than you think,' the boy crowed before throwing himself back into his nest of wool, and waving his writing finger in the air, 'as it is all written up in the lawyer's hand, that without my going there, my inheritance can't be claimed by anyone.'

AT FIRST DAYLIGHT STANTON WENT down on his knees sincerely praying for guidance while from the corner of his eye peered hoping his wife was stirred from sleep enough to see his humility being proved.

They seemed to have signed a treaty without formalities. They would take Titus with them and be done with it.

To save his wife's feelings Stanton resolved that when Titus next howled under his punishments, it would be done in small parcels out of earshot of all. A mind set on action savoured its resources in advance. Even on a crowded sailing ship there would be spaces for instruction, what with waves crashing, timbers groaning, and winds screaming in the sky to cover any yelping out. Stanton as whip handler was come more alive in himself than he had at any time since his conversion when he was eighteen. That was when he lived amazed at the dimness of those without the light, and got such great lessons in contempt of unbelievers, twisters, waverers, complacents, dalliers and the like that he started seeing them everywhere and still knew where to find them.

———————

That morning early Stanton went down to the convict sheds to be sure his stock hands made a decent muster at the start of the day. His habit of close inspection set them grumbling but made their barracks the cleanest in Botany Bay. That notion of course was nothing to the bond stockmen unless it gave them more peace, less pain, which they found it sometimes did. So they scrubbed, scoured and broomed a little harder than they might have done. Even at shearing time they did their chores.

Their hammocks and bedding were rolled out on the stones for airing and sunning by the time Stanton surveyed them in the half hour after daylight. He was already warm from walking down there, in a white sweat with flushed undertones. In the early slanting sun the men sat on their benches elbow to elbow, spooned their bowls of grain to their lips and drowsily chewed their rations of salt meat and bread, sparing the minister his need to say grace over them because they were started ahead of him. The only times the inspection routine was broken was on Sundays, when he preached to them hard, or in wet weather, when they crowded damply indoors, or if there was illness — because when the stomach gripes struck in the close-packed brick sheds they affected them all.

Stanton noted that morning how the regulation jobs were done, the men had earlier washed at their water troughs using the sufficient soap issued them for ordinary purposes. Their bruised and sallow old faces were sere but bright with shine. For them too, thought Stanton, there was something of the bracing, clarifying mood of getting ahead the morning after a night of tears and recriminations. Such had been the mood of his house these past twelve hours that he was glad enough so early to get away from troublesome looks and goading silences into the fresh open air.

'Is you pleased all right with the shearing, reverend?' the bond men asked, while behind their bony foreheads he knew the unspoken question was really, 'Have you skinned him alive yet — that rapscallion boy?'

Stanton ordered new soap for issuing later, and told the convict overseer, Galvin, that if the men bathed fully after the shearing, and wore their clean coats, they would be rewarded an issue of rum and be called to the dedication of the wool hall at four o'clock.

'March them up at the sound of the bell,' he instructed, 'listen for four clear rings, repeated at half-minute intervals three times.'

The morning's response to the minister's round of inspection was satisfying but when Stanton went about the benches greeting the men and tolerating their muted rough silences he detected malevolence creeping up their lines. At first he blamed himself over Titus and glowered; then he stopped being so certain of his own position and observed what was going on. Something was certainly in the air between two groups of men, and where there was conflict that was not up his own nose, there was so often advantage for him that he saw room for himself playing two sides off, in the midst of his wool-taking fever.

The one he admired, Paul Lorenze, sat at one end of a bench; the other, Clumpsy M'Carty, sat at the far end looking as discomfited as Stanton had ever seen a prankster look. It occurred to Stanton that Lorenze had taken M'Carty's seat and stolidly refused to give it up. There had to be more to it, though. It was for the sake of convenient economy that Stanton had the shearers eating with the convicts. But while they saved on salvage, the shearers as free or relatively freer men disliked the idea of being marked by association with filth. There was that kind of feeling between Lorenze and M'Carty — only going well back.

Stanton drew the overseer away into his room. Galvin as sergeant of convicts was a former convict and straddled both worlds with worthy anxiety.

'M'Carty is dancing on hot coals,' said Stanton.

'Well, someone is sitting in his place, and he does not like it.'

'Is that all?'

'There's talk,' admitted Galvin.

'There always is talk,' pushed Stanton.

Galvin was a man in whom Stanton had fairly good trust as long as the question was on the letter of the law. Galvin liked pleasing Stanton and also airily pleasing his charges, and convincing them in their kind of language as to where their rights, such as they were, ended, and their obligations, endless in number, began, and how they would be eased of their worst troubles if they only paid him attention. If Galvin did not walk that narrow path he might wake up one morning to find his brains stoved in.

'They don't like Lehane,' Galvin further said.

Stanton felt for the something deeper down he was after all this time since Lehane was locked away.

'And?'

'Last night I found a knife,' said Galvin, 'being passed round the barracks' room when I went through on the midnight watch, long after they was all settled in. One of our light-fingered gentry, with more skill as a cutpurse than brains, had lifted the instrument from Lorenze's kit. A narrow steel filleting knife falls to the floor and I gets me foot there on it.'

'I thank you for telling me. Lorenze is a good man. He does not deserve bothering. Have you any names?'

'It was Clumpsy M'Carty, that showy man, who flashed the blade around a bit, and boasted catching starlight on its Toledo steel. He held that knife longer than he should have done, when he was heard to say he intended to knife him, Lehane.'

Stanton said nothing. In earlier circumstances, well known, the theft of metal with or without statements attached called for floggings.

Without much help Warren mended smashed hurdles and held aside a dozen ewes that Stanton wanted to look at. Their wool was broken and sparse, some came away in the hands with only a tug, and Stanton told Warren the matter was what the sheep ate. 'Or did not care to eat, for a reason you can help me to find.'

To get his diagnosis Stanton went around grabbing sheep's heads, tipping them back and forcing mouths open to look at their teeth.

'These are the oldest animals I have, they are all my favourite old breeding ewes. I call them the champion ladies of Laban Vale, but they are almost no good any more.'

'They are no good at all,' said Warren. 'We were saving them for last in the shearing in case they died and got in the way.'

'What would you do, that I have not done with them, apprentice sheepmaster?' taunted Stanton as they raised dust around them. Sometimes to keep up conversation they shouted over the sheep's backs.

'They are all broken in the mouth.'

'I can see that, you know.'

'I would not have held on to them for as long as you have.'

'Six years is a good time,' said Stanton, 'in working sheep, in our years around sixty. They have another year in them, according to able practice, taking them up to seven. If they were pets they might live until ten or thirteen. In Yorkshire a sheep lived to twenty.'

'I don't believe you,' said Warren.

They retreated into the shade of the one tree that spread its high crown in the direction of the yards. Twigs fell on the sheep's backs from white cockatoos biting branches and letting them fall.

'Wait till we go "over thar",' said Stanton. 'I shall take you up in the hills. The ones mountain shepherds call *guide* sheep are old wethers kept on purpose to guide and direct the bleating flocks. They live a long time because they are hardy and allowed to live out their span without being put to the knife. We shall live to one hundred if we eat only green food and drink stream water like them and stretch by climbing rocks all day and pray that we're not taken early for our sins. We might see that sort of age of sheep in New South Wales, I reckon, as they walk so far for water. In my home-town hills I once saw a yearling wether that became quite fat with only one tooth. It worked a cavity in the upper jaw where the corresponding central tooth was missing. Sheep are like that, they juice every last fibre and honestly extract victuals from sandy wastes. I knew a young man, when he was true to sheep, unspoiled with ideas of another role — who had a ewe that yeaned a pair of lambs when she was a shearling.'

'Oh?' said Warren, grabbing the next animal so that they could both stand by her, and guessing who Stanton meant from his tone of voice.

'She had two pairs a year for fifteen years, and in her last two years produced single lambs. A brilliant shepherd, but a lesson of care was misplaced on him. These ewes are some of the last of his progeny's line.'

They were sheep that were going to be killed.

'Neglectful of sheep,' echoed Warren, 'was he, but how?' — more to see where Stanton's thoughts were leading than to aggravate him, and not at all to cast doubts on Kale's high place with flocks, which was an opinion buried fast in his blood.

'Say there is someone superb in his work but always drunk on the job. That is like saying, build the timbers of the cathedral, carpenter, then burn the place down.'

Warren turned aside. 'Seven, look, *she* is seven if you go by the mouth,' he said, dipping his head and opening an animal's jaw.

'Seven or eight may be. It gets hard to say. This tooth and that are loose ones. Less than half your age, Warren, is considered old age in a useful sheep. Seven — it is a sacred number in life because ten times seven makes our own blessed allowance of three score years and ten. There was never an animal so finely calculated to serve man in its adaptations.'

Stanton took hold of a ewe that was aberrant, with horns, where the eleven others were polled, and he seemed to want to make the trembling creature stand for all sheepkind before it died its coming death.

'This animal, the God-given sheep, is one of those specially destined to support man with his flesh. Unlike those bullocks of Mick Tornley's over there, it can pull grass up by the roots, when it feels the need. The gassy fermentation of its four stomachs needs mould to neutralise the acids of the gut, and the Lord has made the roots of grasses mouldy, although in this climate, in a form our eyes can't see. It is all one creation. I would fly at Mick Tornley for treading over my home range with his draught bullocks, except the sheep bites closer than the ox — don't you, old Bessie — she was designed in many places to follow the other, and eat where the bullock don't take a single blade. Seven sheep for the seven ages of man seems like a gift we must make best use of.'

'Yes, but the teeth,' said Warren.

'If any of the teeth are loose they should be pulled, and a chance given for the animal to go on. I have seen ewes with broken teeth and some with all their incisors gone keep pace in condition with the best of the flock.'

'It might have been true with your ladies last year,' said Warren. 'But now they are past having them pulled.'

'You are the expert,' said Stanton, fondly rather than tightly, as he liked Warren's bigness of purpose as good as any wit or accuracy. He even liked his rebukes. They had so much trust in them.

'They will live but they won't fatten,' said Warren, 'so they are useless to the butcher, and their wool is broken.'

'You have learned well.'

'I seen it all with my own eyes. You have made a mistake. I wasn't here last year, when they were five or was it six, but that was the time to fatten them and supply their places with the most likely shearing ewes.'

This was all well known to Stanton but he said:

'I consider myself better educated now than when I started out before daylight, Warren. Have you seen your brother Titus this morning?'

'I spoke to him through the crack in the door,' admitted Warren.

'Didn't I say not to go to the hut?'

'Last night you did. So I didn't go then, as you asked me.'

'How did you find him, awake?'

'He said he was tired and going back to sleep.'

'Did you offer to let him out?'

'No.'

'Good, and that is our Titus all over,' said Stanton. 'Why, remember one day he slept until ten, though something told me he was awake half the night, and then there was the time —'

A few more maladroit instances followed.

WHEN STANTON WAS DONE WITH building Titus into a more affectionate frame of opinion, he fanned his face with his hat, drank a mug of water, and felt pleased enough in the coming heat of the day to leave the shearing get on. He stepped clear of the yards and stood with the sun behind him gazing around the open spaces. Warren took a few steps up, wondering if they were all his orders or if there was something more to come. There was usually a word of dismissal at least, but Stanton looked over his shoulder and said, 'They are taking their ease.' He meant the Josephs still waiting for justice over Lehane. He was not thinking about Lehane. The only part of him thinking about Lehane was the part denying he was thinking about Lehane at all.

Across at the Josephs's, smoke skeined up from a fire. There was not much movement, and a feeling of calm to be envied against the stir of the busy day's life.

'Where is our help coming from, saith the Lord. Is it from our friends? I don't think so. Not today.'

'They are not giving me Artie and Solly, their pa said so.'

'That is almost understandable,' said Stanton. 'It is their Sabbath day, after all. So how shall we do it? You can push up the four hundred on your own, with your willing dog, but not hand each man his sheep. The shearers were muttering into their gruel when I met them earlier and I see them coming over now, they'll be here to start before long.'

'The blacks, all husbands and wives are promised a sheep if they put in the morning bringing them up.'

'Give them one of our old ladies, then.'

'One is nothing, they are so thin.'

'Then make it two. Be sure they are sheared first. The wool is tawdry, but every strand counts. Save my old Bessie from the knife when you make your choices, I have a whim to see how long that old lady lives, because I remember the parable of Nathan, in Second Samuel twelve.'

A weepy pride in stock was apt to come out.

'There were two men in one city,' he said, 'the one rich, the other poor. The rich man had exceeding many flocks and herds, but the poor man had nothing but one little ewe lamb, which he had bought and nourished up, and it grew together with him and with his children. It did eat of his own meat, and drank of his own cup, and lay in his bosom, and was unto him as a daughter.'

Stirred by his own sentiment, Stanton went up and broke open the door of the hut, throwing sunlight over Titus who lay on the floor with his knees up under his chin and softly snoring. It was past seven when he would normally be breakfasted but no attempt had been made to break out. The innocence of the thatchy-head boy touched Stanton, his useless dependence, his legs mere trembling grass stalks, and he stood watching Titus a full minute before the tangle of limbs stirred and the boy rolled back his eyes. 'There you are, did you have dreams?'

'Bad dreams,' said Titus, touching his lip, which was scabbed.

Last night Dolly had dressed his few cuts, which were in no way serious, with tincture of iodine, and then without too much argument, except in her eyes, she had given Titus over to him to be locked up.

'Get up, Titus,' Stanton said. 'Do not be afraid. You are feeling sad, I can see. But that is all right. Broken hearts soak up Christian consolation better. Hold this Bible and read the text I finger for you. Read it along with me. Come over into the light. You are limping. Are you sore?'

'Only a bit.'

'Are you sorry?'

'I'm too sorry.'

'Sit here beside me on the bench.'

Stanton liked teaching a lesson where a random text formed the inspiration for a moral and could be twisted into an explanation fitting the moment. Somehow it proved that God was everywhere, when it didn't prove that argument was endless. 'Lord God, guide my inspiration as we turn to your word,' he said, plunging his finger in. He had never been stumped and did not expect to be baffled by so silent and deflated a debater as Titus.

The text Stanton touched and read aloud in the first verse ran:

Then saith Pilate unto him, Speakest thou not unto me? Knowest thou not that I have the power to crucify thee, and have power to release thee?

Before Stanton could draw breath, the reply ran quickly from Titus's mouth:

'"Bejesus answered, you couldn have no power gainst me, cept it was gibben you from above dere, but he that delivered me unter it didden have no power at all."'

Stanton had no energy left in his rage. Only his rage.

'That is not exactly what it says, Titus.'

'I am a no good pluddy reader,' said Titus. 'I can't make it no better. Have we done for today? Am I good enough?'

'No, you are not good enough,' said Stanton, mentally pledging his vow of the day before, to whip Titus repeatedly and hold him over the printed word and push his nose into the clean clear smell of the rice-paper pages of the authorised text until he loved that book as well as he loved his own ragamuffin neckerchiefs.

'Look, Titus,' he took the boy's arm, and grabbing it between his palms twisted Titus's skin in opposite directions to make it burn. 'You are a pest to me and a nuisance.'

'This is hurtin.'

'It is going to hurt all the time inside you until you love God,' said Stanton.

'I lub God,' Titus spilled his tears, and Stanton, with a farewell jab, let him go. He remembered he liked bullying when he was a boy, though feeling ashamed of its easy victories over smaller fry. It was one of the confessions he made when he took holy orders. That he hit lesser boys. Now he had the feeling back with nobler justification.

When Titus's tears were dry they went to a better passage, in another chapter of the word:

'"O wretched man that I am! Who shall deliver me from the body of this death?" Your turn.'

'I tank God true bejesus Christ our Lord. So den with the mind I meself serve the law, but with the flesh the law of sin.'

'That is you, Titus.'

'It's me, I swear,' said Titus. 'My flesh is tore with sin.'

'You do not have the least idea of what you mean, but the

words flow through you, like the biggest river in flood, carrying understanding that glues like mud and debris of meaning. That is all I can hope for. Titus?'

'Yes, Father?'

'Run along and ask the cook for your breakfast. Then go down to the yards and help Warren and your black fellows bring up sheep. And Titus?'

'Yep?'

'No smoking your pipe, as I want your voice peerless clean for singing at our shearing celebration tonight.'

The ditch was dug in length and breadth about the size of a large male sheep, but only about six inches deep. Lorenze supervised preparations under authority granted by Stanton. He relished directing Clumpsy M'Carty with the spade. 'Dig him as large as when he is stretched from his forelegs out to his backs legs pulled as long as a man's.' This instruction surprised Clumpsy about size, and he muttered over the amount of work being exaggerated for the sake of one operation of sheepwork. It was a shallow grave. Clumpsy stared around with warning in his eye, beckoning to Warren, wanting to whisper his worst misgivings about the new favourite (Warren being the only one he could trust) and fancying that after dark he himself might be fitted into this hole a still warm, tormented and very dead Irishman, if his silence was so important to Lorenze's security at Laban Vale.

'What is it?' Warren said.

Clumpsy believed that Lorenze might kill him because he knew too much about him. But Lorenze was listening, watching, calculating, and Clumpsy, resting on his spade handle, ironically relented:

'Your Spaniard is always kind and gentle with his flocks, ain't that true, Senhorato Lorenze, you are a contradictory sort of a race and don't go round castratin every ram lamb, you let em live out their life for the sake of getting more weight in the wool, and when you do have that little operation to do on the eggs, you don't use no knife, no siree, you are all tenderness as you go squeezin the scrotum and twistin the sphermatic vessels more kindly. Though I have heard of it done with stones on a man, it's like an appeal is made to you by the poor craythures, dear things, they beg for their lives, you understand their bleats better than anyone's words, and you deal out your pity.'

'Forget the heggs. Come here this ends,' said the Spaniard. 'Cut hims down and across.' He showed where the earth was to be dug. More people came down to watch and Clumpsy was made dumb by their presence.

The second ditch, slightly shallower, was worked across the top in the shape of the cross that bothered Joe Josephs so much when he and the parson had talked, although the shape did not hold Joe back from watching now. He was cured of resentments by forgiving his enemies their sins and his friends their ignorance in his morning prayers. He wore his top hat to protect him from the greater power of God, having made his meditations under a gum tree and anyway being of a consuming curious temperament, hating to miss out on anything interesting going on, just in case he was brought bad luck by not being in it.

The place was prepared at the side of the wool hall on bare earth. Joe was crowded either side by his two sons and his daughter. Solly with his head stuck through his father's spindly legs kept asking, 'When does it start?'

'When they do it. Stand back.'

'**D**OES A SHEEP FEEL PAIN?' Leah said.

'They feel like us, they don't like showing it, but it is soon over for them,' said Warren. 'They are either strung up with their throats cut, or they are let go, and soon they are back on the grass just as happy as they ever was. Their life is pretty good.'

The answer did not seem to please Leah as much as he thought it should. 'Thank you, Warren,' she said.

'Leave Warren to his rams,' said Stanton.

He wanted Ivy to go back into the house and rest.

'I'm not sick,' she said.

'You are looking pale.'

'It's just that I am feeling something, but not in my stummick,' she said.

Ivy took Leah's hand, clung to her, leaned on her. They sat on a log with their wide calico hats shading their complexions. They placed their hands inside their sleeves which they pulled well down, and seemed to burrow into themselves. Ivy resented her father with poisonous concentration of betrayal while Leah feared

Stanton yet retained a sense of what her power was. These were their separate interior thoughts when Stanton came over to them again, having worked out a plausible threat. Leah's father was with him and Stanton made it sound as if he and Joe were of one mind:

'Well, Leah, I shall let you decide for Ivy's own good. Take her home for a rest as soon as you can, or she shan't be able to join us at four, when the bells ring the celebration.'

As Stanton met Leah's eye she lifted her chin provocatively.

'If she allows me, sir.'

'You must do as the parson says,' said Joe.

Loving her own father complete, Leah only somewhat pitied him for having his weaknesses and thanked herself for strengthening him, without his having any idea that his lame daughter was able to do it. Her difficulty was in believing there was any part of a living body where pain could not reach. There was a point where hard horn grew into flesh and feeling. It was like the cuticle of a nail.

'Don't they feel it in close?' she asked Stanton, standing and stumbling a little as she always did when rising. Blood rushed into her worse leg with a sheeting tide of pain. Turning back to the sheep subject kept everyone concentrated on being understanding with each other because sheep were their attachment in common when they had nothing else lending to kindness. When a mob of sheep bleated it was like a hundred pleading hands.

Leah touched her temples, the seat of her most painful understanding, and made it clearer what she meant.

'Warren says they hurt like we do, he's seen it in them. But they forget a lot sooner.'

'It is reasonable to think so,' said Stanton. 'They are given no sense of time, that is their consolation. We have a sense of time but we get our consolation much higher, through the knowledge of mortality they are born to ignore. Our need of their contribution to us beautifully balances their condition. Certainly they are glorified, as well as put down.'

May be Leah did not realise how obviously it showed why she wanted to know. Just to watch her was to see her wince, when she thought nobody was looking. Her burden of pain was the paleness seen sometimes under her olive skin — flickers of white fear, tensioning of nerves. Pain was her closest companion with a character all of its own. It spoke to her of the world, but she loved the world. Otherwise she could not live.

Stanton placed a hand on Leah's head and gave a consoling chuckle. May be as a boy in a baby's smock he once asked the same sensitive questions. Now he was past feeling too much where it did not count.

He said that while bone and horn grew out of the same nerve ends, they spread in contrasting directions through the devices of nature. The blow would be struck where it would hurt no more than a fingernail being scissored.

So Ivy said, 'Then why hold him down?'

'It is not like you, darling, to dwell too much on finesse. You are more like your mother, with a touch of that understanding oppression, dare I say kindly cruelty needed for survival in this land. It must be the influence of your clever friend,' said Stanton quite openly nasty, as he told the Josephs: 'Usually the girl has no compassion for animal feelings unless they are pets, certainly in any circumstance that I ever remember.'

So this was on Titus, and Ivy frowned. It was on Titus being trapped against a tree and whipped like a dog.

Stanton placed a sheep between his legs.

'Come here, girlies. Feel it here, along these ridges,' he said. 'Numb bone.'

They felt in among the greasy corrugations, but all they sensed was the fragility in the bumps of their own heads, as Stanton's voice peaked saying where the bone should be cut. He let the sheep go and demonstrated by pointing to the sides of his own forehead with his two index fingers like the horns of a devil.

'Neither too close nor too far out. Mind, don't slip,' he warned his working men.

Neither of the mothers wanted to come and see. They were in the wool hall sweeping the floor and stringing up decorations now that the wool was bundled to one end, and the shearers had finished their work. They had little to say to each other, being only polite. Their husbands and children might have mutual advantages to enjoy to the level of friendship but not the wives. Dolly Stanton carried on a running commentary on their home voyage to England. There was a cottage with low doors, where May bush grew along a brook, an old dappled cow in a barn, there were apple and pear trees in a hollow squared in a stone wall, and white sheep spread along a hillside, not brown sheep dirty with dust as they had here.

'Oo, England!' said Martha, seemingly going along with Dolly Stanton in her longing to see an old home, and the ancient couple that lived in it, spending their days weaving in an attic and going to church on Sundays.

Not that Martha ever had an old home to be called as such in the stews of Whitechapel, where they all lived in one room, three generations together until their parents died and some strangers pushed in. Nothing to be called a home anywhere else fixed on land, either, except what satisfied her here — for these days she wanted for nothing more than she had on the move — a carpet, some cushions, tarpaulins, stools, and trunks of household treasures making a transportable kitchen that could be unpacked and readied in as short a time as it took to get a campfire blazing, which was never very long in a country with sticks and logs for the taking lying scattered around the bush everywhere.

There was a thrill in the heart of Martha Josephs that she would never have to go back there, to London. Never! Her sentence was for life transportation and she was an exile and thankfully so. The only part she missed was the sound of the bells. She too was born within the sound of St Mary-Le-Bow, in Cheapside. When the men fitted the bell into the tower of the wool hall they tried it out by ringing. It took her right back. When the tinny echo stopped she only laughed. 'Enough of that, then, me lovelies.' Still, she responded as if enviously every time Dolly spoke a word and it was all she needed to say:

'London! Home! Fancy! And all of you going?'

'Yes,' from that wire-lipped, precise little ferret-like woman's mouth.

'Hurrah, then, eh?'

'Hurrah, yes, Mrs Josephs, hurrah.'

Martha returned to the waggon to prepare for the festivities that would be signalled by the ringing of the bell. As she came around behind the big tree she saw their camp in the sunlight deserted by them all. It was given over to the birds, a pair of wrens who swooped through the thin smoke of the campfire, and a team of swallows who darted in to wrench strings of fibre from the doormat Martha had in front of the waggon. Nests were everywhere, some of feathers, some of twigs, some of mud, some of jute. Over by the creek there were other birds unseen but making their calls like tin whistles, like clarinets, like glassy bells. They were all piercing beautiful and strong, even the calls of birds no bigger than a baby's toe that lived in the thorn bushes. Gratitude overwhelmed this small, stout, energetic woman who was equal to her husband in the business of concealing and selling varieties of stolen goods, artful in the practice of forging signatures and altering letters of ownership on valuables lifted from safes.

AT THE HORNING PIT THE moment was arrived. It was hardly a joyous atmosphere generated but rather a feeling that if anyone put a foot wrong there would be another lesson of opinion.

'Get the boards up,' Clumpsy M'Carty was told. 'Do what Lorenze tells you, man.'

Clumpsy had the shadow of death rising in him and was waiting for nightfall to get away. They said that when you were the chosen one, and your number of days was up, there was a limit to the dodges you could make, the Deil would be there before you: call him fiend, adversary, old scratch, old gooseberry, old horny, his satanic majesty, or the harrowing minister's sheep shearer in person, the Deil's deil, Lorenze.

The Spaniard lifted his hand as if to deliver a blow but was only shading the sun.

In the upper ditch the plank was fixed to support the head of the ram being marched over. Warren and Titus struggled him across, one on each side of the horns. The Spaniard waited with his mallet ready to strike.

The ram was worked in, stood, inspected, lifted, rolled, and collapsed on his back, the plank supporting his head. Then the Spaniard lay in the ditch forming the trunk of the cross. The side arms of suffering were the horns themselves. Stanton gave the signal, at your own pace proceed. Clumpsy M'Carty knelt, stretching his body over the whole body of the sheep. Pass me into your hide, he prayed, as I believe you are to be saved and I am not. As if he was having a woman for the last wild improbable time Clumpsy held the noble head forcibly to the board with one hand by grasping the jaw, while in the other hand he held a large bolt chisel, weighing four or five pounds and darkly thick. The smile on Lorenze's lips was satirically reversed from the way it might have been, had he been the one in Mudowey forest. He brought the mallet slowly up. The girls decided they had seen enough and went to the wool hall to help their mothers.

'Take your last look at their glory,' said Stanton of the horns. They reached either side of a grand old head that was white-whiskered and strangle-eyed with fear. This ram would never have looked at the sky before unless cast on its back in unfortunate circumstances — say by being tossed and spun through the air by a rival sire. Now he was held and the horns were exposed to the sky in their full unwinding and addressed the sky in their helplessness. Hard-ridged, dirty-yellow as poor men's teeth, showing a mess of nicks and cuts, the horns made a scraping bumping noise on the board. Horns were the cage in which a ram's days were passed but lucky the ram as he carried his cage with him and trawled it over the grass.

The Spaniard's dirty boot was wedged against the butting plate of the ram's forehead, where Slumberous had fought his lifetime's mating battles and now faced compacted sheep shit on a hobnailed sole of leather.

'Would that our brains were as protected as his,' said Stanton to his dwindled audience. 'You see, a very small portion only of that which actually covers the brain can receive the concussion in a ram fight. This is an evident proof of design.'

Clumpsy's fingers on the chisel were slippery with sweat as the hammer was raised. Men watched from above.

'What do you see?' said Stanton conspiratorially.

Not wanting to indict anyone, Joe said, 'I see they are ready.'

'Do you see who trembles most?' said Stanton. 'The one lying prone is my man. A most egregious Irish convict dissembler, M'Carty by name. As soon as he gets up from finishing the rams I shall have him confined and a constable sent from Parramatta to lay out the charges. He is ready to blab already. By jolly, I have long wanted to flog him deep in his rotten flesh and now is my chance.'

The candour of the minister around his decided actions was as excellent to Joe as it was categorically offensive.

Lorenze brought down the hammer and the horns fell off clean.

The Irish flashed their eyes at him, and their mouths said oh.

The first ram done, the boys rolled Slumberous to his feet, freed him into the yards and brought over the second one. Stanton picked up the broken horns and presented them to the trader. Joe carried them over to his waggon, one on each shoulder with his thumbs stuck in the hollows of their broken ends. He set them down on a sack, admired them for a minute thinking how long they would be when elastically straightened in the heat of a fire built over sand — dirty yellow horn made nobler and stretched into gleaming trumpets and blown in the direction of God. They would make a rough plaintive scratch of sound, far-travelling music, harsh with pain and longing, and true to the experience of living man. Joe would not like the parson to hear it, for what horn told was not life always being made better or complained against or imagined into a kingdom come. There was no sort of pledge in twisted horn: just an appeal.

Just thinking about it made Joe gather his loved ones into his thoughts — Martha with her shrewd brain used for protection of their family and getting on; Leah and her lovely long face uplifted to the light, her eyes always swimming a bit in tears, her tears diamonds squeezed from the pain she carried, that was never getting any better, and broke their hearts thinking about it; Arthur with his music rousing joy in the dust of New South Wales as he began the craft of wool sorter, only avoiding the dodgy part of Joe's career in making his pa the model of persistence. Finally there was Solly, young but drawn to his eventual destination, stuck to their ways like a barnacle at the same time as he was their authentic wild colonial boy in the making.

Stanton told Joe he would try Lehane in the morning and sentence him. Joe said very well, then he would tell Mick Tornley to have the team ready to roll out when it was done to their satisfaction.

But it was all Joe could do to refrain from telling Mick to harness his bullocks straightaway, so they could steal off without delay, from depth of shame in witnessing how it went at Laban Vale. It was all Joe could do to refrain from hissing the wronged to himself, that they might ride with them on their bullocks' backs as far as they wanted.

After his arrest for the too fanciful crime of saving Desmond Kale in the Mundowey forest, Clumpsy M'Carty was put in the police cells with Lehane at the far end of the barracks' room sheds. The door was bolted and padlocked — top, bottom, and centre — with a loud and important slam. Sergeant Maurice Galvin attached the keys to his belt waist and marched away to report to the minister that M'Carty was tight held. 'I have written myself inter the ballad of Desmond Kale,' said Clumpsy with glum satisfaction. 'I have purchased me fame.'

Galvin returned in less than half an hour to raise a lantern to the sombre grille and ask the new prisoner if was he was all right.

Clumpsy lay on the bricks with his hands behind his head keeping busy count of the few stars he could see. 'I have tobacco, soup, a bone with meat on it, and you have already promised me that when the boys come back from being spoiled by my accuser they'll bring me a little rum.'

'Here is a blanket,' said Galvin, pushing one through the bars. 'Are you all right in yourself? Do you need any more comfort?'

'You mean as one who might get himself hung and wants to confess his innocence?' said Clumpsy. 'Nay, I'm done.'

'I'm a great lover of the Church and clergy,' said Lehane from his corner, 'willya send me a praist? I've been unjustly accused by a Perrotestant one, but don't let that out too loud. I would not like to spend another night behind lock and key, thank you.'

He made it sound like the prideful sulk of an heroic man, but was terrified of his new cellmate and soiled his pants.

'Who would pray with you I'm not sure,' said Galvin. 'There ain't a blessed father for close on fifty miles, Lehane, even if one was allowed to travel to you, or could be bothered. Paugh, use the bucket.'

'No one'll stick up for me more than one that gets the mass preached,' said Lehane in a soft whimper. 'There's one named Kevin Cahill.'

'Listen to the eye of reason,' said Clumpsy, 'Robespierre's vindicator, the republican's voice box they call him.'

'The sufferin sick are helped and consoled by a praisthood generally doin what it is their special business to do — to lighten the cares and troubles of the poor and encourage em in their daily struggle.'

'I hear something lively,' said Clumpsy. 'It sounds like the magic scream of a fiddle.'

The two men inside the cell and the one standing outside fell silent.

'That is a great piece of fiddling,' said Galvin.

'Oh, I'm mighty pissed off and fecking jealous I'm not there,' said Clumpsy. 'I'd be singin with fire in me veins to that uncanny music, as the one thing you can say of himself, is that when he wants to roll himself out drunker than the rest of us, he makes sure we are pissed to the gills so that he looks good. They say there's somewhere he has the name of a reformer and a marvel with making some poor souls happy. I don't know where that place might be where he has that good repute, but I believe it is some-where else, a long way from here, in the missionary fields of the Maori islands, where they think he's a benefactor and pray for him.'

If Clumpsy had a prayer it would be to Kale and ugly Tom:

'It is your old mate M'Carty calumnified and a raid must be mounted to unshackle him fast, as he's runnin out o'breath.'

HORSES WERE SIGHTED IN THE haze of late afternoon and Stanton declared it was evidently the start of an expedition seeking out land.

The animals appeared down a line of track a mile away. 'It has to be someone,' was the informed opinion of a shingle splitter razing a tree near the front gate.

Rare gentleman adventurers travelled in a quick exalted style, threading through the bush like accelerated shadows. The leading pack animal's head swingled low, where the likely alternatives in this country were bullock dray and foot — or was it the carrier of fleeces, J.J. Tharpe? 'See who it is, anyway,' said Stanton, sending the shingle splitter out to ask, on a day when all were welcome: 'Would the strangers like to come in for a glass?'

The man wasted no time when he saw who it was:

'Your old servant Clumpsy's in the cells down yonder,' he told Ugly Tom, 'and he don't like his chances, seeing he's been thurrily dunned.'

The two riders needed no more urging than that, to turn in towards the gates of Laban Vale.

Stanton was mightily confused, and a little amazed, to see that one of the riders was Meg Inchcape (not very skilled on a horse, sitting awkwardly astride wearing a man's serge trousers raked up in the leg and showing red-chafed shinbone from the stirrup leathers). The other was undoubtedly Tom Rankine, of confusing reputation. It was their first meeting.

Stanton could only dissemble in the face of him with thoughts running wild. He stumbled as he walked out. Recovered. It would take him a few moments to steady himself, while the two dismounted.

'Good day,' he said, then half turned his back. 'Dolly,' he called to his wife. 'We have people.'

At the garden gate he made introductions:

'Dolly, darling, it is Warren's dear mother, and her, what shall I say now, "protector"?'

'Officer protector,' admitted Rankine, rather sardonically in the face of Stanton's red-faced bluster. His spinning mind was controlled by ironical detachment. 'Husband' was a word they were saving to say first to Warren.

'That is what I mean,' said Stanton. 'Officer protector.' But regretted the underlying slur in his tone, an affront to Meg Inchcape, though he'd not meant it intentionally towards her.

Then the two men smiled (smiles being the fog of diplomacy) and looked each other over. Their previous haunted sightings gave only a shape. Stanton could hardly remember what his imagination had detailed Rankine into. Look at him here: a man of average height (Meg taller), slim, grey, well proportioned, disfigured to a handsome extent by the pox scars peppering his cheeks and neck. He wore a coarse felt shirt open at the collar, old blue riding trousers, red-piped, high dusty boots and a sombrero hat.

Stanton forgot how his daughter had disgraced her sex by dressing as a boy. Mistress Inchcape could never be taken as male despite the men's clothes and felt hat she wore, with dents pushed out making a dome pulled down almost to the level of her eyebrows and with a pretty style of swagger. Her shirt was open three buttons down her flushed throat.

Rankine looked at the bulging-eyed Stanton in his frock coat and stockings and saw a dusty frog of a man, moon faced, pot bellied, springy legged, almost as wide as he was tall, with a vital energy so extreme it almost squeaked his gristle every time he twitched.

Stanton directed the party on with their horses. 'Over this way past the house yards, follow me.'

They fell to walking in opposite pairs.

Dolly irked Stanton by chatting rather too freely with Rankine as they walked along. Though gone quite silvery grey this Tom Rankine was still quite a young man, and she liked young men — flirting with them incessantly (admiring Rankine's mare, she 'loved a spirited mare') and Ugly Tom Rankine answering to her mood of excitable reference ('Arabian bloodstock and the latest arrived standing stallion are my two consuming passions').

You would never know from Dolly's chirps that when she and Stanton were alone since Titus was flogged she sent him to Coventry. You would never know from Rankine's murmurs about horseflesh that his consuming passion was sheep.

A groom reached the horses and followed behind.

Stanton lowered his head, chewed his knuckles, and looked around from under surly lids while taking breath and licking his dry lips in order to speak. 'Come along now, come along,' he croaked.

'Is Warren all right?' said Meg, as he escorted her across the dirt way. 'I never dreamed I'd see him today, not thinking I would, but oh how I wished to — here we are! Thanks to you, thanks to you for your kindness at Laban Vale. You are very kind.'

Stanton inwardly cursed Rankine for embroiling Meg in his plots. The lovely dear woman was babbling almost from fright, he supposed, over being put in a situation that Stanton was fairly sure (though not entirely sure) he understood. All except Dolly and including himself were in a condition of fright, and that was the case! Stanton felt shame for his own part in remembering how flushed and anxious to please Meg was, when he'd visited her hut — how her agreeableness must have meant fear, even then.

'Stop it. Please,' he heard himself chuckling to Meg. 'Warren is in the wool hall waiting. He is better than all right!' Stanton angled his shoulder to exclude Rankine and Dolly, and his own worse self: 'Let me hurry you along, ma'am, and say, Warren is better than he ever was, and up to his belly in wool. As to some news, I am full of it, but cannot speak of it.'

'News?' The word evidently startled her.

'There's been a rider from the governor with it.'

The look of questioning pain in her eyes — he would not stand for it.

He consoled her: 'Great news, that I shall leave Warren to the pleasure of telling you, madam, and then it shall be my turn to ask you a question, whether you will agree or not. All shall depend on your answer.'

They heard the bell pealing across the paddock. It was a brassy irritable dinging made for convict ears. Stanton told the groom where to hobble their horses. It was satisfying there was no feed for pack animals in the paddock selected but Rankine did not seem to notice the quality of the slight. Anyone else of his class would have complained and set Stanton to finding them hay. Rankine's mind was on some other impression. The fellow was palpably watchful. 'With good reason,' thought Stanton. 'The governor will have told him what I said. Is *Tumbankin* feeling a few hot turns on the roasting griddle? I'll give him a few hot turns more before I am finished, the slippery eel. Why did he accept my call to refreshment, instead of streaking off in the other direction, when he knows I'm on to him? That is the question.'

They came by the house. Meg held still and gazed at the whitewashed homestead with its wisteria-roped verandahs, quarried flagstones and rows of fruit trees in dusty leaf. It was the sort of house she wanted for herself one day, she confessed: 'An oasis.'

'You are quite the ambitious mistress,' thought Stanton, 'you are set on material goods,' and he swelled with liking of her.

'There is hardly a better house in the colony,' he admitted.

It was an evening of outstanding emotions. Stanton found that the moment Meg expressed her opinion about anything much he felt kindlier towards her disgraced father. The connection forced itself on him. He'd never felt any such softness towards Kale. But he began having a sentiment at least, if only to soften her regard, if she detected it.

'You have a clock,' she said. Warren had told her of it. 'You wind it up. Upon the hour, half hour and every quarter hour a bird flies up.'

'We have such a clock. It barely loses five minutes in a week.'

She herself had never seen a cuckoo clock: not even the governor had one. Stanton promised her the chiming of it later, if she would be so kind as to call on them at their house! (Rankine had declared they would be camping the night with the Josephs.)

She kept turning her head back and murmuring, 'Ooh, it is so shaded in there.'

'We could sit in,' said Stanton, 'under the grapevines.' Though it would be well after dark.

He thought with heartfelt poison that if Meg had not arrived on Rankine's mare she might have come to Laban Vale one day as a domestic. He could not help also thinking, stealing a glance at her as they entered the wool hall, that in their games and dances he would like to touch her waist. But that was only in another living of his life: where if he'd committed to being a bad man instead of being a good one, for example.

Throughout all this he never once took his eyes from Rankine.

It was a strange captivation took place in the hour of failing light on the sandy track leading in from Mundowey and passing his homestead and yards. The two strapping and nervously honoured guests — handsome as love allowed them to be, which was pretty high handsome indeed, and Meg a woman most strikingly beautiful in every respect — were seated on a bundle of fleeces in the Stantons' wool hall with a scrubbed, laundered Warren beside them and holding to his news to keep them guessing. Meg had scraps of wool caught in her raven hair from what was floating in the heated atmosphere of movement and naked flame of lights. There was the reflection of flame in her eyes and the light of loving fire. The wool and the light were hooked on her when she gazed at Rankine.

Stanton played with hooks in his mind like a miser with precious metal.

THE WOOL-HALL CELEBRATION THAT dark, still, New South Wales night, in that isolated encampment of lamplight far from the only town, was as distant from the green fields of England as it was possible to be — as far as a separate planet made of coarse dry leaves and rough clay ground spinning through the nothingness of black.

The celebration had a theme of English pastoral glee in which came musical and spoken poem recitals, and a choice of old-time games: skittles and shove halfpenny, leapfrog, blind man's buff, hunt the slipper, hot cockles and snapdragon so that children could learn how things were in the youth of their parents and those past youth could do some remembering on their feet.

Now there was a violent and abrupt Punch and Judy show performed by the Misses Stanton and Josephs, Ivy and Leah — much beating with a stick upon a soft rag head, followed by a song from Titus Stanton, native boy tenor, about the care of Jesus for a sparrow's fall.

Stanton stood before them lacking only his whip to pass for circus master supreme; dressed in frock coat, starched Geneva collar, and wearing a broad-brimmed black shovel hat, curved up at the sides with a projection back and front. He was so tight and lumpy in his breeches, that when he flipped his coat aside a stallion would be envious of his purse.

'There are no sparrows in Titus's country,' he said, after Titus's applause. 'Our Titus has no idea what sparrows are, except he is told they are like the emu wren or "wawguljelly".' Stanton at once turned wistful. 'We ourselves sorely miss the sight of sparrows eating crumbs from a doorstep, or a flock of starlings darkening the sky and bursting into curious shapes.'

Next singer was the Reverend Stanton himself with Ivy chorusing the 'Majesty of Love' (God's love), and then Mrs Stanton standing near the door where she could be heard by the bond men outside, reciting a tribute to the shearers in the poem by Dyer.

'What is going on in this strange house?' Meg whispered to Warren, but was sorry she said it, because half Warren's pride was fixed in the wool hall where the production of his sweat was on display, and the other half was in the paddocks and sheep tracks leading up to it, where he spent his days.

Rankine peered through the wall slats. There before him was a man he knew, green-faced, looking up at him from among the bond men sitting grouped awaiting their next ration of spirits.

Stanton, on a duty of missing as little as he could, saw where Rankine peered. He bared his gums in a red smile.

'Ah, that one there, Lorenze,' he said, 'he does get around. I sometimes think shearers run all night to be ready for the morning, bidding on someone else's flock before break of day.'

Rankine thought: Why is he here, then? Was the Spaniard taken and Stanton his master? Could a man be arrested, assigned, worked and owned in such a short space of time? Was that why Stanton was so jolly hospitable, because he had near all of them pegged down, one way or the other?

'"Lorenze", is he one of your prisoners?' said Rankine.

'That man is no prisoner, he is my best shearer, and the only prisoner I would like to make of him is to take him hostage to my needs, as I am thinking of putting him on as my steward, ha ha, if you don't nab him, sir. Which I won't allow.'

'"*Lorenze*,"' repeated Rankine.

'A Spaniard,' nodded Stanton.

When Rankine looked back the Spaniard smiled ferociously.

'I am encouraging him to stay on with me,' said Stanton. 'All I need's his free consent.'

'You are kinder to your convicts,' said Rankine, with disciplined ease of manner, 'than other landholders. Their men will be rioting when they hear how generous you are with your rum.'

'On this night nothing is too good for them. It is how I say thanks in a way they understand, for their struggle in coming round to me.'

'How so?'

'Their willingness to try harder cutting out swearing and malingering. There is one I have just arrested, though — God knows he is stupid — a false martyr to a cause. I wonder if you know him?'

'How might I?' said Rankine.

'As an officer. Sworn against causes. By your loyal oaths.'

'Then of course,' said Rankine uneasily.

'I winkled out of him that he was involved in the springing of Desmond Kale.'

Rankine managed to ask, as his throat closed tight: 'A confession?'

'Not quite a full confession, sir, I must admit. Not as you might say to the letter of one. A circumstantial fit of the terrors, more like.

Hanging shall be too good for him. You see, I arranged a dumb show over a supine sheep, held down for horn taking, and it all fell out as it must have done at Mundowey, that dark day with Kale — the shattering of chains, the partnership of malefactors between hammer and spike showing the scene all clear. The Spaniard assisted me. There was the smell of flinted horn, the whiffy smoke of the strike. You should have seen the Irishman quake. Understand, I already had the tools used, or what remained of them without handles. They were consumed of their fittings when recovered from the ashes. Solly Josephs is a bowerbird for putting his claws on objects. The only element missing was a mob of sheep and the owner of those sheep bringing them up to sweep Kale along into their disappearing dust. But I saw the figure ghostly enough, as it were through the trees.'

'Saw?'

'An officer of rangers.'

'That has all been settled,' said Rankine. 'The governor has reviewed the events of the day from every slant. Rangers were the escort detail that day.'

'So they were. Isn't it interesting. And so shall I tell you something, my dear captain?'

Rankine could only raise an eyebrow. The rest of him was frozen.

'It is you — I have you under suspicion as the officer involved.'

Rankine with wild inspiration held his wrists up to Stanton.

'Very good,' said Stanton, smiling wanly. 'You invite the shackles. You do not even quake.'

'*But if I don't get out of here with Clumpsy, I'm done,*' thought Rankine, experiencing the intolerable sensation of exploding inwardly, in his mind. The thought he now had was to leave Meg in the care of the Josephs as soon as he could, turn back and admit his involvements to the governor. That way neutralise Stanton by baring himself without shadows. And get his marriage papers signed.

'I would rather have Kale than you,' confided Stanton in a whispering rush. 'I would be kinder to Kale than I ever was before, if I had him in irons. I do heartily regret any distress I have caused his daughter, except that what I do, in my courts, the malefactor gives me best reason to do.'

Then Stanton threw his head back, and said, in a vomit of opposite feeling: 'You must like old coats, sir.'

'I do beg your pardon?' said Rankine.

'In your dalliance with women. Wasn't she spoiled enough by Marsh and having a child out of wedlock, and whatever officers found her willing, right up to the governor, for you to ever dream of turning her petticoat hems honest?'

Rankine decided that one day, when he could, he would strike the minister in the chest, break his jaw and kick him to the ground, and feed him to the dogs in pieces. Smaller and smaller, hoping every one hurt.

There was a long trembling interval before Rankine answered.

'Well, let me say, I think you are better on the subject of sheep, sir, than on the honour of the woman I love.'

'Ha, I think I might be. Though you tried to get my ram, Warren tells me — nothing is hidden between us, by the bye.'

Rankine saw how the minister worked. Stanton didn't need whips at all. His manipulations were various.

'You were seen at the croppies' parliament arguing the toss,' Stanton said.

Rankine answered at once.

'We hopeful breeders have our eyes open, it's true. I badly wanted a superior sire to start me off. Not that I can hold a candle to the master of Laban Vale, but I do fancy myself in the manner of livestock, you follow — as a beginner in sheep, so to speak, where I am making a late start.'

Rankine dabbed his forehead with a handkerchief. They were both hot with jousting. But heat radiated from Stanton as from a buried fire.

'Well, I like you better, Captain Rankine. I might even let you have a few of my ewe culls to take where you will. They are progeny of a line leading back to Kale, my rival in sheep matters. Kale means to damage me but I have my hostage to fortune in place, Warren Inchcape. It is the best I can say of Warren's natural father — I have been told it was Marsh, you see — that the late George Marsh was an impactful sire, leaving Warren enough of his intelligence, none of Kale's acid, and mostly his mother's goodness of spirit to go on with.'

AT A SIGN FROM THE minister, Artie Josephs lifted his violin from its battered case, snapped it under his chin, and stood before them playing the notes of a peddler's jig that Stanton hummed to him.

After a few notes Stanton joined in with words, and everyone picked up the rollicking sense of it: 'Come buy of me, come; come buy, come buy; Buy, lads, or else your lasses cry, Come buy!'

For the moment Rankine was free of his attentions. Stanton was carried away in blind man's buff more than the other games. When he was blindfolded he caught Meg almost at once, and exercised his privilege of getting his 'buffet', his three buffs or pats for the blind man having caught a player.

But when he wanted them to join in with hot cockles, strictly a children's game, in which, he said, one player kneels down with his eyes covered and lays his head in another's lap and on being struck has to guess who gave the blow — then he was dragged away by his wife. Snapdragon, he said, was a game drunkards liked to play, when they were so far gone they risked their eyebrows being burnt. He had a shallow dish of raisins (that had been dried by Stanton from his own grapes) poured over with rum and set alight. Then he challenged the players to eat them while alight. And the winner, although certainly no drunk, was Rankine, because when it came to risking his face, he was the one to chance it even unto eating into the minister's fire.

'They are all games brought from England,' said Stanton, when they were winded from running around and slipping over on the greasy floor and he was set to speechifying. 'There is an unbroken line of innocence in the shearing-shed frolics of which I am very fond. Please drink from the clay cups provided. I am not one of those pastors who thinks a little unsteadiness on the feet is a crime against God, otherwise — I ask you! — it would be a crime to be a toddling baby and a sin to grow old and unsure on your toes. In happy exile, I am a vicar of the country sort, a livestock breeder who goes out every weekday and governs his sheep and on Sundays takes his theme from the word of God. Our Bible is not just worded in the gathering of flocks, but is refreshed throughout by drink! It is called "the wine that cheereth", and says "the king was merry with wine"; elsewhere finds Esther "at the banquet of wine", and calls it "the wine that maketh glad", "the wine that maketh merry", concluding with the eternal soberation that "only His Love is stronger than wine". Charge your cups every one of you from that tub in the corner. Our homely concoction is a punch of orange juice laced with sugar, cinnamon, and a generosity of rum. Not so much as to inebriate too badly but enough to make you merry. God bless you all, and Sergeant Galvin, pass among the bond men giving them a last good strong blend of grog apiece and let them toast the king.'

Stanton seemed to be inventing a style of Botany Bay gentleman as he went along: religious, roasting, rough and ready. There were partygoers numbering around twenty, the numbers swelled by a dozen of his former smallholders (those he called strugglers) who had gone to the bad until he bought them out. They had withdrawn to the biggest river, where they lived envious much-reduced lives. The strugglers turned their heads and saw through the slats of the end wall the eyes of the convict stockmen peering in. They had convicts themselves but were not so likely to include any of their own in any such celebration. 'Give them an inch they will take a file,' was the ditty justifying close control. Hadn't the minister himself fallen foul of such a rule, with Desmond Kale, and had his metal rake taken? But then the strugglers, unlike Stanton, did not hold the whip hand so close: if they wanted punishments, they called on Stanton as their nearest magistrate to do it. But this next part of what Stanton said was not so popular.

'I would like you to meet Warren's mother,' said Stanton in the following interval between items, as he steered Meg and Rankine around the floor to introduce his pious guests. Stanton was the strugglers' leader in all styles of excellence but this was going too far, to hang onto the arm of such a free mover. He was mad, bad, or even wonderfully released from himself, and they lacked the wit to get their heads around all three in a man sworn to eternity. They wondered about the warmth of friendship he showed a captain of rangers and a wild convict's daughter. A glance at Dolly Stanton's narrow face under her pale blue bonnet showed that her husband might be a little outside her control this night.

Ivy and Leah could not take their eyes from Meg as a model of hauteur and grace they would like to follow, if they ever got the chance to grow wonderfully like her. It made them smile at Warren more, to think such a natural woman was his ma.

There were more jigs and country dances, accompanied by a

sheepskin drum played by a struggler of whom it was slyly said, poor sheepskin, how it brawls with him that beateth it! With their rapid exchange of partners, there was hardly any touching allowed, except for a quick brushing of hands. Leah Josephs sat against the wall with an indistinct smile and looked as if she had a lot better things on her mind than getting up and spinning around a creaking floor. But she was grateful when Warren sat beside her. He said nothing and sat with his hands on his knees. Then her mother came and found her, and asked for a turn, being careful to support Leah so she didn't trip. When they came near the sheepskin drum a subtle frenzy seized them, which the drummer saw, and obeyed despite his little skill. They tipped back their heads, closed their eyes, gyrated their trunks without moving their feet except to swivel on the balls of them, and snapped their fingers high. Leah fitted her balance to the mode, seeming to overmaster her lameness, and so resembled a ribbon of smoke from the lamps, in her grey smock with orange ribbons trailing from the sleeves of her upraised hands, that Warren wanted to grab the ribbons and unravel them down to the naked flame.

At the head of the hall, against a rampart of piled wool, Artie Josephs unpacked his harmonium and blew straw from its parts and wiped its glass bowls with a clean rag. His father brought over a basin of water and helped rig the uncanny instrument for playing. As a wheel turned, glasses entered the water basin and came out shining wet, which Artie translated into wavering hums of sound.

It was at this moment that Warren leaned over, cheeks full, eyes shining, to whisper to his mother that he was sailing on the *Edinburgh Castle* as the chosen one of the Stantons, as their apparent son in a cabin of his own with Titus — this last exclusiveness a boast, a prediction born of pity wondering if Titus would finally be allowed to come at all.

All night Warren had teased Meg not letting it out, asking her to guess the news between him and the Stantons.

'It is all acoming to me now,' said Warren, and Meg was not so sure she liked the smugness of his expression. 'My father's belongings and my old bird Car'away, my inheritance that I'm the only one's allowed to see what it is, and take it away.'

When the moment was right, Tom Rankine took Joe Josephs's elbow and steered him outside.

'What is it?' said Joe.

'What is it you know about me?'

'You're the governor's man,' said Joe. 'I carry your load of goods, you are close to me as my family, you and your wife; there's no more to you can be said.'

The discretion of them both was to be tested over what next was needed to be said, however. For Rankine, at least, it was a risky trust.

'Someone was taken for that Mundowey caper.'

'One of the Irish,' nodded Joe.

'It's my old campaign servant, Clumpsy M'Carty. I have reason to know he's innocent.'

Then it was Joe's turn. He took Rankine's elbow, and guided him farther into the dark on the pretext of the two men getting some fresh air, emptying their bladders, and filling their pipes. They would not have very long on their own as the Stantons were a most insinuating pair, 'Except they are so needy of advantages,' said Joe, 'and so honest in their cravings, that a bloke is half inclined to love them.'

'Here, we can sit on this log,' said Rankine.

'Watch out for the ditch,' said Joe. 'It is where the ram was chopped. I got his great horns. Here your man M'Carty was picked out by our very good friend as he lay along the sheep's belly and bunched the chisel in his fist. They say he's a capon, is it true?'

'He is cut,' said Rankine, chopping a fist into the palm of his hand. 'Some Spaniards made him one, with two flat stones. Since then he's mistrusted the race.'

'I wish you had not told me in that fashion. It shrinks me up in my vitals.'

They drew on their pipes. Long light shining from the gaps in the wool-hall walls flickered over them. Small flying ants tickled their noses and climbed into their hair; moths butted their foreheads.

Rankine said:

'Under the far end of Mick Tornley's waggon — I saw this when you loaded my goods — there are nets, slings, and tarpaulins suspended by ropes.'

'Are there, now? You would be the one to know, captain of rangers. I have never looked under there as far, past where we spreads our rugs, nor shall Mick either until I shift my goods and Mick gets his return load of wools and hides up, and unties the coverings to rope them tight in the weather. So I ask you, what is that end of the waggon to do with me?'

'By asking that question you have answered the one I was going to ask you, Joe.'

'Always ready to oblige,' said Joe, warily satisfied that nothing was compromised either way in his dealings with one man or another, and that a friend was enabled to do what was needed. What that might be he would not start guessing, even to himself, except to warrant it aided the unprotected, and he would go a bit further with that idea, than he would with its opposite.

THE CONVICTS WERE LONG SINCE marched back to their barracks' room sheds and those that were shepherds sent away with their flocks before dark to find their night's sheep camps. Each of the bond men saved a snort of rum apiece for Clumpsy M'Carty in his cell with the cur Lehane wakeful in the diagonally opposite dark corner. They did it by tipping their portions into a common jug brought around by Galvin. It would allow Clumpsy enough to frazzle his brain through the night, and torment Lehane with a sip or two, if he chose.

Titus was the other one locked up now with his own hut doors bolted, a prisoner in all but name, still, and Warren told by the parson he should sleep in the woods that night lest Titus taint him with pity.

Some time past nine o'clock the wool-hall benedictions were given by Stanton. God declared all things good through the mouth of a minister finding texts fitted to his needs. The tallow wicks were doused. The owl that had taken up residence in the rafters looked out for mice. Last to leave, the strugglers were sent on their way, urged to their distant beds before their Sabbath began, though it would take them some long while yet to get home and say their prayers as they lived by foot many miles and would milk their ewes past daylight.

Stanton and his wife with Meg and Warren following made their way by starshine to the homestead where the minister promised to show off the cuckoo clock to Meg before they snuffed their candles. Stanton made his preposterous offer of two hundred culls, to be delivered in the morning. Rankine had no choice but to accept them.

He then excused himself, saying he was going across the flat to the Josephs's camp to get their blanket rolls ready and make a place for Warren near them.

But he diverted from the intention as soon as he was clear of the others, after fetching two bottles of brandy from his saddlebags, and went to find the Spaniard, to test his honesty by putting him to a task.

He found the Spaniard drinking rum with the barracks' room sergeant in the office room of the barracks' sheds, and called him away on pretence of looking for a wandering horse that had lost its hobbles. The Spaniard followed close by his heels and out into the dark until they were a hundred yards under the night sky, where they could neither be seen nor heard, except to each other's peering presence, and only sensed by bats, the size of winged mice, that shadowed out from a hollow tree branch nearby, and sliced past their heads.

'You can pull your fingers from your ears, Paolo Moreno. Open up to me, because if you don't tell me the truth I shall be heart-broken by you.'

The Spaniard shielded his forehead believing that all bats were blood suckers, and if these Botany Bay varieties weren't, as

Rankine always said, then he would not wait to have it proved by himself, thank you.

Rankine offered a slug of brandy, which the Spaniard accepted by wrenching the cork between his teeth. There was ever a blocky resistance in him needing loosening by drink to reach his deeper talk. Rankine could almost hear the hiss of brandy down his tongue.

'Senhor Paul Lorenze, drink up. You looked green when I saw you through the slats. Did you get a jolt seeing me in the Devil's wool shed? I think you did.'

'I thinks you did,' came the accusation flung back. 'It must have been greens wools from Laban Vales sheep,' he said. 'No goods diseases.'

The bottle passed back and forth. It took very little for Rankine to feel fired up, whereas Moreno had great capacity, a slower, smouldering intoxication. His sprees were days long and furtive. *Soledad completa.*

'When are you coming back to shear our good white sheep? They'll be looking better since you saw them last, spread out over a high grassy country, dropping their lambs, many twins, a few triplets, in the shelter of granite rocks, some as big as houses, which nourish a light but fertile sand so the Irishman says.'

'There is too much winds in the high lands.'

'Sheep can always find a place to lie down, where the big rocks are. When winds comes from the south they find shelter on the other side. The land rises and falls to the far horizon, gets better, he tells me — from his times with Marsh — broad swamps of water-fowl and reeds between, and the best shelter among low spreading trees for their camps and sheepfolds. There is a bidgee sort of a river. The air is clear as glass, the sky deep blue, far stretching.

When you climb a hill you see the next bend of country mirrored in the sky. It is out there the blue bush grows.'

'You forgets I was there. I saw nothings like it.'

'This is farther along.'

'*Y que?* You forgets they have brown wool in their ears when last I cares for them, some in the folds of their necks.'

'That is true. But didn't we agree, there always has to be advancement, and when it comes to breeding, it cannot be done by councils.'

Rankine was well away on Kale.

'Why does it matters I never comes back at all?' sulked Moreno. 'The browns are culls you say let hims do culls, *pues, que sean todos blancos*, make them all whites, get rid of the browns, the *moreno*. You givens them away, me with them. Kales is a bad shearers, he use anothers mans blades, takes from the mister's sheds, no hang on to his owns, no treats them better.'

This droning whine Rankine knew very well, and chose to ignore. Moreno a few months back had risked his life for the very question.

'I have told you before, my friend, my tactic is to follow the sheep, while my strategy is to find us the land. Kale is a great breeder and you are a great shepherd. Each one of us is needed for the other.'

'What is Rankine's greatness agains?'

'To play the fool and find us the land, to put my hand in my pocket for silver, to break bread, now with the governor, now with the parson, which neither you, nor Kale, is able to do, because how can you brandish influence?'

'I cans,' simmered Moreno.

'Kale is an outlaw, you are not English, you are not regimental.'

'I passes for English, a trooper, when I walks hims free.'

'And peerlessly bravely too. But it proves my point, Moreno. If it was left to just one, or even to two — an Irish rebel and a foreigner whose fortune is his dagger, his loyalty and his ancient north African name — how far would any one of us go? Kale would still be in irons. You would be buggering shepherd boys and goats in Estremadura still. That is to say, if you had not found yourself a gentleman by the name of Rankine. But do not try and take me by the end parts, Paolo Moreno, my very dear, my very dear old friend. I have told you this often enough, and you have trusted me well enough until we got them away from the forest.'

Moreno looked petulantly withdrawn.

'Each time the land is any goods he says no, "travels on", and you don't fights his opinions. You finds the place you wants, ducks moles reach, but you lets him decides it is wrong. All will be lost in unknowns country, sheeps disappears like water in the cracks, crows pecks their eyes out. You have courage under fire but against Kales nothing but weakness. I am fearless enough. I have breedings knowledge enough. While you have Biddy Magee there is no difference between us, but since you have that dream, with your brains in your testicles' bag, you are all for Kales and all for the sake of his daughter's fuck. That she refuses you.'

'She refuses me nothing.'

'To please her,' said Moreno, 'you no longer takes from the priest Stantons, you take from me. I am still here on Labans Vales after the shearers vamoose. You wanna know why? The priest wants me over his flocks while he travels to Englands with his friend boys. I have said yes.'

'Moreno, that is splendid,' said Rankine, who did not know why, but the arrangement relieved his conscience at the same time as it alarmed his interests.

'May be it is my turns,' said Moreno, 'I takes what you say I never can have, and lets me tells you, it is so easy to fix hims you would laugh to hear how easy.' Moreno stared at Rankine, challenging him, daring him under a roof of bright starlight to put him down from the step up he'd gained:

'May be I learns from my master, Ugly Toms. The priest watches me, and so he trusters me. The governors watches you, and so he trusters you.'

Rankine examined the stalwart face of the Spaniard, studied its cracks and folds. The planes of a face like slabs of stone, steadfast in solitude. What a face it was, sculpted by living rough. Shaped by a country. The poor soils, bleached rocks and broken tree branches littering the place fed their way into it. Spain and now Botany Bay hammered in the features. Mulligrubs and brown moths sweeter than chestnuts spat from his iron pan. A curse on this country of thieving crows and shy marsupials: it grained itself into Moreno deeper than into Rankine, who sometimes thought that there was a year ahead of him, to which he put a date around five years hence, when he would return to Yorkshire a rich man and reclaim his green acres.

Moreno with his fists against the bottle tipped back his head. Rankine told him to keep it, the whole square flask, as there were a good few ounces left and here was another one — which he pulled from his pocket — to share with the sergeant of convicts, until the sergeant at least passed out although never Moreno, whose liver was made of iron.

'It is not possible to serve two masters — it is difficult and a strain. Service is worked to breaking point between us, Moreno.'

'It is all differents now,' agreed Moreno.

'One more thing, I ask. It is to free Clumpsy M'Carty when Galvin is safely drunk.'

Rankine spelled it out to the Spaniard — 'I promise it will go without trouble' — and the Spaniard pulled at his lower lip with his forefinger and thumb considering the question.

He made an idiot sound at the back of his throat.

So it was decided.

But walking back into the dark Moreno thought again. 'Rankines is taken my sheeps away and Stantons gives almost as goods a sheeps in the care of me. It is all rights to do what Rankines wants but it is all rights to do what Stantons wants better. Rankines is dangerous crazy his ways and Stantons is dangerous crazy his ways. Stantons give me the wools. So. That is more better.' He would speak to Stanton.

Rankine made his way back to the Josephs's camp seeking Meg. He walked as a bridegroom, feeling his way in the dark, with a light hurried step.

THE WHIRRING INSIDE THE CLOCK began. The small doors rattled and threw themselves open with a backwards jerk. The noisy painted bird began its ten repetitive curtsies. Warren giggled, held his stomach, and Meg laughed with him. It was a wonderful gaiety her lightness of laughter had, but gaiety was the least of the merits the minister valued in her this late. His head whirled from the punch being mixed too strong and he wondered what sins of joyousness would plague him in his bed when he shuffled through his mind, looking for delights mixed with disgusts, sleep evading him.

'Well, madam,' he said with a sigh. 'Now to the question hanging, which I have granted you the power to decide. Are you allowing us Warren on our voyage?'

Meg surprised him with her answer.

'What of his wages? Am I to lose what he brings me in, because you are taking him away?'

Dolly Stanton held her nightdress and sleeping cap over her arm and worked them against her stomach.

'Even to ask!'

'There was always an arrangement and his given word on the amount each year, which your husband swore, with no mention of any change in the pact.'

'I shall now make you a new pact,' said Stanton, 'a better one: that Warren shall have his money on all parts of the voyage as best I can manage, less those times when he is taken around, as when we do the sights of London and our travelling up and down to Yorkshire where he'll get more instruction in wool in a day than Botany Bay gives in a lifetime, and that is saying a great deal.'

'How will he?' said Meg, and Dolly matched her in the same breath at the same time, as they chorused together in the minister's face: 'How will he get his wages, when he won't be working?'

'That is for me to calculate,' said Stanton, 'but you both of you have my promise,' and he waited for their answer like a pasha playing to his harem getting two houris for the one desire guaranteed.

'All right,' they said together.

So it was that Meg allowed her consent to the plan for Warren to sail away and not come back for two years; and so it was that Dolly Stanton had another lesson in swallowing her tongue.

Warren was pointed into the night air with his mother. She held his arm as they crossed the open ground. The Josephs's campfire guided them from afar. Meg felt lonely and confused, with a black gulf opening around her, and she longed for the assurance of Rankine's embrace.

When Stanton and Dolly were in their bedroom with the door closed, he said, before she could start her attack:

'Listen to me, my wife, who knows nothing of sailing ships despite being brought to child on one, and that with the lone aid of your husband. There is always a place on a seagoing vessel for a boy to work the galley or take his turn as a seaman for the whole passage through, paid for out of a captain's account. If you put more trust in your husband you might guess that taking the boys shall be more beneficial than you think. Have I got that into your head, or would you rather not have a carriage when we arrive in London, and a pair in hand?'

Dolly bowed her head, and agreed that she had married a clever man. She knelt at their bedside and said her prayers. At the thought of Titus being driven to scramble away up a mast in a wild storm she almost cried out. But having seen that high-cheekboned beauty Meg Inchcape in her house, leaning against her wall and looking up at her clock, with her sceptical gypsical eyes, and so resoundingly proud of her own distressed origins, and giggling at someone's better pride in a clock striking ten, Dolly was more decided than ever in dealing with the woman's son in her own way. The higher Titus went up his mast so please God the higher Warren went up his, until the heavier, less nimble boy lost his grip and fell into the waves that ran over him like lace tablecloths.

With his wife at prayer, Stanton withdrew from the room and went outside where he was unable to find where the slops buckets were, and so brought up his belly into the hollyhocks, which had been nurtured from treasured seed brought from England, and counted into the ground when Ivy was an infant. There, done: his meat and onions went into a lump on the ground where they would doubtless feed the soil if they were not to feed the minister himself any longer that night.

After washing his face, Stanton wriggled into his nightshirt and climbed into bed. While he rattled through his prayers as far as amen, his wife snored across from him, her thin nostrils flaring in the beam of starlight coming through their curtains. Altogether it was a fairly good day. The strugglers were all impressed. Rankine was tormented. Stanton's standing with Meg Inchcape was raised. Rankine was roped pretty much where Stanton wanted him. Meg was soothed. And as there was to be no help from the law in the matter of Kale, and as Stanton was a law unto himself, here they both were — Stanton and Rankine — surely positioned exactly where Rankine himself wanted to be: at the nefarious service of Kale. It was a joining of forces on the almost spiritual plane, where nothing was proved, but all was connected. Tomorrow Stanton would go out and select a few hundred culls for Rankine to take with him. *Noblesse oblige*. The best of the culls would reach Kale and he'd make them better — they had another two or three lambs in them — until such a time as Stanton returned from England with Marsh's maps and the wherewithal to corner Kale on his pastures, his illegal flocks multiplied without Kale having the least idea of whose benefit he worked towards. It had a rhythm worthy of a ballad, the whole idea. There would be a new governor by then. Change benefited those on the side of the law. Distant country grew closer by the year.

It left Stanton with the question of Patrick Lehane, and his promise to the wronged Josephs to have Lehane corrected at law. It was late but no easy answers suggested themselves. Stanton bit his knuckles and spat small black chewed hairs from the tip of his tongue. Justice by morning. How to achieve?

But then a rap tapping was heard on his homestead's back door, and he jumped up annoyed, while Dolly slept on, to find he was saved. It was the Spaniard standing there; at once, it was plain in those sullen beast's eyes lit by orange candlelight how all Stanton's answers were come at once.

'Dear fellow, Lorenze,' he began.

So the night went on. The Spaniard returned to the barracks' room sheds.

Moreno savoured his French brandy while Galvin let his run into his veins. The more Moreno watered his thin the more Galvin demanded his stronger. In his pocket Moreno had a milk cheese Stanton had given him, that he pared and fed Galvin who washed its pungency down with brandy each swallow.

'I don't mind his cheeses at all,' said Galvin, inhaling the ammonia fumes. 'They smell better than his prayers. It is what the ewe puts into the pail, when she squits her pebbles, that does it. I've seen the men skimming it off, with their fingers yolky and greasy from the wool, but not all of it, the black berries of sheep shit milling around. It all comes through and gives it bite. Very good, very nice, and what's left in that bottle, Senhor Lorenze?'

'Is somes more,' said the Spaniard, tapping his pocket, where the second bottle hung ready to be unstoppered.

'Good, grand, capital and all of us beautifully wasted,' Galvin said. 'Them two in the clink, the minister cross-eyed from it, them puritanical strugglers drunk on their dreams, and now you and me sinking it down. I am only half sorry for Clumpsy M'Carty. There is a blessed lot of Irishmen who are for him.'

Galvin sang, smoked, drank and poisoned his liver blacker. 'You know it becomes the Irishman to drown the shamrock when he can.'

As Galvin drew breath for a new chorus of hope, around midnight, he faltered, slid on over his table, and raised his eyes with the confused appeal of a felled ox. He saw nothing, felt nothing as he dropped. It took a good minute for the Spaniard to work the keys from his belt waist, and then he was round the other end of the barracks' room sheds breathing the sugary oiliness of rum and the odour of piss and vomit that came through the hatch of the three-barred door.

'Allo, M'Carty?' he whispered, unlocking one heart-shaped padlock after another until all three dangled loose.

Almost at once two shadows lifted from the floor and hoisted themselves up all stained in their canvas jackets. Clumpsy offered himself to Moreno first, open-chested with a plea: 'Which is the better, the wind pipe, the belly, or the vascular organ Mr Paul fecking Lorenze with your Toledo blade?'

Moreno only partly understood the rattled words but well understood the obsequiousness of the fearful as he opened the door a little wider.

'Come out!' It was addressed to both men, on behalf of two masters, but at first only Clumpsy responded.

Before Moreno could demonstrate himself friendlier than Clumpsy knew he was, the prisoner ducked under his arm, lurched past him — stopped only by Moreno's thrusting out a leg.

'As one Caytholic to another, spare me till I make me peace,' said Clumpsy, thrown to his back where he rocked on the dirt, pushing air up at the looming Spaniard's knife. 'Nor! Nor!' he said. 'I won't tell Rankine it's you sucking the Deil's tiddy.'

'Rankine warnts you,' hissed Moreno, despising last moments cowardly framed. He pricked M'Carty all over with his knife point, like a picador.

'Aye, that would be heaven,' said Clumpsy, getting the first suggestion that Rankine had come for him, but hardly believing it. Thinking more that he was stabbed.

'Over there by the creeks, see by the campfires, shut your mouths, and run.'

Moreno stood back heaving space between them as Clumpsy clambered to his feet, clapped his hands to his head, groaned and ran off.

Lehane came crawling out on all fours. He looked up at the Spaniard — an infatuated man with a trickle of saliva on dry lips and bloodhound pouches under his burning eyes.

'I'm to go?'

'It saves you,' said the Spaniard. Lehane kissed his boots, and stood up. Swaying off into the deep forgiving dark. Oh he would convert to a Protestant for this, he would. For this, he would go straight to the governor, and get his all right.

THERE WERE TIMES WHEN A good, courageous man of this earth was all animal arousal, a creature of idiotic fear, fleet of foot with a galloping pulsation in the kneecaps and a meaningless flailing of the arms. Clumpsy M'Carty crossed the wide farm flat squawking like a pullet and praying to Mother Mary for assurance that all the wet warm liquid flowing below his waist wasn't blood.

'The bastid has stabbed me,' Clumpsy told himself as he slowed, creeping along the edge of shadows, farming his fingers down the inside front of his clammy crotch. Blood was thinned down to pissifaction and he was a pismire complete with a trickle of shite on his scalded thighs.

'Halloo, M'Carty!' said a voice he supposed with a start was Moreno's come back again. The disembodied call came from the dark in front of him, where Moreno might have got round to torment him.

'Yaiss?' Clumpsy replied in childish humility, because having met the Devil, there were possibly angels as deceiving in this place. 'Yaiss? — please?' His hands looked black when he held them out in front of him, searching in the dark, but not black black as they should be from blood in the dark. So he wasn't stabbed after all, it seemed.

'This way, man.'

There were two fires, one burning low red and another, brighter, kept up with sticks, away off the far end of the bullock waggon where the traders Josephs had their camp. People were still up, moving around, getting ready to shift at daylight. Would that Clumpsy could dissolve into them as he'd wanted into a sheep, Clumpsy a shape shifter and fairy hiker of the marshes and skylined ridges if only this cursed country allowed the mythologies in.

'Clumpsy!'

It was Rankine, then. He stood at the end of the waggon wearing a pale shirt and dark trousers, no ghost of the imagination at all but the handsome captain of rangers. Rankine held up a corner of dog blanket, inviting a motion, and, thought Clumpsy, forget that rancorous Spaniard and his hornswoggling ways, here was a challenge to dive upon better than any the foreigner knew when fighting bulls or driving spikes to within a quarter inch of a man's brains — a suspended dark space or cubby fitted out with blankets and smelling of safety and dog.

Clumpsy was aware that he was in the middle of a camp of strangers both ends and one side of the waggon. They were all favoured visitors to the minister's ground, and here was Clumpsy M'Carty most favoured among them. Wasn't that something?

'Hush but you are a good man, Ugly Tom Rankine.'

Deeper into the underspace without a word or a question Clumpsy went, jerking his ankles to get his forward parts wedged in tighter. It was a released convict's private prepared cabin between the axles under the long chassis of the waggon — between the two ends curved up like a boat. Heaven could wait. A caterpillar had no better berth in a cocoon of silken web. There was a slung blanket. Rolls of tarpaulin. Coils of rope. 'I shall be sailing on the morning tide,' thought Clumpsy, 'with instead of water under my feet there'll be sticks and dry leaves to look at.' When he was wriggled full length and tight, nose poking through a slit, eyes peering around, he was little inclined to ask the whys and wherefores. Not a breath was he capable of escaping from himself loaded with common sense: only in babbling gratitude could he express himself here. May be tomorrer he'd talk it over, when they were well away from accursed Laban Vale and the reach of the minister.

Rankine brought the dogs over to smell Clumpsy so as not to be alarmed when they tried leaping into their cots and found a man inside them. Clumpsy the hedgerow attorney whispered: 'I am rehearsing me arguments, faster than I can get me breath, on the subject of where I stand with the prayst fellow, and feel I'm pretty right. See, I'm not even an absconder now as I've been set free by the parson's own man, Senhor Paul Lorenze. Am I makin sense?'

'You might be freer sooner than you think,' said Rankine, in a voice so soothing it would soon have Clumpsy nodding off like the rum-guzzling baby he was. 'I have paid Mick Tornley with a promise of your labour, and sworn your innocence to Joe Josephs over the freeing of Kale. But that is not the best part, Clumpsy.'

'As to my freedom it couldn't come better.'

'As to your freedom I'll swear to the governor you are innocent, and I'll request you back in my service, as my assigned convict servant.'

'Like you did with our Biddy Magee,' said Clumpsy with a wicked grin.

'Just so. Stay put till it's done.'

'I have been transmogrified. Heavens be praised and I promise you won't be sorry. It will be a great story to tell the boys, if it has a good ending.'

'Sleep through into morning, don't make a noise.'

'Only me bladder'll be a bucket of straw.'

'Use the gaps of the hammock if you must. Stay tight until I call you, then you'll be safe. By the time Stanton learns you've been assigned it will be too late, as a ship, the *Edinburgh Castle*, will be sailing in through the heads of Port Jackson any day now, and they'll be on it with their wool and crossing the Pacific Ocean and rounding the Horn before we even get to the duck mole reach and unload our gear.'

'Now there's a name oughter have capitals,' said Clumpsy, falling asleep to the idea of a ballad recital at a bright campfire — a story in which a famous convict escapes, an officer of rangers is outlawed, a woman decides on love, a boy is given trust by the one with wool round his wrist, a black boy is treated like shite by the same old devil, and the days roll into each other under the throbbing ball of the sun over the height of a sturdy waggon hauled by fourteen bullocks and carrying a band of hopefuls in the direction of Desmond Kale.

It was late, very late, when everything was done. In the shining darkness of that country, it was luminous past midnight. The stillness over the dry creekbed was remarkable. It had an effect on the minds of sleepers and on the attention of those still awake greater than offered within reason. For it was said the creek had an underground river following its way below. Crickets, small movements of air twittering the branches. The clatter of a leaf descending could be heard. The call of a nightbird came clear as fracturing glass. The creek was alive with life you could and couldn't see. In the night there was the power of prophecy: things would get better, because feel how beautifully soft they already were, rich below.

Meg Inchcape turned the planes of her face to the sky and almost sang with love. It was like strewing flowers this feeling of excitement she had, beginning her voyage into an unknown country as mysterious as could be.

It was late, very late when Rankine came past the end of the waggon with starshine in his hair and she knew he'd finished putting their camp visitor at his ease. Blankets were spread on the ground, made easier by a sack of clean straw pounded flat, laid underneath, with more blankets piled over and a canvas flicked over the top to protect against dew.

Meg muffled shrieks of laughter as Rankine showed her how to get her legs into a stockman's bedroll without bringing any sand in with her, as he promised there were no bugs and crawlies in with them for he'd taken particular care to brush them out. Close bound to each other's warmth, they were ready for the few hours that remained of the night. But not so ready for sleep, as they were ready for each other, seeking the hungry touch. Meg found herself looking into Rankine's face lit by starlight, cupping that willing pocked visage between her long fingers. He returned her gaze and then they were in each other's arms for love. This was not pleasure-seeking of the kind they lately knew how to take, it was more an hour of their lives assenting to a promise that was already made, they knew not how. It told they could live through their separations when they came. That promise, unspoken, was prophecy, deep felt, and it went along under them like that river. The shadows of trees could be seen with the starlight shining through the narrow leaves and around the ends of boughs where the leaves hung in bunches. The clay earth was alive in the deep night's breathing. The harder tested of their two was going to be Rankine — he that swapped advantage for hardship. She would remember that in the morning, and the morning after.

Before first light Rankine left the camp for Parramatta, whispering that if he was not returned by the time camp broke, she was to stay with the Josephs until he caught up. With a stroke of Meg's cheek, and a tender look, he was gone.

With sheep in the morning, Warren came to say goodbye. He brought the two hundred culls from Stanton, herded now by Joe Josephs's boys and their sister, who would lose a few, and find a few, before they grew much older.

'Ma?'

It was too much for Meg, this farewell as she clung to Warren. He broke off. Came back. They looked at each other in the dust. Meg's heart was great with love for him, but she broke from their kisses and holdings-on, and separated finger from finger, bidding adieu, for reasons of the life yet to come for both of them, with their backs turned to each other, travelling to either end of the world.

At noon Clumpsy was still with them, slung in his unlikely cradle and pissily reeking. Behind were the sheep and the boys hup-hupping them along.

Tramping at the side of the oxen was their bullocky, Mick, a lover of jam and pickles, a man whose brain was a stone inside a tin dish rattling and striking; whose concentration of person had the benefit of rhythm derived from a natural gait. Each flick of his whip was matched to a loud oath. When the bullocks heard Mick cursing they twitched their nerve ends, strained their haunches, lowered their narrowly muscled shoulders and shook them of flies, getting on their way.

Mick and the Josephs and you might almost believe the wary bullocks themselves kept their eyes open for Patrick Lehane, that cur lucky enough to find freedom in the swing door of a cage but undoubtedly stupid enough to squander its benefits under his messy feet when he next got the chance. Just let him try.

Mick coiled the whip that was tired from chasing a black boy, wielded by a parson, allowing his bullocks to carry on whipless as they chose. Its painful effect they remembered in their bones as well as any black boy was able. Oaths on plain beasts saved on lash, and if only a ballad could do the same for a person it would be brilliant, please God. There was a singing from under the waggon seemed to hope so.

Except where was Rankine now? Gone from the breakfast fire, gone from their inland direction, and all Meg Inchcape could say the next morning (when he was still not back) — Meg rising from her tangled blankets to join a company of knees seeking a little warmth from a blaze of sticks — was that she expected he would be along again quite soon.

Yet as the days grew perceptibly shorter and they progressed on their way, he did not return. The party of travellers poked on without him, turning around peering back through the wan trees expecting his horse would be seen coming soon through in a haze of sheep dust. Only like Desmond Kale, but in the other direction, Rankine was gone from their world of understanding and quite as if he'd never been there in it at all.

Meg gathered water, cooked bread in a fire of myrtle ash, sheltered under applewood trees in a thunderstorm, and every day walked up the nearest hill to look back the way they'd come.

There was never anyone appearing through the trees.

Chorus of the Fifth Part

Where Kale is sought abroad

A MUMMIFIED ANIMAL OF THE marsupial race, with ground teeth pulled back in a smirk, mocked from a bundle of wool. It stank from a bed of shrivelled blackness, showing shreds of pelt, glued bristles in a frame of ribs. It was about the size of a small pig, deflated.

Blaise Cribb poked it over with a cane and cursed. From the other side of the globe he was taunted by criminal filth.

'Consigner: J.J. Tharpe', he noted, and went to the side door of the wool store where he gagged, before coming back to see what was under it.

These were the worst days when Cribb felt his life was fairly well wasted at forty except he was not quite finished with wool.

He would take a brief look at a bundle now, and a better look tomorrow, when there was more light. Stuffing samples in his pockets, he left for the Inn of the Four Bound Sheaves, and quite soon, Cribb was drunk and reeling.

Out of a long, narrow pocket appeared a bone flute made from the shank of a goat, carved in Sicily, which Cribb played to rouse the melancholy of his soul and to charm his listeners as they drank.

It was a plaintive high-pitched instrument. He seemed happier tonight, it was noticed. Light on his small feet.

Later there was a drunken argument with his friend Dud Hardcastle, the village schoolmaster, a forthright rational man which Cribb wasn't, quite, despite the absolute demands of his trade, because he reserved a particle of the universe for unaccountable mystery. Mentally there he retreated into what Hardcastle called a spiritual bag of tricks and did so the harder his friend pushed with atheism, paganism, Jacobinism, or whatever inspired him fitfully — with a fair swerve of Wordsworthian nature-adoration and advocacy of walking cures thrown in.

As a radical materialist and promoter of unfettered love, Dud Hardcastle was a supremely happily married man and regular as a Methodist in all respects of his life except when giving out opinions. If Cribb could not advance his return arguments with logic — and there he regularly failed, being morosely inarticulate with emotional states too large for him — he drew up his fists. At this, Hardcastle surrendered for the sake of companionship. A blow bounced off anyway — look at Cribb tonight, fat-pocketed on every side.

Hardcastle asked for a closer look at what he carried, and they touched foreheads either side of a lantern while Cribb spread his material out. The medium of devotion was imperishable gossamer spun from the skin of an edible quadruped, and if Hardcastle rashly cursed its enchantment, thinking to appease Cribb when *he* cursed it back and forth, beware.

They went outside into the windblown cloudy night and began their long walk home, discoursing on the way.

Hardcastle loved Cribb and believed he would be a happier man if married. But in affairs of the heart pessimism had spoiled Cribb for a settled life. Disinheritance proved he would never have a decent roof over his head, he argued, showing to the world he was incapable of offering any bride a place worth her hand. Of course, the piteousness of a circumstance suited Cribb very well. Only adventures would do, and of a passionate concentration until success was assured, and then Cribb showed a side of himself that could only be called vague, indecisive, unreliable; most unlike him at all (except it was). Avoiding breach of promise suits, he did so merely by the chance that his determined fickleness was played out with married women.

Hardcastle said that when he met the love of his life he would be felled, split, cast to the winds and destroyed completely — quite deserving every particle of his humiliation and despair. Cribb said he'd already met her, and her name was Dolly Pringle. Hardcastle knew the old story of that bold young woman and her conversion to better ways. Everything was remembered in wool that Cribb had ever done, binding his entanglements in love crosswise into the material of his vocation. His son, Johnny, was now a raw eighteen and a woolstapler's boy in his own right and puzzled by love of a father and obedient to a father's soul, not so much to his father's expectations, as they seemed to bypass Johnny and called somewhere wider. Cribb might say he was finished but that was a lie to Johnny and lived out every time Cribb gave an offhand instruction to the boy and cuffed him around the scone for making a fool of himself, which Johnny gladly did, to have his closeness guaranteed by hot attention. While Cribb worried his personal fate, Johnny awaited the fuller declaration of their alliance and a freedom they would one day enjoy together as Cribb & Son, Wool Brokers — north of England's foremost, may be? In this Johnny was like Cribb himself, when younger, who had shown such loyalty and hope, to his stepfather, and to his trade, whereas Cribb gave no sign that he saw any resemblance in Johnny and cursed him for his tinker blood which apart from dark good looks meant mostly an easy friendliness and a compliant smile, that made him over-trusting rather than sly as tinkers were known to be.

Cribb was not well from all the standing, eating, drinking, fine discriminating and exact disputing that made up his day. He was a man who after a great deal of riding through rural parishes sorting and buying wool found himself too much under the one great roof as his expertise grew in demand and reputation. It was a couple of years since he last rode to hounds, or joined Hardcastle on a walking tour of the high tops, each with a book of verse in his coat pocket. There was no time for anything more than the getting of coin through the offer of quality and profiting on quantity. Congestions of dirt and fatty oils brought from afar thickened Cribb's lungs. Come winter a cough clawed behind his ribs, persistent as a rat in warehouse rafters. Blood flecked his handkerchief after too much strain, vexing his son who stayed at the farm with him, when he could, hard by the waterfall — in that damp unhappy purloined place at the edge of the moors. Whether the cough meant worse than Johnny dared guess no doctor was consulted by Cribb to confirm. Johnny was given a bloodshot stare (as if Cribb's eyes were doused in vinegar), a wincing challenge to be gone, and Johnny gained the feeling it was a failure of manhood in him even to throw a blanket over Cribb when he snored drunk in his snow-melting coat. But he loved Cribb and would go past his father's expressed opinion to have him warm and did so.

Next day it was still there waiting: bin 871:D of colonial wools, with its dead marsupial badger rolled inside the mummy case of fleece, with its stink as pungent as any Cribb had ever broke open.

He cursed the desecration and muttered the name of the fool who seemed to think his bags would be sorted anonymously and never traced back by letter or reputation some fourteen thousand miles. 'J.J. Tharpe, hard by the duckmole rch.' But when he unfolded the outer binding there was a surprise within, fuller than the few fistfuls he'd plucked the night before, in dimmer light. A bundle of fleeces that were fragrant and soft. Two styles in all.

He wrote in his report:

'Superior softness of texture . . . Clean of thorns and wire grasses . . . Comparatively very peculiar qualities, a softness and silkiness . . .' — words of description carrying a sense of superb character cherished by his chief buyers, Addison and Roper of Bradford, if they could only get their hands on some, which they would not succeed in doing, as there was just this one tantalising bundle to hand in the whole of Britain.

Though after a moment, Cribb, while holding his breath, dangling the fleece at arm's length into a better light, corrected that conclusion.

For J.J. Tharpe's exceptional pearly bundle, which Cribb now spread on a window ledge, like a piece of washing to air of its too close companion, set him thinking.

It was the direct relation of the one that came into his hands a few years past, of that he was sure, the fleece marked 'Kale' he'd retained hoping for better days from the prison colony and its flocks. It was stored in a sack on the farm and soon he'd go and have a look at it, whether it rained starless cold and sleet or snowed or what. And more to the point, mixed in it was prime Spanish wool, improved from a style of wool that went to the colony on the backs of Rankine's Spaniards.

Hardly surprising, then, that Cribb excused himself from duty and went down the back of a high stone wall and clambered down a slippery stone stairway to the chilly mud flats where it was his oblivious habit to stand when he wanted a pull of drink. Once he could see for clear miles over banks to the hills, but no longer. As mills produced clean woollen goods in quantity of incessant tons it followed that lewd chimneys grew from their honest walls, spreading smuts among gorse flowers, sooting the buttercups of springtime fields, staining the golden harvest moon with their filth, and blackening the snow in winter. Their outspills were a congestion on the breathing earth and here, downstream of a woolscour on banks of a muddy river, grew burrs, woody weeds and saplings strange to see in England. A few years ago Cribb walked these banks with George Marsh, who made Cribb smile by likening the stray Botany Bay seeds to jewels in a sad beauty's hair (fair England's) — a washed fleece's cargo of winged seed and sprocketed burr heads plentiful and stubborn, growing a world away from their origins.

Cribb took bread and cheese from his pocket, and when his stomach was ready lined he fed his spirits down into himself in a whisky braid.

It was not widely known that Lord Bramley was the important money behind Thomas's Wool Brokers. A few years ago Thomases married into the Lloyds of Caermarthenshire, a continuing line of lawyers, horseflesh fanciers, and money spenders, and when it came to sheep they liked the mountain sheep of their Welsh landholdings best, for no better reason than that particular sheep's character of almost unmanageable wildness was their family emblem. As to interest they had in Thomas's, it diminished as their gambling debts increased. So it was that these days Lord Bramley ruled the company tables.

Bramley put a chapter on New South Wales in *The Shepherd's Sure Guide*:

The first sheep carried there had large heads, Roman noses and slouch ears; they were extremely narrow in the chest; they had plain and narrow shoulders; very high curved backs, a coarse, hairy fleece, and tremendously long legs. From such animals emanated all the improved flocks now in the country.

But even then, Cribb was receiving a few bundles of fairly good Saxon merinos and interesting bundles of Spaniard merinos only part crossed, such as the Stanton and Kale.

Now some of Cribb's reluctance to overenthuse was malice towards his stepbrother. Nothing over-superlative must be said of New South Wales if Rankine thrived there. But here, in the 'Tharpe', was proof that a combined Spanish flock, its wool analysed by Cribb once in England, now again after its growth in Botany Bay, had a part in an advanced miracle, call it glory, served up under the *nom de laine* 'Tharpe' of a cryptic locale, 'duckmole rch'.

The evidence made Cribb tremble and burn to a point of his guts unappeasable by whisky, which in no way stopped him downing more. For he deduced — as no other man was able, through the quantities of threads revealing their sources to eye and touch — that his stepbrother Rankine was behind the stinking shroud and in partnership with the palpable man of beauty. That Kale still lived and worked sheep for their betterment was certain to Cribb as the evidence would be to a saint having kissed the hem of a garment finding it wept fresh blood. Two parcels had been sandwiched together by the one hand. The wool said it all.

No great gifts of imagination were valued by mill owners and landholders in Cribb's part of the East Riding. They liked practical inventions such as the infernally tireless combing machine, which only needed the attendance of an overlooker and ten children, and combed a pack of two hundred and forty pounds of wool in twelve hours to get a job done that was worked by whole villages beforetimes. Application and skill were praised, and the keeping of trust and accurate books in the language of counting and gaining. These requirements Cribb supplied while his genius was called forth anyway, in prophecies of supreme and useless understanding, about equal to poetry, as he plunged his hands into rolls of fleece, drew them apart with a high controlled throw and noted with a narrowed glance from beneath wild eyebrows their quality and importance displayed on his slatted table.

Lord Bramley, for his part — where he circulated at the level of parliamentary committees and royal societies — was remarkable in never needing to take notes on anything much, because he remembered all details of breeding experiments and measurement tables to the extent that he amiably agreed to have his brain pickled after death, to allow science to describe what amounted to perfection in that regard; although that same brain had not prevented his getting a few pointers in *The Shepherd's Sure Guide* wrong, by writing down what he was told. Lately his fingers were stained from printer's ink as he carried around scrolls of proofs in his pockets, to work on putting his sheep man's bible into its eleventh edition.

On New South Wales, he now corrected:

The colony seems to be an exception to the fundamental princi-ple of the paramount influence of blood. My friend Mr Blaise Cribb urges this on me, from his study of fibres. In the first years these sheep were, in a manner, changed; the hair was comparatively gone, and a fleece of wool, of no great but improving fineness, succeeded.

Cribb might sneer understatement, but his lines of life sweated the truth. A very beautiful fabric called the merinos was specialised in Bradford from Saxon wools. It was extensively used in the neighbouring town of Leeds, where Cribb went one day to have his opinions examined by Lord Bramley. Imagine his surprise when Bramley told him pack his trunks, and get ready for a voyage of enterprise to New South Wales.

Imagine Bramley's surprise (as a man getting his own way) when Cribb said:

'No.'

FROM LEEDS, ON A WINTRY day, his lordship set forth with Cribb to London, where he was presented before a committee of parliament at Westminster. For the week members and lords were charged with examining the wool trade. A harder to impress, more confidently superior wool master of twitchy disdainfulness could not be imagined being squeezed for a knowledge of Spanish wools and their uses.

And you would think — mused Bramley as he watched his protégé preening and ticking men off — that Cribb was a sworn minister of the Crown himself, hoisting his figure lofty as he could by jacking his heels and rocking forward on his toes, extending his square jaw to his betters. There was sneezing, a wrapping around of scarf ends, a harshness of coughing, but not from any apparent nervousness, more from a skill in commanding attention by turning disadvantage to dramatic effect. Cribb was grossly unwell and after he put away his handkerchiefs the whole chamber leaned forward and attentively breathed with him, wheeze by wheeze, watching as Blaise Henry Rousillon Cribb grabbed his loose grey hair into a bunch behind his neck and allowed it to tumble free with a grandeur of mane. It was the style of a square-built sleekly devouring carnivore and not the manner of a sick man at all!

Cribb read from a document composed just a bit better than it might have been, polished by a stylist, Dud Hardcastle.

'Was it true,' he was asked, at the end of his first recitation, 'that Botany Bay wools were looking better than best Spanish and best Saxon Spanish wools when milled for fine descriptions of cloth?'

Cribb answered reluctantly in a way that made his arguments more tantalising. Colonial wools were indeed looking better, though only in fits and starts. From Spain, he said, came fine wool but deficient in softness; consequently not suited to rich and ornamental cloths. In Saxony, however, Saxon Spaniards, much the same sheep to begin with, were evolved in a more yielding climate under the hand of cleverer breeders to retain the Spaniards' fineness but better them in softness. Thus under the Saxon hand Spanish wool improved in length and soundness of staple, and freeness of fibre. When it was decided to try if it would stand the process of combing, Addison and Roper of Bradford bought lots, through Cribb, and a new description of worsted goods was produced, so light, soft, fine, and rich, as to compete with silks and satins for ladies' dresses.

At Botany Bay, Cribb then agreed — if a study of an outpost through the spyglass of fibres had any fix on its peoples — a fitful improvement had been effected under bad management, incrementally over a few short years. It was more thanks to the climate and to God, he declared, than to the hand of wisdom, and he concluded by asking, as he glared around the room: 'What results might not be attained with more intelligent husbandry in that distant clime, which had come under the orders of a band of officers without much breeding instinct between them?'

'Toughly said!' murmured Bramley when Cribb was done, detecting there was more to be unravelled here, from something more held in — a discovery that Cribb was too defiantly proud to tell. None except Bramley knew enough to sense the full man while the rest of the room was satisfied. 'He's too jealous of Botany Bay, vain of his knowledge,' thought Bramley. 'What Britain needs to hear most, he keeps to himself — for reasons he can't possibly confess. Having a French mother annoys his patriotism, it can't be helped, and since his brother inherited it's a hundred times worse.'

Bramley made a deduction, later proved correct: that Cribb had tested his more excellent samples and found recent Botany Bay lots giving a milling quality equal to Spain's, with softness equal to Saxony's, and without the defects of either. It was like finding grains of gold in a rusty dish and looking up at a wild mountain knowing they were washed from there, but hardly praising the mountain for what it threw out.

Cribb flicked back his coat tails and sat down. Bramley was beginning to understand there was an even greater fortune in the man hunched in front of him spitting into a bespeckled white handkerchief than he'd already decided. He'd said no to a voyage of investigation, but if persistent in refusal, Bramley would give him no choice.

Bramley waited until Cribb was finished with his lung clearing, completed by hoarse breathing, thumping himself on the breastplate with his shoulders wide back and nostrils flared.

A fortune, yes, but only if Cribb lived out the year in good enough health to carry on. Then Bramley considered something else: it was not just sheep that gained their feet in Botany Bay privations but men were turned onto her shores rarely better than skeletons and ran to fat fairly soon.

The parliament's tableau was lit by smoking lamps and fugged with tobacco smoke, crowded with representatives jostling for space, with documents piled everywhere on the floor and loose papers bound in scarlet ribbon and men stepping over them. Cribb was their attaché of breeds in waiting.

Hadn't the two men often talked of Cribb getting away from England for his health? — to Egypt, the Levant?

Cribb liked the idea of winter months in hot dry air eating dates and drinking ewe's milk on the decks of a dhow drifting the Nile. Bramley gave him the picture, otherwise it was beyond Cribb's pocket. So nothing came of this either. Bramley was reluctant to annoy his friendship with a prideful man by meeting his bills of travel. It still might be, though, that Cribb's intelligence alone would cover a passage to the right place, because wasn't Botany Bay a veritable Egypt with food of a dry and stimulating nature for stock, but without the miasmata afflicting sheep closer to the Nile (and without any Nile or river like it, it had to be said, that had yet been found)?

Luckily there were no New South Wales gentlemen in the room just then, to hear Cribb imply they were more stupid than they needed to be. But some were in the building having sailed dangerous seas to be there, at risk to their lives and prosperity. Word went around how they were damned (by a man from the north of England), denigrated for their proudest boast, their considerable sheep and their consignments of bouncy wool pressed tight as trusses of hay, alerting them to ask, through somewhat clenched teeth, 'Which one is Cribb?'

After his first evidence, Cribb was taken by Bramley and shown the woolsack from where the country was ruled. He was then steered by the young lord's elbow to an oak-panelled room and told to wait outside until wanted again. A crowd of men jostling their turn refused to ignore him. Cribb was greeted by alnagers, wool sorters, factors and breeders from the wool counties and breed-of-sheep exhibitions. They thickened the air with their knowing exhalations. Cribb barely acknowledged them, and that was all right among them as Cribb's reputation in wool was matched to a name for high rudeness and temper fits. Such men had been brought to London from their barns and fields for the week of quizzing and gave the room the feeling of a gathering at a fair, getting up a thirst that would be slaked in the evening in a pot house where Cribb would join them and drown his differences in drink — and show less of a temper, it was doubtfully agreed, from mixed experience they had of Blaise Cribb in his cups.

Crowding up closer were a few men of a more peculiar sort and prickly with unfathomable pride.

Their faces had the baked skin-flaked appearance of roasted rocks and they were unsteady on their legs, being not long recovered from six to ten months at sea. There was a colonel, a lieutenant — and one so man-in-the-moon-faced ugly as to be remarkable.

This was the Reverend Matthew Stanton — recently landed from the *Edinburgh Castle*, a ship taking longer than most on her voyage to England, being overtaken by two that left Botany Bay well after her, in a voyage dragging on ten months. It was not true that the elements reliably sent westerlies across the wild southern latitudes to whisk a boat home on a broad run. Too often winds rounded from the east and north and set up an opposition. The *Edinburgh Castle* was a leaky, miserable, barnacle-encrusted vessel fighting contrary winds nearly the whole way and delivering her unhappy pilgrims into a smallpox plague at Rio, where they were delayed eight weeks with careening before beating up the grey Atlantic as winter set in. It was a year of winters if you sailed the southern oceans that plunged from one season to the next with barely an hour's interval and all freezing wet.

S TANTON WAS DRESSED IN A lumpy suit of clothes hastily tailored for the occasion, a sprig of dried wattle blossom dangling from a breast pocket to show his origins, en passant, from the Bay. He carried a hefty cane fashioned from hard gum wood. His coin purse was made from the skin of a wallaby kangaroo. His Geneva collar was woven from Bay of Islands flax. From under the folds of his neck protruded the twin flaps singed by an overly hot steaming iron in the London chapter house where he lodged with his wife and daughter. Long expected from Botany Bay among churchmen, thanks to letters boasting his ever delayed coming, Stanton had a curt response to any who asked if he surely had sons as well as a wife and daughter. Wasn't it true there were two boys of around the same age, to be brought along? Boys described as sons?

The answer was a sharp, defensive, 'No': No sons, and why should you think so?

When there was every reason to think so — from them being boasted of in letters of anticipation, two boys being brought across the seas in an exemplary party of colonials, but had never arrived with them: two boys dark and light, one the father's favourite, Warren, and one the good wife's pet, Titus, but neither any longer referred to by either party as England bound when enquiring churchmen and interested relatives wondered.

Before the Stantons' arrival, advertisements were posted in church annexes and meeting halls, announcing their missionary zeal. There was much interest in how a great matter fared: a sacred adventure guided from London on orders trusted to God. Reports came back too infrequently as a rule, from the Pacific shores, and sometimes even after beloved missionaries had been killed, eaten, or had scandalously gone native indulging their lusts. (God save them all in prayer!)

The Stantons had survived out there a full sixteen years. Word was wanted from the horse's own ministering mouth but nobody quite realised, until they met Matthew Stanton, the extent to which the man had cut his trouble teeth on military commanders and despotic governors, least till he worked his conviction on Church authorities with startling ferocious ease and strutted his opinions on the lecture floor. The churchmen Stanton battled in the archbishop's offices (far less obdurate than a governor's, he found) were for a fact the same sag-bellied authorities who had, over the years, bent to his every whim of conscience when he wrote from Botany Bay seeking guidance, as to whether it was correct to flog convicts and serve commerce by raising flocks. They liked to say there was an arm of the Church flourishing out there on the far edge of imagination, so their answers were always yes, you are on the straight and narrow, sir. But a sense they were well rid of Stanton along with England's most beastly criminals, and Ireland's filth was fairly open in their attitudes, now that Stanton met with them. They were overly judicious, overly refined. He was out of sight, almost out of mind: and he sensed peculiarly not the right sort but peculiarly the right sort there, to deal with matters beyond their grumbly purview. It was verified a Christian trait to adapt, in a weary world, to fight the Devil with the Devil's own pitchfork — except lucky for the archdeacons it was Stanton pricking the beast not them — using whips and the jealousy of getting on, yea, yea, and nay if the result was fear in men's hearts, Church property made safe from governors' hands, and mission stations properly fed. But did it have to be so openly personified, in a toadish rampager?

Thus Stanton was getting (in a few short weeks on land) justly famous for shaping his own role as a churchman and playing it as a right. It was a power of inflated self more comparable with a politician's or a general's: Napoleon being the most recent exemplar of wild confidence on the European stage, and the two men's linkage by analogy not so absurd, when the topic turned to wool, because while Napoleon had destroyed Spain's future in wool by laying waste the land, Stanton was a hope for Botany Bay in answering Spain's loss (to Britain as a supplier) by putting another land under sheep. If you doubted it, ask him, and if his answers wouldn't do, consult Lord Bramley, of scientific fame. He said the same thing.

As Stanton went around London on social calls he found himself despising his old Cambridge mentors as despicably mortal men, while envying their clerical power and cleverer whispers to God. They were getting published in bound volumes of sermons that were selling better than romances and shipwreck tales (though not as well as wool, he jovially reminded them). While their theology still tied him in knots, how he barked at them and saw them retreat to sherry! Answering about Wilberforce he instructed he was a Wilberforcian too — hated slavery, how could they doubt it? — slaves being abhorrent to a man from Botany Bay because a slave was not punished for any sin, by having his rights withdrawn and his labour sold on a block, only a convict was, for sins that were as cunning as original, but with the benefit of emancipation fairly soon following on good behaviour (if recurrence didn't show). That the colony was growing on unpaid labour was not to call it slave labour at all. 'Not even taking into account whips and irons, judiciously applied?' The answer again, 'Not so, sir.'

After prayers at missionary suppers, Stanton told the story of his first days in Botany Bay as a chaplain of convicts, when his poor wife and child almost starved and risked getting their throats cut by rebels. It was a boisterous picture of struggle involving playing down his failure — complete failure, it was — in converting New South Wales native blacks to Christian lives. Only with whips would they bend the pious knee! A small grey fleck of spittle appeared at the corner of the mouth when he said so, which he destroyed with his thumb.

Sheep were mentioned in more favourable tones than souls. It was impressed that breathing dust fleas and chasing wayward ewes was what a missionary mostly cared about.

Stanton's talks were followed by plate suppers with currant buns and five-gallon pots of Cantonese tea. Among good people the rumour grew the larger, the quicker it was strangled in the cot. For it happened that a girl of Ivy Stanton's Bible class, in their London chapter house, pitched tales of a rage-roaring Stanton straddling the decks of his ship. Ivy must have been talking, for her father to arise quite the demon in clerical garb attacking a black boy with fists until in artful desperation the poor fellow bleeding-mouthed leaped overboard, and his adopted brother, encouraged by Mrs Stanton, leaped in to save him: and that was the last seen of either. The family then sailed away leaving their beloved sons in waters off Brazil!

It was hardly to be believed, even of a disorderly sheep-breeding parson. Whispers were told among small groups of Christians rattling their teacups, until Stanton by instinct came in through their clusters, breaking up the very thought of intrigue with more of his wild stories of life at Botany Bay amid Cockney forgers and Irish radicals brandishing metal rakes.

Husband or wife — which had most urged Captain Maule to sail on the tide from Rio, when the wind was right?

The question was one the Stantons asked each other in private, believing it more extremely private a query than any imaginable. 'Dolly?' 'Matthew?' They sought each other out, defiant of making a mistake. But they could not blame anyone else, they could only face each other.

For each had had a reason to flee the Rio roads, as much as a reason to delay. That was the trick of it. Well, they had sailed. Each of them had spoken. As a pair they were opposed that day, but Maule heard them give the identical word of consent, that he translated forthwith into orders to sail. Then the wind dropped, making moral judgement of their haste, and they hardly got around a corner past rocks, and were rebuked a little longer by the shore.

So it was in London they found themselves in moods so strangely contrasting to their expectations of how they would feel in the capital of the world.

Stanton left first for Westminster each day with a concentrated purpose in mind, in the dripping foggy weather carrying his noisy gum-wood cane to announce a progress through the murk.

Dolly wrapped herself in a coat and ordered up the two in hand long promised by her husband as a luxury they could use when they got there, if she went along quietly enough in herself.

Well, she was quiet enough in herself to get around, you can believe. Jaws ached from keeping jaws tight clamped. Eyes stung and ears burned from paying attention to a daughter, a problematical splinter, who was not very thrilled by the thought of going to Westminster, except that some officers of Botany Bay were going to be there, she'd heard, with their families — and in case they saw the king. Ivy was titillated by thoughts of royalty and famished for conversation with anyone who knew what she talked about when describing that wide plain of bleached dreams, her childhood residence, Laban Vale, where dust devils blew and paper daisies never faded nor grew slack. Her mother knew as much as this but only a little of the next thing relating to a passion for the land left behind.

Because also Ivy was starved to know, as her most urgent, less sentimental, and definitely very careful and quite clandestine enquiry, if anyone knew of a naval officer named Lieutenant Commander Valentine Lloyd Thomas. Was there anyone from his family known, a sister, a cousin, the Miss Lloyd he mentioned as a favourite cousin? — Oh dear God Ivy must make herself recognised by some, or die of oblivion. When she used that word to herself, oblivion, she meant oblivion not as a cry of being unknown and wanting fame, but of ceasing to exist. Death by knot of Lloyd Thomases. They were judges, lawyers, horseflesh fanciers and gamblers for high stakes. They would know how to deal with a piece of trouble brought upon them by a sixteen-year-old girl. There was a farming estate in Caermarthenshire where they went at times of the year: to do what, Ivy was uncertain, except she'd heard teach tenants how to grow turnips on neglected lands, and she hoped they were not there now — unable to remember which season they decamped from the city. For didn't Valentine say they had an address kept up in London? Or Miss Lloyd and her mother had? And when he'd said they had, hadn't Ivy too lightly thought of London as a knowable sort of town, larger than Sydney and Parramatta together, of course, but laid out orderly, easy to get around, with its monuments, parks, churches and palaces landmarks you sighted one to the other without losing your direction because the London that mattered was just a few streets — she had seen it in panoramic etchings of river, squares and rows — just a few fine houses, and in those fine houses just a few confident men who stepped out and organised the world? Men such as Valentine Lloyd Thomas, who, though a legal officer of the Royal Navy, a servant of the king, and a confidential enquirer of the governor of New South Wales, did not give a fig for respectability, as he told Ivy while kissing and holding her against a tree in the shadows of flowering moth vines in Rio. Indeed of the two parties of this world — those who thought Lord Byron a scourge, and those who thought him a wag — Valentine was of the latter cabal.

In the afternoons, in the London season, Lloyd Thomases paid visits, taking glasses of wine, gaming at cards, enjoying music, following the toes of dancing masters into the newest steps. Was there somebody from that side who would see in her, in her green discovered eyes, in her secret panic as she passed in the street looking into dimly lit doorways, who she was, what she wanted to say and lay claim to, without her actually having to say so? 'You are a gift,' Valentine had said, as he lowered her in the leaf mould of a forest's bed, and proper to a gift unwrapped her with hurried fingers releasing hooks and bows. Now he was at Botany Bay and she was here in trouble.

But the London of her arrival! After her previous imagination Ivy wondered what sort of a place she'd been brought into, nothing but houses and streets look which way she would; nothing but houses when she walked for hours together. It must have been two miles in a straight line and all the time wondering how so many hundreds of thousands of shopkeepers made a living, and yet she had seen nothing of London yet. She had hardly even barely come into a sensation of looking for a needle in a haystack. Where were they? How would they greet her at their door, the Lloyd Thomases, when she knocked at the very last one?

In putting the question to herself Ivy knew the answer would not be favourable. But setback, or even shame, would never stop Ivy Stanton (her father's true daughter, her mother's absolute child) from seeking what she wanted in life because she was fearless in the face of it. Otherwise there was no meaning to her name, she contended, Ivy being the hook of itself, the catch, the snag, the lock. She went climbing life's steep wall until she peered over the top. Although now at the beginning of a great check on fearlessness, having made a sorry mistake, she was very uncertain whether life after a certain date say a month hence would be worth living for the shame revealed. Skinny naked in her mirror she was no more protruding than a piece of string with a knot tied in the middle. But that knot was the tie.

Dolly, only sometimes able to read her daughter's condition of mind, and not at all this furtive matter concerning her 'condition' *per se*, was full of her own justifications of a similar headstrong nature.

Dolly, each day, had the carriage waiting that her husband supplied despite her not keeping her side of her bargain with him any longer, although to be precise about it, nor had he. For her word on all matters of mutual satisfaction was rendered void by the non-arrival in London of Titus. All she had promised, when they'd bargained at Laban Vale, was to stop opposing Warren's passage in return for Titus's coming. After that she believed she was free to work her means.

Dolly had an idea that was never to be. It was born of seeing a bluebell emerge from velvet green grass in a graveyard, and of wanting to throw herself down alongside it in shocking relief, like a person dying of thirst finding water, or a wanton her lover. Her idea to put to her husband was that she stay in England longer than he, with Ivy set to finish her schooling, while Matthew returned to the colony alone and she looked after their business this end. Whatever his objections might be (and they would be loud) they could be purchased, she considered, by picturing her return to the colony with the wildness in their daughter tamed and the girl quite eligibly married off in about four years' time. They would fairly certainly be comfortably rich in that number of seasons, the way things were growing with their wool, and while it was their devout shared belief, as Christians, that money was never to be sought as an end, it was always a good recommendation of higher virtues to have some in the bank.

AT THE START OF THEIR voyage, ten months ago, Dolly put an obstacle on her sleeping arrangements by declaring she would no more sleep on straw than fly to the moon. 'A donkey's breakfast,' she said, was how their ship's mattress was made, proof against mildew from wet oak planks: two wide sacks filled with straw and dried seagrass, sewn up with sail twine. 'I will not, I cannot, and I shan't,' was what she'd said, and a move was arranged by their obliging Captain Maule. In the cabins amidships the accommodation was dry and the mattresses stuffed with feathers where she bunked in with Ivy, while her husband agitated over his connubial rights — just where were they to be taken, how? — and picked on Titus more.

Alignments changed among the five of them. It was a revelation how Warren baffled her husband, of a sudden, since their voyage began. The sadness was that Titus paid for it on both sides, in a displacement of rebuke and none of it Titus's fault.

Dolly had always been pretty cool at cutting off heart passions in the name of the next practicality coming along. In the matter of Warren she'd always been open enough not wanting him on their voyage and that didn't change. Was her husband then to be surprised at losing him? You would think so by Matthew's acting out the loss among street folk and beggars. He was convinced that the two boys (grown malicious in his imagination) had already made their way to the great capital. He'd got into the alarming habit of seeing them in every smudged face.

Dolly had left the final plotting of breaking free from Warren until Rio. There'd been no landfall since the Bay of Islands (their one port of call after Sydney) where she could have unloosed him sooner. If Warren *had* fallen overboard she would have been sorry. But the lumpen hair-sprouting boy had a distinctive sweat she could smell in a roaring forties gale and hardly bear. It was an amalgam of sheep grease extruding long after it had soaked in, of pickled cabbage, rancid pork, issue of sailor's grog, and a feeling of something else, to do with the muddiness of his eye. Discount the bullcalf-longing to jump upon anything that moved, that was betrayed by a hand in his trousers and his eyeballs rolled back when he thought nobody watched. There was the annoyance of his wantingness, of course, how could that be borne? The craving of sentimental deprivation, wantingness and something more that thickened the air. She did not know what it was for a long time. Whatever it was, it hardly touched her pity until he was gone. As for Ivy, all through the voyage she called Warren brother and used him to fetch and carry, otherwise was wrapped in Titus as her mother was and more. 'Where is Warren?' she asked, idle as a kitten wanting her things picked up where she'd dropped them. The answer was coiling the ropes, picking through the rice for its weevils and grubs, feeding the pigs on deck in their smelly houses, or climbing into the rigging as high as he could go. 'Oh, be careful what you say — he's at the door!'

Warren had changed, but the worst of the change was that he'd only intensified his differences.

He talked much of his mother and called on Dolly trustingly when he twisted an ankle dropping to the deck from the ratlines under bosun's orders, and asked if he could lie in her bunk, because the sway of his hammock hurt him. She supposed that disgustingly yes he could! And when he fell below, shivering cold from his watch, he came to her and asked her to hold him, to warm his bones. He talked of wonders like the squid that landed in a sail; and repeated stories sailors told, of ghost ships and treasure. He seemed to need something from her that he couldn't ask, which she had not in herself to give. Something half seen. Something half heard. To do with her husband and the officer of rangers, Rankine.

Dolly swooned whenever Titus was whipped, and found a sailor was posted to keep the women below. She struggled on deck and screamed her fury, a madwoman protecting her imp as much as her husband was the madman beating him down. Yet they went to their prayers kneeling, a pigeon pair, while the timbers of the ship oozed wetness that dripped in their faces. 'What have you done to Warren?'

'I have no idea.'

Why to be honest, Dolly had wished Warren only as much harm as he needed to carry — say a small amount would be all right. At the very end, at Rio, she'd seen him make it safely to the shore, clamber to rocks, turn around and look back with a long stare and apparently a shaken fist before going in under the trees. Then she wished him no harm whatever because he was gone from her life. Oh, but the loss of Titus wounded her spirit.

If Dolly had thought harder she would have realised that the something worse troubling Warren since their voyage began, and splitting him from her husband so unusually, had not been mere wantingness — more yearning for trust on the basis of information received. It would be some time before she found out — that the answer was terror! — terror aiding Warren to jump overboard when she urged him, and terror sacrificing his gift of coming to England . . .

It started with their anchoring near another ship — when word was passed like a poisoned cup between sailors cavorting on a beach eating boiled mussels and trading favours with savages. A ship's boy from the vessel *Allorah* (a boy of convict family, and full of clandestine knowledge) befriended Warren and told him what was known.

It was, that a captain of N.S. Wales rangers was arrested on Parson Magistrate Stanton's sheep station and taken in chains by constables to Parramatta and to Sydney, and given a flogging when his pleas were fallen on deaf ears and, after a secret trial in Sydney where the governor was called, was exiled to Van Diemen's Land.

But worse than that was told: because when the captain reached Van Diemen's Land as a prisoner aboard the *Allorah* the lieutenant governor of that island was handed a letter from the governor of New South Wales. Officers came out to the mooring in a cutter and showed the captain an example by taking him personally in charge. A heavy resentment was laid on him. It was to do with sheep. Nothing more was known than that. The captain was removed to a second vessel, a prison boat that set off for Hell's Gates on the westerly end of the island, a hard-beating voyage into the teeth of westerly gales, reputedly taking weeks of foul sailing, though it was barely two hundred miles off.

Hell's Gates — everyone knew of Hell's Gates. Nobody could follow there or had so far escaped. It was a closed trap against the rampages of the southern oceans, whose waves rolled unstopped round the planet until they thrust themselves at a narrow opening of land choked with a sand bar. Imagination was unable to exceed the penalties of the place. To survive the crossing to the dark waters of the harbour beyond Hell's Gates was perilous, and the saying was, that to give prayer for being saved in crossing that bar was to spend one's days in bitter despair of God for allowing your crossing at all.

Warren was sick to his stomach hearing of it. Though he'd had his differences with Rankine, that was all over now, and he thought of his mother. It seemed Stanton had turned around from all his affectionate chaffing and liking of Ugly Tom and had him took, without warning forthwith. Mistrust fell on Warren like the shadow of night in the middle of the day. No wonder he continually faced the wildest seas to find what other sorts of surprises he could go up against. His own master had shown his worst, tipped off the governor, and the governor had struck.

Every doubt Warren had over Stanton came back to him, the stronger for having been curbed, for a long time, in the name of sheep. Every accusation hurled at Stanton that Warren chose to ignore he now learned was under a scab of conscience and festering since they first met. He was the earth's last fool waking to rub sleep from his eyes on the last day, beguiled by sheep and the vanity of knowledge around them. In his mind he went back through the sequence of events. What a deep silence must have fallen over Parramatta and its sources of information when Rankine was taken, and no wonder! Apparently nothing was wider known of the disappearance until the officer was bundled aboard the cabin boy's ship and taken roughly below. The *Allorah* had sailed for Van Diemen's Land that same night, taking her prisoner with her as she winked down the purple harbour and out under the Heads of Port Jackson at daylight. Silence then until the *Allorah* hove to — near the *Edinburgh Castle*! and the two crews had fraternised at that pretty musselbed bay a few miles from Cape Brett. Warren told himself the sequence over and over, until time and feeling were tangled.

It seemed the parson did not need to be told what he already knew. All his excitement was on missionary matters and the band of tattooed Christians established in the next bay along. After a few days they'd got under weigh with a supply of pigs and potatoes. Stanton was farewelled by the missionary and his natives with a ceremony of taking leave — after they pressed noses, some of them squatted on their haunches with tears rolling down their cheeks and were so terribly sorry farewelling the man who'd brought money for their little church and given them a few pounds of gunpowder for their muzzle loaders.

WARREN THEREAFTER SAT ON THE upturned ship's jolly boat with his fists grinding his eye sockets and his brain alert with sparks. The ocean rolled under them and the *Edinburgh Castle* slid backwards down waves, never getting very far, week by week straining into months as they put south until they saw icebergs and then sailed north seeking a safer course. Whenever the crew grumbled and wouldn't put their hammocks out on deck, to air the forecastle, and complained how their meat was too old, it shrank and they weren't getting their agreed weight at mealtimes, Captain Maule gave them their meat but stopped their grog for a few days, and so they were brought a bit more under his control. Warren and Titus groaned with the crew and sang shanties when the crew sang, cheered when they got their grog and together shared the life of the ocean. They learned they would not be putting in at Tahiti nor Valparaiso unless it was needed to fill their water casks, but sometimes when the weather was squally the rain poured down and they caught hundreds of gallons of water at a time and so kept plunging on. From his vantage point on deck, when he wasn't serving his watch, Warren saw anyone coming and decided whether to avoid them by going around to the leeward side, almost awash. He calculated he was a great lump of deceived fool that the arrest of Rankine was old news when the *Edinburgh Castle* sailed. It meant Rankine's seizure was close to the date, may be the same day, that his mother and the Josephs left Laban Vale with Stanton's hearty blessings and two hundred gifted culls. Warren felt his opinion of the minister shrink into its newest shape, a hot burning lump of hate. All this time Stanton knew where Rankine was truthfully gone? In irons? Forsaken? Could it ever be asked?

No. Warren on his own could not ask, because he knew Rankine had fatally courted danger; and so waited disagreeably until Stanton let something out.

One day at breakfast Warren heard Stanton musing with his finger dipping into a cup of hot toddy, about all his years of sheep dealing. The listener was their Captain Maule eating his oatmeal, as Warren drew nearer the door and heard the name Van Diemen's Land.

'Now there's a pleasant island pasture to benefit a sheep man with a breeding nose if one is plucked from the prison filth,' said Stanton.

'Is that likely?' said Maule.

'I have known one or two one half worthy. Unless they go to the Hell's Gates, where it's a whole lot harder to get free.'

'A puir place for a sailor, there's a mean sort of a bar. I know there's a few low rocky islets, shoals more like, where they maroon their worst rebels, unshackle them, set them up and they live on kelp and pippies naked as the day they was born. It's cold, there, and it constantly rains. Men stand up to their waists in freezing water getting logs for the shipbuilding.'

'They could do worse,' said Stanton and astonishingly so, and Warren, coming into the stateroom to collect the captain's chamber pot, which he did at this hour, lingered to hear what else would be said unguarded from those brown sugared lips.

'It would be the same as a shipwreck, being so prisoned,' said Maule, a firm but affectionate tyrant in the estimation of his crew and all including Warren, 'that I wouldn't like at all. The very thought makes me shudder, aye Warren? What is it noo?'

'I have come for your pot.'

'You are lucky it's empty, as I'm gummed up in the gizzards. Look in that cupboard and see, there's a jar of poultry bran, it should do the trick. Take it to the cook and see he makes me a gruel for my parritch. Inchcape's a good strong lad,' Maule turned back to Stanton, 'a ship's lucky to have him. He's learning to be a seaman good as I hoped.'

'Until the day we land.'

'Isn't that our bargain,' agreed Maule.

'If you ever chance a landfall at Van Diemen's Land, Mr Maule, some day in your weavings around the world in this nutshell of yours, you might do worse than take a Warren with you — he's a shepherd before he's a sailor, recall — there might be a profit in bringing off some stock from this shore or that. They would be worth many pounds a head in New South Wales. I give you that suggestion free of charge, sir.'

Warren went aft clutching hold of a mizzen stay; he rose and fell with the stern end, dunking himself in the cold ocean of a following sea as if he was hotter than any burning coal, and coming up wetter than a drowned bird, and crying tears of salt. It was where he went to sluice the captain's chamber pot dependent on winds and today felt dumping himself over would be lumpier.

But did not, and never would with the spirit that burned in him too fiercely. He'd developed, apart from whiskers and an itchy crotch, what the captain called a topsail yard voice. Anyone on a part of the ship could hear him call aye or nay. Thereafter avoiding Stanton, above decks with plenty of places to climb aloft with Titus, his chosen shipmate, he worked the duties assigned him far out on the yards and made conversation with albatrosses. It was said they were birds that circled the world a few times while a ship beat a slow passage one way. The birds of the world favoured Warren all his days. What did albatrosses see casting their eyes over the rocky wastes and islands of the world, when the tearful salt wind parted the feathers of their foreheads?

Warren imagined Ugly Tom and his gaolers — Rankine if lucky being given privileges to make him comfortable enough, as happened with gentlemen in bondage to their own class, even at prisons as cruel as Hell's Gate, according to what was said. But then he remembered how Rankine's stomach turned while he made cheerful conversation with his equals, how he went to lengths unmatched in the annals of Botany Bay to be sure somebody down-trodden was as comfortable as he himself. Then it seemed sure that a man in prison rags resembling Rankine would be dragged scraped bleeding from cuts of oyster shells, would be marooned on one of those rocky piles that made strong Captain Maule shudder but the minister stay thickly silent, unmoved, and change the subject back and forth to sheep.

Sheep, sheep, and sheep, thought Warren. He almost remembered them in the same way he remembered himself before he began his changes. As a reason for morning excitement and a reason to be proud at dusk, when all were brought in. A horned head would turn looking at him from monotonous eyes and he would accept, from its alien gaze, some sort of tribute. Now he saw they were creatures with no reason to like him or anyone else. Their mistrust was complete. Their herding was about as liked as if a school of whales was caught in a net and dangled above the deck and milked of its fat. Dust choked them and they sneezed and coughed and made more dust with their trotting hooves. It was a fine dust composed of dried crystals of pissover and shredded sheep shit and sand. He was better off without them and wanted nothing more to do with them as he sniffed the salt air.

Below decks was the quarter where Warren knew his mentor was rarely likely to be present, his beloved teacher in morality and wools — that part of the ship where Ivy and her mother made nest with oak planks and featherdown mattresses as comfortable as heaven.

Down there Ivy had her kittens, her sewing boxes, and a small coal stove that was fed with a pair of metal tongs from fuel in a basket. She was never seasick and roamed the boat when everyone else was down spewing, getting into corners with Titus when she wasn't allowed. She and her mother and the captain's wife and ugly daughter made a four to compete in needlework as best they could in the smeared, smoky light of whale-oil lamps, with the rocking motions of the ship making them sleepy. Warren knew he wasn't welcome, but found a corner for himself out of the way, nonetheless, where he made his stolid invasion of overgrown limbs and loud breathing through his nose; but was sometimes asked if he would kindly thread a needle or hold a skein of wool while it was balled, or to go to the galley for some two-decker, as sea pie was called with a double layer of crust, that great favourite, and it was a good enough reward for an exile from bad feeling, was it not? They were fabricating dresses and costumes for themselves to wear when they made their landfall in England. Underneath them while they improved on scraps of lace, chiffon, crepe and velvet — by cleverly sewing them into whole pieces — swam whales, sea sharks and giant stingrays to which they hardly gave a thought, except one time when there was a low thump throughout the ship and the captain sent down word: it was the head of a giant octopus nodding against them, and they all rushed up in time to half glimpse it sliding away. It stayed in their dreams and in Warren's made nightmares of long fingers crushing out life.

When he climbed the mainmast and looked into the sea it was clearer looking straight down. He saw, in rare calms, the shadows of those creatures sliding under them. Also sometimes when Warren looked down, there was another sort of shadow this time crossing the decks. A red-haired variety slipping under the jolly boat where the ship's tender was stowed inverted. That little shadow was more dangerous to safety, thought Warren, than a sea creature was: and he feared more for Titus than he did for Ivy crossing the decks. For those two, going in under the boat was a place like climbing the fork of a tree, except now it wasn't so much joy that lit their faces when they made their meetings, it was more like sullen need and stronger over them than any punishments forthcoming.

On Sundays Stanton performed divine service even when seasick to please the Lord. If he needed an excuse to whip Titus he found one, keeping a pocketbook where he added wrong deeds between one and ten. Upon reaching ten he broke out the whip and for the lower numbers there was an almost daily cuffing.

INTERMINABLE COURSES MARKED CAPTAIN MAULE'S charts like a cat's claw raking the bottom of the world looking for where to pounce, until they rounded the Horn (in a lull of rare good weather) and were safer — released from fogs and gales and their worst dangers.

After a creeping progress up a low coast they reached Montevideo and were allowed to take water but passengers were forbidden ashore — it seemed for the reason of driving them mad except it was claimed to be political and there were reports of shootings! Two weeks more afloat, and they reached Rio on a port tack on a warmish tropical evening, but were denied a fair wind and stood off for two more days impatiently waiting and smelling the wood smoke of landsmen. If they thought this the end of their torments they were wrong.

They went over to the town in the jolly boat as soon as allowed and at the dockside felt their legs slumping under them after too many months at sea. Stanton fell down on all fours on the flagstones and kissed them in prayer. Titus, his humour bright as his bruises, and loose in the legs himself, mimed kneeing his master in the rump, to the delight of bystanders. Stanton was warned by their commotion, chased Titus with his stick, couldn't run, fell, and cursed all slaves as much as pitied them. For they were slaves or freed slaves in their rags and tatters who watched and found him a joke. It was ever the minister's fate to be paraded, on an unwelcome stage, closer to the earth's misbegotten than where he wanted to be. Meantime Titus elected to take his freedom as he found it — on the shores of a foreign land.

Where Titus disappeared for three days roaming not even Warren knew. When he came back Titus knew every tavern or stew in which a mortal could get drunk for a song or a penny. When Stanton finished flogging him and next time reached for his cane Titus ran away again — one statement Warren heard him make was that if Stanton touched him ever again, he would kill him. Though upon return, to Stanton's face, he merely bowed his head and called him master.

'I am not your master, Titus, I am your father.'

Stanton smiled saying this probably for the last time, putting some meaning behind the words, but not much, as if his love for Titus had life left in it, but not much, and Warren knew that the minister had forsaken Titus in his heart. Titus was no longer a representative of a native people worth saving. If there was a tribe on earth worth saving they were the Bay of Islands islanders: they seemed to like putting on snowy-white chemises and singing in choirs of salvation numbering as many as made a sweet sound.

'The word "master" is a bad one,' said Stanton, souring his lips in a smile — sure sign of a crueller pleasure, when you knew him better. 'Because in this country, Titus, a master has the authority to sell his servant in the slave market. Though I doubt you would fetch many dollars, and none at all if an honest man did the spruiking.

You are better off being disobedient within reach of my right arm, let me tell you.'

In that interlude of loitering on land there was never a day when Warren stopped off adventuring nor Titus running wild. Ivy bloomed into coppery beauty (white-shouldered, small-waisted, tiny-plum-breasted), was declared a fleet favourite and taken to receptions on board vessels and met ships' officers who were around her a few days and then gone on the next leg of their voyages as if they had never existed on the face of the earth, and the more offhand they were in losing her gaze, the better she liked them.

The best that Warren did was to become friends with a boatman, Peres, by name.

Peres was that poor commodity — a freed slave. Together the two of them rowed out to ships and carried captains and midship-men all around the bay. Sometimes they took Stanton. It kept Warren interested in boating matters and gave Peres a spell. Warren took up the oars willingly. It was the same as when he became a shepherd and sheep herder. The sea and the means of crossing it filled his mind, because what call was there for knowing sheep, when there wasn't any land? So Warren answered to water, formerly to dust. As long as he was certain Titus wasn't getting murdered, he was pleased. Titus was safer among brigands and cutthroats in Rio than he was on the deck of a ship with his master.

One day Warren rowed Titus to Peres's camp on the beach, expecting he might get finished with sprees, but as soon as Titus woke under a palm tree and shook off his bad head by diving into the waves, he was looking out for grog and shortly found a few companions of a like mind to indulge him with their sugar spirit distilled over fires.

The *Edinburgh Castle* was taken away to be beached and scraped of a crust of barnacles and if the Stantons thought they would find another vessel with berths for five (as they daily applied) they were marked for sure disappointment. The peevish bureaucracies of the Portuguese were as nothing compared with the tarrying of the British consul. The only one happy in it was Ivy, observed by Dolly (but not yet by her father) to have busy flirtation in mind, particularly where an older officer was concerned. She met him, Valentine Lloyd Thomas. He was made to match her need. Dolly, if she were not so ill every day with the heat and the belly gripes, might have seen where Ivy was taken during the time he gave her because she had been there herself, at the same age, and only luckily come through: although not steered by such a practised diplomat in getting agreement without much opposition. His blue eyes, black hair, and expression of need were the same strong forces effective on women that he applied in his work as a royal commissioner. In the evenings they walked in the gardens with Ivy's chaperone walking a few paces behind. Mrs Redway was a Portuguese woman married to an Englishman, and came with recommendations. When required to look the other way, she had her price.

Daily confronting the British consul Stanton made himself an enemy of the one person who might have helped shift them off before they grew mildew from the rains or had their brains fried by the sun. Of course, if he paid his own way instead of doing their journey on government warrant it would be quite easy to get a vessel. But he still had that stubborn idea of himself as a consequential chaplain of the Crown.

Appearing off shore in the glittering Rio roads were some

convict ships bound for Botany Bay. Their next port of call was Cape Town and then Sydney. As well as people, they carried livestock, cattle and sheep. Stanton, Dolly, Ivy, Titus and Warren — all five — elevated their noses when a pungency of sheep's dung wafted over the water and for a moment they forgot where they were, it was such a wavering banner of home.

From those convict ships Stanton was sought by officers and a party of free settlers with farming plans. They were ill equipped with rural handbooks telling them what to do about cows, horses, pigs, dogs, bees, and sheep when they got there. They asked which breeds were best for a colony where the seasons were reportedly turned upside down, and it was fairly well known that it did not rain as much as at home, except when it did bucket down and there were tremendous floods on the biggest river. As Stanton knew of no books being any use at all, unless it was a few chapters in Lord Jeremy Bramley's *The Shepherd's Sure Guide*, he told them that all breeds were pretty scarce and wanted in their own way, but they would have to wait and see. If they wanted his wisdom they might have to wait a bit longer. Why should he give out for nothing the wisdom gnarled into him by sweat?

'All very good queries, ask me again tomorrow,' said Stanton, his head filled with visions of being beaten at his own game. He feared newcomers were set to inherit a man's advantages unless he closed on his security quick, reached London, found maps, recited his needs, and received his land grants from the king according to where the maps showed best land. The new men were a fairly serious sort of traveller and some were rich, going abroad with their wives and families, their overseers, their servants, their leading shepherds as well as their best bloodstock lines including bulls, rams and stallions.

From them (as they'd been briefed in London) Stanton learned that Sir Colin Wilkie was sacked as governor of New South Wales and since five months past a better man was on the water, wearing cocked hat and gold braid, to learn how much harder it was to rule prisoners from Botany Bay than from Britain.

Hiring Peres's light dory and Warren as boatman Stanton used his time going around preaching to ships' crews at Evensong and Sunday Eucharist, picking up what information he could, which was very little. His daughter was more up than he was on officers' knowledge but ask her what they talked about and she said they talked about her, and very nicely too. At night, tossing on his sweaty bed under a breathless muslin net, Stanton applied in his prayers for acknowledgement of all he had done and for strength for what he would do when released from confusion over his wife and child. His wife being ill, his daughter pining for a man who sailed off on the morning tide, and who Stanton learned — too late — had in his keeping the next New South Wales governor's secret despatches! Moaning with inward defeat, approaching Ivy with any sort of question regarding Lieutenant Commander Lloyd Thomas was to risk perdition of a poisonous rage casting him as whoremaster to his own daughter's usefulness. The Stantons made a dismal show of life ashore among bananas, goats and coffee beans, in a bungalow with one servant and a well of putrid water.

Fevers swept through the town and carts groaned out carrying bodies marked by smallpox.

Storms raised thunderheads and squalls whipped the water. Peres got up a small sail, with Warren at the steering oar and Titus in the bow to give their dory weight in a rough sea. They put around a few miles to the slip of a bay with its sandy white beach and a clear stream running down. The motion of the dory was easy in a rough water, better in a beam sea when Peres balanced the centre of motion around which the boat pitched so they didn't get thrown about in a seaway. There was no fever in the boatmen's camp, it never reached them from the steep ridges of the town. Warren and Titus, little they knew, were getting ready for their life as independent providers of their own needs, which they barely fancied as a future, even yet.

Warren learned from an old carpenter how to steam boards in a curve and peg them tight ready for sealing with oakum and tar. Bearing beamwise to the shore in an offshore wind, using sails cut down from an old schooner, Warren learned his captaincy of a small boat. In a squall he was almost knocked down, but came up drenched holding the rudder angled hard and luffing up to the wind.

WHEN THEIR WORST RUPTURE CAME it was not the usual cause — the contrived, inflamed impression Stanton had, that it was the next high moment for a whipping — but a real commotion Titus produced coming out on deck dressed as their captain!

Only the day previous the *Edinburgh Castle* had returned from careening and there was a lot of excited work restoring items to the chests where they spilled when the ship was laid on her side.

There was even an impression of Titus being forgiven his worst roamings (after a light lashing only, though which he seemed to have mutely resented more than most): but oh then, how he eased on deck like a piece of silk being puffed in light airs, cuts and bruises covered, floating up the captain's companionway wearing a three-cornered hat with a seagull's feather in the top, a high-collared cutaway coat, grey in colour with blue piping and brass buttons. Braces made of plaited string ran up under the coat. The trousers were of white cotton with a blue silk stripe down the seams, and his long feet were bare. In the time since they left Sydney Titus had grown a wiry beard. He never trimmed it, it was not enormous, but it grew quite dense and smart; it twirled to his upper lip like a pencil and pushed forward from under his lower lip like a small thick box. There he posed, a hand upon his hip, as he would always be remembered, while Warren, who was in on the game, asked him to turn one way and then another which Titus gladly did, as if posing for a sketch.

Accounts were to vary on what happened next, but there was never a court in judgement to establish any record for the keeping — as there was no crime as Stanton willed, in that instant when his fingers flexed and he reached for his hand whip and remembered it was down below in its sack, like the licking viper it was. There was only a crime in the insult so thunderously delivered as Stanton looked around for Captain Maule, to be certain the commander of their safety knew he was being ridiculed by his lowest rig scrambler. There was Maule, standing in the wheelhouse, only looking bemused. 'By God, am I the only one? Always the only one?' Stanton bellowed, and looking down at his right hand, flexed his fingers that were used to turning pages of the Bible and thumping lectern wood, to see if they were really as strong as they needed to be. Which they were, and so like a bowler lurching to the crease Stanton went a full twenty-two yards down the deck and knocked Titus backwards with his balled fist. It was not a strong blow, but Titus's next action was to roll, hardly a fall, over the side: so to drop lightly into the ship's tender knocking against the stern, pause there a minute keeping his balance in a barefoot dance like any good sailor might. Then he peeled off his clothes and stuffed them into the capacious admiral's hat he wore, and slid into the water naked and began swimming ashore about one mile. Laughter was heard from every watcher leaning out of hatches, hanging from the main topgallant yards one hundred feet in the air. Even from the captain, mildly, though he was out of good moods — for Maule's government passenger, the reverend, was worse than any limpet that could be scraped from the belly of his boat, and he was stuck with him. It was an exhibition, to be sure, of the power of a suit of clothes — now all that could be seen was the bundle of hat apparently bobbing across the water at a reasonable pace and growing smaller.

'Oh you lump, you gob, you chunk, don't save him, will you!' screamed Dolly Stanton, throwing a piece of soapstone at Warren.

'Hey, what?'

She took him around the neck and dragged him to the stern.

'Go after him, or don't you love him like the rest of us? S-s-s-aaa-ve him!'

'He's saved hisself,' said Warren, as the demand in all its importance came clearer; therefore follow him he would, despite Titus being a swift swimmer, and as he hit the water and went gurgling under remembered he was losing his inheritance by doing so. They were making ready to sail and if the captain didn't give the order any minute (in a stiffening gust that would push all swimmers to landward) he would find himself driven like them to a lee shore. With a spluttering gasp, Warren's head broke the surface and so many of the crew ran across to see the fun that the deck swung noticeably. As Warren pulled at his shirt and loosed his trousers for a swim, the longest of his life, he reasoned there were easier ways of getting back what was owed him, but none of those ways were honestly his any more to choose.

Turning around, treading water facing the ship, he filled his lungs with air and trumpeted:

'Stanton, you're the next, you horribilis cunt, and bugger my eyes if I don't get hanged for it!'

This was when the captain asked Parson and Mrs Stanton if he should wait or go, and they both of them said set sail.

Dolly was handed the captain's telescope. The good man held it steady into her trembling arms. Last glimpse of Titus under the trees. Going and gone through her lashes blurred with tears. Then came the last glimpse of Warren turning, shaking his fist.

At evening they'd found themselves becalmed and the next evening, drifting close to shore, a tide carried them near what seemed like a ghost barge made up of hulls of old fishing schooners, ten or twenty of them roped together and their decks patrolled by yellow dogs. Families clustered around cooking pots of fish heads and meat bones. As the *Edinburgh Castle* made her way past this vision of dismal hell without much choice (her boats rowing her in the calm) Dolly stood in the stern and her husband stood in the bow as far as they could stretch from each other without stepping overboard. It had been such a day of awful, immutable silences.

Stanton was fairly sure he saw Titus, Dolly was fairly sure she saw Warren, their boys taking shelter with the misbegotten escaped slaves and wretched of the earth who found shelter neither on land nor upon the waters there. Husband and wife, each one of them saw, or decided they saw, the one person they did not want to see and good riddance to him too. They both said nothing. It seemed to bind them as there was a rivalry grown between them stronger than other disappointments that carried them on in a picture of agreement. Dolly always had it in mind, now, if she could not curb him, to harm her husband as carefully as she could having tested her means on Warren and found them effective enough. As for Ivy,

Titus's loving playmate, companion of touch and tingle of touch, she would miss him all her days — but was in another state of confusion altogether, now that fun was finished, from which if rescues were needed, could she please be found by the Lloyd Thomases of Caermarthenshire and London, and taken to safety, or she would ruin her parents' happiness even more than it already was.

S OME OF IVY'S YORKSHIRE COUSINS came to see her
in London and she was marvellously rude, saying she did
not like them at all, they would not last two summers in
New South Wales — declaring it was her sister Leah whom she
loved most, missed most in this awful London, and thought of
always as moving through the Botany Bay bush with rainbow
parrots flying around her head.

'Who is Leah?' the cousins said.

'A young Jewess,' intruded Stanton, with a cautious controlling
eye on his daughter, 'who writes every day a journal of her experience, and already some packets of letters have come to Ivy. They
leapfrogged our boat by faster ship and waited for us in London,
although what is in them, and where Ivy keeps them, I might as
well ask the sparrows.'

Ivy said nothing to this. Her silences were more aggravating
than a torrent of accusations. The memory of Leah Josephs came to
Stanton, those dark eyes, those high-thrown black eyebrows as he
asked his wild questions of her — that she effectively be his next
watcher in line — when he'd promised, after whipping Titus

through the creek and under the trees at Laban Vale, never to harm his own daughter.

Stanton recalled the way Leah pursed her lips when she made the request — an effect like a branding iron making the sign of zero scorching her agreement as they parted. And that was the quandary he was in. Whether to make it pay. Because to get what was wanted from Ivy meant smashing her hiding places in those very sorts of action he was pledged to avoid. To quiz her on Valentine Lloyd Thomas, RN, and impugn her virtue irrecoverably, probably as well. Yet he wanted to maintain in his daughter a few shreds of respect lost from his wife.

For the strangest result of their voyage was that since the loss of the boys Ivy gained the ascendancy. The eventuality of a highly placed lover, if only a Welshman, and the friendship of a lowly trader's daughter, if only a Jew, were connected elements in Stanton's need as he faced his losses. Ivy was in London and the other two in New South Wales. Say if they were all in the one place! — then if Lloyd Thomas were able to say where new country was being opened, Leah Josephs might already be indicating where the choicest particles of it were grazed, Ivy could draw out required knowledge with her affections, and Stanton would be happy as sin!

His longstanding application to the colonial office was for land a mere twenty or thirty miles beyond Laban Vale. Now he begged for a change of locale, country much farther out. 'But where?' he was asked. It moved around in his mind like a cloud rippling shadow across rock ramparts, and he could not say. Yet he argued: what difference to the king if it was two hundred or ten hundred miles from Laban Vale, as long as it was deserved? It was just as far from London. What difference if the quantity was ten thousand or ten hundred thousand acres, either? What was any wasteland to the king? He'd been New South Wales's ruler for five and twenty years and hadn't shown much interest in expanding past the biggest river. Stanton was told that a grant was pending, but the locality required a description good enough for a government surveyor to go out one day and make it legal.

Then Stanton's heart hammered with excitement of what was nearer to him in London than anywhere else. He excused himself from a day of appearances at Westminster to worry that a hint of Kale's location was under the roof of his London chapter house in letters, and exult how much was at an Inns of Court lawyer's office in maps, George Marsh's old maps — if only Stanton could claim them without Warren, which he believed he could fairly do, wearing his minister's cut of clothes and clutching a Bible.

Leah Josephs's mail packets were probably hidden somewhere quite obvious, for Ivy was too emotionally honest to be devious, but when Stanton pried under Ivy's bed when she was out with her cousins, into her sewing baskets, and jabbed between the pages of a book (though not into her Bible through superstition of its sanctity), there they were not. Stanton's hunger to know what progress Joe Josephs was making in discovering where the best wool was being grown and in tracing Desmond Kale was so very strong in him that as he set off almost running through the streets to find the lawyer, Ritchie, guardian of a cockatoo, he suffered heart palpitations.

It happened within sight of the Inns of Court: his chest buckling with a loud thump. He fell over onto his knees and jarred the bones of his hand on the stones.

'Oh Lord, where is thy beam of light?' he found himself on his knees asking, quite unable to breathe.

He'd long expected, near death, revelation as a source of knowledge. Nothing came of it except a small voice enticing him that he was of the Devil's camp, if he wanted a way.

He remained down on his knees staring at the grey cobblestones, head spinning in a beatless, hapless moment when he heard himself addressed:

'Mister?'

He looked up, rapturously drawing breath. Being alive was quite splendid after a reeling blow. Two ragged boys held their filthy hands out to him. 'Are you all right, mister?'

Dirty smudged faces, ears pointed at the tips. 'I am all right, thank you, boys.' The most remarkable haunting impression was of Leah Josephs and her brothers in the fathomless softness of the two undernourished boys' eyes.

'Are you Jews?'

The boys grinned wanly. '*Marsel toff*,' and they touched their cap brims.

They guided him to a horse trough where he wetted the back of his neck.

Then the boys led him over to some grimy steps, and he sat down. Stanton was obliged to scrabble for a farthing, and told them of a paradise he knew, not like this foggy London, but where Jews lived in the wide open spaces, where boys giving good work could raise to be princes if they did not run away.

Truly, since arriving in London, Stanton could hardly open his mouth without making a boast of some sort about Botany Bay. Even his charity was a boast. For he was sick with remembering the deafening noise of cicadas, the scraping cry of cockatoos, the lumpy-backed, ever moving progress of a flock of sheep through the skinny trees. Happiness narrowed down to a stinking hoof and a twisted horn. Impossible for anyone this side of the world to know the wrench of experience in a place of pitiless desolation. But the two boys listened.

'Will you wait for me here?' Stanton said.

'We shan't run away,' the boys answered, as the minister gave each another coin, and looked around to find he was already nearby where there was a name board, telling him it was the rooms of Alexander Ritchie, attorney at law, at the very top of the stairs where he sat.

As he slowly climbed those stairs he thought to himself:

'Laban Vale — I do wish I was back there — where my sullen marvel, Paul Lorenze, is getting on with breeding plans; where my man, Galvin, sergeant of convicts, is keeping the bond men up to shepherding; where the dim Lehane circles the district with crazed sensitivity on my behalf; where all shall be restored to order when a boy appears, cap in hand, and waits for his day's commands.'

The name of that boy tormented him all the way up the stairs until he reached the top.

'WARREN!' STANTON HEARD THE NAME squawked as a door swung open before him. He was met by a bald cockatoo sitting on the shoulder of an elderly man of old-fashioned military bearing. Erect, metallic-eyed, guarded — both of them.

Scotch, the man was revealed to be:

'Weel, halloo!' or words of that dry sort. Though it may have been the bird that spoke.

Stanton made himself known, stated his business. Placed the Bible on the counter. Told the sad tale. Boy. Lost. Fled. Boy sad victim of attachment to native rascal and expected on ship any day, following to London, but not arrived. Tut tut, very well able to handle himself, but gone.

Ritchie said little causing Stanton to talk more.

'That boy, Warren, effectively my ward, sad owner of maps, papers, and one cockatoo of venerable scalp. Hello cocky!'

The bird grumbled a grey tongue. Stanton pulled a downcast look, and said, 'I knew Marsh as a young man. I had the privilege of tending Warren's mother's soul in her poor simple cottage.'

'You are well briefed, sir.'

'By Warren good soul himself. I wish to make myself more so, on his behalf,' said Stanton, stating his next desire, with some assertion: it was to satisfy himself, he said, that Alexander Ritchie was an honourable attorney, for such an honourable boy.

'And how do you propose to examine my integrity, then?' said Ritchie, a little more tightly than Stanton hoped.

'Oh, by seeing the maps left him,' said Stanton. 'And whatever else there may be. To be sure he gets what's coming to him, when he appears.'

The bird waddled to a corner of Ritchie's rooms. It had a dish of corn to crack in its dismal blue beak. But instead of eating, it hauled itself up a shelf of tomes via beak and claw.

'Wha'ever and wherever,' said Ritchie. 'There's a great store of estates I have to govern, but ye shan't have your revelation, Reverend Stanton, ye shan't be shown any maps, sir.'

Stanton watched close as he could the direction Ritchie's hand wandered when indicating the bulging cabinets holding legal papers. Then he closed his eyes and prayed for calm. Enough for now.

'Until tomorrow or the next day,' Stanton bowed out of the room. He grinned with laborious strain. 'I am sure we shall be friends.'

'Tuesdays and Wednesdays I'm in court,' said Ritchie.

At the bottom of the stairs the boys waited. Stanton led them around the corner and pledged to meet them there again. It was another five days until Tuesday, and if he wasn't warm glued to Ritchie by then, there was a door, and a window, he wanted them to watch.

———————

Then it was off through the streets dodging carts and beggars, sheltering in doorways avoiding downpours, and generally despising himself for being unable to be in three or four places at once. He wished his mind would stop going over the same matters all the time, when there was so much to be fixed settled and done. A painted apparition grabbed his elbow. 'I'm yours, master, for a gold coin,' she boasted, hardly fourteen years old, and he shook her off with an unkind word. When he looked back to correct his sharpness, she was gone on the arm of a soldier. Why, she reminded him of the most reluctant consideration he confronted! — the power of fornication. Ritchie in denying him had used the word 'revelation'. Well, here was the connection — when he was a theological student he'd been set to write a sermon: 'Revelation as a source of knowledge', and better if had been the coupling of animals, he might have won a higher mark. A young man newly wed had the world at his knees and he thought only that far: sweating over pages, scoring out words and fitting others in, never settling his mind to the question. Revelation he appreciated as the word of God. Knowledge he knew from his sensations. The word 'source' — he did not notice as he wrote, but his examiners replied, ' "Sauce", as you have spelled it, is a warm, flavoursome substance, either savoury or sugar, that is used on meats or puddings.' And that was only a small part of revelation on a day of test. A devil splashed in the bathtub where he frolicked with his new wife and she glowingly splashed in his mind. It was a great tiled tub in the palace of the bishop where they found themselves taken as penniless students for their bridal holiday while sitting his viva voce and written tests. He'd had knowledge of his wife on the steaming tiles, once twice and more, till he was pleasantly squeezed of desire. On one of those nights of release Ivy was conceived. Knowledge of his ineptitude as a scholar was delivered to him in the verdict of his advisors. A suggestion was made that God was calling him afar. Rather than go on with his degree mightn't he answer the call head up — be ordained and go to Botany Bay as a chaplain of convicts? Thanks to fornication he sailed.

Now, in the shortness of the same year in which the mere child Ivy Stanton became a woman, Titus and that bitter twist, Warren, newfound seafarer and moral judgement maker, had entered their manhood phase. It was there in them, the moment they came aboard that ship eyes flashing. Two juveniles of passable innocence overnight changed into braw jack tars with lust in their eyes and opposition in their heads. Their voices boomed, their chests broadened, their arms grew stronger. Their gloss of carnal excitement shone on their lips with unappeasable hunger and foul jokes. It had not been Stanton's imagination that on a ship of two hundred feet the distance Warren Inchcape went to avoid him was more like two hundred miles. They were seen going to the ship's doctor one day and Stanton wondered to the doctor if he was shown, by that pair of grubs, any blains of vice on the genitals, and was given an assenting answer.

They had all of their voyage a sailor's perplexing ways, and knew their halyards, sheets, and eight-hour watches very well — thanks, it should be remembered, to the employment Stanton settled on them with the captain of the *Edinburgh Castle* from their first day! Titus said he liked it better, as a job of work — scrambling up rigging and staying high as he could until dark — for which Stanton whipped him, naturally enough, as mostly it expressed rebellion for failing to serve his master at a given hour. Every day unlucky for Titus there was something the boy said, or did, for which it was justifiably needful to chase him with the whip around the narrow decks, saving the good Captain Maule the exercise of a masthead flogging that might be harsher than the minister's by far, if any more justification was needed, which it wasn't. But now scanning faces in the street and hoping, wouldn't Stanton give a lot to be able to say: 'Forgive me!' and get over this constant running of thoughts through his head and sudden stoppings of his heart to do battle. Especially if it got him those maps without the Devil's work.

BLAISE CRIBB'S PHYSICAL APPEARANCE STANTON had strangely imagined into a tall and loosely limbed, irresistibly affectionate man with a burr in his voice that melted milkmaids' reluctance to butter (and this after his wife told him Cribb was pugnaciously intense and moody to a fault).

But then with Cribb pointed out in the halls of Westminster — 'the one standing rigid, in the short brown coat, holding a handkerchief to his jaw' — it was impossible to remember any previous imagining, including that St Blasius was beheaded after performing his magic on women.

Stanton gave a low moan of alarmed satisfaction. Why, the fellow was no better looking than he should be. In his mind he brayed: 'I have won the prize of your youth and am the better man for it, sir, having had the joy of your hedgerow bride these seventeen years, and just as my wool must make you bite your elbow, my whole life betters yours to a height unscalable.'

As Stanton was about to go to Cribb, to make himself known, an attendant beadle tapped him on the shoulder and whispered that his wife and daughter were arrived at the door.

Stanton was obliged to attend to Dolly and Ivy, settling them on benches under a high window, where other wives and daughters waited in excitement of getting a look at great persons. It was learned that the king would not be coming with those of his court, as hoped: 'But the king's cowman is here somewhere,' Stanton offered, 'he was chaffing me a minute ago, and lives in a lodge opposite the queen's gardens at Frogmore. See over there, a dozen or more under-secretaries and ministers.' At which both mother and daughter stood up and sat down again. There was the excitement of being at the centre of the world even without its crowns and tiaras. They themselves were of interest! — and how these farming aristocrats were unafraid of showing it, despite the snobberies prevailing in England, a contrast, if you would believe, to Botany Bay, where society lived no better than in a camp, divided ten times into ten, and to look at someone with too much interest was to shame your position and betray your safety.

Mother and daughter wore identical brown capes as favoured by evangelists but under hers Ivy wore the 'grenade silk', her grenadine cloth dress sewn together when they sailed at latitude 45 degrees south. The nap had flashes of cold sea colour matching Ivy's eyes. It was worth remembering she was born on the ocean and came into her second life on the ocean: now she was spilled onto land, a deep-sea treasure. When she loosened the laces at her throat, Stanton helping her off with her cape, he saw how she dazzled the room with her look of flashing eyes and unbonneted fiery hair. 'I have fathered a beauty,' Stanton reflectively touched his chin, remembering Dolly with something of this appearance, except in humbler fabric and with a more teazled mop, and a higher colour. Ivy looked fearfully pale.

Barely before saying hello to her father, Ivy excused herself and was off on the other side of the room and there embraced Sophia, daughter of an officer who'd bought his founding sheep from Stanton (absolute culls). This was Major James Agnew, who'd gained a ship after Stanton, but wouldn't have managed to do so except by the downfall of the governor. The minister caught Agnew's eye for an ascertaining moment, and when he was sure he was recognised, cut the man off with barely a nod. The whole factional giddy-go-round was somewhat octagonal. Agnew was a sworn enemy of Sir Colin Wilkie, deposed, and on an opposite factional front an opponent of Stanton and therefore of God. Amazing how coming thousands of miles reversed some feelings irrevocably but left other feelings intact. Stanton was sorry for Wilkie now. That officer, Agnew, was one of the party denigrating Stanton's breeders, not to mention his condition of soul, morality, purse, and whatever else, though it was hardly to be known how such officers could judge of anyone higher than themselves, or of a sheep, as they were made rich by dealing in rum, duping governors, befriending judges, and by taking concubines from the female factory to breed their Sophias. Oh, and then to boast lambs from Stanton's originals as a pick of New Holland's bunch, purifying their reputations with wools that weren't even legitimately bred in their own advanced name! It was, as well, a pretty good question if those wools had authentically improved since they went to Agnew. Stanton would like to ask that of Mr Blaise Henry Cribb, for hadn't Cribb said, in the committee rooms, that Botany Bay wools improved but their breeders did not?

'There is your man,' he whispered to Dolly. She hardly knew whom he meant. 'Your Blaise Cribb,' he hissed, to awake her, which made her blush and sit up.

'I say, let me through!' said Stanton as he scuttled into the crowd. There was the feeling of wanting to appease an attacker before a blow was struck. It was how he'd met God as a young convert. It was a feeling he'd had with Kale, but turned on its head.

Stanton pushed through the crush until he reached the less bustling end of the long room, where he seized Cribb by the collar, making a pleadingly sour announcement at the same time as tugging him around:

'Cribb? Blaise Henry Cribb? Are you the Cribb, agent and wool buyer who sells under the name of Thomas's to Addison and Roper, Garnett, Woods, and Co., on behalf of colonial wools?'

Cribb stared phlegmatic agreement. 'Who are you?'

'Lord, I am your best supplier, sir, under the brand of Laban Vale, mark of the twisted horn; I am Stanton, Matthew, Rrreverend, of Botany Bay,' he crowed, turning a few heads nearby who believed there was a person not quite gentlemanly standing in the room. 'How do you do, sir? How do you do?'

In a gust of breakfasted breath (kidneys, bacon, and scrolls of butter on yeasty baps, well soured on strong coffee) Stanton leaned into Cribb's face and the two men — of the same stumpy height — seemed started on a ritual dominance contest, but then pulled back.

'I DO, AS YOU SAY, very profitably, I hope,' answered Cribb after long hesitation, with a withdrawn, almost shy smile, and eyeing the other wonderingly, and in some surprise.

The man before him impressed Cribb as so needfully wanting that he challenged his understanding of where to begin. With his wool? With his wife? With an enquiry after the welfare of the engaging Tom Rankine, of Botany Bay? It was too soon for that. The topic of a brother would have to be prepared.

'I trust that Mrs Stanton is in good health?'

'She is in strapping condition, as you may see,' the minister nudged Cribb with an elbow, and pointed across the room. 'Our voyage took a few pounds off, but good roast beef, potatoes and jam puddin's put it back on.'

Cribb gave the room a slow lighthouse sweep.

'You missed her, sir,' said Stanton in a pandering disappointed tone, as if there was something whisked from Cribb's plate that he wanted to urge amorously and it shook like a jelly and twinkled like sugar, so give it a jab.

And there, not twenty feet away, sitting on a bench facing Cribb, was a woman of improbable grandmotherly age in a pamphleteer's cape wearing a righteously tight bonnet with springy mouse hair poking out. She found herself a pair of spectacles, upending a cloth bag with the combativeness of a bear tipping a jar of honey. Dolly Pringle, it was, in full possession of her character, though not of her domination over Cribb's heart, he was suddenly given to know after too many years of grinding recrimination.

He felt himself examined. Dolly packed her spectacles away. When Cribb looked again she was gone from the room. A paroxysm of coughing left him standing feebly, held up by one hand on Stanton's shoulder, the other clamped over his mouth, not daring to look at his handkerchief lest it was speckled with blood.

Cribb excused himself, found a bench, and wondered how he could like Parson Stanton in any reasonable way at all. The minister followed him attentively, helpfully, not finished with him. There was no incentive to be charitable yet Cribb felt himself oddly moved. This minister's nose hung like a bell. His bulging, tortoisey eyes seemed affronted over whatever he said of himself, as if half the time he didn't know what was to come out: a man tied to convulsive self-truthfulness. The few strands of hair combed over his baldness were noble as strings of spittle. Well, either Cribb liked him or was doing some work for the reputation of the woman who'd spurned him those eighteen years ago and was at last welcome to lie in the bed of her own contradictions. Could the ugliness of the man truly be what Dolly Pringle had chosen over him? Stanton must have been handsomer once, more redeemable as a young saint. That, or she was truly perverse. More time than

Cribb could credit had been spent sweating over what the victor was like, and now he could only assume what he'd been told was true, that Dolly had undergone a sincere conversion to Christian aims and the match was designed to further herself with God — who was irreproachable unlike herself or the one she'd liked best to grapple with, in days gone by, on dungheaps.

Cribb swayed where a gush of fresher air came through a door opening. A young woman left the room, showing a crop of hair like a bursting bronze bud. Cribb had the heart-wrenching impression he must have known her before, somehow, somewhere. She had a thin nose, a small chest, pale freckled skin, green eyes, a broad pale forehead. Hers was a beauty of the exhausted kind that argued against beauty and lost. It was dim in here and she was picked out in shadow. Cribb realised that while he went on staring at her it was rude to Stanton. He turned to him.

'You are getting your good prices, in the main, now, aren't you, reverend, and your Botany Bay confrères? Haven't I just been talking in the other room, advancing your colony's name? Its climate? Its good hard going? Its ability for the Spaniards — whose best wool, after washing, is white without spot? I say the breed is contented there, *il devient citoyen du lieu qu'il habite.*'

'I suppose that means good,' said Stanton, lowering his eyes. 'But whose wool is white without spot? Did you say? You see I wasn't there in the committee rooms to hear you talk. The impression going around this room is that you were less than flattering to all.'

What Stanton wanted to ask, but could not manage, if ever! was whether Cribb had lately sorted any over *supremely* fine fleeces from New South Wales and, if he had, what please was their origin by name of grower and address if it wasn't Laban Vale?

To learn he was trumped would be unbearable. Stanton found himself grinning unhappily to know an answer. His lips pulled tight across his teeth. Keeping up appearances was never his strength. As in wools, so in life, vanity to have oneself known would out.

Meantime Cribb, only barely holding his post, stayed mute over what he wanted to ask Stanton on the very same point as Stanton felt towards him blindly — namely, confirmation of his guess: the true origin of that fragrant sample wrapped in filth.

'Tell me about your life there,' he said.

Stanton set off on a rant. There was the word 'progress' and the phrase 'fascinating stage'; there were the words 'limits of settlement', 'redcoats', 'sheep', and 'drays loaded as ships of the line'. As Stanton spoke he tugged at his clerical collar and with a clatter of studs managed to tear it off without quite meaning to. It was shoved in a pocket. Bit by bit before Cribb's amazed eyes he removed the evidence of his vocation — but obliviously, disregardingly, in a way of his left hand not knowing what was done by the right. It appeared now that Cribb was being delivered a mercantile proclamation in spoken form advancing Botany Bay as the setting for a panorama of breathless purpose in which, Cribb deduced, Stanton was getting ready to raise the value of his wool in every breath. It was a speech propelled in tones of ebullient anxiety, and if not to be endorsed by the listener, then it would be devastating to the speaker. Such was the look of vulnerable pride in Stanton's woeful face when he finished his rant and stood heaving with emotion and lung pressure.

'How marvellous,' said Cribb, obedient to what was expected, then sank back into his thoughts, his breathing more controlled.

'I have an idea,' said Stanton, 'which you may think impossibly foolish. It is a recipe for stupendous excellence of style through sticking to the one breed and mixing its differences under a suitable sky. The eminence of blood is being disproved every day, though the experts don't think so. I am after good rams if they exist, but only if they suit my habit of crossing like to like. Nobody I think has thought my way before in Botany Bay, I mean, except look at you, your expression says otherwise. Were you born with a frown? No matter. I have taken a few Saxon Spaniards as far as they can go and it's time to bulk them up. One flock at a time, seeing how I go. Nobody has tried it with the pinnacle of the breed and that is where I think thrust will ignite — best to best! Size of frame and quality of fleece! My breeding records are second to none. Copies are in my valise, they go back to the early days of the colony. I have folded them in and in. My steward by paradoxical marvel is a Spaniard — hard to come by, trained in the wool of Estremadura and with a face baked flat as mud in the New South Wales sun. He's a great shearer of sheep and shepherd par excellence.'

'Where did you find him?' said Cribb.

'He was sent to me in our last months before we sailed.'

'Sent?'

'A disbeliever would say, by fortunate chance. Lorenze, for that is his name, if he's not half sheep is at least half goat and the better part of one — my men are afraid of him, which is all to the good — he leads, orders, knows, and rules. He's keeping the lot in good heart, and consigning wool off to your house every shearing while I'm absent, unless the new governor plays tardy with ships like the old one. Anyway, that is the wonder of our material, don't you agree, it is preservable and can wait unlike ourselves. Am I moving along too fast? I suppose I am. Next I shall be asking if you know that man, over there, see the one —'

'Lord Bramley?'

'Bramley!' said Stanton. 'The cleverest farmer in Yorkshire. All New Holland travellers carry his "Sure Guide". But he should not listen to every word he is told.'

'There is a new edition, now.'

Cribb saw Bramley breaking off from the conversation he was in. Bramley would be over in a minute to relieve him of Stanton and the occasion altogether.

'THERE IS A GOOD FLOCK, you know,' said a voice at Stanton's ear, 'upon the king's lawns.'

'Yes, well, you are quite right, of royal merinos —' Stanton turned, saw who addressed him, and said, 'my lord' — then lowered his voice. He would agree to anything at all in the face of one of his betters. But only for a suitable pause.

'I was talking to the king's cowman, then,' said Stanton. 'His merinos don't do well, a blind man from Botany Bay could have told him so. I'll stake my walking stick of berryergro-box-tree wood on that; by the look in his eyes when he praised them, they are,' and he tapped the stick knob against the lord's sash buckle, 'rotted, cottled, and mottled in the staple.'

Bramley turned to Cribb and raised his eyebrows. 'Are you going to make him known?'

'The Reverend Matthew Stanton,' Cribb bowed, ever so slightly, as he made the introduction, 'senior chaplain of Botany Bay.'

'I am only a simple farmer,' said Stanton. Neither man knew what this meant, except he looked more like one, with his clerical garb awry, than he did a minister of God.

'I have heard of your wools,' said Bramley, who was a tall, plain-looking man of around forty, with straight black hair and an expression of innocent, enthusiastic surprise. He would always be called 'young Bramley' even on his deathbed which would not come, surely, until he was around ninety-nine. He was alert as a heron standing in marshland, narrow as a sapling from ankle to chin, with a sharp nose and supple, expressive fingers.

Stanton smiled, squeezing his eyes into rolls of whitish fat, in what seemed a friendly way to the charitably inclined, among whose number Bramley seemed unaccountably to be declaring himself belonged!

'So you've "heard of my wools"?' said Stanton.

'Indeed.'

'There's only one person might have told you,' preened Stanton. 'He's tight as a clam, except I think he knows my valuable best wool intimately, sir, as you hint, and as I say, quite as close as he once knew my wife — in other circumstances.'

This was fairly astounding! And fearlessly droll.

Bramley was trained up to Cribb's stories of a few husbands' challenges, sometimes dangerous, sometimes sad, but he'd never heard of one so forthrightly put, so woefully out of tune with itself and wrongheadedly fearless either. Here at last was the unlikely evangelist who had won Cribb's love, Dolly Pringle — too many years gone by to count, and Cribb the loser in it, to his enduring heartache and wonder, and to Bramley's mystification, but then, he did not understand the human heart as well as he tried. Rather than gloss over the old affair, as Stanton was privileged to do, as any gentleman ought, the minister played the insulting fool by seeming to blame Cribb for his own victory! It was a ploy of original style leaving Bramley feeling definitely affectionate towards Stanton, and Cribb oddly seemed to feel the same. It began Bramley thinking of a possible partner for his Botany Bay agricultural company nine-tenths launched: a foot on the ground with Cribb.

'She chose the better man,' bowed Cribb.

'That is for heaven to decide at the last trump,' answered Stanton, 'as we are Christian people, depending altogether on what is written. Now I hear, before he makes his escape, sir, that Cribb is God driven as well.'

'How so?' wondered Bramley, deciding that Stanton was both monstrously sarcastic and freakishly perceptive. For yes, Cribb could be said to be God driven, in his thinking; anyway his standards of reach were the ideals of creation. At the last trump the last sheep called in over the last hill of Blaise Cribb's world would be a mystical ram with its horns on fire.

'In the committee rooms where none of our colonial parties were invited — I hear it was to the Lord God he gave credit for our achievements in Botany Bay. Isn't that right, my Lord Bramley? For weren't you there too? As a clergyman, I can hardly argue the point, but as a farmer, Cribb has injured my pride.'

Bramley was astounded. 'The three of us might indeed have something to share,' he thought. 'My capital, Stanton's knowledge of Botany Bay sheepwalks, and Cribb's peerless expertise plucked from the lip of the grave.' Looking at his friend tenderly, you might say, Bramley no longer believed that only a little more encouragement was needed and Cribb would agree taking the voyage to New Holland. Because it mattered not at all what Cribb thought, his health gave no alternative. Bramley would exercise his power and organise the sailing, and if need be have Cribb delivered to the ship in an invalid's chair and placed aboard by marshals. Would he survive the voyage? Death's door was behind Cribb where a beauty lurked — that young woman who'd come around asking after the Lloyd Thomases, and Bramley had told her to go away. But she wouldn't go away. Now Bramley had seen how Cribb stared at her showing what life was in him yet.

'As I recall, I gave God credit, yes,' said Cribb, 'to a high degree, as one must, for his creatures.'

It could not be put less pompously! — unless Cribb went back and reinstated the edge of sarcasm he'd given the credit in the committee room.

'Amen to that,' said Bramley. 'You are far gone, my friend. Take my arm.'

'To which I say "amen",' said Stanton intrusively, and hurried on. 'While I am loathe to bother you further, Cribb, yet I must say — if you will forgive me before his lordship — for the reason that it is written that the Lord helps those who help themselves, I beg of you to answer: what opinion do you make of my very latest lot of wools? They came on the *Edinburgh Castle*, that slow-going East Indiaman she drove us quite insane, being short-sailed through having miserly owners and rotten spars, overtaken by a pair of vessels that left Port Jackson after we did, one of the ships bearing the sacked governor, Sir Colin Wilkie.'

'There is a new owner now,' said Bramley, without giving away who it was — first ship of a Bramley line if it came home in profit.

'I hear she reached your wharfings with my wools. Ten bundles of heavy weight apiece?'

'She did too, and your wools,' said Cribb, 'if I remember aright, were a record weight. Fleeces averaged four pounds each, to the weight of between four and five thousand pounds total.'

'You do remember aright. It had excellent fineness, then?'

'It had only moderately excellent fineness, over all, yet made good price at auction.'

'What are you saying?'

'Density of staple was the lack. I am still saying a great deal.'

'Is he always quite as offensive?' Stanton asked Bramley, as rudely as he could manage without twitching for a strap.

'Fairly often,' said Bramley with the sort of smile that an aristocrat did get away with.

'But you praised it to Lord Bramley here, as he testifies,' said Stanton through his teeth. 'Was that before you saw something else?'

'Oh,' said Cribb, discovering he was caught out on his main hidden subject.

'What was it you saw after mine?'

'Nothing much,' said Cribb — and left the room.

As he passed through the half-opened doors into the anteroom Cribb saw the young woman again — the purest yearning, reddened golden doe that was ever startled out of a hide.

'Is Lord Bramley going to be long?' she said, jumping up and standing in Cribb's way.

Cribb shook his head. 'I think an age with that man.' She ignored this slight on her father in favour of her only wish.

'Do you know the Lloyd Thomases?'

'Of Caermarthenshire?'

'That's them in Wales — but here in London, I asked the man with the buckle sash, and he knew them, but couldn't remember their houses, or untruthfully said he couldn't. They're here aren't they, tell me they are!'

This was consistent. Bramley's greatest fame, apart from his 'Shepherd's Sure Guide', his wealth and his wondrous wife, Hetty, who rode to hounds five days a week, was that he forgot nothing he learned in life that passed for a fact, including all numerals, whether alone or in long-division calculations which he computed without a pencil. He would certainly know Lloyd Thomas's connections. Cribb guessed he took the young woman for a bother, and held back from telling her what she wished through fear of unwanted involvement. Bramley could be aloof in passion. His position gave him wealth, power, entree — the privilege of admission to any house in England — but very few adventures except in commerce. Whereas presumption in a young woman gave Cribb nothing but excitement burning north of his kneecaps.

They went to the bench. Cribb steadied himself, pulled out his purse and found the London addresses of the fairly well-known judge advocates and fading wool brokers. In the time it took for her to decipher details, Cribb's intuition told him more than he wished to know about the young woman and her needs. She had been wronged. It would be by the younger brother who had gone into the navy: Valentine, the rake. The knowledge covered Cribb with sadness over a young beauty's needs, which were nothing to do with his needs on fire at all, now that he saw her distress was real. But he still wanted her.

'What is your name?' he said. And as she suddenly stood to leave he grabbed her wrist tight, an unpleasantly needful grip from a man that any young woman would detest, and remember as wrong, but Cribb was drowning, and she could see that, too — as much as she was able to see anything else going on above her own distress.

'Let me go.'

Wishing her a kindness, he did so, and she was gone.

'CRIBB IS THE FOULEST MAN I ever met,' said Stanton. 'A bullfrog, an ogre. I would cease my cultivation of him if I didn't need him, and I would tell him that although I am *crawling* at present, I never heard of him until he wrote of my wools, rather niggardly I must say, and the rest barely a year ago, when my wife popped out her confession.'

There was a movement of brown cape in the crowd to which Stanton answered: 'There is my wife back again, now that he is gone. She is going around the room asking questions of returned travellers, who arrived in England in boats later than our own. She is terribly heartsick for what was left behind, a breakage, a swelling of that female organ, the heart.'

'In there is a great mystery,' agreed Bramley, with a vagueness of wisdom meaning nothing very much, except his dislike of getting away from conversations about livestock. They talked about the wonders of Botany Bay in that regard, where sheep might grow to the size of horses if unchecked, with their wool sarked dense around them as chain mail.

Stanton talked about the wool rush on; if a man had money where it would grow.

'I do think about the prospects there,' said Bramley, uncertain whether to broach his plans. He would go on sizing up Stanton until he decided.

'The entire population of officers and administrators wants a hand in sheep,' said Stanton. 'They are mostly great fools. They spend their time scrapping and mending their pride when they should be minding what bleats. All the greatest advancers of their own name are in this room as we speak. One of them is Major Agnew, over there. You are better off talking to me than to him. Be careful he doesn't impress you. I hear he's very plausible.'

'You hear? You don't know him?' said Bramley.

'Hardly at all.'

Bramley was amazed. It would seem that in a small colony gathered at the edge of an unknown continent, where every man must reach a hand to another, or die, suspicion, selfishness, stupidity and exclusivity ruled.

'I wonder if you know an officer, a man named Rankine?'

'I might, if pressed,' said Stanton querulously.

'A breeder of Spaniards.'

'It sounds unlikely,' Stanton paled.

Bramley sensed Stanton's unwillingness as nothing more came out.

Of course, thought Bramley, there is a hideous Botany Bay etiquette being observed. They have such haughty opinions of each other all round: murderers, gaolers, republicans, shepherds and garrison priests.

Bramley decided to force the subject on.

'No mention of Rankine by Cribb?'

'No, why should he?'

'They were raised together as brothers. Stepbrothers. Cribb is the older.'

Stanton tremblingly shook his head. 'Rankine, a breeder of Spaniards, you say?'

'As pure a flock as ever left Spain. The Spanish thousand. Seven hundred of them portioned to Cribb in satisfaction of inheritance disputes. Three hundred shipped to Botany Bay with great care, and I hear most survived. They'll be up to a good number and thriving by now.'

'I don't think so,' said Stanton, staring from a frigid mask. 'Your Captain Rankine would be pretty well known, to do such a thing, and all on his own. You can't have best sheep in that place and pretend you don't. They must have died, or something else.'

'Never with Moreno.'

'That is a sheep like any other, if it don't get food and water.'

'You misunderstand. Moreno is Rankine's shepherd. A Spaniard of stolid cunning, brilliant with sheep to the point of uncanny devotion, but in other ways deviously strange. Ingratiating, treacherous, I would have thought, like most foreigners swears by the knife.'

Remembering it all — as a blow to the heart — and seeing the light in Bramley's eyes, Stanton exclaimed:

'Have you any idea of the pits, the dazzle of pits in that deceitful country, into which a man might fall?'

'Tell me,' said Bramley.

'Think of a maze, a labyrinth, a meandering confusion drawn in a wiggle, plunged hundreds of feet deep with every entrance a dead end many miles up. All of it thickened with vegetation, thorn bushes, vines, great gum trees growing high as the cliffs they guard, by watercourses choked with boulders, not that there is ever much water in them, but when it comes, how it comes, flood water pouring over the jagged rims and lightning and thunder thrashing. No man, nor beast, nor mortal insect, my lord, can withstand such an onslaught. Except imagine — imagine on the other side of some obstructional wall — some other sort of country.'

Stanton gave these words a low, hissing authority.

'Some other sort of country? Now this I have heard about,' thought Bramley, examining his fingernails as if merely considering their shine. Bramley remembered visiting Sir Joseph Banks with Cribb, and the contretemps they walked into was tremendous. The explorer naturalist Marsh was there — having returned from New South Wales with barrels and trunks of specimens. Marsh had been superb in collecting flowers, buds, twigs, animal and bird skins of all sorts, but in other ways had exceeded Banks's commission and made a pest of himself to his employer — to the extent that fathering a child upon a convict girl and spending his allowance three times over while writing demanding letters was only the beginning point of trouble. There was also a black man, named Mun'mow or Mr Moon, who was accommodated on Banks's estate. He'd been Marsh's guide into country far from any known parts of Botany Bay, where Marsh was not allowed to go, and as a reward for that persistent misdemeanour, Marsh had voyaged his Mun'mow to England and kept him as a servant without particular duties. 'Marsh presents him as a curiosity,' Bramley recalled Banks objecting. 'He does not know why he may not keep him, as some of our neighbours do lions and tigers at some expense. He thinks the amusement I have in his conversation will fully repay me. But observe, the polished manners and comfortable living of Englishmen make not the slightest impression on him. He sits huddled in the corner in the cold, with his eyes turned inwards, and I am sending him home forthwith.'

Bramley frowned slightly remembering the account, making a tight pinch above his eyes, by which he was usually able to get a pretty good handle on something heard long ago. It explained what Stanton just said, which Bramley echoed:

'Some other sort of country already reached?'

'Well, but it's never been found,' said Stanton, looking up so steeply to Bramley that his jowls disappeared into a stiffening of whiteness. 'Unless by those with maps.'

Stanton felt this inside him, then — that one of those great dry boulders he projected so bitterly onto a cliff edge for Bramley's impressment did its work and began to move. It teetered on an axis so fine, that the touch of a finger — this finger jabbing Bramley's bird chest would do — or the push of a slightly expelled breath — this breath Stanton held in, while frothing it with spittle, lest it explode with sensation — both did work and rested on the stone and the stone moved. It started slowly and then went bounding, springing, racing away inside Stanton until it smashed to a thousand fragments on a broad plain and every one of its particles of grit, when the dust cleared, was a fine woolly sheep. And not a single one of them had Stanton's mark of breed on its forehead.

Chorus of the Sixth Part

WHERE KALE IS CONCLUSIVELY PLACED

L IFE WAS SHORT. DREAMS WENT longer. When Cribb
woke from his worst fevers into a rational sequence of
remembered life he was able to make decisions, or could
say, at least, that Jeremy Bramley made decisions and he gave way
to them for the sake of this and that.

In doing so, Cribb let slip his old life and began his new, in a
break that wasn't clean, but was progressively complete to the point
where there was no turning back. If it wasn't to be death, for Cribb,
in these weeks after coming to London, it was to be like death in the
respect that namely, he was the next in line to learn how everything
became opposite of what it had been before, when there were
dealings to be done on the underside of the world. Call it his stepbrother's lesson in getting on up. Those that were down were up,
their wrongs made right, in a place where governors profited from
crime, criminals made themselves rich, Irish gentlemen sprang free
of irons, sheep improved themselves in the rough, and ministers of
religion ran flocks on a scale of many thousands. While the roads
of Botany Bay ran nowhere into its interior, as Cribb was told, he
learned in these weeks how one of them led back to London.

Bramley brought Cribb's son, Johnny, down from Yorkshire. He slept in a cot in a corner of Cribb's room. Throughout many nights he was up tending the fire. They were always able, those two, to spend time in each other's company without much conversation at least on the boy's side, while Cribb made his difficulties that Johnny overcame with his good nature. Yet the son's nature was better than good — it was greater than Cribb's, unless Cribb saw to himself in extremis and very fast made himself over decently and agreeably as a changed person. Bramley saw not for the first time how the boy loved Cribb. Bramley trusted Johnny with all his schemes and this was the fuller declaration of an alliance that Johnny waited to seal with his father.

It fooled nobody that Cribb feigned indifference to the fuss being made of his illness and the plans growing out of so much going up and down of stairs and through the banging of heavy doors and unloading of delivery carts blocking a side lane. It was a support to his pride to be as vague in giving way to persuasion. That was about all the resistance Cribb had left in him. The rest was do or die at Botany Bay as Bramley dictated.

The next Cribb knew, Dud Hardcastle, his wife, Rosalind, and Barney, aged ten and a half, and their three little girls, twins, aged seven, and the baby at two and a half, were down from Yorkshire and at Cribb's bedside telling him their excited news in a milling of awe, screeching, and thumb sucking. They were coming with him.

The much maligned tub the *Edinburgh Castle*, after discharging its wools on the Humberside, was sailed down into the Thames and was undergoing refitting at Lord Bramley's expense at London Docks in the Thames upper pool, not far from the Tower of London. A bit more than a spit and a hawk away Cribb lay ill at ease rattling his lungs and possibly dying in Bramley's spacious residence on Rotten Row. Cribb told Hardcastle: 'If death wasn't so desperately ordinary it might be something profound!'

Cribb was indelibly Catholic, though. It went against Hardcastle's beliefs, but friendship pulled stronger, and the schoolmaster sent for a priest.

At the door a portly, judgemental man, Father Daubenton, looked Hardcastle in the eye. Exiled from Paris since the early days of the revolution, the old priest picked the schoolmaster as an excitable romantic, an English variant of dreamer about as far removed from political realities as a man on the moon.

Cribb and the priest carried on a conversation in French, of which Hardcastle knew enough to know he was treated condescendingly. Soon the room was full of incense and Cribb was coughing out his last confession, as it would be, unless Hardcastle bustled through the room to the window latch and caused an explosion of pigeons by swinging the window open to the rooftops and the best London offered in gulps of pungent air. It was not very good, but was better. The old priest scowled, stroked his grey throat, pulled at his red lower lip, and looked like a turkey gobbler.

Hardcastle went around London with a list of requirements, putting together chests of books, shoes and linen, strong clothes for a family and all the housekeeping conveniences needed for five or six years of adventuring and schoolmastering in an unknown country.

Bramley sent him to see Stanton and get some advice. Hardcastle found a sorry servant ushering him into the small, square parlour of the chapter house with its pallid evangelical contrivances of grey antimacassars and neatly stacked pamphlets of recent sermons lying in wait on every available surface. He picked the pamphlets up and threw them down. There were instructional novels written by literary clergymen, about dairymen's daughters and Negro servants, telling of new ways of thinking unknown to the human brain except through prayer said a certain way and intoned many times.

Bramley had warned Hardcastle to dampen his rationalism if he wanted sound advice. It was going to be difficult. Bramley had said not to make an outburst as he usually did to clergy about invisible trinities and puerile moralities. In the minutes before he actually met Stanton there was barely a chance to shuffle the literature disdainfully before there came a noise at the door, and the beginning of a shape like a disturbed but inquisitive, black-clad bulky animal backing in. The man who greeted Hardcastle was unshaven, badly dressed, obviously blearily the worse for drink, shrugging into his going-out coat as quickly as he could, 'to get them to a public house by noon'.

There, it was Stanton's turn to be amazed, and not just by the amount the curly-headed, boyish Hardcastle was able to drink without affecting his steadiness too much, but by how it mattered, not at all, how venomously entertaining and bitterly sarcastic Stanton became in the advice he gave. The schoolmaster wrote it all down.

'What should I take?' said Hardcastle. 'At my new school, if I start one, I want to teach all the practical arts. With enough land, and the help of my friend Cribb, when he gets back his health, I'll want to fence in a couple of fields, and show boys and girls how the mental and the physical spheres are one.'

Despite his promise to Bramley, this was a barb to a man of the cloth, which Stanton either ignored or didn't understand.

'Iron tools,' said Stanton, 'are the rarest commodity in the colony. Iron is worn as decoration by the most prominent men: I refer to ankle iron.'

'What tools are most wanted?'

'Hatchets, spades, axes, wedges, reaping hooks, sheep shears, locks, bolts, staples, latches, hold posts, scythes, saws, nails, screws, pots and pans. I did not say rakes, did I?'

'Rakes,' scribbled Hardcastle.

'Take a few rakes, or they will disappear from under you.'

'I have been learning and observing the habits of bees,' said Hardcastle.

'Anything that stings,' nodded Stanton, 'does well.'

'Are square boxes used instead of straw hives, to keep them in?'

'You would have to say so. With iron bars, too.'

'I once took the trouble to learn shoemaking. I can sew and heel shoes,' said Hardcastle, 'and can sew patches on. I have leather lasts and tools. As I expect we shall be some miles from any town this will be a great saving of money and trouble, and my boy can help me.'

'Boots to kick and trample are the thing,' said Stanton.

'Captain Rankine took a tent,' said Hardcastle, looking up from his page.

'Did he? I never heard of tents belonging to a man of that stripe.'

'Well, it was a large one, sent after him, fifteen feet by fifteen with a central pole, lightning rod, and other proper supports. It was erected in a field and bought in complete order. It looked like a cottage with the sides perpendicular, and when sheep ran against it, they couldn't knock it down.'

'If there's a Rankine,' said Stanton, looking lofty, but troubled, 'I would say he lives somewhere more solid now. More like a palace of stone, with a grim roof, and those bars of iron that are indispensable to the quality of advancement where you are going, young man.'

'You mean he's a prisoner?'

Stanton looked thumpingly glum.

'I would not know. I do not know. How should I know? Do not ask me.'

T HE SICK MAN, CRIBB, AT the centre of a vortex of energetic emigrational enterprise, resolved that when he
regained his strength he would oppose his friends; but more
and more, in the weeks that followed his collapse, he saw that
opposing was only an attitude, a hollow defence. Life lay in agreement and the agreement in this matter was life — to the best chance
Cribb had of it, at least. Hardcastle was playing his part with
Bramley relishing his position as organiser of enterprises — through
his powers of thoroughness, concentration, and unlimited funds.

Hardcastle returned from his meeting with Stanton not much
wiser about the needs of a rational colonist, but convinced of
Stanton's irrationality. Hardcastle's head whirled from drinking
strong ale without any steak and kidney pie to bed his senses down.
In the kitchen, where Bramley took food standing up, the two men
went over the news about Rankine being imprisoned. So Rankine
was in trouble. Cribb should know. They went upstairs and told the
Cribbs what they had learned. The sick man listened, absorbing
the possibility that a severer form of justice had been dealt to
Rankine in the remote geography of exile. Improbably worse than

Cribb's daydreams of revenge. Bramley decided that with no more information being squeezed from Stanton, he would make a call on the returned governor, Sir Colin Wilkie, in lodgings at Chelsea, and take him a gift of best highland whisky, to which he was said to be fatally addicted as an antidote to the shame of being recalled.

The talk of Rankine at last being called to pay for his blithe existence changed Cribb's thinking, as he faced what lay ahead. Just as much, it was the distressed young woman of dusty pale beauty who caused a swerve of direction.

After the vision of Ivy's loveliness and a few feverish lusting hallucinations, came the vision of her life as it truly was, as worth his interest, for her life was something desperate, frightening and fraught. It had all been revealed in that minute when they sat together with hardly any words and certainly no confession that she was how many weeks gone with child, except what feeling showed to be true — what Cribb rapidly deduced. If Cribb was wrong in this reading of her barely restrained alarm, his experience of life went nowhere.

As Cribb had given her Bramley's address and promised aid of whatever vague sort, it was good that one day she came around to Bramley's house in desperation that was not without curiosity and spirit. The Hardcastles were arrived and well settled when she knocked on the door and was received, and Rosalind was presented to her — Rosalind taking one look at her and loving her, asking to see her every day. Rosalind learned from Ivy that her parents mistrusted even a good woman's maid as company for their daughter, and if there was to be any going out Rosalind herself would have to call for Ivy, at least at their beginning, which with some enthusiasm and no persuasion, she did, and brought Ivy back to Bramley's house many times.

There was a back door, a front door, and a side door enabling Ivy to come and go without encountering those she wished to avoid, two of whom, it might be guessed, were soon to be her parents cultivating Lord Bramley and investigating Cribb as hard as they could — but never at the same minute if it could be contrived, as the two were so at odds. While Parson Stanton sought Bramley, Mrs Stanton would look out for Cribb.

Ivy told Rosalind everything she needed to know in desperate confidence while Cribb at the top of the stairs learned some of it. The comet of purpose that watched over Cribb's life swung down its lanigerous tail and brushed him with a better sort of understanding. Rosalind saw the understanding in Cribb and liked it in a man she had often despaired of ever liking for his fickleness. Though she said: 'Mightn't she almost have been your daughter, in a swerve of life's chances?'

Cribb agreed, having soon learned whose daughter she really was. But there was no helping it. He would wait.

Dolly Stanton came up the stairs one day, carrying a bowl of lamb shank's broth, mooned with yellow fat, and after settling a stool at Cribb's bedside, spooned broth to Cribb's lips as if he were her ailing child. When the napkin was folded and the spoon put away they talked of old acquaintances living and dead, and things went on so ordinarily fine they might only have known each other well enough, and not too passionately, on a distant day, except Dolly was still slightly crazed in the force of her feelings: for wasn't it like her, to appear at Bramley's door encumbered, and burst in with her quart pots of broth, practically swimming with secrets? — none of which she spilled, but the whole house was beginning to know them.

Each day when the Stantons left after making their calls, Cribb, Hardcastle and Rosalind decided on various stratagems to save Ivy.

Their greatest question was wondering if she was safe, not from her parents and society — but as to the likelihood of drowning herself in the Thames or drinking prussic acid. It helped she was colonial born with robustness reassuring to know. She was a young girl of forthright certainty and out of hardship extremes appeared to have grown into something finer. Hardcastle and Rosalind made no judgements of how she was fallen in sin, through Hardcastle's rational theories of passion, that held our bodies were to be enjoyed and the consequences accepted as rational enough. It helped that Ivy was Dolly Pringle's daughter in boldness, said Cribb. It helped that now Ivy — as she related in tears — in placing herself at the mercy of two spiteful spinsters, Catherine and Jessica Lloyd Thomas and their gambling nephew, David Lloyd Thomas, brother of the rakish Valentine, had experienced despicable contempt and slammed doors guarded by unfriendly footmen, and concluded that nothing worse could happen to her.

And so it helped she was thrown back on her parents, to tell them the truth. It helped that the truth she told them was not accepted by them, or if it was, for an interval of disbelieving shock and shame, it was only to collect their thoughts and wonder aloud: 'What if the child she is having — God save us — is not fathered by Lloyd Thomas as she swears, but by Titus, a black boy?'

In the Bramley house it was a daily topic to wonder what material the parents were hammered from. An impression of Parson Stanton emerged as quite monstrously peculiar in the thoughts and deeds he planted on others, including his own daughter.

One day when Lord Bramley went to the ship he made enquiries of Captain Maule, asking what stamp of passenger Stanton had been, on that vessel, before it changed owners. Bramley found Maule downright uncomfortable and not forthcoming at all. Maule being a good man and true, this was enough of an answer for Bramley to persist with enquiries: and so he set to work putting together the story of the voyage pretty much as it was known to the rest of them coming over. By the time Bramley finished working his investigation on first mate, second mate, the rest of the officers and a few of the remaining men, there was hardly a detail of the business overlooked. He was left with an account of two shepherd boys catapulted into the service of the sea, one of them whipped around decks until he finally leaped overboard, and the other following him into the shades of Brazil. Bramley's opinion of Stanton by then was fairly low, but he continued allowing him to visit his house and quizzing him on sheep husbandry.

IT WAS ENOUGH TO KILL decent people stone dead, Ivy's news. But Stanton and Dolly would survive it, Ivy believed, because while holding themselves to be decent people all through, and going about accordingly among good Christians and bad, the two of them, her parents, were not at all so very decently inclined at all. Their daughter knew it about them better than anyone: unseemliness was their saving grace in regard to her predicament — impropriety the undercurrent of their virtue. She'd learned it from them only to improve on it over them, to make of it something more honest, because they did not know it very well of themselves, if at all. She hardly knew she pitied them this way more than fearing them. She would not go as far as what she'd heard them called. The father tyrannical fool, the mother foolish tyrant. Insupportable labels to bear. Horribilis crumpet was far enough.

Torment came out fairly naked and supported them better than prayer, when her father was without his whips, her mother without her servants, without her saddle horses prancing about like demons, and without their boy Titus to practise passions on. They trod the London stage of their choosing, horribilously roused. While they raged, wept, and asked what was to become of them, they became what they always were, only more so.

At last Stanton got up from his knees and a pointlessness of prayer, wiped his mouth of spittle, and decided theologically speaking what experience showed: that God was not interested in New South Wales, the Devil was, and very much so and should have his own patch entirely. One day Stanton started to say such things as, 'When I was a good Christian I did so and so, and so on.' When he heard himself he wept, and after weeping, smiled.

In preparation for the Devil knew what, only with his mind cleared of doubts, Stanton went to a gunsmith and purchased himself a pair of small, fine pistols. One, the larger, he kept in a walnut case under his bed. The other, the smaller more personal of the pair, he carried in his coat pocket where it made a bulge hardly more noticeable than a pottle of brandywine.

They moved from their church quarters into lodgings nearby. It was a small but quite clean house that was going for six weeks renewable, complete with a maid and a man, and was fairly afford-able to a minister whose bank account made him a wealthier cleric than any he'd met in the county of his birth or those adjoining, before leaving to minister to convicts. It was all scrimp and save and put aside with country parsons and theirs, even among those who hunted to hounds in the week and had barely the time for their prayers on Sundays.

From a small window Stanton viewed up and down the busy street. Some days he stood there twitching the curtains for hours. He wondered, as he studied the lewd, deprived faces of passersby, what he would do if any one of his principal enemies turned up. It was mostly a speculation but fed his anger pretty well. Would he ask them to turn their backs before firing, or would he shoot them honestly in the face? If they all came at once would it be too many for his pistols which were double-barrelled — he knew it was fancy matter, but flexed his fingers — seeing that the count of betrayers whose lives were forfeit to his brainstorm amounted to a good few more than he listed when he left Parramatta. There was Kale to the fore, there was Captain Rankine, Paolo Moreno alias Paul Lorenze, Clumpsy M'Carty, and Warren Inchcape, of sorry fame, together with Titus Stanton — fled — and Commander Valentine Lloyd Thomas and a few other hangers-on to a young woman's freshness of beauty who'd raked their eyes over Ivy quite blatantly lustful including the arrogant Blaise Henry Cribb.

There was a limit to alteration, however. Unseemly as Stanton and his wife were, unseemly as everything in their lives had become, they pretty soon decided they could not have a grandchild out of wedlock. That was understood between them. Dolly was never one to vent rage like her husband but in this they were welded back into their marriage vows as one.

'Suffer, suffer, suffer,' she cried.

They decided the ragamuffin sinner their daughter whose defiance was quite heart-rending, was inventing her encounter with the lieutenant commander inspector advocate to give grandiloquence to her fall. From Stanton's description of when he found her under the jolly boat with Titus feeling up to her waistband there was little left to imagine. Ivy did not deny it, you see, neither did she confirm, but sat with her hands in her wilful green lap allowing the little bows in her hair to droop all awry, the slackened curl of an overlooked, abandoned temptress's sorry locks sticking to her cheek with cold sweat. Altogether their Ivy matched a blowsy image of what she could very well become, in this life, having made a start early on a path of debauch. Unprotected experience had begun for her early — when never at all would have been early enough.

'You must never go back to Botany Bay,' said her father — banging his hard stick on the floor and saying never, never to the ghost of a dear gone persuasive child, who'd played out her wiles in a game of consequences, and was now, for the first time! come under his fidgety consideration for a thrashing — from one end of their rented house to the other if he could be sure it wouldn't be heard by the servants.

'Certainly we can't go back there. How could we?' said her mother. There was one consolation in it. Dolly was at least pleased that her argument to stay in England longer wouldn't have to be put. It was won by Ivy being enjoyed which she daren't picture, except with an arm over her eyes. Yet where might they go? It could not be to Yorkshire and several villages of righteous cousins on both sides. There the ancestors of this problem spark dusted their leather-bound Bibles thrice daily and read hard lessons. They had waited almost eighteen years to bless her, they could wait one more! Something would have to be said to explain that delay for eight months or seven until the infant was out, and then, after due search for a good family, taken away from them. It was an area of experience where Dolly shone, the gathering up and farming out of sucklings. And she was sure she meant it, too.

'Mother?'

'I have spoken.'

'Father?'

'It must be.'

London was a vast, anonymous place, her parents agreed, heads together plotting. Together in want they had always plotted best. When they found their agreement, their truest, strongest marriage was in the creaking bed of pleasure where much if not all was forgotten for minutes apace.

Ivy could hardly disagree that London was where to hide, having traipsed the streets bewildered until she was spurned as a liar by the Lloyd Thomases and saved by Rosalind Hardcastle instead. London was a maze and a thicket, that wondrous dirty town, and if a girl went through the streets with a shawl wrapped around her and a belly getting bigger, who was to care? Already a few old wives sensed it on her, not from her size, but from her desperate pride — it meant only one thing apart from her being a colonial, and so she had nosegays thrust into her hands, wishing her well. They were formed of the daffodils and snowdrops coming in as spring peeped out a warmer eye before shutting it away again. Who could ever be ashamed of due pride? It was something to take anywhere. And so she had returned it, day after day, knocking on the door of Lord Bramley's house in her mood of courageous abandon; there to be greeted by Rosalind, that energetic, pretty woman of thirty, with golden hair, red cheeks, blue eyes, and greatly mischievous smile. Of the friendship, her parents hoped for the best. Her virtue was no longer a question among Christians let alone freethinkers. After all Ivy could hardly be ruined twice.

Dolly's mind went racing ahead. 'We can take rooms in Hampstead, say, and allow we are from the West Indies. I have heard of ladies from there, whose grandfathers were slave owners, and there is a taint they talk about, which is shameful, of course, but of such high colour it's almost a distinction of shame to be born into it. Or to have a child coloured so. They are good church people, too. Necessity has made me used to hard work,' she added, 'if need be.'

'No need,' said Stanton sternly, as if it was her fault; he'd provided for her over the years, and still was able.

'Remember I was born to something else, in a small cottage of weavers and ewe milkers,' said Dolly. 'See what I made on the voyage, that turned our daughter so vain. My fingertips are callused with sewing it all. If it wasn't Titus she loved, green is the colour of a grown man's envious lust and he wanted what wore it, uncaring as a ram.'

She wept. Stanton comforted her with an arm around. It did little good. But he left it there, dangling.

Dolly thought: 'This will ruin his respectability and his believ-ability for the final time, they are already rough used, but when we get back to the colony — thank God — everything will be the same if there is no child to justify. I am respected enough. Matthew is often enough disliked, but he does get ahead. He is my strength and keeper. He must get a London parish for a year and bury himself in good works. We shall make forays to Yorkshire separately, satisfy-ing our obligations there. We have the money to keep us while the other one of us keeps watch over Ivy.'

S IR COLIN WILKIE'S LONDON ROOMS were located in a meanly furnished house, close to the river, that Wilkie's aide-de-camp complained about as below his general's needs, but that the returning governor assured his visitor would do.

'I am a great despiser of comforts,' said Wilkie, 'having slept enough nights in heather, wrapped in plaid, with icicles formed on the tip of my speculative nose, having my preferences hardened into a vanity of roughness.'

Rotting stained walls, shaky stairs, flaking gilt cornices and a mouldy cellar were small inconveniences after a lifetime of living rough. And this was not even to begin listing his times of campaigning in the Peninsular War, where a staff officer's billets were as good as they were found, and mostly open to the weather. Wilkie, he told Bramley, had served in Spain with the 88th Foot, later 1st Battalion Connaught Rangers, dubbed by General Picton 'the Devil's Own'.

'Lord Bramley,' bowed Wilkie, accepting a pint bottle of the Athol brose Bramley handed him as a gift. He asked his servant to draw the cork and leave the room. Then he raised his glass to the light. 'It is a good drink for a Scot to taste in the morning.' The Athol brose was a mixture Bramley had his man prepare. It was made from old whisky, strained honey and sweet cream beaten together in a certain order and in the correct proportions. Men had been known to fight to keep drinking it after being offered their first glass.

After taking a lick, Wilkie continued his theme of tolerance. 'I have in recent times taken a few damned roistering tours around the prison colony of New South Wales, seeing how it might improve, until the imperatives of my position and not so much the privations of living caught me out. Nobody was willing to live rougher, in that heel end o'the world, and I would not have slept under canvas, either, except a charming captain of rangers convinced me it was better for my aching bones. Later, when I thought about his extreme fastidious-ness on my behalf — coming and going and proving he never went anywhere — why, and seducing my handsomest laundrymaid away from me — it came as a warning, and I began to have him watched. There was an outrage involving sheep, and the Irishman, Kale, offen-sive to every faction of opinion except the prison gangs'. Even after his being watched I trusted him like a son. Will ye take a wee dram of the Athol brose?'

It was ten in the morning as Bramley accepted a brimming glass, and said to the yellow-haired Scot:

'Might that same captain have been —' but Wilkie cut him off with a raised hand. Bramley was about to ask, might that same captain have been the one arrested by the ministering magistrate, Stanton, and sent to perish in Van Diemen's Land? But he would come to it soon enough, as it preyed on his plans.

With a patient expression, like a grazing old horse, looking this way, and that, Wilkie said:

'I would rather talk about principles than give out names, until I am sure of your protection, sir. Then I shall be glad to confide in you more about the venal factions eating away at my good name, hungrier than the white ants of Parramatta. There is to be a committee of enquiry over my administration, and I need a friend before the table, speaking on my behalf, as I have very few friends left to me any more. Major Agnew is here to do his damnedest. I don't trust many since the new governor was sent.'

Then Wilkie finally admitted, with a defeated air: 'While I am happy with the roof over my head, whatever the condition, it tells you I am yesterday's man, and that is a humiliation.'

'Where there is talk of livestock,' said Bramley, 'I am often called down from Yorkshire, and believe it's my duty towards His Majesty to oblige. There is much to do over sheep at Botany Bay. I have reasons for asking. Are they the cause of the outrage you mention, committed by that officer you resent, against his own kind? I know the officers all have em, and aren't they all set against each other over sheep? Are you a herdsman yourself, Sir Colin?'

'I am a soldier plain and true. The great set against me concerns men as cattle.' Wilkie narrowed his pale-lashed eyes, apparently willing to go further, now, in the direction Bramley led. 'In a place of cruel punishments I was regarded as lenient, having invited improved convicts, emancipists, Irish balladeers and ticket o'leave birds to my dinner table as equals. This despite daily floggings and hangings proceeding around me apace. I have signed away hanged men, aye, and women too, and ordered them lashed for all manner of evils, for arson, rape, forgery, buggery, burglary or house breaking in the night-time, housebreaking in the daytime, shoplifting above five shillings, stealing linen from bleaching grounds, stealing sheep and killing sheep maliciously. Y'see, as a Scot, I am a child of the enlightenment, which favours instruction, but as a loyal servant of the king, I am an agent of calibrated punishment. That is the reason I was recalled — as you see me before you, wiping my tears — each and every day a conflict of duty most intolerable to my masters, in their rule books, but to me in my heart. Then at the end I was enraged, and used all the authority I had to bring a man viciously to heel, although I am not sorry. I want you to know that I am not sorry.'

'I understand. You are not sorry. That is clear but it is the only matter that is clear, Sir Colin.' Bramley frowned enquiringly and threw back his heady mixture. 'Who was it you brought to heel, now, can we get to that man?'

Without yet answering Wilkie poured him another, and a larger one for himself, which brimmed over onto the table top, making a brown stain, causing Wilkie to lament under his breath: 'Ochone.'

The two men did some staring into vacant space as a servant came into the room and cleaned up the sticky spilt drink, Wilkie tugging at his untidy hair to busy the silence, Bramley severely smoothing his stockings at the knee. Bramley was a man of compassion to the extent that he disliked having his conscience pricked. As a landlord of forty thousand acres, and sitting locally as a magistrate, he often had cause to be quite as severe as Wilkie lamented.

The servant backed out a pair of closing doors. Wilkie glared after him and raised his voice an octave:

'He is no doubt listening, being in the pay of the colonial secretary, may he profit from the nonsense I am peddling you, Lord Bramley.'

'I am interested to know your opinion of Parson Stanton,' said Bramley, as they took their glasses over to the window, and talked more confidingly. 'You see, I wonder whether to join Stanton as a partner, when applying for land in New South Wales.'

'If he's not mad, you must be so for considering it.'

'You think him a doubtful prospect, then?'

'He is not certifiably insane,' said Wilkie, 'I've had that looked into by a medical wise head; but he resists careful definition of soundness, by all standards except those of his livestock keeping.'

'He seems near to weeping over the smallest matters,' said Bramley. 'Then he peers out at you, red of eye, to check his advantage. Everything is needful to him in a particular light. I wish that understanding people wasn't required. He challenges understanding. There is a nakedness to his feelings under the skin, but what are those feelings worth?'

'Like an owl without feathers,' said Wilkie, 'who won't admit he's no longer covered, and hoots the day long.'

'Were you ever so close to him?' said Bramley.

'I was, at first, through his tremendous obsequiousness and his wife's species of charm, which I was rather more drawn to than to his, for it seemed more on fire in the seat of the passions than self-servingly righteous and interfering. We got along well enough until Stanton discovered I was a reformer, that I spoke the Irish tongue through command of Scots' Gaelic. He was very suspicious of my meaning when I played the pipes. He went around saying I played a little spring in a very ranting manner, as if the force of an opinion carried the logic of a dislike. Yet my first six months there he called me his friend. I could noo get through a day without he or his wife calling in, leaving a mutton ham for my table or requesting some concession or other, which I was glad to sign over. Importation of horses was always on her mind, as much as his was on rams. They had lockfast chests of trade goods, meant for cannibals, which

I believe they sold at a profit to smallholders who desperately wanted nutmeg graters and pretty paint boxes to brighten their huts. Conscience walks a wide path in that land, my lord. I'd barely completed my first six months' rounds of inspection and made out my reports — the tenor of reports that finally brought me down — when Stanton led a case before me, asking the limit of fifty lashes be lifted from a magistrate's orders. I certainly refused him and would have taken away his power of the lash altogether, had I the reach. While limited to fifty, he worked an art of renewing the lash for a separate offence the next day, or the day after it more, when the scabs were still fresh, and if the offender had information he wanted, it suited him to extract a confession by this means. Always at arm's length, mind — he's sworn never to attend a flogging for fear of letting emotion intrude, has my quondam friend.'

'That is wise, his hide being thick with exposed feeling.'

'At a quarterly church parade, that Stanton insisted was required to preach governors — under orders he brought with him to the colony many years past, that none of us wanted kept up but he saw no reason to stop — he exceeded good manners as a mark of right-eousness, and made me out to be a devil through analogy. It was done with heavy humour. He winkled out that my two regiments were both called the Devil's Own, you see. As a young man, before I went to the 88th Foot, I was adjutant of a territorial unit called the Inns of Court Rifles. Because it consisted mainly of lawyers, and some good Scots lawyers, the king called us the Devil's Own as a piece of humour against clever attorneys. The strange effect was, that the wilder the parson raged in his pulpit the more his portrait of the Devil resembled himself. Holding a mirror to hatred he sees his own face. There he is, at the trick of exposing himself naked, that you observed so wisely, scouring me while he scourged himself, and rousing as much pity as amazement. Something about him suggests, och, merit through a debasement of what he stands for. That is about all, and why that is almost worth something, is a mystery that annoys me at the same time as it very reluctantly prevents me from dismissing him utterly to hell. His destructiveness has one undeclared object — himself. And it sustains him. Carries him on. There have been times when I've wanted him hung. I think it shall happen, too, before he's much older. Then he will be complete.'

'I can't have a partner on the gibbet,' said Bramley, closing his fingers over his glass while Wilkie gestured an offer of more, and then helped himself quite generously. 'Thank you for this warning, anyway. He's become a regular caller at our house. We are all colonial sheep experience men, of a sudden, lapping up knowledge. We do pump him for facts.'

'You'll find no better in flocks.'

Wilkie stared at his glass, asking the question a drinker will beg — a little mair? — and then to sip its peaty medicine, almost reluctantly, as a deserved treat. 'Weel weel, as you are a livestock man, Bramley, you might do worse. He is conceded best sheep breeder in the colony with the exception of the man at large, Kale, who was his convict shepherd and his bosom friend, when they were all younger, starving for bread and grinding meal from wattle seeds, in the early years of famine.'

'Kale, I remember being told,' said Bramley, 'was the author of Cribb's most remarkable fleece.'

'Stanton would rage to hear it,' said Wilkie. 'Now did I tell ye: she, I declare — Dolly Stanton — tried to rid me of two little children I fathered by different mothers — all four of whom, mothers and bairns, are now in this house drinking chocolate in the kitchen below stairs. I am proud to claim them as my own, by warrant of the love I bear them.'

The topic of children made Wilkie sentimental, as he wiped away a tear. He was drunk and they had still not arrived at where Bramley wanted to have him.

BRAMLEY WAS NEVER A DRINKING man, and found, as the clock struck eleven, that the dim light entering Wilkie's poor sitting room broke into crystal points and inexplicably exploded with a quiet, nauseating puff, making it difficult for him to focus his eyes. Wilkie rang the bell and ordered up coffee. The house being near the river, the muds of low tide mingled their smells with the aroma of the brew when it was presented and poured.

'Do go on,' Bramley encouraged, when his senses were more settled.

'Stanton's obsequiousness when he petitioned a ship more than anything turned my stomach,' said Wilkie. 'I refused him a long time. Then I was mickle pleased to get him one with a good captain, but a leaky bottom.'

'That ship, *Edinburgh Castle*, let me tell you,' said Bramley with a bright, defensive smile, 'is done over snug as a walnut shell and lies in the Thames near Shadwell Basin, and its new owner, for a voyage to Botany Bay, I am pleased to tell you, is the man who sits before you.'

'Is she still under Captain Maule?'

'The same.'

'Then she will do all right. And so will you, Lord Bramley, if you listen hard. Speak for me at Westminster, how I stood for common sense, and I think I may be more useful to you than Parson Stanton shall ever be.'

'On the question of land for sheep?'

'I should very much hope so. My career may be over, but I have a resource. I know this much about you, you were born a Tory and became a Whig, through open thinking. You keep in your household a radical dominie, Hardcastle, and his wee wife, Rosalind, who's from the Borders? You cannot say nae to me on account of heart. For you have one, Bramley, while you strain to keep it hidden. There is also the greatest wool man that ever lived, that you care about, Blaise Henry Cribb, whose life and fortune you are bent on saving by getting him to a dry climate.'

Intrigued, Bramley said that the colonial secretary was not the only one gathering information. 'Where did you find this out?'

'Och, it's a small world, I'll tell you how much smaller than even you think it is. The quartermaster of those disbanded territorials I spoke about, the first of the Devil's Own, was a fatherly man to my younger man's soldiering, a true spirited Scot, a servant of the Inns of Court named Alexander Ritchie. We stayed connected over the years as I rose in the military lists and he attended the courts facing a melancholy truth, that among the variety of actions men are daily liable to commit, no less than one hundred and sixty have been declared by an act of parliament to be felonies without benefit of clergy; in other words, to be worthy of death at the end of a rope.'

'It is vexing, to say the least. Though the injured, through compassion will often forbear to prosecute.'

'Ritchie does not like seeing a man hung. He attends the courts with petitions every Tuesday and Wednesday, for little personal reward, except the joy it gives him when a soul is saved hanging. The rest of the week he attends to estates and bonds. He was lawyer to the naturalist, Marsh. He is Marsh's executor for his last will and testament.'

'I once met Marsh, at the home of Banks,' said Bramley, leaning forward with particular interest. 'He seemed to know more about the outlying parts of your colony than any man alive. Cribb went with me, and obtained a fleece of great beauty and style, which remains his model of excellence. Did Marsh find sheep country, which he never divulged?'

'It seems none went farther into the interior, but how far is speculation. Now that he is dead, matters have changed, and we are in a position to find out what even Stanton can't discover by flogging. Marsh's papers are in Ritchie's care, awaiting their rightful claimant. The maps were always rumoured, never proven, and to sight them, believe me, would be something of a Holy Grail for our friend.'

'I would very much like to see them too.'

'The owner is the boy that Stanton alienated. I hear that Stanton visits Ritchie pushing a claim, making a nuisance and a clamour.'

'Does he have a case?'

'By boasting your acquaintance, he blusters to be given materials into his care. He puts forward several arguments, some of them more persuasive than others, but Ritchie gives no ground. Stanton swears he is of your settlers' party.'

'I've made no offers, as you know. I may have hinted more than was wise. If I took him on, I'd need some way of keeping control, but he's uncontrollable by nature, so there you are.'

'Know that he threatens Ritchie with your wealth and influence.'

'That's forward, I must say.'

'He describes the innards of your house and its inhabitants, from the sick man under your roof to the housemaids in your scullery, to prove himself the insider.'

'How very demeaning,' said Bramley. 'But what of the maps and their rightful owner?'

'It could easily be you.'

'I daresay,' said Bramley, restraining emotion. At last he'd come to where he wanted to be with Wilkie. 'How?'

'On my long voyage home, which I spent mainly standing on the deck with my arms clasped behind my back and shouting against the elements as they streamed either side of the rails, I made a stop at Rio. The British consul placed me in a villa with a terrace overlooking a sparkling waterway. I learned how Rio is fairly like the world itself, wonderful in perspective but hideously stinking in detail. I was luckier than most, having only a week between sailings. Our Parson Stanton was held there much longer, I believe, and when he sailed, his two boy passengers, adoptees from Botany Bay, one black, one white, were obliged to remain on shore.'

'I have heard of them,' said Bramley, 'from our Captain Maule. It is a desperate low mark against the minister, the way he treated those veritable sons. They are on Maule's conscience, for obeying his passengers. What happened after they disappeared remains a mystery, still?'

'No mystery at all. They shipped out on a New Bedford whaler, the *Betsy*, bound for Pacific waters. The vessel lost crew to the fever at Rio and took on hands. The lads hoped on a voyage to

Sydney, if whales can swim that far. I made the arrangements with the captain myself, to be sure they weren't being hoodwinked. He seemed a good enough man. Their chances of getting home looked pretty fair, as they are brave resourceful lads, and thanks to Stanton making use of them on their voyage, and the attention of Maule to their seafaring knots, they've become extremely handy in their own survival.'

'Did they seek you out?'

'Not quite. The first I knew of them was a feeling I had, of being selected. Smoking my first cigarillo of the day on my balcony, I found I was watched by a mulatto and his mate. They came down to the port every morning from a hide of thatched banana leaves and oilskin rags where they huddled. The darker of the two boys interested me as a type of Negro I had nae seen before, but when I called him to me, and was in my comparative anatomy lesson, marking flatness of nose, breadth of forehead, curl of lip, and so on, the youth called me "gubna". I recognised Titus Stanton. The last person I expected to find in South America was a New Holland autochthonous.'

'What of the white boy?'

'Warren Inchcape? You'll have cause to remember that name, as he's George Marsh's natural son and sole inheritor of his maps.'

Before Bramley could ask how this knowledge gave him any advantage, in the way of rights, Wilkie pulled a fold of papers from an inside pocket.

'Has it ever been your lot, my lord, to severely punish a favourite child, with hideous regret, to damn someone you loved, for a transgression?'

Without waiting for Bramley's answer (which would have been no, he was never so morally divided) Wilkie continued:

'I have done it. Many true men of the world have found them-selves so tangled. Our braw good intentions oft gang awry. For this reason I am prone to go soft on Stanton even for alarming his sons; but what I cannot forgive is the fear, nay the terror, he finally inspired in them — to turn their backs on him, aye, in tears and melancholy confusion, forgoing their long-promised sight of England in his care. For they are changed bitterly against the English as far as two good hearts could ever be, and I, traduced in my own fashion, by my own masters, took upon myself the role of trustee to Warren Inchcape.'

Sir Colin spread out a fold of documents on a side table.

'Here are sworn papers, notarised by the Portuguese governor of Brazil and countersigned by the British consul, Leatherbridge, to the effect that I, Colin Wilkie, am sole authorised person to represent myself to Alexander Ritchie and take into care letters, papers, journals, maps, and a scrofulous cockatoo, property of said boy, the whole collection of "finery" to be placed in the care of an honourable person bound for Botany Bay — if I cannot carry them to Inchcape myself, which I cannot, some other shall carry them forth where aye he may be found. Soon again at Botany Bay, it is to be hoped. Hoots, I am naming you that person, Lord Bramley.'

'But I am not travelling to Botany Bay. I am sending Blaise Cribb.'

'Would you trust your Cribb, as a man of honour, to seek out the rightful heir?'

'As long as he remains alive, I would,' agreed Bramley.

'Then let us go and find Ritchie,' said Wilkie, 'and get this done. Before we do, there's a guid finger of Athol brose waiting to be rinsed on the backstairs of our tongues.'

Bramley watched the great sad man, Wilkie, spooning out the last quantity of drink from the bottom of his glass. As he did so, Wilkie told a further story of sadness impenetrable even to his own deepest understanding.

It was a confession — that an act of justice allegedly committed by Stanton, so frightening to Warren and the black boy, as to drive them off, had not been committed by Stanton at all. It was committed by Wilkie — against the hide of one Captain Tom Rankine, of the N.S. Wales rangers.

What Wilkie hinted around earlier emerged bold and clear.

'I'd long loved Tom Rankine, as I told you, though had my disquiets, when a scabrous informer, Lehane, threw himself on my mercy having no friends left for his protection. He tipped the balance with uncontestable reports, in sum: while enjoying himself as my boon companion, Rankine, using forged passes, arranged the impersonation of a soldier on guard; stole a prisoner under charge of gaolers; hiding massed sheep from the colonial tally Rankine grazed them on public lands, behaving jauntily while concealing his hand; oh, at the end, entering my rooms within an hour of Lehane, resigned his commission and when faced with my brace of reports made seditious statements tormenting a governor's conscience to his face — to the point where I brought down my hand. Pleased I was to pass sentence upon my own indictment.'

'That's allowed?'

'The royal cipher allows it in that country, where justice is rough as the ground is cracked. Many are sentenced just the same by magistrates less kindly. May I continue? In justified anger I condemned Tom Rankine to the prison wastes of Van Diemen's Land. He made no statement, no complaint, merely bowed with acknowledgement of an affidavit signed, by one Patrick Lehane.'

'He deserved his comeuppance, I am sure,' said Bramley, thinking of Cribb's resentments against Rankine. 'But isn't Van Diemen's Land the hell on earth of the convict cosmology? Need you have been so harsh, Sir Colin?'

'What was my thinking, you ask, when Rankine came bursting into my office, resigning his commission and asking pardons for servants, as if my sack of preferments was bottomless? I acted from offence, and when a man acts from offence, he creates in himself possibilities he never knew for anger. There is a souring of justice comes with emotion. That same day, to my intense surprise, my commission as governor was withdrawn; and as Rankine was carried from Sydney to the pretty town of Hobart I heard that even greater cruelties than before were being practised by the new lieutenant governor there, in the name of Christian instruction.'

'This you told to the boys?' said Bramley.

'I could not,' said Wilkie, 'for the love of them and the contempt I had for Stanton, which I would leverage with a pitchfork, if I were able. I left them believing that Stanton was the wurrst of the two of us.'

W HEN WARREN INCHCAPE AND TITUS Stanton
signed on with the *Betsy* of New Bedford and sailed
towards the whaling grounds of the South Seas they
took aboard with them a sea chest containing white shirts, red
shirts, cloth trousers and duck trousers, shoes, and several hats. It
was near all they owned in the world and not very much. Yet it was
heavier to lift than it might have been because Warren, using the
tools of the boatman Peres, worked down into the bottom of
the chest a neat floor of shaved planks and under that platform
concealed bags of gold and silver coin.

For it was not just revulsion at Stanton that decided Warren
against the charms of England. There was another reason for putting
his faith in Wilkie and giving him power to make the inheritance
claim, by means of a few shaky wriggles on parchment paper, and
passed across. They were close to desperation the day Wilkie found
them watching, when they were hailed as New Hollanders, and soon
confessed they were ready to go back there. They were not so poor
as they looked, nor so down on their luck as Wilkie said, only
haggard for good reason, because of the life they led in the town.

Word was out that a black man was thieving houses in partnership with a thug. A nightwatchman was beaten and tied up, the act done with enough violence and quantity of bruises to carry conviction of purpose. A split skull and a chest full of cracked ribs: such injuries showing that when a beating was called for, it was better to strike with force. Warren, you might say, was educated by his former master in application of force, standing aloof from a result but not from consequences.

One night a man was threatened and submitted to being gagged. He squealed, upon release, that though he hadn't seen his assailants clearly (it was dark, and they wore bandanas on their faces) one of them wasn't a slave. He was a white man.

Afoot past midnight, a moonless night, Warren and Titus circled back to the grandest house of the town. Warren crouched nearby, to whistle warning while Titus scaled walls within. Warren was equal at calming dogs with Titus who was better at passing through bolted doors. A few times, in shadowed rooms, Titus was seen but not grabbed, nor did he rouse an alarm. When he was seen he perfectly made sense they had so little idea of their slaves — once by taking a chamberpot away, emptying it and restoring it; once by holding out a hand and accepting a coin from a lady's devotee in the name of discretion; and always muttering a blessing in Portuguese from the shadows, giving a giggle of high, strange amusement, which made people feel admirable in response, even as it allowed them to be robbed. In one place, a lady cried out and took him into her bed. He said she was ugly but gave him a good ride.

They were shown their great kindness by the former governor when he took them to meet the American captain, Ashcraft. Unheard-of courtesy cured them of desperation. They were saved from the chance of prison or death, the choices Dolly and Matthew

Stanton had left them. Sir Colin Wilkie told the whaling ship captain that Warren and Titus were farm boys in Botany Bay and asked if they might sail with him for the sake of Warren's dear mother — saying she was fine as any good woman on earth. What did the captain think? Would they make it back to the Bay? Ashcraft replied in his wisdom that if whales went there, they might, and there was no better combination suited to his ship, than a farm boy turned sailor, for city boys were often hard cases. Nor did Ashcraft have any objections to taking the black one in, if he proved himself a mariner. They'd had some Negroes in their crew, who died when the fever swept her. And at this, Ashcraft turned solemn.

They learned as the *Betsy* set sail from the Rio roads that a warrant was out for their arrest; and Warren noticed with a glad heart that the boatman hired to row a gendarme out to the vessel was his friend Peres, and the harder Peres pulled at the oars, the wider the gap separating them grew. The more the gendarme waved his arms to attract attention, the less notice was taken by the Americans. At this interesting complication, it was noticeable that Captain Ashcraft engaged in a conversation with the officer of the watch, his back turned to the pursuing boat.

Charles Ashcraft was a New Bedford man of about thirty-five whose entire concentration was upon the whale fisheries and the welfare of his ship. His manners were cordial ashore but catch him in command and there was never a question of his authority being anything but strong. Then his face would redden, his voice lift and twang. They respected and properly feared him though they were soon very remote from him, at the other end of the ship. In this conjuncture of their existence Warren and Titus were lucky what life taught them to beware — that it did not ruin them, when it bewared them of the Stantons — because trust came back, trickle by drop, and along with trust a few dribbles of happiness. It took so little for it to happen, but there it was — in the sad contortion of their hopeful smiles.

'How goes it in New Holland?' echoed Warren to his new shipmates, who gawped with open, gullible faces. 'It goes free and easy — the people go naked, nothin but a bowline round the midships is the rule, made of hooman hair, and a bit of paint here and there.'

'We don't have no dinners,' said Titus, 'but keep dinin all day off goannas and snakes. If we wants any puddin we climb a tree where there's honeycomb.'

'Where do you go to bed?'

'Anywhere we please, so long as it's under the stars.'

Titus had his reasons and slept wherever he chose on their ship. It was his pledge of freedom and would not be taken from him. On one occasion in a calm, before they left the warm latitudes, he was found up in the cross trees, taking a nap, a hundred feet above the water. Warren feared he was in for a flogging, but soon learned better. Titus was allowed his persistent freedoms in honour of devotion and pluck. Watch him in a storm as they worked on reefing the mainsail, scrambling out along the yards with never a care; listen as their captain declared him a favourite and laughingly opinioned that Titus was quite possibly a Turk in another life, for in the Turkish navy they had no chests but used rugs, in which they wrapped their belongings, and sought no hammocks, but slept, like Titus, wherever they fell on the decks. Warren asked if all American ships were like this one, and was told that for his sins, he was on a lucky one.

They heard of a sealing vessel called the *Salamander* of Boston, that was connected to the *Betsy* through a partnership of their owners, but in no other way compatible. The sealer was under the command of Captain Martin Sykes. The *Betsy* had a commission to meet with Sykes in the South Seas, and take his bundles of sealskins aboard. The *Salamander* was a smart but fearsomely miserable brig, make no mistake, and Warren was told to watch out and beware, when their two ships rafted up in some remote bay. For by bribery, charm or necessity Martin Sykes would do anything to secure himself crew, and once he had them, was reported by the necromancy of his frothing eyes to hold an entire people prisoner, until they were ghosts of their former selves, and destined to haunt whatever seas Sykes sailed them into, even as far as the southernmost quarters of the globe, among icebergs, fogs, and moaning horizontal gales.

On their mess's watch Warren always knew where to find Titus and fetch him to his duty. Warren kept an eye on his friend and cared for him and would die, it was reckoned, before he would allow Titus ever again to be whipped. In this respect Warren was not so much warned as half crazed by recent experience, and would never again be so easy, trusting and straight as those who loved him remembered him. All the strong feeling of his former being was concentrated into the hard, well-nigh murderous omen of his fists, which if Titus was ever whispered against, he raised. Fists threatening like hammers, and mustardy eyes with a smoulder of red.

One person aboard woke up resentment against the two new hands: a junior officer named Harry Dugdale, who was covered over with curled black hairs clustered on the backs of his hands, sprouting from his ears, matted around his low, thick neck, tufted from his knees, and rising from his chest like a spill of inky foam. Those chest hairs in particular collected crumbs of the broken sea biscuit that were called midshipman's nuts by the men. Everyone called them midshipman's nuts but when Warren did so Dugdale took offence. It was learned he'd been a midshipman on a man o'war before he sailed with Ashcraft.

Harry Dugdale was English born with plenty to say about Botany Bay (where he'd never been). As Dugdale was the boxing champion of the *Betsy* it was unwise to argue with him too much, for he would bend a nose and fell an opponent with a level punch as good as reply to a word, meantime wetting his lips with his biscuity tongue and leering insufferably from large damp eyes. Dugdale said that an uglier set of men and women had never been found in England, as the convicts that were thrown onto hulks and taken to the Bay in 1788. They were about as different from people who went to America as dirt was from cream. Their complexion was shallow and putrid, he said. They had a flatness of feature, caused by want of rations to cushion up their cheeks. They were short as monkeys, with bowed legs, jutting thick jaws, an inability at arithmetic, an inability to write their names, except as a cross, and the only benefit of them was in saving of ropes, as less was needed when they were hung.

'Your mother was a convict woman, I hear,' said Dugdale. 'Didn't the captain get told, when he took you aboard, that he could have her as a real beauty, if he liked, by God, when he got to the Bay?'

Warren stared back at Dugdale and said nothing. Only the judgement of his eyes said there was one bad egg in every basket, and he would come to that bad egg when he did the counting. Because otherwise, by a rule of observation, Warren reckoned the *Betsy* was a good enough ship. She was tidy, but not overly so. Warren knew enough to know it was a rule, holding that too tidy a ship meant there was a tyrant at the helm or a tyrant in the person of a first officer roaming about looking for victims. That would not happen until Harry Dugdale got his promotions.

Warren thanked God there was no chaplain aboard, as they'd had their chaplain in Stanton. Whenever there were prayers to be said, the readings, the business was performed by Captain Ashcraft in good simple order. The fourth of July, a date neither of them had ever heard about as important, they soon learned meant a riot of drinking and boxing matches.

The weather was colder and the captain warned it would be their last chance for a holiday in a long time, as they would need to batten down to round the Horn. He was not as particular as their captain, Maule, of past experience, in keeping the deck spotless at all times, and in all weathers.

But on the morning of the fourth of July there was a great bustle. It was a raw, cold morning, but fairly calm, when the holystones, prayer books, and trumpets came out. Men kicked off their shoes, rolled up their trousers, and knelt to their scrubbing business with good will. They did more scraping of wood and polishing of ring bolts than the ship had seen in a good long time. Indeed they had their noses far down into the grain of her decks where they smelled every strip of whale meat and every dried jot of whale blood and dribbly wasted whale oil that had ever been soaked into her planks and passed into her floating body to keep her prancing across the waves.

Later in the morning, when the weather was reckoned settled and they were lying in the arms of a sheltered enough bay, as ever was found on the coasts of Patagonia, at least, with the anchor holding, and pennants flying from the topmast, the captain ordered a doubling of the allowance of spirits to the men. You can be sure that most were hoarding an extra allowance of rum too, having brought plenty from shore on the day they left Rio in expectation of their national holiday and other consolations. The decks were given over to drinking and at first it started quietly, with the captain and officers moving among men proposing toasts to presidents and generals, and to a renowned old sailor they had aboard, who'd been a boy when America was won off Britain. They saluted the memory of lost shipmates and those green boys who died in the recent plague; they toasted their wives and sweethearts, if they ever had them, and Warren toasted his mother and Captain Ugly Tom. 'To freedom!' they roared, and when Warren spoke that word, he felt the irons fall off men far away, though he saw Harry Dugdale sneer in his direction.

Quite soon men settled into more solemn drinking, turning every now and again to remember their American flag, which hung from the stern, and of which they were so proud. A defensiveness crept into the celebrations as the Dutch, French, and Irish sailors they had on board, and a lone German too, remembered they had a nationality, or if they were still under a foreign yoke, would fight any man who said they couldn't have a country of their own. Sailors reeled about the decks singing songs, howling joy, chasing each other with buckets of water, dressing as devils and injuns, and fighting. Bare knuckles were the order of the day and a few old grudges were settled, as well as some clean athletic contests being sorted out; a champion of the ship was to be declared at the next match on the quarter deck, when the bell was rung.

'Rum, tobacco,' said a man, grabbing hold of Titus between the legs, and shoving him up against a stanchion, twisting his cods to extract favours, 'what more does a man want?' Titus laughed and pushed him away with a hand in his face:

Jack dances and tsings, Jack is always content,
In his vows to his lass he wurrunt failer;
His anchor's atrip when his coin's all tspent,
Eeow! tis the life of a tsailor.

It was what he'd learned in the Stanton's parlour and sung in his fine soprano before his voice deepened, when he'd never seen the sea, nor could imagine what it was, unless like a flood on the biggest river, with treetops drawn into the currents and the only way to get around on the waters to kneel on a strip of bark lashed both ends.

Titus's song started Warren remembering Laban Vale. Tears. Men so crying everywhere. Amid talk of home and loved ones it wasn't so very noticed how Warren sobbed more than most. They passed around the fiery jug that drowned the souls of those who drank it, in the invitation of its fumes. Warren wasn't the least bit drunk, though, as he watched Harry Dugdale quaffing it back and trying to find out who his challenger was to be at the sound of the bell. It was to be Warren Inchcape but for the moment only Warren and his second knew. It was their names on a fold of paper passed to the captain.

Men were calling for shanties from every part of the ship and they asked Warren what he knew. He swore loudly as he splashed his lips and spat rum out, that he knew a ballad when he sang one! The rocking motion of the ship gave the rhythm, and the lofty masts indicated how far into heaven a feeling pierced. The attentive faces of the crew that could hear him, were the roads where the ballad dusted.

Warren was a tuneless singer, his bad notes could make you wince. Oh but the trembling heart of his manner, and the bellow of his heart in the bellow of his lungs! — sailors broke from their brawling and listened to his story:

You lecherous whoremasters who practise vile arts,
To ruin young virgins and break parents' hearts,
Or from the fond husband the wife lead astray —
Let such debauched stallions be sent to the Bay.

('Hooray!')

There's whores, pimps and bastards, a large costly crew
Maintained by the sweat of a labouring few,
They should have no commission, place, pension or pay,
Such locusts should all go to Botany Bay.

('Hooray!')

Now should any take umbrage at what I have writ,
Or find here a bonnet or cap that will fit,
To such I have only this one word to say:
They are welcome to wear it at Botany Bay.

('Hooray!')

DRUNK BY CLOSE OF DAY, each day of the week, Parson Matthew Stanton found this stool or that bench, this serving window or that low door reeking powerful drink, leading into a few London streets of haggard hope that he took to, now, in the time since Ivy dropped her confession and he arrived at his estimation of Botany Bay as the Devil's exclusive domain.

In slips of the tongue's reasoning, Stanton even called Botany Bay home, in drowsy moments when the soul slipped its ropes, when he thought he had dust in his nostrils and the riddly cry of rosehiller parrots in his ears. Dressed in flowing black robes, he found himself roaming there realer than anything — riding a snorty horse into abandoned sacristies and violating altars and gleaming crosses with spit and piss puddles and piles of steaming dung before cantering off in a sweat. One of the chapels he despoiled was his own, St Botolph's, left a smouldering ruin of wattle and daub, where the roof fell in.

In the weeks since meeting Cribb and Bramley at the wool committees, Stanton found himself doing his London rounds in agitation and befuddlement as much as in purposeful achievement. His missionary duties he neglected. On his almost daily visits to Ritchie's chambers, the man showed contempt, mistrust and disbelief. Thrice weekly Stanton went to Bramley's house as boaster and supplicant, buying friendship of doorman and staff, and getting lordly good manners but little more than sheeply interest from Bramley. Stanton's brains were picked but his pocket was not flattered.

Indeed, Stanton daily felt that, of his family of three, he was the chief one being pushed aside while having most to offer any enterprise being planned. For in that tall, wide, deep and important house, Ivy and Dolly were busy on other floors where he was not taken at all. A pretence was kept up they were not even there at the same time he was. Another pretence was that Ivy wasn't in trouble, only her father was, just by being himself. The great peddlers of pretended ordinariness around a girl's foolish sin were the merry little Hardcastles, whose hair was golden as clouds, who moved past Stanton in the hallway nimbly begging their pardons, a pair whose way of dealing with disastrous experience was woefully positive! Stanton disliked them except for their three lively little girls and their boy, Barney, who asked keen questions about sea voyages and sea monsters while Stanton sat in the parlour and awaited his next interview. He very much liked this boy who was sharp, with a good turn of phrase, having the eyes of a dreamer and the hands of a blacksmith's apprentice, a stocky lad made for colonial experience once he got there, and grew into it.

'I always have need for a boy, to benefit him,' said Stanton, with wistful awareness of the vacancy in his heart, and that strange homesickness for a country where he had not been born.

The routine with Bramley was the same, week by week, until the most recent call Stanton made at Bramley's house.

Stanton was shown in, as usual, by the footman, Wetherell, and waited for Bramley to come in. Stanton met him in the hall. Bramley, shaking his topcoat of a downpour, said he'd been at the Inns of Court — and why did Stanton suddenly think, of all the persons there, Bramley was closeted with a particular resistant Scotsman by the name of Sir Colin Wilkie? Well, it was that Bramley reeked of sweet whisky fumes; and his eyes were particularly veined in opposition.

Bramley called for black China tea, and said he had a headache. 'What do you want, then, Stanton?' he said, quite rude as he was able.

Stanton, as usual when pleading, smiled in a stricken sort of way, and reminded Bramley for the hundredth time of his eminence in wools, as testified to by Cribb, however scurvily, in his classification of colonial fleeces. Of money, experience, and stock Stanton lacked nothing, and Bramley tiredly agreed — said he didn't question it, but opened his palms admitting that unless Stanton was personally in the colony when the proposed party of Cribbs and Hardcastles arrived there, he was of little practical use to him. They needed more than a partner — and less — they needed a reliable, loyal, experienced manservant and guide. Somebody lower down the social scale, perhaps.

'A convict bond man, is what you want,' said Stanton. 'If I knew the name of a good one, practised enough in sheep, I would tell you where to seek him. They are lazy rascals and rogues, one good man in a thousand. The only very good one I ever knew is gone to the bad.'

By degrees, however, Stanton tempted Bramley with larger ideas. His important station, Laban Vale, he suggested, could be made available as a staging post in a process of setting up. If Cribb wished to assemble a flock he had Stanton's blessing to lead out from Laban Vale. Why, when their acres were totalled, Stanton and Bramley owned pretty roughly the same amount of land on opposite sites of the world! They could both afford largesse. Of course, on his forty thousand acres Bramley had a hundred farms and a thousand tenants, factories and towns, salmon runs and green hills, sheep tight-packed not scattered — while Stanton's station was one great dry bap baked miles wide and split with gullies and rocks, parched creekbeds, no habitation except the homestead, the barracks, and a few shepherds' huts made of stringybark. If there were three acres to the sheep he was lucky with feed.

'I have a man there, on Laban Vale, of exceptional brilliance, steadiness, and sheepliness of eye,' said Stanton. 'I do think you know of him. Paul Lorenze he calls himself today. A louring, pouty individual who persuades me by his sullen possessiveness that my best interests are safe.'

'Obviously, Rankine is abandoned,' said Bramley.

'From what I have heard,' agreed Stanton.

'It does not sound good.'

'No. We do not always get everything we deserve. But in his case, Rankine will be held as a gentleman convict, a particular beneficial class. They never fare badly as the rest, aren't as flogged, aren't as hung. Indeed, if they want to hang a man at Hell's Gates they bring him back to Hobart Town. Or so I have heard.'

'That is a consolation,' said Bramley, taken aback by Stanton's blithe summary of a system. He wondered how fast his emigrants would get past the prison towns and into the interior, which he imagined so peaceful, so empty. 'A bit like the moors, only hot,' he'd heard it described, 'and with savages.'

'As for Lorenze not being my man's real name,' said Stanton, 'a false name in that country is a sure sign either of an outright rogue, or of a man intent on improving himself. My judgement on the fellow tells me the latter. I have a great trust. It is something that inspires me, trustingness. I have charged Galvin, my sergeant of convicts, with giving Lorenze what he wants. A word from you, Lord Bramley, and Galvin shall be at your service as well! I mean to have all of my lands and waterholes at your disposal!'

Bramley seemed not to be taking the bait. He motioned to the sick man upstairs.

'I have not heard Cribb coughing, today,' he said. 'On other days it is quite distinctly heard, all through the house.'

'If he is better,' said Stanton impatiently, 'shouldn't we ask him down?'

'What if he's not better?' said Bramley, picturing the scene three floors above them: Dolly Stanton holding Cribb bare-chested upright in his bed and bathing his sweaty torso out of a basin with a white cloth. It seemed Dolly had the strength for nursing and making Cribb better with her sudden devotion. She was up there tending Cribb a good part of each day. She was up to something and she was most of the reason Cribb was improving, but Bramley was reluctant to admit Stanton into that knowledge. There was no benefit stirring a man already stirred.

Stanton walked home to his house in the rain. Most of what made Bramley uneasy around Stanton's wife did not make Stanton uneasy at all. They were in this together.

For Bramley, in allowing Dolly under his roof and up into the gods of his house to nurse Cribb, gave Stanton the opportunity to hear from her what she had learned.

Today, the only morsel, and a nicely confusing one, told of superb wools from a location that sounded like 'plotops'. The best wool Cribb had ever seen, he coughed it out to Dolly, into his basin, was a word sounding Greek.

'Cribb knows less Greek than a Hottentot,' said Stanton, 'but Bramley has a first in classics. He gives nothing away. When he admits me to his house I find, to my chagrin, that I'm no better than a peasant babbling out my service to his lordship and getting little mercy for my pains. Bramley would rather cultivate failed governors and peevish lawyers than successful graziers of sheep. I will get to the bottom of this.'

Confirmation that Bramley was seen with Sir Colin Wilkie at the Inns of Court was brought to Stanton by his beggar boys.

They lived in shadows, up stairways, below window panes. They ran at night through sewers and up the inside legs of painted ladies who shrieked with delight in gin shops. Stanton walked past, angling his head to beckon and learn how other lives were lived. Very soon, as instructed, they would bring him a key.

He next learned, from Church sources, that a whole week's missionary engagements were cancelled by the archdeacon in charge of arrangements, and he was surprised that his own reaction was a shrug. Without enquiring too close why, he was glad enough without his afternoons and nights of hectic storytelling. New importances were in the air. The only times he looked in his Bible now were to argue with the old sheep-herding prophets in mental debate between divided parts of his brain. Any thought of opening his New Testament and Gospels — which was to say, the Christian parts of the Book — left him cold in the nostrils. Hinted to him was news that a Church committee was preparing a report to a committee higher up, on the question of whether Matthew Stanton (B.A. Cantab., failed) should be deprived of his Botany Bay chaplaincy. The only trouble with that suggestion, and why it would get nowhere, Stanton patted himself thinking, was it could scarcely be followed in a population of clergy where half of them were nice to the point of cruelty to others, and all over England without even setting sail to the Bay. England was a country where cuffings and canings of lessers was known to be beneficial even without consent of law, and Botany Bay was her child.

A S AN OFFERING TO HER parents whom she loved, feared, and had despoiled — but to whom there was no word of sorry to be said — Ivy Stanton went to her Bible one day, balanced it on her knee, opened it around five-sixths of the way through, and just as her father was busy mentally predicting which Gospel text she was likely to spout as justification of her deeds (but finding himself unable to, from the distaste of Christianity that had come upon him), she removed a bundle of envelopes from the box where she kept her Book and handed them over to him. There was an intense red coal of hostility in the gesture. The journal of her friend who promised to include details of interest to her father was just as likely to damage him.

'What is this?'

'They are my letters from Leah. They were in my Bible box and not even hidden.' She could not resist asking: 'Didn't you look there?'

'It did not cross my mind,' he said honestly wicked, appreciatively surprised at himself, with something like his old playful smile from before they set out on their journey to perdition. 'That body of text is inviolable to my thinking.'

It was the truth. He could not go there even for his own greatest advantage. 'But what about these letters, my dear? What treasure is in them?'

'Don't spill anything,' Ivy warned, as Stanton left the room to console himself with information.

When tipping the letters open, dried flowers and trickles of coloured earths fell from the bundles onto the writing table in the small side room, dried leaves like veined scimitars, fragile as thin smoked glass — twigs, pebbles, feathers, bird bones and a perfectly miniature snake's skull cleaned of its flesh by ants and dried white in the sun. Stanton knew every word written would be true when he remembered the eyes of the writer, though when he began the first few sentences of Ivy's letter cache there was a heightened excitement of vision that only passionate young ladies could express.

For, in Leah Josephs's account of her life in the New South Wales bush, days were brighter, pace was brisker, nights were starrier. Intensity of attachment was revealed over many lurching weeks' writing as a waggon proceeded west and south. In Leah's cleverness of eye. In her rightness of words.

As soon as he could, Stanton closed the door and turned up the lamp to read the pages through, but reached only page two of the small, sloped, characterful handwriting in half an hour. All pages went across in one direction, left to right, and then covered themselves down over the top of what was already written to make the material fiddly to read, like a mesh of twigs. It was how postage and paper were saved but very frustrating. Where were Stanton's hints and signs as promised if he saved Ivy from his fury? He hunted up and down the frugal lattice. Came through and out the other side of pages one and two. There were many good reasons for rage, now, but he would like to tell Leah Josephs that more was being done to save Ivy than could ever be imagined by her. So give him his secrets!

Upon reaching page three, a while later, Stanton heard the chimes of noon, ran his tongue around the inside of his mouth, and went into the hall where the coats were hung. He buttoned his heaviest overcoat, found his warmest (and wornest) boots, checked for his pistol, tucked the letters in a pocket, and set off walking a good pace to the Drayman's Inn where if any hostelry was comfortable for a livestock-raising country parson to make himself nameless among habitués of steaming dung and hairy hides, then this was the one in the whole of London.

Stanton looked around for the two quick boys he had in his pay. He met them there daily watching the front door and rear passage of the rooms where the cursed lawyer spent his mornings. A dropped key, an impression of one, a duplicate lifted, whatever. The boys reported that Ritchie rarely worked past two of the afternoon, and on days when he hurried to court with a jingle of keys he barely lingered in his office at all. Today was a Wednesday, a court day, and as Stanton settled himself to wait to hear if they had slipped themselves a lock springer, he said good day to his fellows and passed for one who belonged there, by right, a scabbed-looking rotund man from a butcher's stockyard slaking a bloodied thirst and running fresh foam down his chin.

'Good cheer to you, sir.'

'And to you, my good friend.'

It even felt quite homely hearing the Irish brickmen call for their drinks: 'Would your highness be after granting us a swallow of the craytur, on such a blustery miserable day as it is, beyond these hospitable walls?'

It occurred to Stanton's battered morality that it rather suited him best of all, this life, standing with an open collar inhaling a farmyard stink in the centre of London. But of course he was not deprived of choice, as some were — his choices were only narrowed down a space, becoming more concentrated, like pitch. Pray they would take fire soon. He'd drunk Burton ale at the Salutation and Cat in Hand Court, but liked the Drayman's better. He was in the grip of inevitable feeling and no more liable to question inevitable feeling than ever.

Benches in the stableyard allowed daylight to fall on Leah Josephs's pages where Stanton took his pot of strong beer and flattened the creases with his forearm. Great heroine of the cobwebby-inked narrative was Meg Inchcape, daughter of a convict of old, wife of a convict of new. Rewarded by a mood of forgetfulness inspired by reading her name, Stanton reflected that if Rankine suffered, it pained him, but only through her. He even forgot for a time the crafty promise he'd extracted from the author of the letter. Forgot that his craftiness asked for Leah Josephs's craftiness in reply, crosswise through Ivy, and if it was not given, he would burst a bag of blood and take what was wanted!

In a short while Stanton would remember this hour and the emotions it roused. How he stood there with Kale forgotten. Rankine forgiven. He would remember and it would seem a thousand years past he dreamed, drank, and ran his finger along the closely written lines in that warm-hearted ruin, the Drayman's Inn.

'Meg's hair piled high.' 'Meg's arms with her sleeves pushed up almost to the knobs of her shoulders.' 'Meg on her knees washing clothes in a stream.' 'A clear sparkling stream.'

A clear sparkling stream? This drew Stanton up short. Where was any clear stream that ever ran in that country of muddy creeks and stagnant waters? Watercourses when they coursed at all ran mud green, mud brown; thick with clay; when you drank their tea it left a gritty sludge; at best they reduced themselves to chains of ponds clotted with gum leaves and stained with tannins. In the warm heart of winter the stream of Mundowey ran clean over sand, it was true, but it soon dried. Eighteen years in New South Wales and he'd seen too few of those. Soon dried and pugged by animal tracks and the bootprints of heinous man.

Meg slapping washing on clean stones and Leah Josephs valiantly twisting the other end of sheets and shirts and draping them on bushes to dry! How the butterflies and shell-backed beetles flew up! In the mornings small honeyeating birds tossed themselves through treetops like water from flicked fingertips of branches! Meg was some kind of good woman for certain. Back and front as the waggon creaked along, Meg's name travelled fore and aft of the one precious sheet of paper before Stanton turned to the next, numbering them to page five before there was any mention of an illicit passenger, M'Carty.

Some of Mick Tornley's bullocks went missing and there was a long report of it made by M'Carty back to the bullocky. 'Lost from the duck mole reach, three working bullocks, a brown and white, MT off rump, with lopped horns, very large bell on when lost, one brindle and white, ditto, cocked horns, MT off thigh, one straw-berry bullock, snail horns, bullfrog bell on.'

Who needed such a close description? Stanton did. Leah was telling him something. The duck mole reach. Close by a stream of sparkling water. Or was she temptingly mocking him? The bullocks weren't lost in England. There wasn't a notice posting on tavern walls. Only here was the minister, bewitched, raising his eyes to the door and expecting to see bullocks in a powder of dust!

— in a place of that whimsical name, duck mole, meaning platypus. Lord show him a map as a cross reference! Page seven and the bullocks had not yet come back but a note came from a wild man, a bushranger! saying he would return the bullocks and the two horses that went missing when he finished making use of them, which was going to be a while. Oh the honour among interesting thieves in that rivalling country where Stanton wasn't, how he longed to equal them! The bushranger had a limp, a deformed ear, and spoke with a foul mouth. Thus Stanton knew him as well as anyone who'd ever had a curse of precise unspeakableness thrown in their face. Here written in barely decipherable lines was another piece of information conveyed by the girl, and about as useful to Stanton on this side of the world as a sprinkling of fairy dust.

And now there was a boy tugging his sleeve. A boy in moth-eaten rags. With a dirty face. With fathomless eyes. With a curious puckered and whispering mouth.

'Eh! E's not innit!'

'Key?'

'You won't need no key, master.'

S TANTON SET DOWN HIS JUG and touched his left side like a man with a not quite unpleasant twinge of colic. The small pistol was there. He followed the boy down the lane and around the corner, along damp cobblestones to the foot of the stairs. The boy ran off.

Stanton climbed three landings and up a count of forty more steps. As he went he primed his pistol, just to be cautious, and stowed it back under his jacket. A loud creak every step of the way. The door stood half open into Ritchie's chambers. 'Well settled, my boys,' Stanton thought. A daytime lamp spat yellow light onto a green baize table. The rooms were empty and laid wide for his wasting. Closing the door behind him with a satisfying nudge, he was blatantly alone.

But when he edged farther into the chambers he received a shock. At the far end of the table stood Lord Bramley with papers spread out before him. The bald cockatoo sat on his shoulder. Stanton realised he was expected. Perhaps a little early but expected. The cockatoo turned a sorrowful pebble eye on him, itching its bare crown on Bramley's neck. Expected and betrayed.

'Oh, I say, Parson Stanton!' said Bramley, looking up with tense joviality.

Gathering his papers Bramley leaned forward and scraped his chair on the floor. The sound brought Alexander Ritchie stepping from an alcove. Behind him, heaving with noisy breath, was Cribb.

'Why, Stanton!'

'Cribb,' said Stanton, 'such a sick man, and up a great lot of stairs too.' In a surge of unchecked emotion he found himself drawing the pistol from the inside fold of his jacket. To get this done, Cribb's hulking wellness was a motive. All three of them with their exclusive gaze making him do it. The Devil making him do it until he grinned.

Bramley said, 'What is your meaning, Stanton? Are you deranged?'

A minister's guise dependably paid out on astonishment. For while they were all three made ready for him in this tableau, it was seen from their pale faces they did not expect his advantage of arms.

'Give me the maps,' said Stanton. 'As the fiend is my judge, I must have them.' He raised, and levelled, his pistol.

'Stanton, be a good man,' said Bramley. 'This leads the wrong way.'

It was then that Ritchie moved, advancing like an ox. Otherwise even the Devil might have withdrawn to consider. Stanton fired at once, at the Scot, and then following the smoke of that jolt, which appeared to miss Ritchie altogether, only turn him shaky, and smash a cupboard door, Stanton shifted his aim onto Bramley.

'Do give me the maps,' he said.

'You have frightened a harmless bird,' said Bramley. An effect of the shot was to send the bald cockatoo clawing up bookshelves to the ceiling, where it perched in shadows and looked its one hundred years.

The peer maintained such poise with a pistol pointing at his heart, that it was how aristocrats did die, no doubt. Quite deliberately Bramley folded the maps back into their component concertinas, and held them out to Cribb. 'Very beautifully drawn. Exquisite hachuring style. Marsh was an inspired cartographer. His son should be proud of him.'

'*Cribb* is to have them?' said Stanton. 'By what possible right?'

Ritchie dusted his lapels, cleared his throat, and said:

'By power of attorney vested in Sir Colin Wilkie, by Warren Inchcape, in writing, notarised by the Portuguese proconsul in Brazil, so passed from the boy, missing, to Sir Colin Wilkie to Blaise Henry Cribb, before me, Alexander Ritchie, until such a time as Cribb, travelling to New Holland via Brazil, locates Warren Inchcape and restores him to his rightful estate — maps, papers, and aged cockatoo, as above.'

If Ritchie had wanted a gun, to venge himself on Stanton, he would not have found one to go off in Stanton's face with as much force as this statement.

Stanton turned to Cribb.

'What is "plotops"?'

'I have no idea,' said Cribb.

'But you mentioned it to my wife. It sounded Greek.'

'It is not Greek,' said Bramley.

'No? Not Greek for machination, or something like it? Treachery. Conspiracy. Double dealing. Everything done behind my back?'

Cribb coughed, and there the word sounded again: 'Plotops.'

'Plotops . . . platyops . . . it's platypus,' said Bramley, 'platty puss is Greek, meaning flat of foot. Why, there is your "plotops", Stanton.'

Platypus, or duck mole, reach. It was where they all were! It was where the noblest fleece was bundled! — that his wife told him about, not realising what she heard, while making Cribb better! Where Mick Tornley, the Josephs, Meg Inchcape, Clumpsy M'Carty, and quite likely Desmond Kale himself and whatever branded bullocks remaining were camped, all of them, all of them in the place of superlative sheep!

Stanton felt he only needed to fire his pistol again, and when the smoke cleared he would be with them: hailing them from the throw of their campfire's light.

'A platypus is an enigmatic mole,' said Bramley, 'duckbilled, that lays an egg. It stays hidden and has poisonous claws. It is normally quite shy, according to the best authorities.'

'They are everywhere,' said Stanton. 'Do not give them too much credit for being rare, if you know where to look.'

'I'd say you don't know where to look, or you shouldn't be here, old fellow,' said Bramley.

This was not appeasing. It was possessive to a hideous level of contempt. Stanton waved his pistol around. Three shies at a fair faced him. Cribb stared back at Stanton from livid, bulging eyes, his shoulders heaving dogwise, as he made ready to jump.

'Stanton,' he taunted, 'the finest, densest packet of new wools in God's universe comes from there. From the platypus duck mole reach. Shipped by a man named Tharpe.'

'There is no such scoundrel in wools.'

'Of course not. It is Kale's. You brought it with you in the holds of the *Edinburgh Castle*! Kale's wool. Isn't that a great thought, Stanton? To be second-best? Always lagging? And yet up there at the forefront in aiding your rival?'

'Why, this is insufferable,' said Stanton.

'You have the gun at our heads,' Bramley pointed out.

At this reminder, Stanton fired his second barrel, without decisive aim, through a blur of angry tears, and Cribb fell down. Smoke cleared and the solid man lay on his back, blood staining his jacket, with Bramley on his knees beside him holding a handkerchief to his heart.

'Seize him!'

Stanton dropped the pistol to the floor and raised his hands in abashment. His thought was, 'If Cribb lives, all will be well.'

He did not know why the thought. It was a strange consideration, as Ritchie grappled and held him down.

NEVERTHELESS, SOMETHING OF THE WAY of thinking was in Stanton's argument of defence when he was brought to court two months later — after being refused bail as an attempted murderer and spending his time in Newgate Prison thinking up ways to explain himself; not so much busily justifying himself, either, as anyone knowing Matthew Stanton might have predicted. For you could say that in a world in the business of turning itself around he'd managed a most completely profound rotation. It was not for nothing, the denying fullness of his heart. It always had a purpose.

At Newgate it was said there were only two choices could be made to survive the misery of a gaoling there. One was to sink into misery, the other to study villainy.

But Stanton found a third way, which was to fortify his own sensibility in a place where it was close enough to a picture of hell for him to fancy that hell wasn't so ugly after all.

It was to realise that in getting what he wanted, if he wasn't going to be hung (and that was a fairly large condition), he might after all have come only to a mere halt against these high stone walls, windowed and grated with the king's iron; and that he was perfectly headed in the right direction to make his life out better than anyone realised. For, in other circumstances, there was no way he could have justified turning around to sail straight back to the colony unless he was a convict. And being back in the colony was where he had to be, as fast as the maps could be taken there. Land grants, a good part of his reason in coming to England, were beyond his reach. Land grabs were not.

The only trouble with his argument was that he was more likely to be hung than not. Even with Cribb recovered. Yet he would face that rope when it dangled. Meantime he learned that fear of shame was hardly possible in a prison yard where the law had no power, religion didn't penetrate, the lewd held court with the lewd, and the audacious provided inspiration in rising above a bad situation.

Newgate was like the streets where he'd already made his introductions to the underworld of knowledge, except of course far worse, being more crowded, diseased, and venal with appetites on a rampage of people gorging themselves stupid. It was like the London streets in miniature with all the milling around being done except Newgate had no exits. It was so entirely criminal, and despairing, and sometimes so vengeful a place, that Stanton feared for his prominence as a dispenser of punishments. Sometimes a man was bludgeoned for his past, knifed or strangled on a whim of resentment. It was not pretty but soon Stanton learned he was respected for his fall more than his rise, admired for his clerical collar reversed as a yoke. He was liked for his posturings of wealth, too, a man with treasure stoked in quantities of land and sheep. 'I am wealthy as a duke,' he boasted, 'but cannot get at my treasury. My enemies have made sure of it.' The statement pursued a line so familiar to old lags it made Stanton one of them, and what did it matter, they liked him even if convinced he was just as big a liar as they were.

Thus Stanton saw himself changed, but not as much as might be. If he didn't hang or die of typhus from the rats biting his toes he might be all right. Certainly he was changed in every conceivable circumstance. But that was from the outside. What a relief it was to be no good! The deed done, his whole life seemed to have been spent in making the journey to greet the wrong. Each day now was spent in a near happiness of filth and sin and the greatest uplifter of himself was his pride in the lowness of Newgate. His face was in the awfulest dirt. He was saved by not being saved.

Newgate was so jostlingly overcrowded that in the first part of his stay there, before he was removed to the press yard, where prisoners were kept waiting to be executed, he got by through remembering sheep yards and how sheep managed being jostled even when they lay down to sleep and how they were trodden in their faces and still got up. By night he gazed out through a hole in the roof avoiding streams of rain and watching for a gap in the clouds where a star came out. There were no cells available and he slept hard by a wall. He remembered how a sheep was held against a wall or on a hurdle being stilled having its throat cut and hoped to be resolute at his end. Each morning he gathered around him a gang whose best reward for crime was going to be transportation. Stanton was far and away the greatest expert in all of Newgate, in all of England, he corrected, in advising convicts how to get on if they reached Botany Bay. He imparted his advice without charge in a place where every sharpish prisoner had something of cost to impart, or extract from a pocket if it wasn't their own.

How Stanton managed to keep himself clean among so many unwashed bodies was an exercise in achievement. He'd always been fairly deft in that regard and was now more attentive, without being too plagued by the need. They'd all of them lived from one shallow dish of water some years at Laban Vale and none of it very clean. Streaks of human faeces on the stones, decaying food in corners being gnawed by rats: these were the decorations of his new house's carpet, but he gained in weight, wore clean clothes every day (the only one there who was able), and through being privileged to purchase wine from a wardsman was satisfied in his thirst. It was all mainly thanks to the roster of visitors who came bringing baskets every day that he counted himself lucky — his wife, daughter, and the Hardcastles. The Hardcastles proved their merit. They believed in the Devil as little as they believed in God, no matter how much Stanton glared at them to prove them wrong. Just when he went to the bad, here they were assaulting him with good.

They brought news of the preparation of his case, which was being underwritten by Bramley's wealth, leaving unanswered the riddle of how a man wronged was willing to save his attacker while being part of the trial against him. Stanton was changed, but not so soft as to have an answer to such superlative kindnesses as made him believe he was being played along on a leash of condescension. It was one irritation, and the other was that every week a deputation of catechists came to pray with him and their main object was to castigate him and shrive him of his sins. At the same time, they brought the news that he was bit by bit divested of his clerical titles and positions in the Anglican Church. He was spared the discomfort of the bishops and archdeacons coming to tell him this in person by their regal reluctance to make the walk to Newgate, on the grounds that he'd cut himself off from their interest quite wilfully. How they ever understood they were Christians wasn't plain unless it was the case as he'd found in his own life, that what was pledged wasn't done. Stanton went through the prayers by rote with the catechists, and when they asked him to sink to his knees, he did so, but otherwise his heart was stone. They asked him to think on the suffering son of God, but in the faces of those around him he saw all the suffering, joy, hope and despondency that he ever needed to know, or, because he'd never been close enough to it before (from always standing back to control his purpose) hadn't ever quite seen yet.

Stanton's triumph in prison was in discovering how his strangest intuition was proved right, and that a step over a line brought him to the Devil's domain and living there was less shameful than pushing the limit of Christian understanding. However, it had to be conceded — his mind came back to it — chance had fouled his timing in going to Ritchie's chambers and surely the day would have unfolded otherwise had the Bow Street runners been waiting to warn him off on the outside of the door instead of arriving minutes later than organised by the plotters, to arrest him within. It was the last vestige of his whining, needful self to put forward this explanation, for the strangest part of it was, that while under remand, he spent his days playing chess and skittles, drinking wine and gin that was fairly easily obtainable, and making the acquaintance of his whole new circle of hard-bitten friends and learning that while the wages of sin were death, the wages of pleasure were countable in a few smuggled sovereigns and in the rabid fumbling of fornication in corners and under piles of rags. Whenever Stanton wavered in his faith in the path he'd been thrown upon, and was tempted back to the straight and narrow (it was usually on Sundays) he only needed see how life was lived in the stink of forceful aggravation at the level to which he was reduced. Oh, and he wanted his wife to know (if she ever doubted it) he was not so disordered in his morals as to be party to fornication, either. He loved her dearly, longed for her visits, and Dolly discovered through heartbreak and humiliation that she loved her husband whichever way he turned.

'"Chance", Parson Stanton?' said the judge, roused to the point of outrage by a claim. '"Chance" in your mounting up those stairs, with primed pistol loaded with hard ball, showing murderous intent? And "plotters"? Weren't you the one plotter, sir? A conspiracy of yourself?'

The judge looked at the statement of charges before him and uttered a tormented sigh. It was plainly understood that if Judge Pidgeon could not have Stanton sentenced by three in the afternoon and hung by morning light, his amazement would then be complete. Until then he was all disbelieving looks. The jury had only to read his face to know their verdict some long time before they retired to consider it.

A constable's timing was the only matter in the whole unravelling affair that depended on chance, answered the prosecution — led by the famous Erskine — not having too much trouble in persuading the judge, either, that it was better not to address the accused by the title of Reverend. It might give the impression that Stanton was some kind of agent of moral force, still, and as justifiable in his ambitions as his defence counsel came close to arguing, but was soon enough discredited. That Stanton was formerly an Anglican priest only proved he was once certified capable of appreciating right from wrong. Therefore was guilty as could be. Wasn't it shown by his years of preaching in Botany Bay, that he was clear on morality? There were several churchmen, witnesses for him, who, although they had struck him from their register of clerics as soon as they could, volunteered their very fine feeling by testifying they had known the prisoner twenty years and a man more humble, more inoffensive and less likely to commit such an outrage was not within the circle of their acquaintance. There was not much more to be said for him. Major Agnew of His Majesty's N.S. Wales rangers was examined, and although Agnew tried saying his best for Stanton's reputation as a sheep breeder it came out he was a flogger. The information went back to Newgate and Stanton spent an unhappy time being clawed and mocked until his sentencing came around, when he was left alone from pity in the press yard. It was his lowest point. He was like a bag emptied of lumpy seed-potatoes gone wrong and ready to be thrown away, a piece of sacking. That a bullet wound to the chest had opened Blaise Cribb's ribcage and drained his lungs of pestilence while he lay knocked back on the bare boards of Ritchie's rooms, giving him back his health several hundred percentage-wise, so that he sat in the body of the court breathing freely, bright of cheek, quick of step, shining of eye, was not even raised. But that Stanton had loaded his pistol with something a little more powerful than swanshot and powder, which was to say, hard ball, was made much of: the intent to commit murder was plain.

The presence in court of a powerful friend had some slight effect upon the judge in deciding what sentence to pass, but it was not sufficient. That the powerful friend was the same Lord Bramley who'd come under the nose of Stanton's pistol, and indeed that all of Stanton's house remaining, his wife, his daughter, his (too obvious) unborn grandchild, were under the kind protection of Bramley and his friends, including Cribb, the man shot, and the Hardcastles, known reformers, only added a certain urgency to getting the world rid of the origin of all their misery and charity: the morosely glaring prisoner in the dock, Matthew Stanton.

At the end, a plea was allowed from Alexander Ritchie, on behalf of the prisoner. Ritchie was against the noose even if it was himself shot and killed! Such a statement never having been heard in his court nor in any other the judge knew of, he asked for the jury to retire and consider.

Very soon they were back:

'*Guilty, Death, aged 53.*'

Chorus of the Seventh Part

WHERE KALE IS UPON THE WIND

T O BE TAKEN FROM A rotten cell of the Hell's Gate
prison of Van Diemen's Land, pushed along an oyster-
bladed shore by a resentful guard, placed in a rowing boat,
made to take up the oars while manacled, and then, still wearing
prison rags, and under the worst incessantly raging sky experience-
able that end of the planet, under dense cold clouds that could be
reached up and touched, almost, if one had the will to meddle with
such dripping smoke — then ordered from that boat shivering cold
and led up a rocky path, there to be greeted by a prison governor
detested, to have iron rivets removed by a waiting blacksmith, and
be told there was hot water and a washtub being made ready —
was, you would have to agree, the most fairly refined sweet torture
of any experienced during the convict age.

But more of it on the compelling side of experience was to come
for Tom Rankine. His captivity, he was told, was over — if he
wanted to believe it.

Men were chained like beasts to a wall each night, after doing
their day's work. Men were made to stand to their necks in freezing
water moving great logs floated across the dark harbour, while

Rankine, for his sins, had been given a clerk's ledger and better rations, and except for being locked in a windowless room for twelve hours each night was allowed some of the gentleman convict mitigation that was dispensed to the few prisoners of his class, called the white handers. Small mercies saved lives in descriptions of pits of hell. When beaten, it wasn't as hard as some. Rankine shared what he could with those worse off: a stale crust, a rancid chew of salt beef, a trickle of sugar onto a horny old palm, with a grunt of gratitude directed at him. He lived, with nerves badly blown, and flinched at any noise, saw shadows of slinking creatures that weren't there, gave malicious willpower to a blade, a rock, a marlin spike, and having been biffed around the hairline once too often, swingled his head louringly on a lookout for blows. It would take him many months to lose the habit. More than a year. And what of the companions he made, the revelations, attachments, consolations and narratives of life's misfortunates transfused to a sympathetic heart and soul? Those fellow prisoners were the salt and bread of Rankine's four hundred and twenty days. They were the magnified, sorriest expression of what he touched in Kale. Through networks of sympathisers he learned that Meg was safe, with friends, and awaited him: but there came no privilege of letters, and no assurance his messages smuggled back in the other direction ever reached her.

While he was splashing in that bath house, clean clothes were laid out for him, and almost fainting from the confusion of the switch, from cursed to cared for, Rankine was surprised to find they were his old uniform coats, with the insignia of rank cut from them. That was all right, as he believed his resignation of commission came before Wilkie's move against him in the order of their final interview. His regimental pride was not so very dented (procedure still counting), while more to the point, he believed he was removed from further punishments in courts of N.S. Wales rangers.

What he wanted very much now was to get the word through to Meg, that he was all right in his way, at least alive, and better still, hoping, loving, and trusting the word he received of her safety. He longed to learn how she was faring with the Josephs and Mick. How to do so from the teardrop-shaped end of Van Diemen's Land was a question soon to be answered.

Better — or worse, depending on the finality of the outcome — was to succeed this moment of surprise for Tom Rankine in that fourteenth month of his captivity, when from Hell's Gate he was taken by ship to Hobart.

There he was informed how legal opinion, rather than any compassionate clemency, had turned over his conviction; apparently it was a free pardon; no apologies, no recompense, and none expected, far from it; but an order signed by a new arrival at Sydney Town, an officer unknown to the colony when Rankine was in it — by name, Convict Commissioner Valentine Lloyd Thomas, RN.

Was this the Val Lloyd Thomas of Thomas's Mill? It could be no other. They had played together as boys. Their fathers were friends in the years when the Thomases thrived on wool. At twelve, Val entered the navy. Rankine in latter years heard of his brilliance in law, his recklessness at gaming, his appetite for sexual conquest. When Napoleon wreaked havoc they went to their separate wars, Rankine's in Spain, Lloyd Thomas's at the Admiralty, where he was greatly admired for winning indictments against troublesome captains.

It looked like what seemed fixed in the rancorous universe of whips and gallows had a second guesser. The commissioner's charge was to question everything concerning the public purse and the dispensing of justice. Broad powers of request. Enforcement of answers. Rankine was called to give evidence in his court of enquiry. As well as the summons to attend, he was handed a warrant of ship's passage to Sydney Town, and a packet of letters.

Now his blood began to warm. The letters were from Meg. A cornucopia of them spilled from red string. His fingers trembled gathering them up.

Rankine took the letters to the room where he lodged awaiting a ship back to Sydney. There, overlooking cold Derwent water, he called for a glass of brandy, stoked his pipe, and with a window open to the free movement of air (he was never again to tolerate a closed room) learned that Meg was safe as far as the sequence of the letters went, in the journey started without him, with Stanton's offloaded culls setting a pace for the waggoners and his return daily expected — until the word came (after long delay) that he was taken and held. Most of a year was given to him in the letters, and he cursed the cruelty imposed, in regulations keeping the letters from him.

Rankine read of how they were bailed up by Lehane who brought an offsider to make sure the job was more certainly done this time. How Lehane took bullocks, and a barrel of gin. His accomplice a black fellow, Crouch. M'Carty set off with a friend-lier black fellow, Piper, to find them. M'Carty returned in a week saying he saw bullocks, and Lehane by a fire, close enough for his curses to be heard, but on the other side of a limestone ravine six hundred feet deep and no way down or across.

Solly, Arthur and Leah Josephs drove those sheep hard and tight until they arrived at the duck mole reach, with few losses. Rankine smiled. He almost disbelieved the trouble taken. He knew that country too well. He could only imagine how many times the waggon was unloaded, dismantled, a bullock team packed and driven over riverbed and gorge, then the waggon refurbished to get to the reach. He could only imagine nights of sheep in sapling yards, guard fires lit, warregal dogs howling the perimeter. They were not at the duck mole very long before the word went back towards civilisation and a straggle of settlers arrived in their waggon tracks; and so, while Rankine was forcefully held, distances altered, condensed, and walking paces became easier. There was a ramshackle inn set up, by name of Tharpe's. It was no more an inn than a bark hut and stockyards, with horse rails and a wooden watering trough.

On some pages, Leah Josephs took over the writing from Meg (she made it more vividly seen). Rankine learned that Mick Tornley and old Mother Hauser shared a camp. So, smiled Rankine, Mick was welded to their ways, and the old crone, seen through Mick's eyes, mightn't be so old, or so cronish, either. At night they could be heard singing along, as revellers struck up. Artie Josephs won favour with his fiddle. M'Carty went on a binge. Tharpe's was sworn the greatest hostelry in the land, as well as the loneliest one. Potatoes were planted and maize, by the settlers, a kitchen garden dug, poultry housed, pigs styed; next to establish was a black-smith's forge. Lehane's blacks came in from the bush, bargaining for tucker. Mick shouted an express order for them to spear Lehane and drive his bullocks home.

They thought Mick a great laugh, with his beard slapped to his belly, his stumpy rage, and his long-reaching whip. When they were too far away for leather he fired after them, across the dance of trees, where they disappeared.

The waggon stalled, throwing a wheel, and was unloaded into three light drays. Rankine deduced the drays were built from waggon parts. From there they blazed a trail as far as an old camp of Kale's, referred to as the gentleman. From Leah's description it was a camp beyond where Rankine had ever come, at the edge of a wide, rolling plain, grassy, cold and windswept. Kale? He was gone out to the blazes with Biddy Magee — except, in a ballad sung at Tharpe's, it was said now, that the gentleman found a broad river that flowed to an inland sea. McCarty set off with Piper to find him.

The letters were not in any order. In every one the assurance came through that Meg was cared for. Rankine saw that anyone reading them wouldn't know where the country was, exactly. Only he guessed it through joining the parts. Pulling one out without forewarning Rankine learned that Meg was pregnant. It was difficult to read through the tears. She'd waited a while to be sure she was carrying. She hoped it made Rankine happy. Happy? He threw the letters down and went to the window, took hold of the window frame and leaned out into the night. Being alive, having such life heaped on him that his heart ached from joy. Now it was like Meg was with him in the room, when he turned back in, Meg walking him about, looking him over and gazing at him with love, shaking her head wonderingly as she covered his face with her hands — warming his cheeks with her fingers — and stopping the shakiness Rankine had in him from a good few hard beatings that he discounted as not as bad as others were dealt.

That there was to be a son born to them — wrote Meg — a son and not a daughter, she precisely emphasised — was winkled through enchantment spun in two sticks bound across a third, and suspended with string over Meg's protruding navel by Martha Josephs.

Rankine counted on his fingers. The boy would be seven months old now.

THREE WEEKS LATER RANKINE ARRIVED in Sydney a ghost of himself, impatient to find a horse and busy avoiding any face he knew. He was bound to attract attention — a twitchy man with drawn, pale features, an air of great strain, with resentful reaction to curiosity and a colossal reputation to face down. Everyone had a story of bad leading to worse. Rankine's, leading from better to worse, challenged the ordinary sequence of progress. Many lives were ruined in struggle, but there were few volunteers in the ruining of their own lives. He was traitor to his own class. Fomenter of Irish delusion. Defier of laid-down regulation and deceiver of authority. How he escaped a hanging was the mystery, and now, incomprehensibly honoured with a pardon, his hold on life, though revealed, still remained a riddle. 'Report daily or lose your freedom' — that was dislikeable to Rankine and his resenters both. Why should he have his freedom at all? asked the offended class. If given it, why must it be partly checked? asked Rankine. To the Irish he was proof of miracle, though some wondered if he'd turned coat.

His pardon, he learned, was free but conditional . . . He was free to find lodgings, but required to wait about. No straying beyond three miles of Farm Cove in any direction. The gritty, humid, southerly wind whipped a busy, greedy Sydney Town of sandstone and raw timbers, windmills, brickpits, cesspits, taverns and dusty prizefighting rings. Ships arrived every two weeks or three and sat on moorings in the cove besieged by speculators. Since Rankine was dragged in from Parramatta it was more than ever a gambler's paradise expended in a variety of sports. Lloyd Thomas's name was more than respected, it was feared — whereas the new governor's was not so much. The convict commissioner's runners took wagers on boxing matches, dog fights, horse races. When the flags went up, Lloyd Thomas went to his telescope, with a long view down the harbour, and then to the ships, Rankine learned, to look over the newly arrived women, choosing the unspoiled, where such were to be had, or to carry away the wildest, most beautiful whore on deck.

Rankine walked out daily, taking a heel of bread and an orange, making his way round the foreshore, until he found a place to fish. It gave him a look of belonging, without inviting conversation. After a week of such waiting he was more anxious than ever to get going.

On the eighth day Commissioner Lloyd Thomas had him brought to his office without too much fuss. No sign was given that they had ever known each other. It was all formalities. A stenographer took the record. Coal-black-haired, gimlet-eyed, hungry of attack, Lloyd Thomas was an authority to be reckoned with. There had been an air of forceful certainty, even as a rivalling boy. Now it was given the full authority of the Crown.

First came the sally, that Rankine learned was loosed by the commissioner on all those of experience, following a tried routine:

'Have you any complaint to make against Governor Wilkie?'

Rankine deflected the shot. 'I have no rights of protest in this.'

'Come, do not be coy.'

If Rankine did have complaints, they were at the level of personal relations — and thought the commissioner might not care about those. 'Not at all,' he was assured, as Lloyd Thomas was passionate in everything. But Rankine remained reluctant, because when it came to leniency — one of the indictments against Wilkie — Rankine was for Wilkie's inclinations of mercy more than another's, and always had been. It was why he'd fallen silent the day he rode in to resign his commission, leaving Meg with the waggoners, he thought but for the day, to discover he faced Lehane, who'd galloped ahead of him on a saddleless nag, bridled with string, to acquaint the governor with 'Tumbankin', at which the governor asked, 'Is this you, Tom?' As Rankine dropped his head, half proud, unashamed, he said it might be, and found himself, within minutes, clapped in irons.

'You were charged with springing convict Kale from a punishment gang.'

'I was,' said Rankine.

'And you had?'

Rankine blinked, confused. 'Sir . . .'

He was not about to make the same mistake twice, of blabbing his way to perdition, as had happened faced with Lehane's affidavit, that morning with the governor. But hadn't he just said so?

'Well?'

'You have the records,' Rankine hedged, 'my transportation and treatment reports. You have clerks of the court at your bidding, to bring them out. Fourteen months and never being dry, or warm, though better regarded than most, yet, it's all comparative, commander, and I bear some scars, it's true.'

'Not so fast in humbling yourself, dear man. Wilkie appears to have erred. There is no record of evidence.'

'None?'

This must be a snare, thought Rankine.

'Not in colonial files. If you'd been hanged, he'd have a bad conscience. There is, of course, a chance you'll be tried again, if evidence should come to light.'

This made Rankine sit up, although —

'I am set against Wilkie, not against you,' he was told by the commissioner. It was all so nicely put. A veiled threat, presented as generosity of bias.

At this point Lloyd Thomas asked the convict stenographer to step from the room. Then, removing his jacket, shooting his silk cuffs, he went to the fire and removed a jug of coffee where it warmed on the coals. 'Tom Rankine, Tom Rankine,' he said. 'How are you, my good man?'

'I am knocked sideways.'

Lloyd Thomas poured two cups, passing one to Rankine, who held it between his trembling hands. It was a warm Sydney day, the first of September, the first day of spring, but Rankine's bones were blue cold.

'If a man sets forth on an expedition, Tom, what sort of prisoners should he take? Think about this. In my position, I have first call on the best transported artisans — drovers, wheelwrights, blacksmiths, grooms, transported females of various crafts and wiles: I can take them from anyone; Nero had not such powers. The best available I am proposing are yours, for an enterprise of exploration. It will reverse your fortunes from where they now stand. Rankine? Do you hear me? Lift your head, Tom. There is nothing for you to look so far down about. To the extent you have a motive in mind, to prosper Kale, my interest is the same. Do you remember me, Tom?'

'I do,' said the trembling returnee. 'Raindrops running down a window pane, the fertility of a dean's wife, steeplechasing by moonlight, anything and everything grounds for a wager.'

'I am not changed. In the wager I lose myself, as in love. I come back to my duties braced.'

'Is this a gamble, then?'

'On you, a gambler yourself, you princely dog. What I am asking is nothing more than a stake in your interest in Kale.'

'Over sheep?'

'Not over sheep. I believe he's found a river.'

'The duck mole reach,' said Rankine, with nothing to lose, as what information was in Meg's letters would be thoroughly read.

'The duck mole reach, indeed. Nay, what I seek is an inland sea, fed by a great river. It is called the Kindur.'

'I've never heard anyone speak of it.'

'That is hardly likely.'

'If the Irish bandy a name, it's often poetical,' said Rankine.

The commissioner raised an eyebrow. 'Don't deny me, Tom, your tangle of secrets is safe. Reach Kale, you will have crossed and surveyed more land than anyone's sensibly found.' Lloyd Thomas rapped the table. 'Tom, in my commission so far, I have interviewed most of the free inhabitants of Botany Bay, over fifty emancipists and hundreds of convicts. You will not believe the number of times Kale's name has been spoken. The man is a boast to the downhearted, a bother to the secure. I have raked together all the dirt and filth, scandal, calumnies and lies that were ever circulated. Kale's name shines through pretty clear. Your name is in there, twisted, but magnanimous. Reach Kale, send word back of the country, and you shall carry on with an unconditional free pardon under my authority as commissioner of convicts. For you and for Kale.'

'Where is it?' said Rankine, wanting the piece of paper.

The commissioner said, 'I'll have it drawn up. I want you and your mistress to dine with me — your lovely Meg Inchcape —'

'She is my wife.'

'Acknowledged,' said Lloyd Thomas wolfishly. 'And faithfully awaits you, I believe?'

'As I hope and pray,' said Rankine.

Lloyd Thomas turned to a case of Baltic pine, with brass hinges and a clasp, sitting on the floor.

'It holds a sextant, Tom, gifted from my uncle, when I joined the navy as a boy. I could hardly carry it around, and was laughed at. It is a precious instrument. Of little use in my present game, though it is barely all I have left of my rightful inheritance. My talents, more forensic than oceanic — anyway, I was put to the study of courts martial, and thrived. As a midshipman, however, I learned enough to know that once navigation rises above the category of a chore, it becomes a science of consuming interest.' He handed Rankine the box. 'I want you to have it.'

'I cannot.'

'Come, now. Take care of it for me, put it to use. Since enlisting in the rangers you play down your service with the 95th, as quartermaster-general's surveyor. You can still take a star fix. Take it, and push on. There is a horse in your name at my stables. I would put Lord Bramley not far behind us.'

'Bramley?' said Rankine.

'His eye is fixed on Botany Bay. Bramley would never take on the voyage himself — but shall send an agent, and that agent when he gets here shall start pegging country down until he owns a good share of it, in Bramley's name. Money, tied to purpose, meets little resistance. Purpose, without money, cannot catch a horse.'

'Acknowledged,' said Rankine.

'Ah, but purpose, allied with power, beats money, Tom, if it uses its head. Bramley's purse is bottomless, once Bramley loosens the strings. The day I left England, Botany Bay wools were the topic in Bramley's corner. There's been mail this week bringing confirmation. His agent, addressing the houses of Westminster, made a great splash. That was, by calculation, six months ago. His agent, you should know, is most likely on the water and halfway across the world by now.'

As Rankine left, Lloyd Thomas called him back. 'You did not ask his name, this agent of Bramley's.'

'No. Your expression tells me all I need. If I was a betting man like you, I'd put my shirt on it.'

'On Blaise Henry Cribb, and not go wrong,' agreed Lloyd Thomas.

W ARREN INCHCAPE COULD NOT TELL. One day
he might. One day he might tell. One day he might tell
how it was — that he was one of the larboard watch.
That the men of the larboard watch were called up early by means
of a great yelling and running along the decks above their heads.
How they did not know what it was coming upon them, but through
a sailor's understanding penetrating their sailors' half sleep they
were aware of a great danger at sea. From the dark, from the night,
a force akin to another world looming upon this one rose before
them. A rent opened in the fabric of the heavens! 'Look up!' they
cried, and saw the mate standing forward, on the starboard bow,
and calling out, '*Luff! Luff!*'

One day Warren might tell how everybody ran forward, and
stared into the dark water. How there was a steady breeze (they
were on their starboard tack) and absolute darkness just penetrated
by a floating star. Only it was not a star, but a light, a ship's light
that the mate must have seen before anyone else and sensed in the
night, apprehended it as they all did now, with horror. Another ship
bearing down on them, on a beam reach in towering silence! They

heard the flap of her topsails and were relieved for the moment that she seemed smaller in reality than she seemed in the gloom when she was an instinctive presence, and might be going about. And how they were wrong about that: because advancing across the waves she was a knife, an arrow, a ram. How they heard a voice echoing their mate's with 'Luff! Luff!' from the other ship. And how that must have been Captain Martin Sykes. How it must have been that man at the helm and as helpless as anyone but he was never going to admit he was wrong, and would need the best story of himself to tell his ship owners when he returned to Boston. How if there was a drowsy lookout on one ship there was a sleepy lookout on the other, and the two vessels coming along and expecting in a few days to meet up with each other in their arranged encounter. How instead of their arranged encounter it was this disarranged encounter and all too terribly soon.

After that? Noise. Blows. Timbers falling around the ears. A strange smell of dust and powder over the wet sea. Loudness of material and men falling into the water. How if there was to be an account of the loss of seventy-eight men, some pigs, some cats, some parrots and some rats, the only one to tell the tale would be Martin Sykes and he would have his side of it — because Warren and Titus would never say anything. They had seen too far and gone too far and wanted towards home. As for the *Betsy* of New Bedford, she was spread far and wide in all her missing parts and crew, a hundred fathoms down.

A raft of lashed planks, half awash, saved them, and their sea chest that floated up from the wreckage. The chest's gunwales, more often than not, were down a foot under water. They'd seen their precious biscuits, threads and nails for fishing lines, tobacco tins, and whatnots sink to the bottom. Maybe they were wanted by the drowned crew waving from the deep. The only good things apart from their chest, that never once capsized, so saved them, were flying fish they grabbed and tore to pieces, and a few squalls of rain, that they drank with their mouths open as it torrented down. Up came the sun after each night into a terrible day, to fry their brains and forget them who they were.

There was a way Titus had, though, of facing terror straight, in trust of his soul's brother, Warren, even when the sharks grazed against the bones of their legs, and made ready to come back for a decent bite, by swimming out wide with their fins slicking above water. At the very last did Titus scream — and just as well — because by then their floating sea chest was close to the *Salamander*, which they were too blinded to see was near them. They said it was Titus's screams that made them look out.

The two castaways were found floating, holding to the sea chest, a weak hail from where the *Salamander* was hove to for her repairs, a whole two weeks after the cataclysm. By immense good chance circling currents had brought them back to the bearings where the two ships ripped through each other.

The two sailors clutching wreckage were brought on board. They were almost deprived of their senses but not quite. Otherwise this story would have no ending known. All the port bow of the *Salamander* was ragged and fractured in her raking of the other ship. Her port anchor was completely gone and its weight, thrown into the other vessel, must have played a main part in taking the *Betsy* down. A huge length of the port bulwarks was taken off her and carried away. All the lower yardarms were broken in the same direction, but none of this was discouraging to Sykes holding to his purpose of staying at sea and catching seals. During her repairs the *Salamander* stood off a lonely atoll south of cannibal islands located a week's sailing to the north of Cape Brett. It was a scribble on a chart, known as a haven for whalers and their shoddier ilk, sealers. Sykes still had a load of skins to carry and would not seek harbour for them: the next lot he was determined would be stowed on her open decks. And he had two extra crewmen hauled from the hungry sea to make sure he did it.

Before they hove into view, a body had been fished floating from the water, the only one found. It was the swollen form of a hairy man wearing a medallion around his neck proclaiming him the *Betsy* boxing champion, and that was the only evidence remaining of any ship at all until the two named creatures swam up, one of them wearing a triangular hat, a cream silk vest, and a white sash around his black, burning throat — hence to be nicknamed Admiral. The other with no trousers and a hideously swollen scrotum — hence to be named Pepperpots. Their skeletal hands clung to their ship's chest with a Christian cross pokerworked into its wood and some ciphering on its lid. It was hoisted aboard and found to be empty. Upon the information that a boxing champion had been drowned, Pepperpots looked startled and for the first time a bit of life came into his eyes.

'What is the matter?' said Sykes, with cunning particularity. 'Did he have you?'

'Nay, I had him,' said Pepperpots, baring a grin, though without knowing what he meant, at all, until his memory came back to him, in shreds and tatters. So that was who took his medal, the one he'd felled in fair contest on a far happier ship.

The sealer was a brig of handsome make, a battered salt and sunwhite craft with rakish masts and yards and manned by a crew of deserters and escaped convicts of several nations. At the end of her repairs she was jury rigged, but workable. Only her moods made her truly ugly and they were vile moods indeed. Against each and every man aboard it served their Massachusetts man, Martin Sykes, to hold resentments enough to be sure they wouldn't run. All including Pepperpots and Admiral had prices on their heads or warrants out against them in various ports. After being cruelly used ashore men laid cruelty on others on the high seas, as if their due. Because it served his ship, Sykes allowed his crew free run against each other, though to be doubly sure of their displeasure, he stayed away from civilised ports for as long as he could, only once in a while consulting the ship's almanac where an appointment was laid down and where if he wished to continue sealing he would have his goods taken off his decks. He slung his skins to other ships while moored in lonely places and thus stayed abroad while his cargo was traded to port. There was a harbour north of the Bay of Islands he used, another at Van Diemen's Land, and a shelter somewhere about Bass Strait, between Van Diemen's Land and New Holland where wild seas clashed, tore, tossed and fumed over shallows.

When the name Botany Bay was whispered around, Admiral and Pepperpots experienced a thrill of silence, lest they betray their hopes: for if they did cut loose they would have their best chance of a homecoming in the Bass Strait.

Among that crew, tormenting them was a sport, and the captain the biggest bully of all. But a lesson was soon learned: it was better to mess with their carnal virtue than attempt destroying their hopes of getting themselves free and back to where they started. They never admitted where that was, for fear they'd never be taken there, except sometimes Pepperpots' eyes rolled up in his head; and he bleated with forgotten joy as he counted whales and porpoises, their backs gleaming, their heads spuming a haze of breath into the grey salt air. How he herded them with his eyes, sorted them in his heart until they reckoned he was a shepherd wrenched from his lubberly beginnings by circumstances too miserable to be told.

Strength regained, Admiral was a hellcat; he couldn't be stopped by any fist, nor by the bosun's whip either, as he took whatever lashes were laid on him for being insolent and nimble — along his legs, upon his thin scarred shoulders, and even on the soles of his naked feet as he lay on his back repelling attackers of his enraged pride. Only Pepperpots was able to calm him, at such times, and that was by sitting attentively to him, and saying nothing, not even looking at him, but twiddling his bulky toes and finding a point on the far horizon to fix his eyes on, where he might see hope in the shape of islands or the long smoky edge of somewhere. If anyone came near them again he jumped up and challenged them even if it was their captain himself. An almost crazed passion of justification existed between the pair of them.

So vitriolic was Sykes's blame on the *Betsy* and her two survivors that no reply was possible from any person, leastwise a pair of half-drowned sailors, in defence of themselves and the truth that their *Betsy* was rammed by the *Salamander* and not the other way around. Sykes cursed them as two of the worst luck bringers that were ever flung alive upon the waters. Wasn't it their watch? Hadn't they been on deck?

They weren't confessing it. Either that, or all memory of what happened was wiped from their brains by the horror of their experience, the wreck, the drownings, the loss of shipmates, the loss of a good captain when his ship broke under him in a reasonable calm sea and its various parts sunk to the bottom, except for a few spars and bits of baggage. Then all those two weeks of being maddened with thirst! vomiting sick from hunger! attacked by sharks! being covered in buboes and scalding rashes! dying!

They believed it was hard for them to die at sea after every way they tried.

One day on the *Salamander* Pepperpots stroked his fingers through the fur of a seal skin, a wonder to himself as well as to the ship's master, who stood nearby.

'Why, these hairs are all silken,' he said, 'they are flat, pointed, harsh.' And this from an ordinary seaman, who was marked by a blistery scorched face and his rib and arse bones chafed, his powers of discrimination dimmed almost to extinction!

'Tell me what you know,' said Sykes, his interest piqued by one so lately waterlogged.

Pepperpots turned the external coat into folds and gave a deeper interpretation. He could not use his eyes too well, they were sore. Smoothing his finger and thumb in the material he said, 'There is a variable quantity of wool in here. The curves are not thickly set.'

'Curves? I should think not. A fur is good and straight.'

Pepperpots recited his understanding, which was less like intelligence and more like comfort: 'In the matter of wools, if the curves are not very thickly set, the serrations are not very numerous. So it might be covered in scales, this fur, but not serrations. It says why its hairs lie all in the same way, and don't tangle to form a mat — why seals' coats are worn by people as they are on the animal, not greatly changed, except for being cut, and sewn. There are no hooks to bind it.'

A FTER THEIR BLISTERS HEALED IT was seen that Pepperpots's ogling features were covered in a reddish, frosted fuzz of beard. Across the side of his scalp, white as oyster meat, was a thick scar where his hair refused to grow back after he was struck his injury when he ran forward to assist. The skin where it healed pulled his eyelids up, leaving him with an affronted sort of expression, and meant when asleep his eyes stuck partly open, in a slit of watchfulness that had the benefit of warning off anyone wanting to sort through his belongings or his mate's.

When Admiral's blisters healed he was seen to be blacker than when he was burnt: a truly black man, indeed, of which race, though, was the subject of passionate ignorance. It made Admiral the lowest on the ship but with his preposterous three-cornered hat he showed refusal to accept how lowly he was. As the castaways were roughened by weather, hard usage, illness and injury, they looked about forty bleary years old, but they were mere mother's sons, both of them, and still short of twenty years of age.

'Where are you from, jackass,' said Sykes, 'where's your home port, suckling?' Wrenching Pepperpots's ear, he marched him up and down along the deck but learned nothing.

After the iron rule of his ship as a means of sadistic enjoyment, the leading motive of Martin Sykes was commerce. When they found a place to hunt seal, his motive was to prevent anyone else from getting skins. His idea was, that no foreigner had right to privilege near any colony that he declared his own. From the decks of the *Salamander* he scanned the blear horizon and sent his boats on.

One day Pepperpots and Admiral were among those in the first boat away. The two close shipmates had made a practice of never taking more nor less than most of what they needed for their living needs in a boat running into a surf. It might be their last chance every time, and like the rest of their crew, they did not always make it back to their vessel at night, but slept in the sea grass, among dunes, or curled in a rocky cave echoing with breakers.

On boards at their feet that day they had all their worldly goods in a calico sack. They had some salt pork between them, a flask of rum, a sharpening stone, a sealing knife, a sealing club, a few poor souvenirs of happier times, and a lump each of dark tobacco. They had little to protect them from the weather in the coming night ashore. They each carried a tin canister of water since a time they were driven crazed by thirst, and whenever there was a squall of rain they always cupped their hands and licked their paws like cats, to save it. Pepperpots owned the clothes he stood in, and that was all, while Admiral — of lean and agile pretension — had a bedroll tied with a leather thong, hitched tight to his backbone.

Only closer inspection might have shown that the way Admiral carried himself, with a careful, forced, and upright gait —

sometimes he couldn't help tilting — was a sign that his bedroll contained something much heavier than the precious sea commander's outfit, for which he was mocked, and which he was wearing — quite sadly bedraggled.

At their back, bucking an easterly swell, the *Salamander* rode with jabbing persistence against a grinding anchor chain on a shallow bottom. They were well enough away from her, and today the two mariners jabbed their fingers secretly in the air and swore silently it was the last they would look back on her.

They had not come as close before to such a difficult beach for setting down. Hummocks and dunes were all the land to be seen past the edge. It was a bay so constantly beaten by strong winds and high seas that their captain believed the seals inhabiting it were sure to remain unmolested until none were to be found anywhere else. The only trouble with his thinking was that seals everywhere were getting into shorter supply, the traders hungrier for them. Indeed had they only known it, in the bays over from this one were six different gangs of men belonging to a Port Jackson sealer, moored from sight, who were there on the same business as themselves, and all of them running short of provisions and on the point of eating seabirds and seals if they didn't find better relief from their wants.

This was the leading boat coming away from the *Salamander.* Four men rowed, one worked a steering oar, while a sixth crouched in the bows looking out for trouble. The other boats followed, some with the intention of standing off to drive the seals back onto land when the killing began. Others would land and begin the dirty work of sticking them and skinning them, leaving their carcases to rot, their fishy dark meat being no use to anyone except the carrion birds and island rats, once the skins were taken.

They watched the *Salamander* shrinking behind them as their boat wallowed in a swell behind breakers, trying for a chance to get in among the rocky platforms. The easterly wind drove the seals up on land. There were a good many of them flopped and basking, shining their backs, their noses and long whiskers aligned to the wind in the direction of possible threat. They had heavy necks and thick manes and looked like a colony that had not been attacked too many times, as they were plentiful with the shore fairly free of bones. They were dense with variations in colour from dark black-brown to golden. Seal fur was wanted for its strength of insulation in coats, hats and mufflers, and for high, warm boots of style. Skins would be bloodily piled at the tide line by sunset. Bull seals raised themselves on their tails, scarred in their fights for females, having chunks torn from their hides and rendering them less desirable as skins. In pauses between waves thumping, males could be heard barking their challenges and the men were ready with theirs. Bull seals went for their opponents throwing their heads up and rising chest to chest, biting each other around the neck and shoulders, making guttural sounds and very preoccupied they were, as the first of the boats came in on a surge and was hauled up the rubble beach to sit above the tide line.

From there the *Salamander* was far off but they knew the eye of Martin Sykes was upon them, his telescope raised and lowered every few minutes and his last and most trusted boat's crew of cutthroats standing by to be sent after stragglers, who might decide that a low piece of land lying in the southern oceans was better than their ship to live on.

There were sealers who lived on land the whole year, maintaining depots, and saving themselves the discomfort of ever having to go back to sea. They kidnapped women for their comfort. This day when Pepperpots and Admiral came stepping on sand, leaping from the boat, plunging up to their chests in foam, they were soon enough looking around for a rock, a lump of coral, the thighbone of a seal, or a piece of driftwood to use as a weapon. There were seals and there were men who lived among seals.

As for the seals, it was bloody work ending their animal life and stepping in blood and salt water. They got among them chasing them down, slaughtering them and skinning them between rocks and leaving their carcases to rot in the wind. It was bloodier, colder work than dealing with sheep ever was, and while there was plenty of barking there wasn't any dog to do it better.

As for men — it was men the *Salamander*'s crew feared most: each other first and then rival gangs from rival ships who might appear any time and dispute the harvest. Pepperpots and Admiral weren't so sure if they feared other men more than their own men. Other men were likely to beat them and press them into their gangs but other men's gangs were likely to go home to port. There were signs of men around, a cold fire where mussel shells were cooked, and footprints in sand. If their men ran for their boats it might be better for the two sailors where they were. They were always ready for it anyway.

In a pause between killing they were both flat on their bellies watching ahead. A gap in the dunes showed a lumpy dark shape nosing around. 'It ain't no seal,' said the Admiral. 'It must be someone.' The figure dropped from sight. So they scurried forward and scrambled to the top of the dune. There they saw a man watching towards them, but through careful manoeuvering they had put their backs to the eastern light and weren't seen. The man must have thought he was safe, then, because he lifted an arm in a signal. He was joined by a few men raising themselves out of the tussocks, all carrying weapons. They set off moving at a jog trot in a westerly direction. It was clear their plan was to round on the *Salamander* men from the leeward side. They would reach them in less than quarter of an hour and each man jack of them would have his hands full.

Having seen what was up, the two friends turned and looked at each other, thinking the same wild thought, and then they ran forward into a hollow of the dunes, a scoop of land at the very narrowest part of the island, and hidden from Sykes's telescope. They climbed the next dune and from there got themselves a surprise as they looked down into the next narrow, sheltered hollow. It was a thrusting animal coming along a sandy track, a womback, and didn't that mean they were in their own country? And wasn't it very tame, quite fearless as it ambled forward into Admiral's arms? Admiral grasped it behind its neck bones, pushing its trunk backwards and forwards as if he'd just met a great old friend and had all the time in the world to greet him. Pepperpots looked to their safety while the womback butted. On hands and knees Pepperpots advanced to the crest of the last dune. There was a wide expanse of ocean to the north and a narrow stretch of beach below. Was there any guard posted? Nobody was seen. Certainly there were no men on that beach, but drawn up on the sand, with its sails furled, was their salvation — a ship's whaleboat about fifteen feet in length!

With a garbled cry of wonder Pepperpots tumbled over the edge of the dune and plunged downwards, running. He crossed the tide line in a few wet strides and was at the bow of the boat. It was heavy on the sand. He dared not yell out to Admiral, but whistled piercingly like the whistling kite, hoping he was heard above the chop of the waves, and spent a few minutes untying knots and readying canvas, glancing around all the time and hardly believing the find. Shouldering the vessel around to face the sea was difficult heavy work and could not be done until Admiral appeared running backwards across the sands, scanning the skyline as he came, and lurching in such a particular disorganised way owing to his bedroll's heft across his back. About that bedroll, which seemed to have grown into Admiral's spine, he carried it so much, Pepperpots thought if there was anyone watching they would surely divine that held in the precious bundle of constant keeping was more than just the finery of a sea commander's clothes and a triple-cornered hat — that sewn into the pouches of the bandolier was coinage of weight and worth. It was held since their sea chest was thrown on the ballast of the *Salamander*. They took their time and removed its false floor, securing their fortune.

Almost buried to the ankles in wet sloppy sand they got the boat turned athwart and heaved her, lurch by lurch, until a foaming wash of tide lightened her timbers and she began floating in a few inches of water. Pushing hard they drifted her across a stretch of shallows until the easterly, no longer blocked by the dunes, combed her stern, smacking the sails. As she began briskly moving, the two clambered aboard and fell into the bottom, from where one grabbed the tiller and the other hauled in the sheets, working the canvas from an almost lying position inside the hull. Anyone chancing to see them would think the craft had got an idea of its own freedom into its head, and was gone skimming over the ocean unattended.

They sailed for an hour not daring to speak. It was well past noon when the seal island shrank to a low pale band on the horizon.

Pepperpots was half blinded by glare but Admiral screwed up his eyes and spoke: the moored *Salamander*, he said, was visible but hardly bigger than a freckle at one end of the island, while the strangers' ship at the other end of it, where the *Salamander* hadn't been able to see it, was no bigger than a pin head. Neither ship showed signs of putting out boats to give chase.

'And pray God they never will, pray God there's some kind of battle royale goin on,' said Pepperpots as he leaned back, keeping the sail trimmed, and grinned his salt lips. 'It will take all their attention, battling for seals. They might miss us by now, seeing as how we showed em the seal fighters we were. By tomorrer they won't know where we's gone, even if we don't know where we are ourselves, cept heading away. I trust our captain's come ashore to get his share of harm. I'd be disappointed if he ain't. I can see his head being split open. I am almost pleased enough to sail back there an shake the hand of the man who done it, who was a big enough fool to leave his boat unguarded.'

Admiral cried out, 'Ooh yah!' and was busy untangling a fishing line in his lap, that he'd found in a storage hatch. It was a generously supplied boat they had, and if they were caught, they'd be in worse trouble for stealing it than any sort of trouble they'd known before. There were other good things in there, under that hatch. Admiral was at the business of hauling them out when the wind changed aft, almost knocking them down. Pepperpots shouted a warning, hauled in ropes, pushed hard at the tiller, came around, the small craft bobbling and wobbling, and it was all right, only busy with slamming this way and that. They hadn't seen it coming, feathering across the green stirred sea: they were in for a time of it.

Wind belted from the south-west and settled in with a howl, bringing whitecaps. Admiral kept his head down. Eventually the two battered mariners looked at each other again with dripping faces and had the same thought. It was that any two who'd sailed a sea chest in a circle of the ocean, ballasted by stolen coin, and lived to make towards home, would be well able to span the whole world in a whaleboat with a standing lugsail and ready rigged as a yawl, when it came to trouble worse than this. For there was a feeling within the narrow ribs of their vessel that its rules of ownership were changed for the good, and a few other rules of ownership were changed as well, and with a little more luck changed for ever. They lifted their eyes to each other and dared their souls to return, that had deserted them for so long.

HAVING THE WHOLE WIDE SEA to themselves for the second time in their short lives they could barely contain their wonder at the reversal of fortune. When they were marooned drifting they'd dreamed of such a boat. Waves slapped the underside of her as she carried them along. One of them worked the tiller while the other stood high as he could holding onto a shroud and shading a hand across his eyes.

'Is anyone followin, yet?'

'I can't see nobody. Don't mean they ain't there.'

The little boat seemed almost to shout aloud that she was in better-deserved hands than she was with a bunch of dirty sealers, and so she'd hurry them along. Why, she was a tighter and more responsive bundle of salvation than two such mortal souls ever deserved. They might even see reason in keeping her and making her theirs if they ever found land! They'd sail her up rivers and pirate their way along in full charge, doing what was needed to get back their choices so lately stolen away. When they reached dry land they might even try out a few lessons they'd learned as ones who suffered but wouldn't no more. One sure thing was, that when it came down to trust, it would be hard to give it to anyone, except each other.

In the bottom of the boat they found waterproof canvases stowed for shelter of the coming night, jugs of water, lucifer matches, salt meat, hunks of bread, hard cheese, and a flagon of rum all stowed ready for an island camp that was never going to happen for a company of rogues. They were good sailors, though, it had to be said, who got their boat so ready for strangers. In this blowy change of wind, it was found that because of the sail layout being so conveniently prepared by those who might by other chance have knocked them on the head, things went very well indeed. When the mizzen was sheeted on hard, then the boat lay comfortably hoved to, head to wind, while the pair of them enjoyed a respite and looked each other over with such unaccustomed smiles on their faces, as they'd been trying out since they left the island. Pepperpots and the Admiral. Was *that* who they were?

They blinked, to find it was safe to say otherwise, when only the wind, and a few seabirds were listening.

'Titus Stanton, is that you, matey, sitting on your arse bones?'

'Warrie inch-long boy, with your balls so black and blue. I thought you bin done with sailin all over the world, mate.'

'Not till we get safe over, I ain't. Till then we have a ship. She's a good one and all.'

'An she is.'

From the direction of the seal island a leaning pillar of smoke came in their direction. It was easy to guess that all the grass must have been set on fire to scare men out in the contest between them.

'I'm smellin smoke,' said Titus, with a look of pleasure on his beloved mug. 'When we get to land, I'm thinkin, a fire is what we want, to warm us.'

'It won't be tonight, mate,' said Warren. He stood in the stern and scanned the northern horizon. 'I don't see no land signs and there weren't none this morning, neither, when I looked.'

'When'll it be, cap'n?'

'That, God knows.'

They were shivering cold and wet, but after they wiped their faces with a rag and took swills of rum they were warmer. Warren attended the helm and swung her back into making way, with the wind on the port side, hugging the tiller under his armpit — keeping her up to the wind. If he'd learned anything at all in the time he'd been flung away from his truest life, it was about finding direction. He believed, more or less, that they were heading nor-nor' east. There wasn't any compass to prove the guess, but in the sea they were in they were obliged to hold her a direction as best they could — just in case they sailed clear past New Holland and back into the Pacific Ocean again. What a trick that would be. Never again to know their land, and the only taste of it given, a sandy hollow with dead seals on one side and a womback in the middle.

Holding the white ball of the sun at his left shoulder Warren kept trying and thought about ways to keep safe in the night. This gale that was driving them was getting stronger. It was coming on faster than they liked. As they crossed the waves Titus crouched sheltered in the bow. He sang a song, a droning melody Warren hadn't heard in a good long time, except it meant he was happy.

And safe. So safe now that in his mind he started to go back and must have arrived on his home dirt already. It was allowed by their circumstances, allowed in feelings long banned from their hearts.

'Remember that Mr Moon, Warrie, that old man belongin to Laban Bale? It's his song I'm singin, y'know.'

'Mr Moon,' said Warren. 'A course I remember Mr Moon. He that studied the ground for prints, when the parson's ram was took — I recollect he mumbled a lot, an if the parson had of listened to half what he said, he coulda had Ugly Tom Rankine by the nuts sooner than later.'

'That same one, Mr Moon, is the one. Him that was called Mun'mow,' nodded Titus.

'Mun'mow? Get along. Mun'mow was my father's servant, in the good old days. My father's servant went to England with him. It is in all them papers, that old Governor Wilkie is getting for me, that are sure to make me right.'

'Well, but it's all the same fella, Warrie — Mun'mow was too pluddy hard for white men to say. England, he said it was no good for black fellas.'

'You never told me.'

'You never askit me, Brother.'

Titus arranged himself under the canvas, pulled his knees up to his chin, and prepared himself for sleep. But it was too early for sleep. Before sleep was allowed, Warren gave a warning: 'Let's get his tub tidied and see what's needed for dark.'

Warren's memories of how they'd dropped nearly all their belongings in the water were his worst recollections of their crazed time adrift. Things went straight to the bottom if they weren't held.

Warren got Titus busy, and the two of them stowed all the loose goods back under the whaleboat's hatches. When it was all put away they had a great feed of bread and pork to get them through the night. Then as a last precaution, they lashed a rope around the waist of each of them, and tethered themselves to the sides, in case they were washed over.

So it was all right for many, many hours of flying along with the tiller lashed to a steady course. The gale dropped to a strong wind, and the sea instead of being choppy eased to long swells. The wind dropped even more and things were most comfortable under the tilting stars, except it was shivering cold. Everything Warren had learned from boats he put to use, and the most he learned for this night's sailing was from a captain named Maule, a captain named Ashcraft, and an old slave boatman, Peres.

From the time they left the island to the time the Cross swung over, in a clear windswept sky not far from dawn, Warren estimated it was seventeen or eighteen hours of swift sailing they had done. He was anxious for dawn in case they made land, though having no idea how far land might be — an hour away or a day away or a week's hard sailing away? How could he know?

It must have been about four in the morning when Warren was wide awake, cold and wet, but filled with elation that the night was almost through, when their boat slid down a wave, hit something — it was surely a whale — pitchpoled, which was to say, turned completely over and landed in the sea upside down.

Warren was thrown into the water on one side of the hull, Titus on the other. They went under and came up, floundered, gasped, went under and came up again. Then they found some sort of grip although where they found it they were later unable to remember, except to wonder that whatever they needed to lay hands on seemed to be at the ready in the dark. They scrambled from opposite sides of the hull to find themselves roped, still, and sitting on the boat's narrow keel, which, they found — all in the same instant — gave enough weight to start righting her! The masts came up level in the water with the sails like a stingrays floating under the surface. Warren had no idea what was to happen next, when the whole boat shuddered and righted, low but standing upright! and spilling Titus down on the side he'd appeared from, and Warren under the other, without either of them having exchanged a word except loud curses and coughs of sea water.

THE GUNWALES OF THE WHALEBOAT were even with the sea and the entire inside of the boat awash. The other lucky shot was that the wind fell away almost completely though there was still a long swell. From the distance came the low pounding drum of surf, and they were in for it; they clung to the sides of the boat listening; and then they climbed back in, or rather floated over the sides back in, and untied their waist ropes in starlight to find all lines everywhere tangled like a nest of snakes. Warren splashed around cutting lines and bringing the sails down. They had not lost very much, considering they still had their oars, when Titus gave a cry:

'Lookit tiss!'

Warren turned around and saw Titus holding their bucket, which was tied by a line. There was no need to tell an old shipmate to start bailing her out as furiously as he could. It was warming work and they went to it until the first daylight.

By then they had her buoyant again, though sloppy with water, riding low, and could see, by standing and holding to the mast, how colour changed and light crept across the horizon. What seemed a pile of dark sky changed into high hills, ridges and gullies and shadowed folds all timbered and coming down to a seacoast of yellow sand and white misty breakers. And there was smoke. Everywhere there was smoke. This was their sought land, surely, and if they ever doubted it, a white cockatoo came over the sea and flapped above their heads before turning back towards land again to greet the morning there.

'Car'away,' said Titus.

Warren shed some tears.

Each time a high wave lifted them they looked around on the sight of land pouring from east to west, coming up from the vague distance and going off into vague distance again. The curve of beaches before them, one after the other running along a fair way.

Grabbing the oars, taking a side each and nosing the boat clumsily stern to the swell, they did not register anything more of it in their busy wet work except the bang of wood on wood, the roar and hiss of waves too close to them. Waves curved, swelled, went silently flat with foam and eddies, and then collapsed away under them. The boat surged nose down, shipping water, but held. They had no doubt of it as they sang out to each other in excitement. 'Heave away, haul away home . . .'

It was not in their control to be brought where they wanted to be. But brought there finally they were.

Now they came in sideways, crossing the bar, struggling with oars in a chop where a gap of water appeared in front of them instead of the beach. Waves creamed on both sides towards them with the speed of bolting horses and the boat was caught in their collision, shuddered and was part knocked down. Somehow she came upright again. Aided by tide, wind, and shouted curses, she rose on a crest, hesitated and then fell headlong down, hissingly gaining speed — and was shot in from the sea at last.

After much confusion they found themselves floating on a salty lake. It was sheltered and they could hear bird calls.

An eddy took them close to the inside shore. They gaped and breathed coarsely like two dying fish thrown in the boat. The water was the colour of tea. It had leaves and twigs in it and these they parted as they made way. Behind them, as behind a wall, the surf they had come through continued to sound. It could not touch them while the tide of it still carried them. Exhausted they allowed the tide to do what it must. They lay in their boat's sides and gazed at the banks where they saw wallabies grazing under paperbark trees and if they had wanted a fish, they could have trawled with their fingers for mullet and snapper, as easy as could be.

She nosed into a bank and they scrambled ashore on grass. The land rocked worse than the sea, or so it felt. Warren tied a line around a tree root and Titus gathered wood at once for a fire. He made two fires with flints they had in oilskin, and cleared a space between them where he would sleep. They discovered a fireplace of stones, with broken clay pipes and bones of fish. There were no footprints or signs of occupation, no tracks of men. There was just an old piece of rope, charred at one end, and a broken bottle showing that glass was worked on a rock and, may be, spear points made from it. That made them look around and wonder.

At dusk Titus went around with bunches of leaves and swept the sand clean for the distance of a good few yards away from the fires. It was a grove of sheoaks where they chose their camp. The wind sifted through their needles with a low-pitched moan familiar to each of them as the sound of the creek at Laban Vale, that so-often dry creek with its trees and sand, where Titus was flogged up and down.

That night they ate fish cooked in the coals, drank more of their rum, smoked their pipes, and went to bed on the ground with their bellies full and no thoughts for the future. They were wrapped in the blanket of the earth and their nostrils were crammed with the smells and sensations they remembered from when they were boys. Although, where were sheep, Warren asked, in this country, now they were back? — their bleating cries as much a part of the air as bird calls, their reek of dust, their habit of breaking down the undergrowth that made any place formerly untouched left changed by them. May be if the trees parted a bit more and they went inland a bit more they would come to a more open country. May be there would be travelling flocks, and people scattered along, in huts and inns, with smoke drifting up from their chimneys (such as the parson used to imagine would be Warren's). They could begin to ask word of a party of traders, Jews of London, the father a ginger-bearded fence, his jug-built wife a forger, their two sons, one musical, the other a mere boy but a horse rider, and their lovely crippled daughter, did she still live? Oh, and a silent man named Mick Tornley with bullocks and stores (silent except when he swore at his teams) — and Warren would ask if they still had travelling with them a woman, tall and long-stepping, Mrs Rankine. And what news of Captain Tom, taken by the traps, and of a man named Desmond Kale? Were Kale's deeds still sung?

The sighing of the wind in the trees asked these questions.

In the morning they saw the sea on one side and steep hills on the other as a barricade.

Titus showed Warren a worried look: 'They come in our camp in the night,' he said, after finding a toeprint in the sand, a disturbed twig. He was despondent. He killed a brown snake, skinned it, and spilled its belly contents in the grass. Then he grilled the snake in the ashes and felt better.

There was a map Warren had seen of New Holland's east coast, and although it was about as complete, in resemblance, as a few half-digested lizards cut from the belly of a snake and laid out in a line on a plank, the known parts separated from the unknown parts by wormy gaps, it reminded him that if Van Diemen's Land was at their backs, then this coastline they were thrown onto ran north, and north again until it met Port Jackson where Sydney was, and where the river led up to Parramatta and so on out. It was the best hope they had — to sail north — except getting back on the sea was not a very strong attraction.

Then the whole problem of getting their boat out through the bar was made simpler when Titus came running through the trees yelling that people were massing at the end of their spit of land; they spoke a bad language and held their spears meaning bad business, and before Warren was even able to throw his gear in the boat, Titus was ahead of him, untying the tether, jumping in waist deep, and pushing their whaleboat off.

How they broached the bar going out was in one part reliant on catching the outgoing last of the tide, which they managed to do with a small sail tugging them upright. But the main part of what drove them on was the cry of strangers against them and, at the last, a spear hurled with such penetrating accuracy that if it wasn't for a puff of wind veering them, they would have been struck hard in the timbers. It only showed they weren't the first comers to this haven, otherwise they might have been greeted in some quieter fashion. Whoever had been through that bar before them — explorers, sealers, or soldiers laying claim — hadn't been liked: and may be had died.

The weather remained fair with a burst of hard southerlies as they put themselves to the task of sailing back to the only civilisation they knew, where there were sheep, redcoats and men breaking stones. It was found always a little ahead of where they were at the end of each day. They went, it must have been, two hundred miles, before they began to ask, as a new promontory loomed up, 'Is that the South Head where the signal light was, where Captain Maule flagged goodbye?' No, it was not, for as each headland emerged from its haze, it was never inhabited nor as precipitous high as the ones at Sydney's Port Jackson, with its crumbled broken cliffs.

Finding sheltered coves they slept on beaches, or up rivers when they found them. They saw few people, except for their fires in the hills, and sometimes on the shore, where they avoided them by sailing on. The sun beat down in their faces. It was an endlessly unfolding country upon their left arm and its rival the sea on the right. They were not always able to find an estuary, but when they did, it was jumping with fish, and a few times they repeated their performance in crossing a bar.

As they came farther north Titus remembered more of his languages, or so it seemed to Warren when they came upon people again — a man and his wife gathering cockles and a grumpy man with warrior scars who showed them where to find drinking water, in reedy springs, and tried to take their fishing gear away from them. When they sat down with him, some intelligence was gleaned. Noisy, he was called by whites. They learned from Noisy of white men who wandered this country lost out of their wits wearing the broad arrow and the canary jacket, some still carrying around their irons cause they couldn't get out of them. These men were afraid of blacks beyond reason. They would rather go back to barracks and be flogged and hung than deal with them after their first encounters. It never surprised them to be speared or have their bodies eaten by meat ants on a gravel mound. If they had no weapons they ran away and slept shivering under rock overhangs or in hollow trees, petrified as cowards. If they had arms, they used them.

Then there was a man Noisy told them about who wasn't an escaped convict at all. The black rogue described him in mime, prancing around the fire until Warren and Titus got the splits laughing. It was done with such respect. It was like another man appeared before them in the firelight, a white man made out of a black man's admiration. He had a deformed left ear, a limp, and he came down from the high country with bullocks and horses and wandered up and down between the coastal swamps, his bullocks speared as they were caught in the swamps and feasted upon by big parties at cooking fires, and bullock fat running down their chests until their bellies were too fat to touch.

I T HAPPENED ONE DAY THAT the two adventurers went up a river, and out of the bush stepped Patrick Lehane.

They watched as he unloaded his packhorse and placed a fowling piece and a horse pistol on a canvas groundsheet. They approached along the bank. All three called out greetings, so as not to alarm, and then stood eyeing each other in mistrustful knowledge of who each was. No surprise to be known in a country of very few souls.

'You two is famous,' said Lehane, as he sat by their fire cadging tobacco and rum: they gave him tobacco, as their rum was gone. Lehane spoke his thanks in a rasping brogue, his hair tangled and lengthy, cursing he was placed in the wrong country for his improvement, but overjoyed to find friends, for his blacks had cast him aside, as he'd done with providing.

Titus that night put on his captain's jacket, quite stained from travel, smelling of stale fish blood. 'Oh, my Lord,' Lehane smirked at the vision. He told of his livestock being speared — by his friends. 'I was only doing my best to keep them intact, such is my thanks. Great beasts they were. There was a strawberry one with snail horns and a bullfrog bell. He was skinny as an orphan calf without a poddy bucket. They was flung down from the high ranges along steep ridges and through rocky creeks hurting their hooves and blooding their hides with black fellows chasing them.'

'Did you duff them, Lehane?'

'You mustn't say duffed. No. They was strayed from Mick Tornley's team. It was my intention to lead them back, to the duck mole reach, and I meant to, too. The trouble is, that Noisy betrayed me. Them bullocks was galloped too far down the ridges to follow — them people who can run down a wren, they are just as able running down a beast of several hundredweights. One of them took hold of the bell and held it by the clapper as they ran. From a ridge I saw the bullocks lying on their backs being cut into pieces and taken away. The leader of the miscreants was Noisy, oh I hate him I do: no bigger than an ant, seen through the tops of peppermint gums, he wielded the tomahawk I gifted from my gear. There was my thanks. Blood so fresh it winked in the noon light way off.'

'How come we're famous?' said Warren.

'For being ditched by the parson and lost at sea.'

'Does everyone know?'

'Word come through the ballad of Desmond Kale, how his grandson was bothered with.'

He did go on. As a sailor of the reluctant rank, Lehane told them, he too found himself pressed into service some years ago, and after a wreck, was marooned on an island towards China. Through a practice of the place (that was on the equator) his ear lobe was stretched according to native ideas of beauty. He was made a convict upon his rescue, on grounds he was a mutineer, and lucky he wasn't hung, though he was here before them to swear, in this judging wilderness, that he was innocent of all charges.

Warren and Titus did not believe him, did not trust him, and did not like him at all. They observed he carried a pocket pistol secreted in his waistcoat. Titus went to relieve him of it while he slept. His muskets were safely out of reach. 'There will be a price on his head,' decided Warren, lying on his blanket with his hands propped behind his head fighting sleep while the fire burned down, waves of injustice and everlasting resentment coming from their snoring companion. 'The place he comes back to is the duck mole reach. Since we've been gone it's established.' Their boat was drawn up on dry land and covered with branches. It was time to leave it be, and strike out on land. Either Lehane took them or they took Lehane — to the duck mole reach, where the bullocks were raided, not strayed, from Tornley's team, and where his mother was, and the Josephs, please God all safe.

The dawn noise of birds woke them. A low, bright sun slashed through the trees. Lehane sat up, looked around at the camp, and then lowered himself back again. In a minute he'd feel for his pistol. Titus never liked getting up either, if he could help it. Now that he was a free man, he embellished his freedom with luxurious sleeps, at least until the chill came from the ground and he took the blanket from over his head. When he heard the crack of a few sticks, as Warren got the day started, he woke a bit more, but stayed snug as he could for as long as he might, the pistol primed and aimed ready for use.

Lehane stirred, slapped his sides, felt in his pockets and swore. Before he could think it through there was a sound behind him, and Warren stood over him with a foot on his chest. Lehane croaked with his ribs compressed:

'Jeez,' he said. 'There's no need of this. I am your friend.' His breath was like wet-packed hay, all broiled and steamy.

Warren agreed he must be their friend as they already had his pistol with inlaid pearl, that Warren knew was the same owned by Joe Josephs.

'Jesus and Mary love yer, get your hoof off me, I'm yours,' he said. Titus collected his muskets.

Lehane warmed his hands to the fire:

'It is purrfectly fitting you should take a bow, because you, Warren Inchcape, are the grandson of Desmond Kale,' and as he said so, he made a motion of tugging his forelock, which Warren did not enjoy.

'You'll take us to the duck mole reach?' said Warren.

'I might, but it won't be easy. Kale will thank me for guiding you. He's on a bit further, always out of reach. Up there, the world has changed. You'll excuse me if I don't go the whole distance. There's an inn, run by Tharpe, who never liked me. A man is trusted one day, spurned the next. A man don't always know his reception from old friends.'

'I'd say there's a price on your head,' said Warren.

'If there is, it's a good one,' snapped Lehane, 'but from the wrong sort, which leaves me respected.'

'All we've heard from you is blather,' said Warren.

'Why don't you shut up, ole man?' said Titus.

'Not till I've finished, boys. Think of the amazement we all felt — on learning, from a ship that arrived here fairly busting with news — that one of the Bay's most conspicuous men was tried for intentional murder after plugging a man in London, over wanting some maps, and was sentenced to death, placed in the bowels of Newgate Prison, and from there was hung.'

'For wanting some maps?' gaped Warren.

'It was the praist fellow, Stanton.'

'My father!' said Titus.

'Hung. Horribilis, I called him to his face, and spat in his eye when he rode past me, to my eternal merit.'

'Hung? You are a liar.'

Titus raised his fist:

'Dat's gammon, ole man.'

Two chilled, shaken hearts faced the teller of tales, who took a stick in his hands and scratched an illustration of a gallows in the dirt. Well enough to say Stanton was dead, but worse to say he was hung. It was delightful to Lehane to score the beams and the trapdoor, to make the sound with his stick of two heels being jounced over cobblestones and thrown into a pit.

'The appeals went as high as the king's royal prerogative of mercy, but His Majesty takes one look at the haitch, an all thoughts of mercy fly out the door of his palace. He throws his petitions an sub-petitions all in the fire. No, bugger im, hang him, he says. Hang the horribilis cunt. All them poor sufferers in Botany Bay deserve a bit of polish in their lives. What is the matter with you two, ain't you happy?'

Their eyes were filled with tears, of a sudden. Their cheeks gleamed wet in the sunlight. They were angry with disbelief. No, not the parson. This was only a trick, to make them love him again. It was not believed by them — only, to be sure it sank in, Lehane elaborated the vision by taking it through until they felt the hairs of the rope that tightened under the reverend's bristly and never very carefully shaved pink chin, which they quite well remembered from the times he kissed them.

'The London papers was full of it, and papers came here on the first available boat, were printed up in the *Gazette*, and was rushed up country for all to see, by the convict commissioner, who's about making evildoers of the upper echelons feel sorry.'

'You saw the papers, then?'

'I admit, I was never that close to getting my eyes on print,' said Lehane. 'I was too far out in the wild bush minding me own business, but you could hear the kookaburrows laughing as the word spread. They must a heard it first. Escaped men brought it through the trees. They was cheered. The only particular was, they never got his last words, a good solid speech of repentance. That would have been the greatest reward. I would have pardoned him, myself, for the benefit of a glorious statement. But too late. It is all well known in Parramatta by now, and has changed the world. No more flogging and preaching two sides of the same coin. Boys, don't look so gloomy, as every cloud has a silver lining.'

'How so?'

'It was reported in them same London papers, that Miss Ivy Stanton was expecting an infant after her marriage to a Lord Bramleys, who is aiming to settle the back country of New South Wales, and for all I know is landed ashore, as we speak, for the time it takes to get across the sea has already passed.' Lehane cocked an eyebrow. 'She might be ruling from guvvermint house be now, the little strumpet.'

Without warning Lehane burst into tears.

'Dear me, I am lonely for love. *Your* loved ones are as far up the arsehole of this country as a civilised party ever went. Excuse me language for once. Your dear mother was there, and I never harmed her, I promise, only she didn't like the way I went on, and said I was a shame to my principles.'

Lehane leaned sideways and exposed his neck, as if to ask for absolution from these two salty strays, and please excuse the ingrained filth on his pale shoulders, where his shirt fell open, as he hated taking baths.

'Now we're getting the truth,' said Warren.

'I sent back a note, undertaking to return everything I stole, except one horse and a pair of boots. Your black fellows have made a liar of me over them bullocks. They've left nothing but bones to prove my honour. No firearms were discharged in any direction. The darlin, the sweet one, Leah — she got a bad fright. I did my best to soothe her.'

Warren's eyes went the colour of dry leaves, on the forest floor most flammable. 'If you hurt one hair of her head I'll strip your guts for mainsheets.'

'Ooh, the boy and his brother got the worst of it,' said Lehane, well away to the music of repentance, 'by creeping up on me, like they do, till they saw which side their saviour was born on, with a pistol in their faces. Mick Tornley was the only one I manacled, and I made sure it was done good, for what he done to me before. He is a man who thinks to be Mick Tornley answers most needs. So I took his bullocks to show him.'

They set off the next day. The western hills rose like shoulders in the blue distance, the greatest hill peering above them like a woolly head. It was mist-crowned lolling in the sky. The duck mole reach was up there somewhere. They walked two days with Noisy's band skipping along beside them. They were strong from feasting on bullock meat. Titus parlayed with these camp followers as they turned their eyes to the hills — it wasn't their country after a certain definable point, they declared, and then it was time for them to turn away. While Lehane was pleased to see the blacks break off, he was almost beside himself to be taken where he came from. He thought they'd be friendlier after he told them the truth, he whined and bickered — 'Please, not this hell's own climb.' So to persuade him, they held him by rope tied to the pack-saddle of his stolen mare. Having no other choice he followed along, rubbing his wrists and complaining if only they would listen. They couldn't be serious. But they were. 'There might be magistrates at platypus reach be now,' he said. 'An troopers.' They followed up shallow rivers and creeks, over forested ridges, up deep valleys and along native pathways nobody knew about, shadowed into existence by bare feet, where the only white man who ever trod them was walking with them. Titus proved himself nimble finding a way in this country he didn't know.

As they walked, Lehane worked his knots loose. When Warren and Titus turned round, he was gone, leaving his horse. When they checked the bandolier of silver and gold, hidden in Titus's best clothes, every coin of it was accounted for. Then they set off after Lehane.

Titus had not gone very far down the ridge when he stopped, and sounded the call of the whistling kite. Warren clambered down to him — depending on which bird was whistled it was possible to tell what Titus found. The kite meant business.

She was a carrion eater and so Warren was not surprised to see a collapsed pile of clothes on the ground, and in amongst that pile the limbs of a man.

THE RUMOUR THAT LORD BRAMLEY was expected as a settler in New South Wales after a hasty marriage to Ivy Stanton proved false; he was already married to Hetty, the Lady Bramley; and he never, ever left England. So it wasn't Lord Bramley coming over the sea with Miss Stanton as his child bride and brought to term rather quickly at all. No such premature elevation of the prison colony's tone was to happen; there was to be no aristocracy of the place except Botany Bay aristocrats wearing chains.

The hanging of Parson Magistrate Stanton was as close to the greatest story ever told. It was to die a snickering death in Sydney or Parramatta, after raising some loud guffaws. He'd joined the throng of those once up, flung down, and never to be raised again! which was the neediest part of the population; he'd joined them most convincingly, next door to the worms. Most of this was guessed from the report in the *Sydney Gazette*, taken from London papers, where the court reporters tersely expressed it: 'Guilty, death, aged 53'. Then the mail ship sailed.

It was pleasantest to know that the fellow he'd shot wasn't too badly hurt but Stanton still got the weight of the law on his voice box.

A good few hard men went to the gallows in Sydney, Parramatta and even as far away as Van Diemen's Land feeling better for the knowledge that Parson Stanton was black-capped by an English judge who thought he was worth the sentence. Those who'd been at Newgate and sentenced to death but were lucky enough to be reprieved to the hulks and sent to Botany Bay told how life was lived in the press yard. It was, they said, where Stanton would have been doomed to spend his last weeks while his family and whatever friends were left ran around raising petitions to save him. He was not a full murderer but a fully intentional murderer and so would have waited his turn at the gallows a lot longer than those who'd done the deed better, and were hung sooner. So the torment was sweeter? Oh yes. For companionship he would have no one better than other murderers, and so did his righteous bones crack in humiliation, or what? And here was the best part. When he went to the church services of a Sunday, which he would be required to do, at Newgate, there were pews set aside for the condemned near the altar. There in front of them was placed a black coffin upon a table. It was to remind them to make their peace with their creator in the face of approaching doom. Ah, then the parson would learn to speak humbly, at last. He would learn the patois where evil was called good. He would learn how a good man was called wicked, and a leader in vice virtuous. He would learn to invert the human heart and reverse the conscience. And learn to blaspheme and grovel to the yard captains. There was pride and much need in corruption of ordinary language amongst Newgate's human congestion. To this he'd been brought down.

The part of all that was true was this part the truest. For even before his sentence, it was learned by Stanton to put everything that mattered the other way around, and shrug off his overstrained virtues, that had been expressed through whips. The gunshot he fired in the lawyer's rooms merely confirmed his direction! He'd already been well into the Devil's camp when the Bow Street runner of Robin Redbreast fame, so called, asked for his surrender; then came the trial; the death sentence; the horror of shame; the shame of horror; then he was in the Devil's camp even further, enjoying the conversation of whores and coiners; Bramley sent money for his gin supply; then the prospect of heaven or hell as the shadow of the noose swung across his imagination; on balance it was going to be hell, he would have to say, and bring it on; then the small black coffin in the Newgate chapel, a pair of greedy eyes shining from the slightly open lid, the eyes of a Thames rat. And then he knew there was an omen of life somewhere. In the coffin.

The evangelical ministers who pursued the condemned at Newgate had a need to make him one of their own all over again, and extract from him an execution-day statement to use in their cause. There they came in their drab jackets and buckled shoes. He refused to talk to them, or pray with them and sing to them their hymns. As for one or two old friends at Cambridge, what could they do for him? They could bring him, while their wives went to Dolly and were given a welcome, a basket holding a pork pie and a bottle of Bordeaux, a crusty loaf and a pat of sweaty butter. They could not eat with him, their stomachs were turned; while Stanton, unfussed, was hungry as a horse — and as heavy a beast as ever was, oblivious to the coming slaughter. Or as big-heartedly brave in seeming so.

But then (if you will believe it) came those visits made to the press yard by his recovered victim, Cribb, talking about sheep breeding when what Stanton wanted to hear was the hour of his execution, so as to get on with it without more pain than Dolly and his dear fallen daughter needed to bear.

While Cribb talked about sheep Stanton felt his brain shrink back into the fumes and straw of a ram pen. The brown light between timber slabs. Swallows building mud nests in the low rafters.

'Qualities too opposite never amalgamate, but only produce a worthless hybrid . . . The defects in breed can only be corrected gradually . . . violent extremes are unsafe.'

'Violent extremes are unsafe,' said Stanton, using sarcasm as he liked to do with Cribb, only in this instance turning it on himself. Why should he cough from the lip of the lime pit such maggots of knowledge as would assist Cribb in his emigration? Who was making a voyage to the colony to breed sheep? It wasn't Stanton. What was Cribb tormenting him for, with visions of greasy perfection?

'Hmm. But there *is* a royal road to perfection,' said Cribb, at which Stanton looked up, startled. Was Cribb trying to tell him something?

He was. For word had come from the king. He was reprieved.

At Sydney there was no ship for a while, so no latest news. Rumours and excitements burned off the colony's imagination like an early mist from the headlands of Port Jackson on a hot morning.

One day, with the sea deep blue and sparkling, the sandstone headlands glowing golden as honeycomb, and dolphins riding below the waves like silky banners, a ship sailed in.

She was the *Edinburgh Castle* under Captain Maule, remembered as the boat that had removed one of the colony's most bothersome characters from its stage, and if he wasn't missed, there was certainly an emotional thrill experienced when the ship went about in a slam of noise with its booms and hinges, off the Middle Head, sounding like a trapdoor sprung under someone. After being rebuilt and given the improvements to her accommodation and her sailing efficiency suggested by Captain Maule, she'd made the voyage from England without too much battling in adverse blows, coming via the Cape and dipping south taking advantage of cold strong winds.

They took on their pilot. She passed up the harbour without much fanfare, carrying passengers of no great notice — except that free settlers were not all that common in those times, and so they were prospectively watched — a Mr and Mrs Blaise Henry Cribb; their baby daughter, Rose (a perfect little object as white as whipped cream and with mauve lips, veined eyelids, and a robust habit of punching wildly when she woke, until she was given all her mother's attention). There was also Cribb's son, Johnny, a gangly, intelligent lad from an earlier liaison; there was a Mr and Mrs Dudley Hardcastle, and their sturdy son, Barney, and daughters; and there was a ferrety-faced servant woman wearing a tight bonnet, by the name of Mrs Dolly; and with her, her husband, Convict Matt — an assigned convict servant to the Cribbs and Hardcastles, a man they had organised for themselves in London, by means of the exercise of privilege. It was said he'd been released from Newgate Prison directly into their care, after being reprieved, by the king's royal mercy, from hanging on a capital charge, just as the hangman came looking for him. Yes, reprieved, but he sent murderous looks if you tried getting close to him. Touchy? There was no doubting it. Undoubtedly proud. 'Wheresoever the body is, thither will the eagles be gathered together,' was written on his brow.

This servant, Convict Matt, was a Yorkshireman, a rubbery, tubby man in his fifties with a sharp eye, which he disliked flashing (only sometimes couldn't help it), and preferred keeping his gaze averted or hooded shut. He kept a black-brimmed hat pulled low on his eyes — had a practised habit of grunting and turning aside when anyone pursued a question. When they persisted he gave them a push. The ship's nonconformist chaplain he particularly disliked, letting it out once, with a yelp during divine service on the afterdeck, that if he was in any sect's grip (when asked for confessions of Christ), it was for the Devil's party he groped. He couldn't help making a comment from the congregation, when the chaplain heard himself disputed on a text — correctly as he later found out, when he went to his Cruden's in a snit — how Abram and Lot came from Ur of the Chaldees, and Abram pitched his tent on a mountain on the east of Bethel, not on the west. When he resolved it, the dear chaplain was saddened to think old Matt had fallen so low, from a worthwhile Christian past, even one so scholarly spent in a sheepfold, as it seemed.

The ship carried sixty convict women to Captain Maule's profit, held in their convict quarters at the other end of the vessel (distant from where some rams and ewes were kept in stalls, but not far enough to blank their stink). Anne Kemp, the prettiest and most flirty of the women, was in business with men from the upper decks the whole voyage, and someone in the Devil's party was just her sort. She made a good try to crack Convict Matt's smile, but never reached him except she showed more intelligence than the paying passengers had between them to get to the bottom of his story. It happened that her wanton's compassion made her a thoroughly good nurse — knowledgeable, kind, willing, and sure of touch — and so she learned from Mrs Dolly and her daughter, Mrs Cribb, by helping them.

There was only one detail anyone needed to know of him, that he wanted acknowledged, at least. He was a sheep man all through. His lack of curiosity about the colony surprised some. Throughout the whole voyage paying passengers, prospective settlers, took every opportunity to learn what they were in for, but not old Matt, he could not care less for the question. Only sometimes he let fly with an opinion on something he couldn't possibly know — the poison of snakes; the call of the kookaburra or laughing jackass or Hawkesbury alarm clock, so called; or that sheep there had better have long legs for walking ways to water. How did he know? Don't ask Convict Matt! His duties as a servant were not very onerous around his master and mistress; he was usually slumbering drunk in the afternoons. As for Mrs Dolly, she was the opposite, wide awake and dedicated the whole day to the young Mrs Cribb and her Rose. As for the young Mrs Cribb herself, Ivy, she had that beautiful, cold, silvery aloofness that redheads in the fullest arrogance of their glory must have by the age of eighteen, or die of neglect, when they sense the control they have over men's desires. Except with her it was remarkable how towards one man, her husband, how extremely cold and punishing she was — as if the ice of the southern oceans (that had formed in their rigging, on the way over) splintered down into her, accumulating and intensifying towards him the longer their voyage ran out. It was noted that Cribb, without too much ceremony, visited Anne Kemp in the curtained cubby she had for her business. As the frosty darling was not giving away any of it, a whore did a wife's duty, it was said. Except you would have to be an intimate to know. In that curtained cubby all they did was talk. Cribb was famished for heart warmth. What Anne Kemp learned among her cushions she kept to herself. It was her quietly spoken opinion, however, that Mr Cribb was in love with his wife.

It remained still quiet enough as the *Edinburgh Castle*, at around two in the afternoon, came to its mooring opposite the handsome town of Sydney. Soon, from below decks, in the part of the ship where the women were packed in, there was heard a symphony of shrieks. Many secreted phials of perfume were broken out, precious lumps of rouge applied, that had been kept ready for this hour the whole voyage. So many various coloured skirts and dresses appeared it was like a bazaar, and the dark-haired, white-skinned, slenderly hipped and voraciously red-lipped Anne Kemp, swirling like a dancer, was the one who would surely go for a price near the top.

It was a sparkling June day, the ninth of the month, the king's birthday, second anniversary of that serene day when Desmond Kale was flogged his last fifty.

Captain Maule congratulated himself on a voyage well run. A good return cargo and the ship's owner, Lord Bramley, might not be much richer, as he was already rich enough — but Maule was made richer by it. As well as a good few thousand, a gratuity of five hundred pounds was already in Maule's London account, having been passed to him by Bramley, on consideration of his keeping to himself, as strenuously as he was able, the intention of his party of settlers under the charge of Cribb.

THE ANCHOR WAS PUT DOWN in Sydney Cove. Signals were made and officials welcomed aboard. Orders of the superintendent of convicts were signed and countersigned. Prisoners brought forth.

'Who is the old chump?'

'His name is written here, on the manifest, male, aged fifty-four, attempted murder, Convict Matt.' The receiving constable took a hard look into the moon face of this Matt, and thought, 'If I hadn't heard old Parson Stanton was hanged, I might of guessed . . .'

'Shepherd and sheep handler?'

'That's what it says.'

Convict Matt sat on a bench in the half dark below decks, his stockings lumpy between his legs, head slumped on his chest.

'Stand on your feet, old Matt, an shake your cods.'

He stood, and pulled his stockings up.

'Where is your master?'

'Over here,' answered Cribb, from the dim side of the passage. He signed where they thumbed him, at the end of a recital of duties — to maintain and clothe the said convict, to give him a ration and clothes equal to that issued from government stores, for which he would perform a government task, as subjoined: and if his master could give him employment for the remainder of his time, which was eight years! at the established rate, he was to do his master's work in preference to any other person's.

The constable said to the convict:

'Understand, it is not all bad here, mate, your master will provide both you and your missus with a sheltered lodging on his farm, or at his habitation, which is it to be?'

'It is on a farm,' said the convict.

'Laban Vale,' said Cribb, 'is the name of the holding.'

The constable wrote it down. 'Laban Vale . . . Laban Vale . . .' he wiggled his pencil, having heard that name.

'Mr Cribb is a little too anxious to belong,' said the convict, looking at Cribb. 'He cannot help himself. But strictly speaking, Laban Vale is the property of his wife.'

'Strictly speaking,' agreed Cribb.

'She is an heiress,' added the convict, showing far too much pride and impulsiveness in the matter for the constable to let it pass, in his guesswork over their exchanges, which were so testy, and ripe with embroilment, that he wondered what Bramley, Cribb, Hardcastle, & Co., were in together, and what could be in it for him, if he put his hand out and touched their secrecy.

'The aforesaid Laban Vale it is,' said the constable, continuing his recitation, 'from which you are not to absent yourself without leave, nor in any case to go from one settlement to another without a pass from a magistrate.'

Hardcastle came down and signed where shown with less distaste than a resemblance of slavery might have roused in a regularly passionate abolitionist, now put over a man as an overseer.

'If either one has just cause to complain of neglect of work, or Convict Matt your servant not obeying your orders, or absenting himself from your farm without leave, you are to report it to a magistrate, and, on conviction, said Matt will receive a flogging.'

'A flogging! — from a magistrate would be good,' said Matt with all the snide humour expected of his class, but so brazenly that the constable struck him hard on the left cheekbone, and forced him back into the shadows.

'I say,' said Hardcastle.

'Learn up your fists, if you're to be his keeper, Mr Hardcastle,' said the constable, who by this outburst had driven from his mind all thought that the convict was someone greater returned from the grave.

(It would not be until the following morning, when the news that Stanton lived went around, that the constable was to remember his guess. The *Edinburgh Castle* was the first ship to reach Sydney since the reprieve, and while it expressly brought no news — London papers were all following in the next ship along — the information among some of its women, that Convict Matt was otherwise than who he said he was, was there to get out, as soon as they were intimately settled with some dispenser of favours and felt like a gossip and a good laugh about their equal under the law.)

Now there was a lot of shouting from a boat drawn alongside, whistles, drums — and firecrackers!

'The bitches are on heat,' said the constable, tilting his head to the sound of bare feet dancing on the decks above their heads. 'And the dogs are primed.'

Here was a party of around forty men, come from up country New South Wales to get themselves wives. They scrambled aboard while the howling, odorous, primped, flushed chorus of women, rattling bangles, pulling up their skirts to thrust out their legs and show their furze bushes, were held back by a party of turnkeys — who said, 'Forty into sixty shall go, ladies' — and stood there getting themselves groped between the legs by those of the front row, to repay them for their humour and may be encourage them if they ended being the ones left out, to take a pick in the lottery of life.

Paying passengers were meant to be out of the way, and ashore by now, for this was a scene of human traffic, and not very suitably exposed to those of better breeding, but as their disembarkation was blocked by the flesh bazaar, there was the chance of being spectators while they waited for their boatman.

Standing forward of the other passengers in a row behind the last of the convict women was the young Mrs Cribb: pale face miserably pinched getting away from her husband's arm. Cribb gave her an angry talk, that morning, about how she was not keeping her side of their bargain at all. It was time to stop it and make a better show, he demanded, as Cribb had hard work to do ashore establishing himself. Their bargain was that he would marry her to save her reputation and her parents' battered pride (done); that he would admit proudly to being the father of her illegitimate child (done); that he would support and protect her parents, as best he could under prison colony law (done); and that she in response might try and love him, just a bit, bit by bit, starting on their voyage to New South Wales (not done).

There was nothing about Cribb she liked, not his hands, his face, his temper, nor even his tried patience in restraining himself from taking his husband's rights until she came to him freely. He loved her, he said, like the open mouth of a furnace roaring, and in other ways, many ways, which when he expressed them she tried not to listen. She liked nothing about him except that he'd rescued her. It only got worse. He was old. She wished she was on this market and could make an escape. She hated the way Cribb held her captive, and worse, the way she held him captive. How pitiable, that if you dreamed to be loved, and were, it came out as the worst thing. It made the man weak, when in every other capacity he was strong. He was brought down leaving you with nothing.

As for her humbled parents, Ivy ruled the family affections as she always had. Her parents were more afraid of her than they had ever been: she had been elevated and placed. It was all in their position now, with their lives reversed. But Dolly in the role of maid found herself giving calm advice she'd never given as a mother, their intimacy now being truer, having restrictive rules, as brought out good and prevented bad. She told Ivy that being loved was not always the worst thing, that love was a story that grew of itself, of its own unintended accord. One day she would tell Ivy about Cribb when all Ivy knew was that her mother and Cribb went well back, to the same little scatter of villages under the moors. She would tell Ivy that out of that passion came the strangest love story of all, when it was properly untangled — the abiding love of Mrs Dolly for Mr Matt. It was seen on the ship that the pair were as affectionate as could be, always with their arms around each other or holding hands viewing the horizon, and sharing the same three-quarter bunk in the same narrow cabin, frogged up together during storms.

The convict women were baying. The men looking them over roared. It did not matter for the day that none of the men coming to claim them was handsome. They clattered around the deck in their noisy boots and then they bunched up and settled, a mob of bulls breathing hoarsely ready for the join. Some of the men were strong, with stone-breaking hands and dusty cold eyes; some were defeated by work, but hopeful of comfort; and some were shy as dry sticks who came with ribboned gifts; others had a bottle or two, for an imminent roister; some drooled; and some looked starved for lightning. Some were foreigners and carried nosegays to offer; and one with that thought, a man who'd been alone too long without civilising himself while he made money, was Paul Lorenze. Getting himself rich, he'd learned, took a man so far — but if he wanted to be richer there were niceties to be observed. You did not get greatly rich without being accepted into great houses, where men made arrangements in each other's favour. It helped most never having been a convict. Oh but he was an ugly bastard, though. And crude.

Of the women, looked at from the men's side, most found no beauty there but plenty of hard-working scrubbers, which was what they had come for: they had eyes for stout arms, solid legs, broad backs and a gobful of teeth.

'Will ye take me? I've got a place — forty acres.'

'All right!'

And a woman would go with that man, taking a gamble. Forty acres was such a lot.

Then a few men sensed each other out, as forceful bidders do at an auction, the ones who count. They looked sidelong and almost died right there for the need they had for that woman blazing into their vision, Anne Kemp wearing a green skirt and a trim red jacket. They'd come with more practical wants on their shopping lists, someone to milk the ewes, do washing, hoe the potato patch and sweep the earth floors clean. Someone to walk out with them across country, and not get tired while carrying a bundle. Anne Kemp might do all that. It did not matter. They had to have her.

Lorenze wanted her the way a man dying in battle wants the hot sword of his enemy to finish its work. But before he could step forward, and make his mark, another man stood in front of him. This man was so much the gentleman that all bidders stood back and let him have his say. It was Convict Commissioner Lloyd Thomas, whose hearings, rulings, and investigations were making them all jump.

'You,' he said, 'with the grey-green eyes.'

The young Mrs Cribb put her hand over her mouth, and gave a short scream. He was looking straight at her through the crowd of women. It was her Valentine with his hair swept back at his temples, his sword in his belt, his smile so eager and wanting, and through the chance of where Ivy stood they were united! Look at him there so unblinking! He was swept aside from his duty just for her, this great man, his heart had chosen her, his mouth, that had kissed her, was speaking, his fingers, that had begun their sure work at her waist to begin their child, were pointing!

So Ivy reckoned, at least, in those few seconds when the crowd gave a soft little sigh, as if a prince had won.

Cribb wasn't the only one who saw Ivy's mistake; Dolly saw it, and glanced at Cribb crestfallen (they understood each other well in their new relation); they saw how Ivy turned white; how her little strong heart fluttered in its cage, before it folded its silk veins around itself, and crushed itself flat.

Anne Kemp stepped forward of the rest, came out on the bare deck, pirouetted in front of the commissioner, who was never said no to in any department of his life — except in getting the worst of a wager — and he was in power to her scent of oils and powders, to her lean bones, her carelessness of eye. He was no longer a man having young girls over against trees and uncovering malfeasance in his committees of enquiry, investigating everything under this sun it was possible to imagine — commissary stores, the rum trade, hospitals, flogging practices, hangings, potato farming, gold, and wool. His power in all this deserted him. Just for now, and over-whelmingly in his feelings. He hardly expected it, but had come to the women's ship wanting it, from the time early that morning when Maule made his signals, which were relayed from the South Head, and it was known there were women aboard the *Edinburgh Castle* creeping up the harbour.

Anne Kemp curtsied.

'You are the prettiest-ankled woman I have seen in my life,' said Lloyd Thomas with a dry throat. He was not aware of a commotion at the back of the gathered females, where a young woman cried to her husband, 'Where are you, why aren't you by me, you never do anything for me, Mr Cribb!' — and was taken below to recover before going ashore. The name Cribb registered, but as Lloyd Thomas did not see him again he did not remember until later, seeing Lord Bramley's emissary ashore.

Nor was Lloyd Thomas aware that from deck level (in the drop of a companionway) he was watched by a sullen convict with straw in his hair, the man whose daughter he had ruined, and that to save that ruin from being final, much else had followed, even to the lip of the gallows — which was why the convict stayed where he stood, and whenever he thought he might be recognised, ducked his head. How could he as the lowest of the low, presume any higher? His best hope was ignominy. He almost liked it. Being so low managed him into some places he'd never been able to slip under so far — such as into Cribb's cabin, and into his letter-case, kept under his bunk, where Cribb kept the troublesome maps of George Marsh in trust for Warren Inchcape. So confident was

Convict Matt within the deepest part of himself that he did not even shake and tremble when he got those maps in his hands (they after all being the other reason he was low as he was). Damned if they weren't bound in strong tape, sealed with wax. But at least he knew where they were when he needed to get hold of them, which might be very soon, if they did as was planned and got themselves past Sydney and Parramatta and reached Laban Vale before sunset of the next day.

The routine of seduction and captivity above decks continued in the bright winter sunshine. Anne Kemp laughed into the dark eyes of the fine man who wanted her. Commissioner Lloyd Thomas frowned, with uncertainty. He was only vaguely aware that he was known as the greatest predatory goat in the place, but seemed to think, because he could never be refused, that he was the greatest master of attraction. It didn't seem to be working on this super-lative bitch. Botany Bay had weathered him more handsomely, doing nothing to improve his insides.

Not that Anne Kemp ever cared to act on considerations of the sort, making distinctions of morality or even looks when her interest was prior. She had been enjoyed by such men and left with nothing. Anne Kemp knew a wealthy man when she saw one, and it was not the commissioner, it was the next man along, wearing a maroon jacket with pearl buttons, and standing on wide legs with his hands in his pockets and his shirt open at the throat, his black hair cut in a pudding-basin fringe, wearing a gold earring and a heavy gold signet ring. A continental, to judge also by the sugar-dusted pink concoction he passed her, with folds of waxed paper over it, each corner neatly turned.

Moreno took Anne Kemp by the arm, and when she had indicated where was her meagre bag of trinkets, he said she could carry them, and they went to the ship's ladder.

'I am galled,' said Lloyd Thomas in a low steady voice. The opinions of the rabble mattered nothing to his pride. It was his greatest expression of absolute anger, and was not to be blocked.

'How am I to bring that fellow down,' he thought, 'and how soon? I will have the woman anyhow.' While Moreno signed the required documents to have female convict Kemp assigned to his care, Lloyd Thomas gave orders to have Moreno traced. When he was sure where he lodged, he would pay him a visit, and bargain for the use of her.

Anne Kemp went down the ladder first, making a celebration event of it as her friends cheered and cried out, and threw their kisses.

As Moreno followed his prize he turned around backwards to get on the ladder and his eyes came level with the deck where he saw a pair of convict eyes watching him —

'That is the priest,' Moreno said to himself, with a confused thudding shock, and already, in his mind, he was off from there as swiftly as he could go. Whether it was the ghost of the parson watching him or the parson himself, saved from the gallows, it made no difference to Moreno. There was enough to be superstitious about inside the boundaries of New South Wales for a long time now and he wanted to get out of them.

Chorus of the Eighth Part

WHERE KALE BLOWS THE TIN HORN OF FAME

EACH OVERSEER OF SECTIONS — MICK Tornley the bullocks, Arthur and Solly Josephs the horses, Joe Josephs the stores, Martha Josephs the kitchens, and Tom Rankine himself over the convicts — was issued with a white bandolier, a veritable cincture of office, a sash to be worn each time the horn was blown for the muster.

That horn was the old ram's horn gifted by Parson Stanton to Joe, worked up to a straight length of four feet in a bed of hot sand, and now, as they dealt with the news of the parson's comeuppance in life — after *not* being hanged — Joe scratched out the parson's names and dates where he'd written them, on a flat part of the trumpet, when believing he was dead. It was inscribed in Hebrew lettering with the parson's old motto — which he left there, anyhow — *Know before whom thou doth stand*. Joe recited prayers for a man whose mystery was that he was liked at all. 'May he live in the world again as a better sort of bloke,' was some of what Joe muttered. 'Blessed art Thou, King of the universe, who gives life to the dead through those left behind.' It was not a request, but stated as something that God was able to do. That was the prayerful man, Joe.

On his ride out from Sydney after being released by Lloyd Thomas, Rankine had ridden through Laban Vale to get himself another couple of horses and to see what Moreno was up to there, with the parson away. He'd wanted to greet Moreno again and get the feeling of him on trust. He was anxious to make his night's camp farther along the track, and to reach Meg within the week. An exchange of horses would allow a better turn of speed.

He located Moreno in the yards classing ram lambs. Turning to see Rankine there, Moreno embraced him and wept.

There were shepherds standing by ready to drag the lambs up to the Spaniard. From the way Moreno dealt with them Rankine could see that he had good authority. There were only a few dozen ram lambs left to do. He was culling those lacking what he liked in a sire and rather than selling them off more cheaply, was butchering them and salting them, and selling the meat. He liked a strong broad forehead, a straight nose, a straight back, long legs, a dense staple of nicely crimped wool, and somewhere about a ram's hocks, some hairs of the burnish that Moreno in his pride claimed as his. Well, was Rankine to differ? The reddish ones thrived. He could not tell they were reddish unless Moreno said so. That reddishness, indeed, came more under the heading of quality of features, as listed. Moreno felt safe with his sheep now; they bought him respect; he no longer hid behind the *nom de laine* of a mucky shearer. If a ram carried the brown it was potent to a high degree.

There were several hundred ram lambs born the previous autumn and many had already proved themselves by serving ewes when they were hardly five months old. These special types were tarred as potent and valued two and three times more than the rest.

Each ordinary ram would bring Moreno a high price anyway, and every one of them had a buyer waiting. A steady eye, a well-attended flock, herbage of the open forest, and without Rankine or Stanton to rule him, Moreno was king.

They talked in Spanish, their language of the heart and of the stones of hardship. Moreno told his workers to make do for an hour, and took Rankine into the house, where all the Stantons' furniture, from the book cases to the cuckoo clock and butter churns and pats and moulds, were draped over in cloths. Moreno lived at the end of the verandah, half outdoors, with his leather and utensils covered in dust, a pair of boots under his cot. They drank rum mixed with water. When Rankine finished telling Moreno about his captivity, there was no more bad feeling left between them.

Next morning Rankine rode on. A week later he came to the silvered plain, ringed by dark hills, where Tornley and Josephs had their run.

There was a star burning on the hillside, the night Rankine found Meg. Too sad for the moment to say what the star remembered, except, when he was closer, and his horse's hooves made a knock on the stones, the star showed itself to be a candle. It was held in the still night air up to Rankine's face so that she could see him. It had a reflector of polished tin. They said some words, ordinary greetings because for the emotions involved, no words existed but I love you yet, I love you still. Before anything, Meg told him how in midsummer there had been a burial on the hill, there by the wattle trees she showed him in the morning (all the blossoms set to seed in brittle bronze casings). Their son, born in August, was dead by Christmas. Meg had named him Tom.

Then she looked at Rankine properly:

'Oh, my darling, what have they done to you?'

There was no call for Rankine to describe what he'd been through, he was too shamed. It was explained in the drawn lines of his cheeks, by his thin frame, and by his lacklustre formerly fine head of hair, still growing back in lumps after being razored off. It was told by his pale eyes burned back in his head. Then — after they went inside, and everyone awoke, got up, and sat around the table — there was Rankine's way of touching his wrists absently as he talked; reaching down to scratch the sores on his ankles, where his manacles had been. Small actions told a lot to anyone living in old time N.S. Wales and knowing the signs. They told of haggard convicts standing in line and never knowing from which direction the blow would come. Privileged as he'd been compared with many, Rankine carried that cringing deflection inside him, and Meg understood. Lying together that night they were as formal as strangers, until their fingers touched and they broke their formality in tears, and were in each other's arms, never again to part.

There was a big hill above duck mole reach. Until it had its trees removed it was never much noticed as a feature. Now it stood over the place in a raw lump. After weeks of getting in practice with sextant, compass, and barometer, Rankine calculated its height at three thousand, two hundred and seventy-three feet, and built a cairn on its summit from which Duck Hill, as he called it, would thenceforth be known as the starting point of a measured line west, on Rankine's survey. On its east flank it erupted in orange rocks, ferns, blackwood trees, and became that jumbled cliff where

Patrick Lehane drove Mick Tornley's bullocks over, that had jumped and survived.

From the back of the hill away down, tall stands of timber were the story of creeks and rivers folding into the coastal ranges far distant; and in the other direction, the west, from which Rankine and Meg came climbing, was its even more parched western slope looking down on Tharpe's at a bend of the duck mole. It was like a battleground smoking ready for tomorrow. Mares were being shod by blacksmiths, wheelwrights went around greasing axles, teamsters worked last scrapes of fat into their leather traces and set doleful blinkers on draught horses. When you lifted your eyes from looking down on those scenes of bullock lines, tents, horse pickets, drays and everybody primed for their twelve miles a day (estimated), then how the ruffled ocean of the country spread beyond. The land west had extended flatness, its trees along scribbles of creeks gave a daylight darkness, a charcoaled look to the parched country, smeared smouldering into the sky where fire cones of natives were seen.

'Coolich,' George Marsh had named the musk lorikeet, musk because of their heads smelling sweet after they'd thrown a fit and died; some flew past, calling; and then there were eagles, a pair of them rising in thermals, with their wingtips trailing out, high above everything. Over from somewhere behind, in the ravines of forest dropping away to the east, the most unusual pipe of a whistling hawk was heard — well out of its place, thought Rankine. Echoey, deep. The whistling hawk was only ever seen over the salt flats hunting for fish when Rankine first overlanded his sheep past Parramatta: it was the first New Holland bird he ever felt clutching his soul. And now as he heard it, he remembered, that a boy used that whistle. It did come from below, from under the escarpment.

Even a year ago you could climb that hill and see nothing out from its trees, and now all the trees were cut down for firewood and railings, cornerposts and shingles. Here was a little storm of congestion, and may be, by the time Rankine's expedition reached its farthermost limit, turned around, and came wending back (six months, a year from now?), duck mole in the scribbly woods would have a proper name, and a main street between its ruptured tree stumps and tethered billy goats. It might not be the venue for a dream any more, the starting line of a ballad. It might even have a gaol, but if it did, it wouldn't be able to fit back in all the convicts that were getting ready to march out under Tom Rankine's lead. The convict commissioner was expected that night, or at the very least, next morning: of whom it was said that if he didn't come, they would not go, as he was their patron in chief, and brought pardons. And echoing such phrasing were a few lewd women of the camp who agreed, if he didn't come, they wouldn't go either.

Each afternoon around four Rankine left off his preparations and found Meg in the heart of the camp, and the two of them walked up the hill and found a log that wasn't burned, that was their love seat. Rankine had a bag of Moreno's rosewater sugarplums, which they sucked while they shared their thoughts. The smoke of a dozen cookfires sent ribbony vapour along the ponded stream as parties of men, broke of their chains after being picked for this service, came in from their last chores hardly believing their luck in the ample quality of freedom found in the work given them, under the charge of one of their recently branded own — Ugly Tom Rankine, Vandemonian passholder, veteran of punishment gangs. Down and across the brittle grass and dry sticks for their supper they came, looking around for him, and saying there he is, Tom, our gentleman Tom, and weaving their way drunk with satisfaction between various kitchen fires to find their man.

The duckbills were like small sticks floating in the water around this time of day, where Rankine and Meg walked down to look. The most of the animal was never seen. They paddled below the surface, platypus coming along feeding, nosing the banks of their underwater burrows, invisible presences and certainly ignored by the clamorous troop of workers everywhere. But each time Rankine and Meg came past, Meg looked for one and remembered what was hidden from her sight and her touch and her love for ever; the child buried with barely a name whose last sign of existence was a distraction of sadness, when she woke.

Out along a broad gully, people not on Rankine's roll of stores, but nevertheless getting a share of them (flour, salt, sugar, tea), ash-daubed themselves lighter than their dark skins would show in firelight, mixing ochres and clays in cupped handfuls of water, and getting ready to sing. They pulled down shaggy bunches of gum leaves and dragged boughs back through the dust and piled them ready for use.

Tents, picket lines, waggons, drays and livestock areas, horse-lines, bullock lines, donkey stalls. Beds on the ground, with just the possessions allowed that could be carried on the back in a blanket roll: it was Rankine's town on many legs, with such a feel of ponderous ability, it bore repeating: only when Commissioner Lloyd Thomas arrived with Rankine's and Kale's free pardon, handed to Rankine, examined by Rankine and confirmed as authentically stamped, would they all get up from the ground, gather and combine their separate portions, and get under way as one.

A plan was rehearsed in case of attack by natives, by coming in every night and pulling the big drays up in two lines sheltering the

sleepers between them from spears and waddies of warriors. Otherwise than this caution, they were a full massed orchestra of bellows
and timber knocks and dinging metal, a music of cow bells, hobble
chains, waggon links creaking. But first Rankine's signal, set for
tomorrow, before anything:

'I will go up on the bare hill, you'll see me on the womback
path. Soon after sunrise, I'll raise my arm, and bring it down. Just
as the light comes, across in the east there, watch.'

A quality came out in Rankine in full command, a very serious
involved concentration. It lost him to Meg at times but that was
all right. He would be easier after a few more weeks, with them all
farther out, on some yellow grass plain slowly moving. Then they
would get back everything that was fragmented. Her time with
Rankine had been short. Broken. So much to look forward to
already finished, taken, never to be recovered. Just the happiness of
anticipation (and most of it consumed in struggle) seemed to carry
the large part of enjoyment in life.

Thin ropes of Artie Josephs's fiddle music thickened into denser
strands of sound as Tom and Meg found their waggon, where
Martha had a pot of hot stew ready, and Artie put his fiddle down
in its case, and the boys and Leah and Joe stood around with
chunks of bread ready to scoop up their share.

They were halfway through eating when a woman wrapped in a
green shawl with a sharply beautiful, sluttish face came into their
firelight, and looming up behind her carelessly like a great ape with
a hand on her thin shoulder was Paolo Moreno.

He gave the woman over to them for her supper, just shoved her
towards Martha and Meg to be accommodated, not pausing to give
her name, only to say, 'Ungry'.

Her name was Anne Kemp, as she straightly told them when

Moreno and Rankine were gone from the firelight to the back of the waggon to deal with Moreno's problem.

Poor thing, she was frightened in the bush. A huge resoundingly empty cold hostile dark dungeon without walls, it did seem to her, so soon off a convict ship and chafed sore from sitting up behind Moreno on a nag when she had never ridden aback a horse before. Artie Josephs stared at her slain with love, jolted from a romantic headspin over pretty girls of whom there were three in the camp that he cared for, but this one could be had for a coin. Solly saw his brother's knees tremble as he tried holding his tin plate of stew in his lap, and wondered why his brother was frightened of her so.

Meg made sure the woman was politely received, but she did not think she would ever like her. Martha, whose own apprenticeship to crime was in a brothel, where many girls died young, thought more charitably how fresh air might kill the poor commercial darlink if she didn't get rigged up in a blanket — it was too exciting altogether for someone who lived on excitements of brutal kinds. Later she thought, 'My Arfur could do worse than fall in love with a whore so long as she keeps her hands off of him.'

It was the last chorus of the last verse of a ballad with the words of the last lines flying over them in a flock of birds, in a torrent of shooting stars, in a handful of gritty dust thrown in their eyes when they hadn't known such a night was coming upon them, hadn't known finality was in the air with the ashes and sparks of so many campfires whisking around their ears crackling promise. Away out where they were going Kale was retreated to the banks of a billabong with twenty-seven remaining ewes from so many hundred, and two greatly horned rams, being all that was left to him after the rest were speared. Biddy Magee was terrified over the bands preying on them, worn thin from excitement when Clumpsy M'Carty appeared with a black man, Piper, who was able to speak to the attackers and persuade them off. They set to work building fences and yards where Rankine in two months would find them. There was a tin whistle Kale carried in his belt, and sometimes called his best rams to him, because they knew, when he played, there was the feast of their appetites among the ewes he picked for them. There was a ram lamb to be born from these last joinings and he was the one, called Supreme Matchless, that Blaise Cribb would send word of to Bramley. In the stud books down two hundred years and more he would be known as the Abraham.

Tom Rankine stood in the shadows of a waggon. He listened standing slightly stooped and considering, cupping a hand to his good ear to what Moreno told him in his low rumble. How getting away from Sydney with his womans he slowed only to find a priests, and paid the priests ten sovereigns to marry thems — how they were followed, but Moreno lost the tail when they got to Labans Vales to gather some last belongings. Lloyd Thomases wanted the womans from him, but Moreno would kill the convicts commissioners if he touched her.

'She stays with us, then,' said Rankine. Martha would see to her, and keep her from sight.

'All rights,' groaned Moreno.

'Anything else, Paolo?'

Moreno said there was something else. As they'd rode into the trees past Labans Vales homestead paddock from the other ends of the track there was a column of dust and they waited. It was a sheeps man new to the country and the sheeps man's assigned convict servant and two boys riding with them. Moreno in his pride of stewardship went back to greet them. The two mens knew him. One from a long time ago in another country, the other more recently, and back from the grave.

Rankine had no need to ask which sheep man it was, which assigned convict it was, knowing very well it was his stepbrother, Cribb, with Matthew Stanton and their party of settlers chasing up, which Moreno then confirmed at prouder length, when he saw Rankine wasn't annoyed — more relieved to be told of it — telling how Stanton was the convict servant now and young Mrs Cribbs the new owner of Labans Vales, she was pleased to the care given on her Labans Vales by a Spaniard.

Leah Josephs thought she was dreaming, as she bent over to the ground, collected tin dishes from a pile, and slid them into a soapy tub where she scrubbed them with a rag. It was in the corner of her eye, on the dark side away from the lantern that she saw him. Incredulous, she was, over the satiny jacket and pair of red-piped trousers that whisked past her, seeming to carry a pair of fathomless eyes in a little bunched cloud of night-time disturbance.

'Moru,' they called it — the whistling kite. From the dark side of their firelight as Rankine came back to their camp he heard it, and saw the crazy apparition wearing the regalia of a sea captain, making the sound of the kite with a set of fine-shaped lips. It was Titus Stanton struggled up from the bush to tell them that just below the jumbled cliff line, in the dark, Warren Inchcape sat with Paddy Lehane the bushranger scared with a broken leg and Warren wasn't going to leave him.

Rankine found men and set off following Titus by starlight.

A dismay lifted from Meg Inchcape's heart then. In worst extremes there was the shine of starlight. She had Rankine back from his sore trials, she had Warren back from his. Or would by morning.

Camped back a few miles from the duck mole reach because his guides were unable to find way by nightfall, Commissioner Lloyd Thomas was aggravated in almost every aspect of his thinking. He disliked being baulked, disliked the dry scratchy irritable native bush. Nothing had prepared him for it. He wasn't told. He pulled his blanket up to his chin and ordered his men to stay awake in watches. But he could not sleep very well under the ring of stars. Carried by the wind in the tops of the trees was a jaunty stupid tune bothering his brain. It caught in the hooks of hollow limbs and poked around like a probe in a broken tooth. A hooting, melancholy sighing, recalling a ballad peddler's tune on a dismal street corner. Bad not to bring a woman with him, either, as to have one would bring sleep. She could be passed into the convict camp in the morning, in exchange for female convict Kemp, who, because he could not have her, threatened to destroy him. In London it was possible to step out and get around and bring back a woman: whores and ballad singers, they occupied the night, and when it was a ballad it was the chorus that counted. How many choruses were there in a proper ballad on a subject — raced the restless brain of the convict commissioner — there's a set number of verses, eight all done, none of them under eight lines; and there's a chorus to every verse; and, if it's the right sort, eight choruses are very good, they'll sell the ballad.

Out in the same stretch of dark bush, in a second camp a few miles closer to the duck mole reach, lay master and servant, Blaise Cribb and Convict Matt. They were guided there by George Marsh's maps so absurdly out of date as to be insultingly, humiliatingly useless (as they barely needed referring to before a deep set of waggon ruts showed, and much knocked-down vegetation to guide along one's way). Near them lay Johnny Cribb and Barney Hard-castle, who both in the course of a few days' hard riding had acquired the affectations of colonial experience, hanging loose in the saddle as they chased kangaroos over fallen logs and cracked stockwhips longer than mythical snakes, only lacking so far some realer experience of dirt to toughen them. (That would come under a withering sky on salty claypans below the horizon; where they would, in years to come, become as hard, mean and unforgiving as the country sheep punched down from paradise over their life-times.) They snored their exhaustion out like a quartet of slumbering wombacks every side of the fire. Nothing woke Matt. Cribb flicked awake every few hours — he was nervous of the New South Wales bush as anyone new, but having looked over Laban Vale sheep for a day was amazed at their improvement in a country so exacting. He was content with so solid a man of experience as Matt Stanton at his side, to say what were wonders, and what were not. All was strange, all was queerly beautiful to Cribb if he didn't get a spear in his side some night. He knew when he got his hands on a flock he would shape something of them. In the night sky the unfamiliar constellations made their show, and he seemed to be able to gather ideals in his hands already and shape them. Getting the nose tight there, under the forehead scroll of wool, and the horns snarled in tight so they would not get in the way of handling too much, but stay open to the blades; and getting the feel of a handful of wool as crimped leaves of gold must feel, when refined pure and leafy.

Cribb was getting to be an old man to be so much in love as he was. His love for Ivy would always be greater than hers — far greater as it was based on some kernel of need rather than necessity, and one day he would die, and she would go on, loving better than she knew how; then she would certainly remember most, that what she grew to feel for Cribb was a good enough love for the purpose it served, and better than that, for the life it gave back to her when she had lost nearly all.

Blaise Henry Cribb was eventually to be remembered as the greatest sheep shaper that walked this thin earth; the stud breeder's stud breeder of origin, he was going to be sent down to his grave marked for fame. Though where he died and was buried nobody would know. The other matter, apart from sheep, that Cribb rose in when he came to this country and began his dealing with it was forgiveness. It surprised him. May be there was no forgiveness in that earth for those who despoiled it, as Cribb was able to do, watching here a run blow away in dust, there a run scour to clay in a decade's only rainstorm; but forgiveness for his stepbrother, Tom Rankine, that was what came. It was already in him, done, finished, cleared out of his rancour when authorities told him the few facts of Rankine's hard expiation. And although they were to meet, within hours of dawn, they never talked about it, never needed to at all. Too much shame, but all of it lived to the full.

As for Convict Matt, all through that night there came no dreams of demons or of anything else to be remembered in the morning from a hefty, unconsciously slumbering, melon-shaped head. Matt's last thoughts before sleeping were: 'Leave the furniture covered in drapes; keep the door of St Botolph's bolted. I love my wife, child, and granddaughter. The Spaniard's done well with my sheep. The redness Cribb finds is a fluked advantage, not in the wools but in the constitution.'

The Devil had come to him and showed a dirty finger. Get out of England, he said (twice). Someone said he was stupid as a sheep, some muttered Irishness: he'd flogged the curser. If he did have any sort of a dream, night after night, it was of a minister of God, bound in ropes and gagged, and of a convict, name of Matt, saying best leave him captive.

With their massed shaken tree branches and painted limbs in line the dancers made their corroboree. It was a pretty good rival to any ballad, that was ended but for one note of play. That night Titus got in the dance, with his glad rags off him. The firelight licked in a circle. Warren sat close to Meg, and Leah on the other side of him, feeding him the best, most succulent parts of the leftovers that she was able to dig out of the pot with her fingers. Lehane in sullen comfort was brought in on a two-pole stretcher bed clutching a bottle of rum to ease his pain, and handed to Mick Tornley to decide what to do with him, and when he was done with him, there was still Rankine to face.

Tomorrow, as promised by Rankine, Titus would be the white man's best hope, and ride with Rankine and Warren, and the whole big company of livestock and people negotiating their way through country of tribes less friendly than this one's — cheeky buggers, Titus would call them, and shoot some. They would find a country to run sheep on. Then Titus would go back east where he came from, and like his grandfather, Mun'mow, live up along the creek somewhere, knowing what he knew.

The dancers took their branches and they danced kangaroos and emus bounding and striding, they danced lizards in the dust, and they danced the wind in the trees with all the boughs massed together and shivering from quick movements, it thrilled the watching crowd. Then they all went back to their camps for the night, ready for the morning.

In the morning when Rankine had his and Kale's pardon securely tucked in his pocket, he signalled the beginning of their march, and the mass of them creaked off through the trees raising dust.

Author's Note

I am particularly grateful to Richard Woldendorp and Charlie Massy for their interpretations of wool culture and allowing me to share in them; to Charlie Massy for a valued manuscript reading; to Rose Creswell and Jane Palfreyman for friendship and encouragement over many years; to Susie Fisher, with love, for unstinting support and inspiration always; and to Donal and Gavin McDonald, who started in wool when wool was king.

Further acknowledgement is made to the following authors, authorities, and individuals helpful to the construction of this novel:

D.B. Adams on sheep behaviour; Alan E.J. Andrews on early exploration; D.W.A. Baker on inland exploration; John and Gwen Bucknall on bush camps; Harold B. Carter and Sir Joseph Banks (and correspondents) on the origins of New Holland wools; George Caley on colonial natural history; J.E.B. Currey on George Caley; Margaret Cameron on wool appreciation and handling; Joy Damousi on convict women; Paul Feehan on wool books; Andrew Dowling on wool country; Jennie and Rob Fenwick on inland travel; John Fogarty on law disputes; Anne Gollan on colonial cooking; J.S. Gunn on shearing words; Alexander Harris on colonial bush life; W.S. Hill-Reid on gentleman convicts; G.N. Hinch on sheep behaviour; Warwick Hirst on convict escapes; Robert Hughes on early convicts; Frankie Japanaga on Aboriginal life; Amanda Laugesen on convict words; J.J. Lynch on sheep behaviour; Colin McCrabb on working dogs; Tony Milner on history and fiction; Sir Thomas Mitchell on inland New South Wales before white men; Bruce Moore on Australian English; Bob Reece on Irish convicts; Stephen H. Roberts on the squatting age; John Ritchie on the Bigge Reports; Johnny Possum Tjapaltjari on Aboriginal life; Helena Valldejuli-Butler on Spanish usage; Sandy Yarwood on Samuel Marsden; Peter Yates on bush life; and William Youatt on sheep breeds, management, and diseases.